Dear Reader,

Christmas is the perfect time to write about complicated families, but the family in this story wouldn't consider themselves to be complicated at all! They're close, and supportive, and they're all looking forward to their annual Christmas gathering. This year promises to be extra snowy and magical, and they are all determined to make it the best it can be – which is why they intend to keep their own personal dramas to themselves. Yes, they're a close family, but close families don't have to tell each other everything, do they?

But secrets have a way of emerging, particularly when people are closeted together (and certain family members are given to interfering!). Before anyone has time to say 'Santa' those secrets are spilling out and they discover that perhaps they don't know each other quite as well as they thought.

Writing a Christmas book every year has become one of my own festive traditions (possibly because cooking a fictional turkey is a lot less stressful than cooking an actual turkey), so it's lucky for me that so many people have decided that snuggling up in the warm and reading a Christmas book is one of their favourite traditions.

I hope this story makes you smile.

Happy reading.

Love Sarah xx

Readers love spending time with

SARAH MORGAN

'Sarah Morgan never fails to make me smile'

'Such a great author who pulls you into the book's world the moment you start reading'

'Sarah Morgan never ever disappoints'

'One of my go-to authors when I'm looking for a heartwarming, feel-good read'

'Always a treat'

'Smashes it every time, delivering romance, emotion, hope, friendship, loyalty, happiness'

'Sarah never lets us down!'

SARAH MORGAN
Read
yourself
happy

Sarah Morgan is the number one *Sunday Times* bestselling author of multiple bestsellers, including *The Christmas Cottage, The Christmas Book Club, One More for Christmas, A Wedding in December, Beach House Summer* and *The Summer Seekers*. She has sold over twenty-five million books worldwide.

Sarah lives near London, England with her family and when she isn't writing or reading, she likes to spend time outdoors hiking or riding her mountain bike.

For all the latest book news, exclusive content and competitions, visit Sarah's website and sign up to her newsletter at

www.sarahmorgan.com

Sarah loves to connect with readers on social media. Find her on:

f @AuthorSarahMorgan

[O] sarahmorganwrites

𝕏 @SarahMorgan_

P.S. Want even more great reads, giveaways and book news?
Follow @hqstories

Also by Sarah Morgan

How to Keep a Secret
The Christmas Sisters
One Summer in Paris
A Wedding in December
Family for Beginners
One More for Christmas
The Summer Seekers
The Christmas Escape
Beach House Summer
Snowed in for Christmas
Summer Wedding
The Christmas Book Club
The Summer Swap
The Christmas Cottage
A Secret Escape

From Manhattan with Love series

Sleepless in Manhattan
Sunset in Central Park
Miracle on 5th Avenue
New York, Actually
Holiday in the Hamptons
Moonlight Over Manhattan

Puffin Island series

First Time in Forever
Some Kind of Wonderful
Christmas Ever After

The O'Neil Brothers series

Sleigh Bells in the Snow
Suddenly, Last Summer
Maybe This Christmas

SARAH MORGAN

All Together for Christmas

ONE PLACE. MANY STORIES

HQ
An imprint of HarperCollins*Publishers* Ltd
1 London Bridge Street
London SE1 9GF

www.harpercollins.co.uk

HarperCollins*Publishers*
Macken House, 39/40 Mayor Street Upper,
Dublin 1, D01 C9W8, Ireland

This edition 2025
4
First published in Great Britain by HQ,
an imprint of HarperCollins*Publishers* Ltd 2025

ISBN: 978-0-00-874439-7

Printed and bound in the UK using 100% Renewable
Electricity by CPI Group (UK) Ltd

For more information visit: www.harpercollins.co.uk/green

This book is for my readers – with thanks and appreciation.

1

Becky

Standing in the airport terminal surrounded by too much noise and too many stressed people, Becky decided that she didn't love Christmas anywhere near as much as she'd always thought.

Usually she looked forward to it, but there was nothing usual about this particular year.

And now this.

She glanced at the departures board. Everything was red, and not a happy Santa red. Canceled flight red. *You're-not-going-anywhere* red.

"Nothing?" She gripped the counter. "Are you seriously telling me nothing is flying?"

"That's right. Blame the weather. I'm sorry." The immaculate woman behind the airport check-in desk gave her a smile that was polite rather than warm.

Becky imagined it being part of the uniform policy. *Knee length skirt, smooth hair, wide smile.*

"This trip isn't optional." If it was, she wouldn't be going. She'd be avoiding a family gathering, the way she'd been avoiding all family gatherings lately. Not that she felt good about it. On the contrary, she felt horribly guilty. Even more so because just last week her mother had confessed how much she was looking forward to finally having everyone together. "I *have* to get home."

"I understand your frustration."

Becky was confident she did not understand. There was no way this woman would have any insight into Becky's current emotional state. If her hair was any indication, she was the type who had every aspect of her life firmly under control.

She tried to stay calm. She reminded herself how lucky she was. She had a job, somewhere to live and she was healthy. She had nothing to complain about. The fact that her inner world was in turmoil didn't count. She could almost hear her brother saying *first-world problems, Becks.*

"How about Edinburgh? I booked a flight to Newcastle, but Edinburgh would be fine. I can drive to Northumberland in just over an hour from there."

"Nothing is flying. Not to Newcastle, and not to Edinburgh. I wish I could help, but sadly we can't control the weather."

What *can* we control? Becky wondered. In her experience, not much at all. But maybe that was just her messy, complicated life.

"I need to get home to my family."

"You and several million other people. It's Christmas and as I said—" the emphasis was gentle but unmistakable "—nothing is flying. Have you considered taking a train?"

"The trains are on strike." It was as if the entire public transport system had conspired to make her Christmas as difficult as possible.

"In that case I suggest a car rental, but you'd better make it fast because everyone here is going to have the same idea. And now if you'll excuse me—" The uniformed woman transferred her smile and her attention to the person who was next in the queue.

Becky knew she should feel sorry for her. It couldn't be fun having to deal with a transport crisis guaranteed to put a dent in everyone's Christmas cheer or to be expected to soothe and placate thousands of irate and upset travelers armed with nothing more than charm and a very red lipstick. But she was too tired to dredge up the necessary sympathy. Also the woman's composure was annoying. How did she tame her hair into something so smooth and perfect? Was it part of the training course? No matter what Becky did, her hair ended up in a tangle of curls, which was why she'd had it cropped short. There weren't enough hours in the day to waste a chunk of them drying and styling her hair every day as her twin sister, Rosie, did.

"You don't understand. If I don't make it home it will look as if I'm—" How would it look? It wasn't as if any of her family knew the real reason she didn't want to be there. No one did. Not even Rosie. It was her secret, which in itself wasn't too much of a problem because she generally kept her feelings to herself. Growing up, Rosie had expressed enough feelings for both of them, and Becky had let her get on with it.

And now she thought about it, she realised that the weather and the train strike gave her a perfect excuse not to show up for Christmas at all. For a wild moment she pictured herself sprinting from the airport and heading back home for a quiet Christmas of video games and walks in one of London's snowy parks.

But then the image faded and she thought instead of her mother's roast turkey and the tiny cinnamon-flecked cookies she baked simply because she knew they were Becky's favorite. She thought of the cheerful red stocking her mother would have hung on the fireplace even though Becky had insisted they were all too old for a stocking (she wasn't too old for a stocking, but she was old enough to understand how much work went into filling it and felt a responsibility to demur). She thought about her father insisting *just one more game of Scrabble, Becky* and the warm, comforting weight of their ancient Irish setter Percy as he lay on her feet.

She felt homesick for Northumberland with its vast starry skies, windswept empty beaches and imposing castles.

She was scared to go home and yet she longed to go home.

"Could you look again? One more time? I really need to get home," she said. "It's not just about Christmas. My brother is having a special party—he's making an announcement. I assume that means he's getting engaged—" she frowned "—and I'm not sure how I feel about that. He only met her two months ago. That's fast, don't you think?" But she wasn't a great judge of what was normal when it came to relationships. She wasn't the sort who fell in and out of love easily.

The woman in the queue adjacent to her nodded. "It is fast. My sister was married after four months and she was divorced a year later. She discovered all these things about him that she wished she'd known before."

"Exactly." Becky turned to face her, relieved that at least *someone* seemed to understand her concerns. "That's what worries me. You need time to get to know a person. Also, my brother hasn't dated anyone seriously since his last girlfriend walked out. That was six years ago, and they'd been together for eight years. Since medical school. It left him a bit broken. We've all been worried about him. Mum, most of all, obviously, because she worries all the time even when we're fine. For years he has dated no one, and then suddenly he went on a business trip and he met this girl and now, two months later, he has an announcement to make. Tomorrow night. He has ordered champagne. I'm assuming it's a sign."

"Sounds like it. Same thing happened to my cousin Martha." The man standing behind her in the queue took a step forward. "We'd all given up on her meeting someone, hadn't we, Ginny?"

Bored with queuing, the woman he'd addressed the ques-

4

tion to hauled her case forward so that she could join in the conversation. "We had. Her boyfriend refused to propose, said they were fine as they were and didn't want to get married, but then a new receptionist started at his work and a month later he left Martha and was getting married. Turns out it wasn't that he didn't want to get married, but he didn't want to marry Martha. He said it wasn't personal, but how much more personal can you get?" She exchanged looks with her husband.

"Heartbreaking," he said. "We thought Martha would be single forever after that, but three years later she was walking the dog and that was it."

"That was what?" Becky was struggling to keep up. People were so complicated. They made her head hurt, which was why generally she preferred to work with computers.

"She met Roland. A month later they were married."

"Oh." Maybe that was reassuring. "A month is fast. And they're happy together?"

"No. They're divorced too."

So not reassuring at all.

She was beginning to wish she hadn't started this conversation because it was doing nothing to soothe her anxiety about her brother. "So you're saying it's best to take your time over falling in love."

"Maybe, but you don't always have a choice." Ginny leaned closer. "Sometimes you can be going along living your life, minding your own business and then wham."

"Wham? As in you walk into something and fall over?"

"No, wham as in you fall in love. Love at first sight. And you can't help it."

Becky was about to say that she didn't believe in love at first sight, but then she thought about her twin sister, now married to Declan, Becky's longtime work colleague (now ex-colleague). Becky had introduced them and that had definitely been a "wham" moment. One minute Becky had been talking to both

5

of them and the next they'd been talking to each other, mesmerized, her existence forgotten. She'd cleared her throat a few times, then banged her glass on the table. Nothing. They'd been so absorbed in each other she'd had a feeling that they wouldn't have noticed her even if she'd danced on the table. She'd always considered Declan to be a sensible human being, but after that encounter all he'd talked about was her sister. Rosie this. Rosie that. *Tell me more about Rosie.*

They were married eight months later.

Was that what had happened to Jamie? What was *wrong* with her family?

"I'm happy for my brother, obviously, but also worried. Although I suppose if I'm honest I didn't totally love his first girlfriend. She was a bit judgy."

Perhaps if you tried to make yourself look a little more feminine, Becky. I get that you work in a mostly male environment and you want to fit in, but maybe you could wear a dress sometimes, or a touch of lipstick. A shoe that doesn't look as if it has passed the health and safety rules of a construction site.

"Try not to worry." Ginny patted her arm. "I'm sure he knows his own mind."

Becky didn't share her confidence. She felt very protective towards her older brother.

She'd been in love once in her life and it hadn't been a quick process. It had crept over her stealthily, like an emotional weight gain, layer upon layer going unnoticed until one day you woke up and took a long hard look at yourself and realised something about you was different. It had come as a shock to her, and not a good one.

But she'd disciplined herself not to think about that.

Her phone rang and a name flashed up.

Rosie.

After a moment's hesitation she rejected the call and a moment later a message popped up on her screen.

Declan and I are on our way! Can't wait to see you.

Becky's fingers hovered over the keyboard but in the end she just sent a couple of emojis.

Rosie was married now. She didn't need to get into lengthy exchanges with her twin sister. And at this precise moment Becky didn't feel robust enough to handle Rosie cooing over how fantastic Declan was—how he'd fixed her laptop again (Becky had often fixed her sister's laptop and had never be on the receiving end of even a fraction of the love and appreciation that Declan was shown for performing the same task) or how perfect Declan was (he certainly hadn't been perfect when Becky had worked with him, and not just because he always left the milk out of the fridge). And honestly Becky was happy for her. She adored her sister, and she believed that if there was ever a moment when life wasn't dumping crap in your lap, then you should make the most of it.

But being relegated to the second-most-important person in her sister's life wasn't easy, and training herself not to contact her sister at all hours of the day required a discipline that was exhausting.

Emojis were okay, weren't they? Emojis didn't intrude on her twin's personal space.

She could hardly register the fact that Rosie was married, even though she'd been at the wedding. This was going to be the first time the whole family had been together since that day in February. Their first family Christmas with an extra member of the family (two extra members if you counted Jamie's girlfriend). Rosie's first Christmas married to Declan. The first Christmas that Becky and Rosie wouldn't be up at dawn poking presents together. Rosie would be in bed with Declan. Sleeping. Or not. Maybe she'd be doing more exciting things than sleeping. Jamie would be in bed with his girlfriend, probably not sleeping.

And she'd be in bed on her own. Or maybe with the dog if she could sneak him into her room without her mother seeing.

Becky felt horribly flat. Not gloomy exactly, but close to it.

Christmas was going to be different. And not in a good way, at least for her.

She wasn't sure she wanted to go at all.

But if she stayed in London she'd break her mother's heart. And very possibly her own. Also, she needed to check out this woman Jamie had met. Turned out the sibling bond was stronger than the need for self-preservation.

She'd be okay. Her superpower was hiding her feelings, not just from other people but also from herself. She worked on the principle that if you didn't acknowledge something, then you could pretend it wasn't there.

She zipped up her hoodie, tightened the laces on her winter boots and clomped her way through the terminal building, dragging her large suitcase and dodging passengers as she followed the signs for car rental. Thanks to the party her flatmate had thrown the night before, she was tired (she'd worn earplugs, but still the entire building had vibrated), and the last thing she needed was to navigate pre-Christmas traffic for seven hours or longer, but it seemed she didn't have a choice. If necessary, she'd pull over and take a nap.

She almost laughed.

She was twenty-eight years old and, if she was to believe the article she'd read on her phone the week before, in the prime of her life. If she hadn't been told, she wouldn't have known. She didn't feel as if she was in the prime of anything.

She'd started a new job eight months earlier and so far it wasn't going well. She was good at what she did and had no problems with the job itself, but in this new place being good at your job wasn't enough. You had to socialize. It wasn't about the work, it was about schmoozing with the right people. She hated playing those complicated political games and she wasn't good at it, mostly because she wasn't interested. Taking the job had been a mistake, she could see that now. One of many she'd made lately.

These days even home was stressful, because she was no longer living with her sister and she'd underestimated how hard that would be. She'd always known she'd miss her, at least at first, but not this much.

She paused just long enough to buy herself a strong coffee, hoping it might give her flagging energy a boost. Juggling suitcase, scarf and coffee, she walked past a giant Christmas tree glowing with lights and no doubt designed to put people in a festive mood. Twinkling stars cascaded from the roof of the terminal building. Most people were too desperate about the travel situation to take any comfort from twinkling stars. What they wanted was transport. No one was where they wanted to be.

It felt like a metaphor for her life.

It crossed her mind briefly that if Rosie and Declan hadn't yet left, she could grab a ride with them, but she dismissed the thought instantly. She wasn't a good passenger at the best of times, and being trapped in the car with those two lovebirds would finish her off. Christmas would be bad enough. She didn't need a preview.

As the woman had predicted, the queue for car rental was long and crackling with impatience and tension.

The man and the woman in front of her were locked in an argument.

"What if we make it to the front and there are no cars left?"

Good question, Becky thought. *What then?*

"They will have cars."

"You don't know that. Look at the length of the queue! I think we should head out of London and try somewhere less busy."

Becky considered that suggestion even though it hadn't been directed at her.

Maybe that wasn't the worst idea. But what if she did that and there were still no cars? She'd be stranded outside London. No, she was staying put and hoping for some luck.

Honestly, could things be any worse?

"Becky?"

The deep voice almost made her drop her coffee.

Oh no. Please no.

She conjured up a smile—if the woman behind the check-in desk could do it then so could she—and turned.

He stood directly behind her, drawing interested glances from the many bored women standing in the queue.

"Will! This is a surprise. What are you doing here?"

He was living proof of the fact that just when you thought things couldn't get any worse, they got worse.

"Same as you I imagine. I was hoping for a quick journey home, but it doesn't look as if that's going to happen." He pulled her in for a hug, which was a standard greeting between them, and it gave her a chance to bury her very red face in his coat.

Typical. It was snowing outside and her cheeks were blazing like a furnace.

She never would have thought she could feel uncomfortable with Will, but that was before she'd embarrassed herself at her sister's wedding. Embarrassed was probably too tame a word. Embarrassed was when you were late for a dental appointment, or you forgot someone's birthday. This was bone-deep humiliation. The sort of humiliation that made you wonder if you should emigrate, have plastic surgery and change your name.

She was just going to ignore it. Pretend it had never happened.

Hopefully he'd do the same.

She stepped back. "I thought I'd hang out in an airport for a while. Soak up some of the festive spirit."

"I'm pleased you're able to laugh about it." He studied her for a moment, his hands still on her shoulders. "It's good to see you. It has been a while."

"Oh, you know—new job, busy, busy—"

He nodded. "Are you okay? You look upset about something."

And she thought that hiding her feelings was her superpower. Not from Will, apparently. "I'm fine. It's just airport stress."

"I can tell you're not fine, Becky. Talk to me."

She almost told him that she didn't feel remotely festive. That she was dreading going home for Christmas. *That she was a mess.* But she managed to stop herself. "You know those train announcements—the ones where they tell you to mind the gap between the train and the platform? It's the same for Christmas. I try not to fall into the chasm between expectation and reality."

He gave her a speculative look. "Okay. Well, if you want to talk about whatever it is that's bothering you, you know where I am."

"You know me. I'm not big on talking about things. I leave that to my sister."

"Hopefully your reality will improve a little once you get out of this place." His gaze shifted from her face to the queue. "You're hiring a car?"

"Yes." What else could she say? That she was standing in line to see Santa? "That seems to be the only way to get up north today. Unless a certain person in a red suit with a white beard can find room for me on his sleigh as he flies past. I didn't see any mention of his flight being grounded. Maybe they've cleared the skies for him."

He smiled. "I don't have a sleigh, but I do have a car and I'm parked here, at the airport. You can come with me if you like. We can drive up together."

She didn't like. She absolutely did not like.

"That's a kind offer, but it will be easier if we do our own thing. I might need to stop on the way, make a few work calls—" She stumbled under his questioning gaze.

"If you need to make a work call from my car, you can make a call, Becks." He was the only person, other than her brother, who called her Becks.

"It's confidential."

He raised an eyebrow. "I'm not exactly known as a gossip."

And given what he'd witnessed that was lucky for her, although right now she didn't feel lucky.

She felt as if the universe hated her.

From behind her she heard a woman mutter *if she doesn't want to get into his car then I will,* and for a fleeting moment she saw Will as a stranger might.

He was tall and he radiated calm confidence. He was a doctor, a cardiologist, and she was sure that any patient who saw him approach the bedside would instantly feel reassured. A smart wool coat emphasized the width of his shoulders and a pair of glasses with a bold tortoiseshell frame accentuated the lean lines of his face. He looked as if he'd stepped directly from a photoshoot for "sexy academic man."

She was conscious of her faded jeans and her comfortable hoodie that she all but lived in. What did he see when he looked at her?

His best friend's little sister.

The thought was annoying. She shouldn't care. She didn't care! She'd known him all her life and he was one of the few people she always felt comfortable with, but that had all changed the day of the wedding.

The memory of that had her reaching behind her for her hood. She tugged it over her head in the hope that it might act as a shield.

He frowned. "Are you cold? Because you can have my coat."

He was already starting to shrug it from his shoulders but she stopped him.

"I'm not cold. My coat is in my luggage because I always overheat in airports. It's just my head. My head gets cold. You lose most of your heat through your head. You're a doctor. You should know that."

"Um—" He pulled a face and pushed his glasses up his nose. "That's a myth."

"It is? That isn't a thing?"

"Not exactly, although of course it's important to bear in mind the effects that cooling the face and head can have on systemic cardiovascular reflex responses, particularly in elderly people."

She loved it when he delivered random facts. "Elderly? I'm twenty-eight."

"I know how old you are, Becks."

Of course he did. He knew everything about her.

She shifted her weight from one leg to the other, wishing she was more comfortable in awkward social situations. This was one of those occasions where, given the choice, she would have shut herself away with just her laptop for company.

"I'm keeping my hood up anyway. In case my head is the exception. I might be suffering from premature aging. Or maybe my head gets colder because my hair is short."

"It's cute. You look good with short hair."

He was trying to make her feel better. Trying to ease the embarrassment he knew she was feeling.

Since the wedding she'd avoided him as much as she could. The last thing she'd expected was to come face to face with him in a busy airport but given her current run of bad luck she probably should have anticipated it.

It was time to implement her extraction protocol.

She was great at melting away without anyone noticing, mostly because she wasn't the sort of person people noticed in the first place, but in this case melting anywhere wasn't easy because Will was looking at her in a slightly strange way and it was unsettling because he always seemed to see so much more than most people.

"Honestly, I'm fine. I'll need a car when I'm up there anyway. I was going to hire one at the airport so that I can be independent because my mother's car has a habit of breaking down at inconvenient moments."

"Is this about what happened at the wedding?" He reached out and brushed a strand of hair away from her face, and if it had been anyone else but Will, she would have slapped his hand away but he'd been hauling her out of ditches and shunting her up trees in the forest near where they lived since she was five years old.

She didn't mind him touching her hair, but she did mind about the question.

She didn't want to think about the wedding. She'd tried to block the whole thing from her mind. But now he'd reminded her and every painful detail came flooding back, including all the emotions she'd been trying to ignore.

"The wedding? No, of course not. It feels like a lifetime ago, doesn't it? I can barely remember a thing about it, apart from the scratchy dress Rosie made me wear. No, this is about what's practical. Anyway, good to see you, Will. I hope you have a good journey home and a great Christmas. Maybe we'll bump into each other at some point." She was tempted to step away but then she would have lost her place in the queue, so she waited for him to do it. *Leave. Please, just leave.*

He didn't leave.

"We're going to be bumping into each other tomorrow. You do know I'm going to the party at your house?"

No, she hadn't known that. If she'd known she would have looked harder for an excuse to stay in London.

This was promising to be the most excruciating Christmas on record.

"Jamie invited you?" Of course he had. Will was Jamie's closest friend. They'd known each other since kindergarten. They'd gone to the same medical school, although once qualified they'd chosen different specialities and their paths had diverged. But if Jamie was having a celebration, Will was going to be there.

"Yes. He said he had something big to announce. I assume it's an engagement?"

"I'm assuming the same."

"I'm happy for him. I know things were rough there for a while." He adjusted his glasses. "So you're going to be a bridesmaid again."

Her gaze met his briefly and she knew they were both thinking about the last time she was a bridesmaid.

Not her finest moment.

"Looks that way. Woohoo. Lucky me. I just hope he doesn't expect me to dress as a fairy like Rosie did. I'm not fairy material."

"You looked stunning in that dress, Becks."

He was just being kind, because he'd sensed she was in a low mood.

"Yeah, right. It gave me a rash, but—thanks." Another thing she wasn't good at. Accepting compliments. "Anyway, you should get going. I'm guessing the snow is going to make the driving difficult."

Will glanced from her to the long line of people ahead of her, as if trying to understand her decision. "If you're sure . . ."

"I'm sure."

But just at that moment there was a commotion at the front of the queue.

"What do you mean there are no more cars?" A man spoke in a loud voice. "There has to be something."

A ripple of consternation passed through the line of people. "No cars?"

"Did he say no cars?"

"What's supposed to happen now?"

It was obvious what had to happen now, at least for Becky. She closed her eyes and tried a few seconds of mindfulness. When she opened them Will was still standing there, waiting. She had to admire his staying power.

With a sigh, she swallowed her pride. "If your offer of sharing your car still stands—"

"It still stands, and I promise not to listen when you make your important phone call."

She wished she'd never mentioned a phone call. Not only would she now need to find someone to call, but she was going to have to make it sound important.

"Thanks."

He nodded and stretched out his hand. "Do you want help with that suitcase?"

"Do I look weak and feeble? Thanks, but I'm fine." She grabbed it firmly and tugged it closer to her, wondering how she was going to survive this. As well as dreading the impending family gathering, she was now also dreading the journey.

"I thought your muscles might have atrophied given the time you spend glued to computer screens."

He was teasing her the way he'd always teased her. It should have felt natural, but nothing felt natural anymore.

"I could still beat you in an arm-wrestling match."

His eyebrow lifted. "If you're referring to that incident on your fifteenth birthday, I let you win."

"No you didn't, but we'll pretend you did if that protects your ego."

"I let you win because you were trying to impress that boy who played in the school orchestra with you. The one with red hair and freckles. Tom."

"Tim." How on earth had he remembered that? "Tim Tucker. I haven't thought about him in years."

"I seem to remember the strategy backfired. He was too scared to go near you after that."

"So you're the reason that relationship didn't work out."

He nodded slowly. "Probably, although in my defence I couldn't see you being happy with a man who was scared to arm-wrestle you. But relationships are complicated. So are feelings."

And didn't she know it. She wasn't good at showing her feelings, but that didn't mean she didn't have them. And she wished she didn't. Feelings were so *annoying*. There were plenty of days when she thought life would be a lot easier if the human body had been designed to include an on/off switch for feelings. At least then when it all got too much she could have rebooted the system.

She noticed the sign to the car park. "We should probably get moving."

"Yes. If we're lucky we'll be there by late afternoon."

Only if his luck was better than hers.

He was checking the weather and the route on his phone. "Mm. If this forecast is correct, the journey might not be easy. It's saying nine hours."

"Nine hours? *Did you say nine hours?*"

"It's snowing. Broken-down vehicles. Lane closures. Don't worry. We'll stock up with snacks and you can choose the music."

The way she felt at the moment her first choice would be a funeral march.

She should have trusted her instincts and refused his offer.

Because it wasn't true that no one knew the real reason she didn't want to go home for Christmas. That no one knew her secret.

Will Patterson knew. And now she was going to be trapped in a car with him for nine hours.

Merry Christmas, Becky.

2

Rosie

I sent her a message and all I got back in response was emojis." Rosie stared at her phone, trying hard to keep all her emotions locked inside her. It was Christmas, her favourite time of the year. She was wearing her sparkly sweater with her festive skirt and boots and the delicate robin earrings that had been a gift from Becky. She was going home and it was snowing. Actually snowing. They were going to have a white Christmas, which was the pinnacle of perfection in her mind. She should be filled with a feeling of warmth and well-being. Instead she was sitting in the front of a freezing car struggling with a strange mixture of sadness and numbness. She felt as if someone had smashed her heart with something heavy.

"Declan?" She turned her head. "Are you listening?"

The back door of the car was open but there was no answer, and she wasn't sure if that was because he was busy loading the car with their luggage and hadn't heard her or because he was still too upset with her to indulge in conversation.

All she'd had from him in the last week was monosyllabic

answers, and it was torture because she was the sort of person who wanted an instant resolution to any problems. But was there even a resolution to this one?

Divorce?

No, no, no! She was not going to think that way.

There was another blast of cold air and Rosie shivered and pulled her coat around herself.

This was their first Christmas together. They should be loading the car with all their luggage and gifts and feeling festive and generally joyful.

Instead they were barely speaking.

They had to start speaking. They had to talk about it. They couldn't go home for Christmas with this atmosphere simmering between them.

She'd hurt him. But he'd hurt her too.

They both needed to move on from it, but to do that one of them had to make the first move.

She took a breath and stepped out of the car. "Do you need help?"

His head was down and he was currently trying to jam a large box next to her suitcase.

"Declan?"

His head jerked up. Snow clung to his hair and the shoulders of his jacket. "What?"

She hated this side of him, or maybe it was more accurate to say she struggled with it. When he was hurt, he vanished inside himself in the same way Becky did. It was impossible to reach him. It was something she'd only discovered about him fairly recently. He dealt with his problems silently whereas she dealt with hers out loud.

"Do you need help?"

"Not unless you can do without one of these suitcases. I thought you said you were going to travel light."

"This is light. I've left a lot of stuff behind."

"Really? Because it feels like you've packed everything you own."

She bristled. "It's not all mine. Some of it is yours."

"One bag." He rested the box on the rest of the packing and winced as he rolled his shoulders. "One small bag is mine."

"It's Christmas. It's hard to pack light at Christmas. What was I supposed to leave behind? The gifts?"

"Normally I go away with just hand luggage and I manage fine." He picked up the box again. "Unless we can make maximum use of the space, it's not going to fit. It's a mathematical challenge."

"Can I help?"

"No. It's basically a giant puzzle, and you hate puzzles." He stared at the box, then turned it onto its side and slotted it into the single space left. "The rest is going to have to go on the back seat and we just have to hope it doesn't block the mirrors. Get back in the car, Rosie. The weather is arctic. There's no sense in both of us freezing."

He was telling her she had too much stuff and couldn't pack a car. Normally she would have laughed and admitted it, but right now it felt like another blow to their increasingly bruised relationship.

She slunk back into the passenger seat feeling useless. Was there really a right and wrong way to pack a car? Why did it have to be a puzzle? What was wrong with just loading everything in haphazardly? That method worked for most people and it had worked perfectly well for her in the past. She was confident that if she'd been doing it, she would have crammed it all in somehow. And who on earth could go away for Christmas with just hand luggage? She couldn't even fit her makeup in a bag the size of the one he'd packed.

But that exchange was further confirmation that Declan's

methodical, ordered approach was completely at odds with her more free and easy style.

They were so different. He changed his passwords regularly and had been horrified to discover that her password was almost always Rosie1. He'd installed a password manager for her and set up two-factor authentication wherever he could, which all sounded very secure and meant strangers were less likely to access her accounts, but most of the time Rosie couldn't access them either. She just wanted her laptop to work—she wasn't interested in the engineering behind it.

And they were different in the way they handled emotions. She'd never been able to sit with a problem. If something was wrong then she needed to talk it through. It was the way she solved things. And if people didn't tell her how they were feeling, then her mind filled in the blanks.

Declan was more like Becky. He kept his thoughts inside, tucked away.

It had never bothered either of them before. If anything, their differences had been part of the attraction. Being with him calmed her overactive imagination and she liked to think he benefited from her more spontaneous nature. But today her spontaneous nature seemed to be a source of irritation, along with so many other things.

At what point had those differences become a problem?

No one had told her that marriage would be this hard. She'd imagined them sailing through the years on the same river of dizzy happiness that had characterized those first blissful months of their relationship. Everything about him had fascinated her. Everything about her had fascinated him. She'd never imagined them reaching a point where they were barely speaking.

Was he regretting marrying her?

Her mind raced forward, spinning worst-case scenarios.

She tried to remember when he'd last said *I love you*. He didn't say it that often, but that was because he wasn't as emotionally open and demonstrative as her. The first time he'd ever said it she felt as if she'd won the lottery.

She tried to put the brakes on her unhelpful thinking. He hadn't *said* he was regretting their marriage, so she was not going to make that assumption. Like her sister, he didn't talk about his feelings, whereas Rosie shared every one of her feelings, and although her family teased her about it she couldn't help thinking that it was easier for everyone in the end. No one ever had to ask her how she was feeling because she usually told them within minutes of entering a room.

She slumped in her seat as he opened the back door of the car, letting in another blast of freezing air.

How were they going to get through the next week? She was hopeless at hiding things. Her family was going to know something was wrong the moment she walked through the door. She could hardly tell them that her marriage was crumbling after less than a year.

They should have taken more time to get to know each other before getting married, which was another reason she was keen to get home for Christmas. It seemed as if her brother was about to announce his engagement and she needed to talk to him. Urgently. She needed to warn him to take his time before fixing a date for the wedding. She needed to tell him that marriage changed everything and that it was best to go slow and take the time to get to know each other properly. She was a cautionary tale, although of course she wasn't going to admit that. She couldn't talk to anyone about this, which was an uncomfortable situation to be in.

It would have been nice to have a friendly message from her sister. She'd called her a few days before, but Becky had been at work and the call had gone to voicemail. And that was happening more and more frequently. Becky seemed to feel that

22

now Rosie and Declan were married she should be giving them space and not intruding on these precious early days of their relationship. She seemed to be imagining Rosie swimming in a sea of pure happiness, and right now nothing could be further from the truth.

One good thing about going home was that she'd finally get to spend quality time with her sister.

She hadn't heard from Becky since Jamie had sent that message to them all telling them he wanted to have a special celebration party before Christmas because he had something to tell them.

Rosie had immediately messaged her sister.

Do you think he's engaged?

It had taken a few hours for Becky to respond, and when she did it was brief.

Don't know.

There had been a time when that sort of message from her brother would have triggered an hour of video chat (admittedly with Rosie doing most of the chatting), but not anymore, and it confirmed what Rosie already knew—that her marriage to Declan had changed everything, not least her relationship with her twin. There had never been a time when she hadn't known exactly what was going on in Becky's life, but she no longer had a clue.

Would she have married Declan if she'd been able to predict the impact on her relationship with her sister?

She was not going to ask herself that question. *She had to stop thinking like this*.

"Is there room for this in the front?" Declan leaned in through the door and passed her a large tote bag.

She pushed it down by her feet without argument. "I messaged Becky and all I got back was emojis."

"She's probably battling mayhem at the airport." Declan was loading the last of the bags into the back seat. He'd planned it with mathematical precision. Large suitcases first. Soft bags. Fragile gifts. Bottles of champagne. Everything fitted.

Everything except them.

Rosie felt her eyes sting. If she'd been more analytical in her approach to decision making maybe she would have decided it was sensible for them to take more time to get to know each other instead of rushing into marriage, but she wasn't analytical. The decisions she made were instinctive. *How does this make me feel?* She didn't make lists of pros and cons. She relied on her emotions to guide her, and most of the time she felt like a passenger, riding those emotions wherever they went. Happy, sad, ecstatic, terrified.

But Declan was nothing like that. He thought things through carefully, just as Becky did. He was a planner. She was the impulsive, spontaneous one. She was the one who'd said *let's go to Paris* on only their second weekend together (they'd stayed at a cute hotel on the Left Bank and it had been fabulous), she was the one who'd said *let's move in together* just two months later, and she was the one who had proposed to him in a burst of spontaneity one winter evening when they'd been walking along the river on their way back from an evening exploring a Christmas market. It had been snowing, lights had been shimmering on the surface of the river and he'd stopped to kiss her, and it had been such a perfect moment that she'd wanted to hold on to those feelings forever. She'd known that she would never, ever feel happier than she'd felt in that moment.

She'd shocked herself by proposing (like most of the things that came out of her mouth, it hadn't been planned) and she'd shocked him too. For a moment he'd stood there, his gaze fixed on hers as if he was searching for something, ignoring the snow that was drifting down and settling on them. She'd held her breath and waited for him to say he needed to think about it and then he'd smiled and said yes. In fact she thought maybe he'd said yes a couple of times, but by then he'd been kissing her again and everything had been a bit blurry.

She was the one who had suggested a small wedding at home in February.

It was only now that she realised she'd driven all of it. She'd been the engine in their relationship. Right from the beginning, she'd had her foot pressed to the accelerator. What would have happened if she hadn't suggested Paris, or moving in together, or getting married? Where would they be now? Would he have hit the brakes?

She felt a shaft of guilt and something close to panic.

Had this whole thing been a terrible mistake? Was he regretting it?

She badly wanted to talk to her sister, but even if Becky had been more available, would she really have talked to her about this? Her marriage? It felt disloyal somehow. And complicated because it was Becky who had introduced her to Declan. They were good friends.

"Becky doesn't usually send emojis. She's not really an emoji person."

He sighed and his gaze flickered to hers. "You'll be seeing her in a few hours so you can ask her then. I'm sure you can survive that long without talking to your sister." There was an edge to his tone and it cut into those soft, tender feelings that she wore far too close to the surface.

"Can we talk about this? I know you're still upset about last week."

"I'm freezing, Rosie. I can't feel my fingers. It's not a great time for conversation." He gave the last box a big shove, forcing it behind the seat. "What is in all these boxes and cases?"

"Mostly gifts. Christmas is a big deal in my family, I've told you that." And this was going to be his first year with them. Last year they'd spent Christmas separately. After her spontaneous proposal she'd gone home as always, and he'd gone skiing with friends, a trip that had been planned before they'd even met each other. She'd been looking forward to this moment for months, which made the current disharmony all the more upsetting. "And clothes, obviously. I need warm layers for the beach and something pretty for my brother's party, whatever that is. And then there's Christmas Day."

"How many pairs of shoes and boots did you bring?"

Seven pairs. Five pairs of shoes and two pairs of boots, not counting her hiking boots, but with the atmosphere so tense she didn't want to admit that. "The bare minimum. I was selective."

He tried to close the car door but it kept jamming against the bags. He cursed softly, put all his weight on it and finally the door closed.

He flung his coat into the back, settled into the driver's seat and blew on his hands to warm them.

"Why did it have to snow?" He peered at the street, rapidly disappearing under a thick coat of white. "Bad timing."

Snow at Christmas—bad?

Normally she would have said it was perfect timing, but right now she was too stressed.

She stared at his profile, trying to read him. "I know you're upset. We *have* to talk. We can't go home for Christmas with this atmosphere hanging over us."

He said nothing but he put his hands on the wheel and she saw his knuckles whiten.

"Declan—"

"Yes. I'm upset. What did you expect?" He sounded tired. "It was my company Christmas party, Rosie. Everyone was there, with partners. Everyone except you. It was awkward." He turned to look at her and it was obvious from the shadows under his eyes that his night had been as bad as hers. "People kept asking where you were."

Guilt made her defensive. "I don't believe that. I doubt they even noticed I wasn't there."

"They noticed. I had to say you were sick."

"Why would you tell them I was sick?"

"Because I couldn't exactly tell them that you didn't want to spend an evening with them, could I?"

She'd had no idea he'd be this upset about it.

Her heart was pounding. She hadn't realised he'd want her there. She genuinely hadn't thought he'd care.

"But they don't like me, Declan! When I joined you all for a drink last month none of them spoke to me. And it was the same the time before that."

"That isn't true."

"It is true. They ignored me. And so did you. You all talked about some obscure computer programming thing all evening and I didn't understand a word of it and certainly wasn't able to contribute, so I sat there like a lemon all night." And she'd felt stupid. Out of her depth. Miserably self-conscious. She'd imagined them all wondering what someone as brilliant as Declan was doing with someone like her. Even her clothing had been wrong, she'd known that the moment she'd walked into the room. She'd worn a sparkly mini dress and she'd felt pretty until she'd seen that they were all wearing jeans and hoodies. There had been a horrible moment where they'd all stared at her speechless, and then Declan had ushered her to an empty seat at the table and the moment had passed. But the humiliation of that evening had stayed with her, which was why she'd had no desire to put herself through it again.

Declan ran his hand through his hair. "We've all worked together a long time. We're comfortable with each other. That's all it was. It wasn't about you."

"But I was there! I was there and they didn't include me. *You* didn't include me. I felt like some—some—*appendage*. Everyone was wondering why you and I were even together."

"You're imagining it."

"Declan, I am not imagining it. One of them actually said to me 'you're not Declan's usual type.'"

He frowned. "Who said that?"

"I don't know. I'm trying to forget the whole evening frankly."

"Probably Harry. Harry Fitch. He tends to say what he's thinking. No filter." He rubbed his fingers across his forehead. "I'm sorry if we got carried away—we've been working on this new project at work which is actually very exciting, and—"

"I know. It's all you talk and think about." And she hated the fact that she didn't understand a word of it. He'd tried explaining it to her. He'd even used a pen and paper and drawn a diagram. But it had made no sense to her. Sometimes she wished she was more like Becky. Becky would have been able to join in. Becky spoke their language.

He glanced at her. "You could have tried harder too?"

It was so unfair she felt her eyes smart. "How? I don't understand what you do, Declan. I don't know enough about computer engineering to be able to join in your conversation. And maybe that makes me stupid—"

"You're not stupid." He frowned. "I have never said, or thought, that you were stupid."

"Well, I felt stupid. And maybe I wouldn't have felt that way if just one of the people in that group could have asked me something about myself. About what *I* liked. Although that probably wouldn't have helped because I'm guessing that 'I make costumes for the ballet' isn't a great conversation starter in your world." It took skill to do what she did, she reminded herself. Real skill. Just not a skill that any of his colleagues would appreciate if the look they'd given her dress was anything to go by.

He took a deep breath. "We need to stop this. We're not getting anywhere."

"We started it because you wanted to know why I didn't go to your Christmas party. And I'm telling you why. My confidence couldn't survive it. I didn't want to spend another humiliating evening standing by myself in the corner like some wallflower feeling bad about myself."

"This is all in your imagination, Rosie."

"No, it really isn't."

"Even if you don't feel you've got to know them properly yet, whatever happened to supporting each other? Isn't that what married couples are supposed to do? Maybe you didn't want to be there, but you could have done it for me. Because I wanted you there. Just as the reason I'm sitting in this car now is because you want us to spend Christmas with your family."

His words knocked the air from her lungs.

"Are you saying you don't want to spend Christmas with my family? You're making it sound like some sort of chore or obligation."

He hesitated just a moment too long and she felt as if the bottom had dropped out of her world.

"Fine then, don't come." The words rushed out of her. Had they really reached this point just because she'd decided not to go to his work Christmas party? No. There was more to it than that, there had to be. "If spending Christmas with my family sounds so terrible to you, then don't come. I would hate to inflict a big family Christmas on you if you're going to hate it."

"Rosie—"

"I'll say you're sick. That's the excuse you gave to your friends, wasn't it?"

She couldn't believe that happiness could turn to misery so quickly. Emotions boiled inside her. She wished she could turn the clock back. From now on she was making lists for every decision she made. And she was going to take more time over it. No more impulsive moments.

There was a tense, swollen silence and then he looked at her and something in his eyes made her heart turn over. "I don't understand what's going on here. I can't talk to you when you're this upset."

The more upset she became, the more he withdrew from it, but how was she supposed to not be upset?

Tears stung her eyes. "Do you wish you'd never married me?"

He frowned. "Rosie—"

"Do you?"

He sighed. "I think we should have this conversation when we're calmer."

So he did regret it.

Her heart ached and she turned her head and looked out of the window so that he wouldn't see her tears fall.

She was so cold. Absolutely freezing. She would have done anything for a hug, but something about this new tension between them had impacted on their usual chemistry. Normally she couldn't stop touching him, and he couldn't stop touching her, but the emotional distance had become a physical distance. Was that her fault? She'd never been good at separating her emotions from her actions. If she didn't feel warm and loved on the inside, she couldn't be warm and loving on the outside.

"I didn't know you didn't want to spend Christmas with me. I don't want you to force yourself so just unload your one single bag and I'll drive myself up north."

"Rosie—"

"I don't want to spend Christmas with someone who doesn't want to be there. It will be miserable for both of us."

He sighed. "Rosie—"

"You think I'm being over emotional, but maybe you should try being a little more emotional and then you might have some insight into my feelings! But you're such a level, calm kind of guy."

"Yes. And in the beginning, you said you liked that about me. You said I calmed you down. Made you feel safe. You couldn't wait to get married. You were excited. You were the one who picked February."

It was all true. Her stupid impulsive emotional nature had been in full flow.

Would he have taken more time? Had she somehow swept him along?

Her fingers were freezing and she tugged on her gloves. "Maybe I should go on a computer programming course or something."

He looked bemused. "Why would you want to do that?"

"So I can hold a conversation with your colleagues. So that when you talk about time series regression or something, I know what you're talking about. Do they do a course called Coding for Clueless Creatives? I'll ask Becky."

"You've talked to Becky about this? About us?"

"No, I haven't talked to Becky about us." She'd barely talked to Becky at all lately, unfortunately. And that was another problem. "This is our marriage. I'm not going to talk to my sister about us. And anyway I hardly see her these days. She doesn't want to burst our happy little romantic bubble."

If only.

"Is that why you're so upset with me? Because you're missing your sister?"

"You're the one who is upset with me. But it's true it does feel weird without Becky around all the time. She has been the main person in my life for—well—my whole life."

She didn't expect Declan to understand. An only child, he had no idea what it was like to be close to a sibling, let alone have a twin. And some twins probably couldn't stand the sight of each other, but that wasn't the case for her and Becky. From the moment they were born—twelve minutes apart—their lives had been intertwined. They'd shared a cot for the first few months of their lives and then a bedroom. They were identical on the outside but inside they couldn't have been more different. Rosie loved ballet and dresses. Becky refused to ever wear a dress and at eight years old her idea of fun was jumping into muddy puddles and creating the biggest mess possible. Rosie made clothes for her dolls—elaborate ballgowns and tutus covered in glittery sequins. Becky was addicted to puzzles and was moved up two classes in maths. Rosie had to have extra help. Despite these differences (or perhaps because of them because they were never in competition), they were best friends.

They'd both gone to college in London—Becky to study computer engineering, and Rosie to study costume production. They'd shared a small apartment and laughed over each other's dating exploits (mostly Rosie's). When they graduated, Becky had landed a job in a large tech company and Rosie had been offered her dream role working for a ballet company. Neither of them had expected to stay in the same place for long, but that was what had happened and for almost five years they'd shared almost every aspect of their lives. They'd joked that they'd still be living together in their nineties, and then Becky had introduced Rosie to her longtime work colleague Declan.

Rosie hadn't believed in love at first sight until Declan, and maybe that first evening hadn't been love exactly, but it had been a strong connection. A connection powerful enough to propel them towards a date, and then another date. Within weeks they were saying *I love you* and a few weeks after that she'd packed up her things and moved out of the apartment she'd shared with her sister since college and moved in with Declan.

He lived in a small apartment north of the river in London that had views of rooftops. If you stood on tiptoe you could see the local park. It was sparsely decorated when she arrived but she'd added bookshelves, upgraded his ancient frayed sofa by covering it in ruby velvet and added piles of bright cushions. She'd hidden his scratched wooden floor under a large rug and filled the place with plants.

They'd offered the spare room to Becky, and Rosie had been disappointed when she'd refused. Instead Becky had rented out Rosie's old room in the flat they'd shared.

You have Declan now, Becky had said.

Rosie had told herself it was fine because it meant she could use the spare room for all her creative projects, but deep down she'd been hurt and more than a little confused.

She hadn't understood it. It wasn't as if Becky didn't like Declan. They'd worked together for years and were good friends. As far as Rosie was concerned nothing needed to change, but Becky seemed to want to give them space.

Rosie hadn't anticipated that being with Declan would change her relationship with her sister.

You two need to build a life together, Becky had said when Rosie had pointed out that they rarely saw each other. *You don't need me hanging around.*

Rosie would have been more than happy to have her twin hanging around, but had decided maybe Becky was right, so she'd put her mind to building a life where, for the first time, she was closer to someone than she was to her sister.

But so far it wasn't working out that way. For the first time in her life she felt lonely.

How could you feel lonely when you were married?

She wanted to tell Declan how she was feeling, but she sensed that every emotional sentence she uttered was driving him deeper into his shell so she said nothing, her stress levels soaring in the tense silence. She wasn't good with atmospheres. They disturbed her equilibrium. She preferred to solve any problems instantly rather than let them simmer.

The family who lived in the apartment below theirs appeared

on the street ahead, dragging a Christmas tree, the youngest child holding out her hands to catch the snowflakes that swirled in front of her.

Spotting Rosie and Declan in the car, the parents waved and mouthed Merry Christmas, and Rosie waved back, her smile an automatic response to their friendly greeting.

She watched them maneuver the tree through the front door, laughing together as the branches got stuck on the frame. They were probably going to make hot chocolate and sing Christmas songs. It was all so enviably cheery. It was how a family Christmas was supposed to be.

And then the front door closed behind them, cocooning them in their own private world of fairy lights and fantasy.

In the meantime, Rose was in her own private world, which was a lot chillier and nothing like Christmas was supposed to be.

Declan was her family now, and it didn't feel the way she'd imagined it would.

He peered through the swirling snow. "We should leave. It's going to take us forever to get up north in this weather. Have you set the SatNav?"

She felt a rush of relief. She'd been terrified he might actually say he didn't want to spend Christmas with her family.

She'd often wondered about marriages that went wrong. Were they always wrong or did they start out right and then gradually unravel? But now, for the first time, she could see how a rift might happen. It was like a tear in a dress. If you didn't mend it right away, it grew bigger and bigger, until it was too big to fix and the dress was ruined.

Or maybe the problem was that the dress hadn't fitted in the first place.

She felt a lurch of panic and pushed that thought away. She wasn't going there.

He stared at the door their neighbours had just closed and she wondered if he was feeling the same sense of envy that she felt. Maybe not. His family was nothing like hers. His parents had divorced when he was very young and Declan had stayed with his father. He'd told her that in a matter-of-fact way when they were exchanging facts about their families. When she'd asked him about the emotional impact of such a major life upheaval he'd simply shrugged and said he'd been too young to remember much about it.

His mother lived in France, but Rosie had never met her because she hadn't come to the wedding (a decision that had shocked Rosie but appeared not to disturb Declan at all). His father lived in Scotland with his stepmother. Declan saw them once a year. It was a very different picture from her family, who were in constant contact. Rosie couldn't imagine only seeing her family once a year. The thought appalled her. She rarely went two days without speaking to her mother, and all three siblings messaged each other regularly on their group chat (although Becky hadn't been doing much of that lately). Rosie had felt sad that Declan had never experienced that same closeness and support, and she'd nurtured a fantasy that her family would become his family. That they'd all blend perfectly.

It hadn't occurred to her that visiting her family might feel like a duty for him. Something to be endured, not enjoyed.

"Christmas is really not special to you, is it?"

He glanced at her and shrugged. "I don't know what you want me to say. Christmas is not really different from any other time of year, except flights and hotels are eye-wateringly expensive and the office closes whether you want it to or not. My family doesn't go for the whole turkey-and-tree experience, you know that."

She knew they had different family experiences, but she hadn't thought it would matter. Now she was wondering if maybe it did. Only now was she really understanding that when you married someone your experiences and wishes had to somehow blend with theirs.

She loved Christmas, and when she'd married Declan she'd

assumed their Christmas would look the way it always had when she was single. A big, noisy family affair. If one day they had children, she'd want to give them the same warm, chaotic festive season that she'd always enjoyed. She'd want to take them to the forest to choose a tree, just as she had with her parents. She'd want to buy stockings that would be hung by the fireplace year after year until they were threadbare. She wanted to reproduce the Christmas she'd had every year of her life. What if he didn't want that? What if, in the future, he wanted them all to go and lie on a beach? What if he said *I don't want to spend Christmas with your family*?

And she realised in that moment that they had much bigger problems than whether his friends liked her.

She adored her family but she was aware that when they were together they were noisy and demonstrative. Personal space wasn't really a thing in her house. What if he found them overwhelming? What if, instead of making him want to repeat the experience, he decided he never wanted to do it again?

She couldn't imagine not getting together with her family at Christmas.

"Rosie?"

"Sorry. I was just thinking." And this time she wasn't going to tell him what she was thinking.

They'd go, and she'd make sure he had the very best time. Yes, that was a good plan.

How could he not love Christmas at her home? The Mill House was gorgeous at Christmas and would be even more magical now that they'd had snow. The thought of going home lifted her spirits. It was just what she needed. The moment she turned into the long driveway that led to her family home, she felt a sense of security. It was nothing to do with the building, of course, but the people. Her wonderful parents. Her grandparents. Her siblings. Whenever anything had gone wrong in her life they'd been there ready to cushion the blow.

"Do you want me to ask my parents if we can have separate bedrooms? Then you can have your own space if you need it?"

"What? No!" He sounded appalled by the suggestion. "That would raise questions, and that's the last thing we need."

Questions. It would raise questions. Not *I want to be with you, Rosie. I can't sleep without you there.*

"I just—"

"Enough! We're doing this. We've bought the presents. We've packed the car. We already had this discussion and agreed to it. It's the right thing to do. Don't worry, I'll survive."

I'll survive.

"Okay then. Wake up those reindeer." She made a supreme effort to feel festive. "Let's go, or we won't get there before Santa."

Declan gave her a look that clearly said *I don't understand you.* Then he started the engine, checked his mirrors and pulled out into the snow-covered road.

Rosie slumped in her seat. She'd been looking forward to Christmas for ages, and now it promised to be a total disaster.

Merry Christmas, Rosie.

3

Jennifer

Christmas.

A time for peace, goodwill and monumental pressure, Jennifer thought as she wrestled the tree through the front door of her parents' ground-floor apartment and found a place for it by the window.

"Hope you approve of this one. It's pot grown, so hopefully it won't drop needles all over your floor. And I bought you some of my cinnamon cookies because I thought we'd need sustenance after decorating it."

Her parents had moved into the light-filled apartment a few years earlier and it offered far more practical living than the old rambling vicarage that had cost a fortune to heat. She'd grown up thinking it was normal to always wear two sweaters.

"I should be telling you that you didn't have to do that, but I'm so happy you did. Both the tree and the cookies." Her mother fussed over the tree, moving a side table and then rotating the pot, first in one direction and then the other, looking for the best angle. "It's a beauty, Jenny. We should be too old to be bothering with decorations at home, shouldn't we? Particularly as we'll be spending Christmas with you at the Mill. It's an extravagance."

"Nothing wrong with a bit of extravagance at Christmas. You've always loved having a tree, and I don't see why age has anything to do with it. You can put it out in the garden after Christmas and then bring it in again next year. It will last forever."

"Which is more than can be said for us," her father muttered without lifting his gaze from the newspaper he still bought daily from the local shop. He did the crossword every morning after breakfast while her mother caught up on her knitting. It always struck Jenny as a very companiable arrangement.

"Ignore him," her mother said. "His bones were aching when he woke up this morning and he has been a grouch ever since. This tree is a pretty shape. Thank you." Her mother tweaked a few branches and then leaned in to breathe in the scent. "Now I feel Christmassy. It's the smell. Come and put your nose in these branches, Brian. It will cheer you up."

"No thanks. They've probably been sprayed with something and I'll have an allergic reaction. Either that or a spider will crawl up my nose."

Her mother made a tutting sound. "They have not been sprayed with anything! Our Jenny got the tree straight from the forest."

"As I said—spiders." He tapped his pencil on the table. "Eight letters—the clue is mood."

"How appropriate."

He ignored that. "Begins with an *F*. The fourth letter is an *l*."

"Feelings?"

"That's it!" Her father looked up, delighted. "I love your mother. Have I told you today that I love your mother? Phyllis, you're wonderful. If we weren't already married, I'd ask you to marry me."

Her mother's cheeks were pink. "I might say no."

"Too late for that. You're stuck with me now."

Jenny grinned. The two of them made her laugh. "Why don't you do the crossword on your tablet, Dad?"

"Because I prefer doing it the old-fashioned way. I don't want to forget how to write. Do you know that the young generation barely write anything anymore? It's all computers. Everything is computers. The tablet has its place, but it's not at the breakfast table." He went back to his paper and her mother shook her head and shared a long-suffering look with her daughter.

"Thank you again for the tree. It makes me think of forests and snow and smiling children. Remember when we used to take Jamie and the twins to get the tree? Martin was always working so we used to do it with you. It was my favourite Christmas activity. And then we'd decorate it."

Jenny felt a pang of nostalgia. She remembered all of it. Occasionally she yearned for the days when the children were very young, but then she reminded herself that memory was selective. Her brain had stored all those precious memories of happy moments and conveniently ignored all the less sunny moments, like the relentlessness and exhaustion that was part of parenting three children (including twins! How on earth had they managed that?) and the way that all three of them had inevitably managed to go down with coughs or ear infections on Christmas Eve.

"I dug out our decorations earlier. There was so much dust in the back of that cupboard I've been sneezing ever since." Her father put down his pencil. "Talking of Martin, how is he? I thought he might come with you today."

"He's having a quiet day. Doing a few jobs around the house before everyone is home for Christmas." Jenny kept her voice bright and cheerful. "One of the showers only produces cold water and the lock on the back door keeps sticking. And Rosie doesn't have a lock on her bedroom door at all so I'm hoping that's on his list. You know how it is."

Did she sound convincing? She hoped so because she didn't want to tell them the truth, which was that she'd begged Martin to come with her just to make him leave the house but he'd stayed slumped on the sofa in his pyjamas, staring out of the window as snow slowly coated everything in the garden. *I'm too tired, Jen. Maybe tomorrow.*

It had been like this for two months, since the day his retirement began, and she was reaching a point of despair. This was not her husband. This wasn't who he was. Martin was an enthusiast who had boundless energy. He was first up in the morning and last to bed at night. He was efficient, kind and not at all given to introspection, which made the current state of affairs all the more alarming.

She'd hoped that the approach of Christmas might shake him out of his state of gloom because he loved the season as much as she did, but so far that hadn't happened.

And she didn't understand it.

After years of working as a family doctor with all the stresses and demands that entailed (particularly now, when the job had become increasingly thankless) he was overdue a break. He'd been exhausted with it all and talking about retiring for ages, so it wasn't as if he shouldn't have been prepared for what was coming. The staff, many of whom had worked with him for years, had thrown a party and made an enormous fuss of him (even the practice manager, widely considered to be the scariest person on the planet and possibly related to a dragon, had been seen with tears in her eyes), and he'd returned home with armfuls of chocolates, bottles of wine and more cards than they had space to display them. But the morning after, instead of waking up and saying *this is the first day of the rest of my life*, he'd woken up and said *this feels like the end of my life*.

And that was the point when she'd realised that it wasn't only his life that had changed, it was also hers. She'd been thinking about retirement as something that was going to happen to him, but now she realised it was something that had happened to them.

They'd been married for forty years, and they'd been happy years (if you ignored the rough patch when the twins were born and didn't seem to sleep at all). They'd had a routine. Martin rose before six, took the dog for a walk, then came back and brought Jenny tea in bed. He was in the surgery by seven thirty every day, which meant she had the house to herself. She'd trained as a nurse originally and had worked for years in the local hospital before taking early retirement. She'd had no problem adjusting. She had her book group, her yoga class, her choir practice, and she frequently met up with friends. They walked, they visited art galleries, they went to the movies in the afternoon when everyone else was at work. She'd filled her days with things she enjoyed doing and was happier than she'd ever been.

Because it had been an easy transition for her, it hadn't occurred to her that it might not be the same for Martin.

Every morning she woke up and hoped that today was the day he would embrace his new life. She wanted him to spring out of bed and suggest they go for a walk on the beach, or out for lunch at the local pub, but so far that hadn't happened. He'd even stopped walking Percy, their English setter, so for the first time in her life Jenny had to drag herself from the bed before dawn and take the dog for his morning walk.

Nothing was the way she'd imagined it would be.

She'd pictured them enjoying a peaceful cup of coffee together in the sunroom, admiring the light on the ocean and agreeing that they'd picked the perfect place to live and raise their children. She'd imagined him tackling all those small jobs around the house that needed doing, but so far that hadn't happened.

When she'd suggested he might fix the bathroom door so that one of the children didn't get stuck and find themselves spending Christmas in there, he'd nodded and said he'd do it, but then he'd retired to the sofa to stare out of the window and listen to a podcast. Still wearing his pyjamas.

The predictable and comfortable rhythm of their life had been shaken up, and now they needed to find a new way to be together every day.

But before they could find a positive way forward, she needed to somehow drag Martin out of his current state of gloom. Only that morning she'd walked into the kitchen to find him reading a new clinical trial on an asthma drug, even though he was never going to have to manage a patient with asthma again.

Maybe she was wrong to keep it from her parents, particularly as they were going to be staying with her for Christmas.

On impulse she sat down at the table next to her father. "How did you feel when you retired? Was it hard?"

"Why are you asking? Is Martin struggling?" Her father put his paper down, his direct look a sharp reminder that at eighty-five he was every bit as astute as he'd been at forty-five.

Jenny was torn between guilt at being disloyal and her own need to talk to someone about it. "I wouldn't say that. It's early days. But he's not as—" she struggled to find the right word "—buoyant as I expected him to be."

Could he be clinically depressed? Was that it?

Her father gave a nod. "It takes some getting used to, even when it's something you want. Martin has been a family doctor here for decades. He's well known and respected. And he was busy, which is both good and bad."

Jenny gave up trying to pretend everything was fine. "Right now it's more bad than good. Did you struggle with it?"

"He did not." Her mother sat down too and picked up her knitting. "He was on the golf course the day after his farewell party. I saw more of him when he was working." But it was said with affection, because Jennifer knew her mother enjoyed having time to herself to read, knit and meet her friends for coffee.

"Martin doesn't play golf."

Her father gave her a long look. "I'd love another cup of coffee, Phyllis. I'm sure our Jenny would love one too. No point in rushing off. Sit for a while. Eat one of those cookies you baked for us."

It was easy to see why her father had been so beloved by the community when he'd been a doctor. He had an instinct for when someone needed to talk and he always made time for them.

Her mother sighed and put down her knitting. "You've already had one coffee."

"Two is fine."

"Don't blame me if your body disagrees." Her mother stood up, walked to the kitchen area and reached for the coffee. "Martin just needs time to adjust, Jenny. Work gives you a purpose. Everyone needs a purpose. A reason to get up in the morning. What he needs is something important in his life. Something to focus on."

She was in his life, and she was important, wasn't she? Why couldn't he focus on their relationship? On having some fun now that they were free of responsibilities. Wasn't that what retirement was supposed to do? Give them more time for each other?

She'd imagined them booking a once-in-a-lifetime trip together, but when she'd mentioned it he'd said that perhaps they could talk about it in the summer.

Her father reached across and gave her hand a quick squeeze. "I've been thinking of coming round and asking his advice on my book. His knowledge is more current than mine. Maybe I'll give him a call."

"Good idea." Her mother made a pot of coffee and carried it to the table along with mugs. "With Martin's help you might even make a start on it. Goodness knows you've been talking about it for long enough."

Jenny hid a smile because her mother was right about that. For as long as she could remember, her father had talked about writing a book on health for the general public.

"Have you made any progress, Dad?"

"Not progress as such. Although I do have a working title. I'm calling it *Lessons from a Life as a Family Doctor.*"

Phyllis rolled her eyes. "It's not exactly catchy, is it?" She put the mugs down on the table. "And it makes it sound as if it's about you. Like a memoir. Whereas really it's going to be about them, isn't it? A self-help book. What can they do to help themselves?"

"Yes." Her father pulled a face. "Maybe I don't have a title after all. Perhaps I could call it *Things Your Doctor Would Like to Tell You if Appointments Were Longer than Six Minutes.*"

Phyllis patted him on the shoulder. "Why don't we leave the title for now?"

"I'll have to give it more thought."

"Brian, I love you but you need to stop thinking and start doing."

He gave her a wounded look. "Starting a sentence with 'I love you' doesn't make the contents less harsh, you know. Writing a book isn't easy. First, there is the sheer volume of information and the challenge of working out what the average person needs to know, and then you have to communicate it all in words that everyone can understand."

Phyllis poured coffee into mugs. "I know, dear, but you were always very good at that part. It's why the patients loved you. Your problem with the book is sitting down and getting on with it. You are the king of procrastination. Just write something, for heaven's sake. Anything! Or I might just have to write it for you. I've listened to you enough over the years to have picked up a thing or two."

Jenny winced. Her mother wasn't known for her tact.

She gave her father a sympathetic smile and he rolled his eyes.

"Your mother's bedside manner leaves something to be desired," he said. "Germs didn't dare inhabit the ward when she was in charge. Anyway, back to Martin. Try not to worry, Jen. He'll cheer up now it's Christmas, I'm sure. And the children will be home soon. That will be a treat. You must be looking forward to it. It will be the first time they've all been home together for ages."

That was true and she was looking forward to it, not least because she didn't know how many more of these lovely family Christmases they would have. Not that any of them had so much as hinted at a change, but she was a realist. Her children were adults now. Someday soon they'd decide they'd rather spend Christmas in their own homes. Or maybe Rosie would have to go and spend Christmas with Declan's father and step-mother. She imagined them arguing about which set of parents they'd be spending Christmas with.

She gave herself a silent telling-off.

This year they were all coming home, and that was all that mattered right now. She should be grateful. If there was one thing nursing had taught her it was to make the most of the moment. There was no point in worrying about next year, or the year after that, because no one knew what life would look like.

And the irony was that a few hours after they'd all descended on Mill House, her home would be filled with chatter, laughter, suitcases, coats and what felt like hundreds of pairs of shoes discarded by the door, and in no time she'd be feeling drained and in desperate need of a moment of peace and quiet, even though just a day earlier she'd sat in the quiet and craved the noise of a busy household.

She loved the idea of a family Christmas, but the gap between her idealized version (visions of cosy evenings spent chatting in front of the fire, or long winter walks) and the reality (a close resemblance to running a boutique hotel single-handed, with no time off and extremely demanding guests) seemed to grow bigger every year.

It was partly her fault. It was her desire to give everyone a perfect Christmas that led her to spend hours in the kitchen. And the pressure was greater than ever this year because Jamie was bringing his new girlfriend, who apparently had never had a proper family Christmas and was desperately excited.

She felt a flicker of anxiety that the Christmas she delivered might fall short of expectations.

Her mother picked up her knitting again. "I thought I'd wear my gold dress to the party. The one Rosie made me for Jamie's wedding. It has a little tear in it but I'm hoping she will mend it for me."

"I'm sure she will. And you look lovely in that dress." And she realised that she hadn't given a single thought to what she might wear to the party.

The party.

It was the party, of course, that had provided the final challenge to her stress levels.

"A party?" Her voice had risen when she'd taken the phone call from Jamie. "A few days before Christmas?"

"I have something special to announce."

And that could only mean one thing. Jamie and Hayley were going to announce their engagement.

All he'd said was *we'll talk when I'm home* and she wondered if that meant he was busy, or that he didn't want to answer any of the questions he knew she was dying to ask. She'd always tried to respect her children's boundaries and let them make their own mistakes (she'd made enough of her own when she was their age) but occasionally she wanted to nudge them and say *are you sure?*

"I'm delighted for Jamie. After what happened with Poppy, I thought maybe he'd given up on love." Her mother put her knitting down. "And whoever she is, she's a lucky girl."

Whoever she is . . .

And who *was* she? That question had been nagging at Jenny in the night. Jamie was about to get engaged to someone he'd met a couple of months ago and had yet to introduce to his family. Why the rush? Did he feel he needed to put a ring on her finger to stop her leaving him the way Poppy had? Did he think marriage would make a difference?

She rubbed her ribs with her fingers, trying to get rid of the ache in her heart.

Jamie was her firstborn, and it didn't matter whether he was three or thirty-three, she still worried about him. They'd had almost five years together before the twins had arrived and changed life beyond recognition. Still, Jamie had loved his sisters, and his steady nature had calmed their often chaotic family.

He'd never given her a single day of worry until he'd fallen in love with Poppy in his second year of medical school. They'd dated for eight years and done everything together, to the extent that everyone in the family got used to saying Jamie-and-Poppy, instead of just Jamie, as if they'd somehow become a single entity. They'd both taken jobs in London, and they'd shared a small apartment where the train rattled past and woke them up early in the morning.

That they would spend the rest of their lives together had been a foregone conclusion, until one day Jamie had called and said that Poppy had left.

And that was that. Her easygoing son had shut himself off. He'd worked, he'd seen friends, but he hadn't dated, and after a few years, when she'd plucked up enough courage to ask about whether he thought he should perhaps put himself out there again, he'd said *if I want pain, I'll just stab myself through the heart.*

Martin had been a rock. It was a type of grief, he'd assured her, and he'd get over it in time. When she'd asked how much time, he'd said that it would take as long as it took.

And it wasn't that she had a particular wish to see her children married, but she did want them to be settled and happy, and she'd never been entirely convinced that Jamie had ever recovered fully from Poppy.

That had been six years ago, and then a few months ago, out of the blue, he'd started mentioning a girl. Hayley. It had been Hayley this and Hayley that, and Jennifer had felt herself relax because finally Jamie had managed to move on. He was having fun again.

What she hadn't anticipated was that he would move on so completely that he'd want to marry her within a matter of months.

"I looked up her social media feed," her mother said, and Jenny, who was rarely surprised by anything, was surprised.

"You did? Since when have you been on social media?"

"How else am I going to stalk my grandchildren? They're busy people, and this way I can see what they're doing and keep an eye on them."

"You follow them on social media?"

"I do. It keeps me young."

"Really?" It had the opposite effect on Jenny. It made her feel old. On one particular platform, everyone seemed angry, and watching that anger was exhausting. On another, everyone was young and gorgeous and everything in the world around them was perfect. Clothes were never wrinkled, hair was never frizzy, food was never burned. Even when people took photos of books, they were perfect. There were no wrinkled covers or turned-down corners or strange sepia blobs that might have occurred when one was paying more attention to the words on the page than the relative angle of one's coffee mug. "You don't follow Hayley too, do you?"

"Yes."

Jennifer felt faint. "Mum, you shouldn't—"

"I'm interested! What's wrong with that? She has a large following, so I hardly think she'd going to notice little me lurking in the background. Anyway, her posts—that's what they call them, in case you didn't know—all seem very wholesome. She's part of the solo travel community, or she was until she met Jamie. She posts all sorts of wonderful photos and tips."

"I thought Jamie said she was an illustrator."

"That's her job, but she's self-employed so she takes her inspiration from her travels. Young people today are very bold. I'm full of admiration, although I do wonder if she gets tired of moving around so much. The girl never seems to be home. She's what they call a digital nomad. I can't believe you don't know all this."

"I try and give my children privacy. Also I'm always scared I'll 'like' something by mistake."

"What's wrong with liking something? I've done that myself several times."

"Mum!"

"What? If she wanted to be private, she wouldn't have a public account. She wants people to look. She has a huge following. Half a million people. Sometimes she posts pictures of her illustrations. She's talented. She and Rosie will have plenty in common."

It occurred to Jenny that her mother, aged eighty-four, knew more about modern life than she did. When Jamie had first mentioned that Hayley was a digital nomad, she'd had to look up what it meant. She still wasn't entirely sure what to make of it all. There were days when she felt decidedly old.

"Is there anything else you've discovered about her that I should know?"

"According to her website, she's a Pisces and her favourite colour is indigo."

"Indigo?"

"Somewhere between blue and violet. I looked it up. Oh, and she's addicted to Christmas movies."

Jenny stared at her. "Christmas movies?"

"The ones where everyone smiles all the time and eats gingerbread without putting on weight. She loves everything to do with Christmas. She admitted as much on her account this week. Last year she spent Christmas in Lapland and posted wonderful photos of the northern lights. She stayed in a beautiful cabin that looked like the inside of Santa's grotto, and she fed reindeer and went on a sledge pulled by huskies. I can't wait to ask her about it. I might persuade your father to take me there, although I don't suppose his arthritis would appreciate the cold." Her mother put her knitting aside and picked up her coffee mug. "And as for Christmas movies, they're the perfect thing to watch while you're doing the ironing, don't you think?"

Jenny avoided ironing whenever she could. "I've never watched a Christmas movie."

"Really? I love a good Christmas romance. I can't believe you've never watched them. They're often on in the afternoons."

"I don't watch TV in the afternoons."

"Well, you need to make an effort. Hayley has told all her followers to stay tuned for some perfect festive posts because she is about to have her first-ever family Christmas and she knows it's going to be the best. Even better than Lapland."

"Is she talking about staying with us?" How on earth could Christmas at the Mill be better than Lapland? How was she supposed to compete with Santa's grotto, reindeer and the northern lights? Jenny felt a flutter of alarm at the thought of half a million strangers seeing the inside of her house. She was going to have to keep it tidy, and that would be a major challenge at Christmas. Did Hayley photograph people? Would Jenny need to be doing her hair and makeup several times a day? "What exactly is she expecting? What happens in these movies?"

"Nothing happens." Her father filled in a few more squares of his crossword. "Sometimes I'm forced to sit through them, and I can assure you that nothing happens, so don't worry about it."

"Nothing *stressful* happens," her mother corrected him. "And really that's the point. You are guaranteed a stress-free ninety minutes. It's not about the plot, it's about the setting and the atmosphere. It's all cosy and soothing."

"In other words, it's nothing like a real Christmas, which is rarely soothing. In a Christmas movie, no one ever fights, no one takes too long in the bathroom and all the gifts turn out to be something you've always wanted rather than something you can't wait to pass on to some other unsuspecting individual." Her father put his pencil down and checked his watch. "Crossword finished in forty-five minutes. Good to know the old brain is still working."

Jenny helped herself to one of the mugs of coffee. "So what you're telling me is that in order to impress my son's new girlfriend, I'm going to have to pull together a dream Christmas."

What did that mean exactly? What did she have to do that she didn't already do?

Her father stood up and strolled to the window, rubbing his shoulders to relieve the ache.

Jenny felt a pang of sympathy. He rarely complained but she knew his arthritis bothered him, particularly in cold weather and the temperature had dropped dramatically overnight.

"It will be simple," her mother said. "Just do what you always do but add more fairy lights. You can never have too many fairy lights."

"Fairy lights? You mean other than the ones that go on the tree?"

"Yes. Put them everywhere, including the garden."

"The garden?" That was the one place she didn't usually have to think about at Christmas, but apparently that was about to change.

"Yes, I saw some very pretty lights that you can hang from a tree."

"At least you won't need fake snow." Her father was staring

52

out of the window. "Looks as if we are going to have plenty of the real stuff. If it carries on snowing this heavily the roads will soon be impassable. Let's hope that doesn't prevent them from getting home."

"I hope so too." Her mother opened the tin of cinnamon cookies Jenny had baked for them and put a few on a plate. "I'm looking forward to meeting this girl of Jamie's. Maybe I could help plan their wedding. And obviously it will be good to spend time with Rosie and the lovely Declan. He's the strong, silent type. Perfect for Rosie."

Her father turned, a smile on his face. "The man probably can't get a word in edgeways so he has no choice but to be silent."

Phyllis broke a cookie in half. "You're not to tease Rosie. You know how sensitive she is." She turned back to Jenny. "I'm looking forward to getting to know him a little better. He seemed rather overwhelmed by us all at the wedding. I wonder if Rosie is pregnant yet?"

"Do not ask that question!" Jennifer went hot and cold at the thought. "That is overstepping."

"I know. You're not allowed to ask these days. But she is my youngest grandchild."

"It doesn't matter where she is in the birth order. You still can't ask that question." Jennifer could just imagine the response if she did. "And don't ask Becky about boyfriends, either."

"Why not?"

"Because young people don't like being asked about these things."

"It's caring. I'm showing an interest."

"No mention of pregnancy and no mention of boyfriends. Promise me."

"I'd better not promise, but I'll do my best. But it would be nice if Becky met someone, don't you think?"

"I want her to do whatever feels right for her. And if she's happier single, that's fine with me."

Her mother scraped up crumbs that had fallen on the table. "I hope it won't be hard for her seeing her brother getting engaged."

How *would* Becky feel if Jamie announced his engagement? First Rosie, and now her brother. Becky didn't talk about her relationships, so Jenny didn't even know if she was seeing anyone. Presumably not, or Rosie would have told her during one of their many chats.

And although she wouldn't admit it to anyone, Jenny was worried.

On the surface, Becky seemed like the toughest of her three children, but Jenny knew that underneath she was as sensitive as the others, possibly more so. As a child, whenever Rosie was upset, she'd crawl onto Jenny's lap and seek comfort. Becky had hidden behind the sofa and stayed there until she had her emotions under control. No amount of coaxing would persuade her to talk about how she was feeling. Of all her children, Becky was the hardest to read.

"Aren't you getting ahead of yourself?" Her father turned. "You're planning a wedding and we don't know that Jamie and Hayley are getting engaged. You're making assumptions."

Jenny forced her mind from her youngest child to her eldest.

"I took a delivery of champagne yesterday." She helped herself to one of her own cookies. "Why else would he order that?"

"Possibly because he's wise enough to know that we're going to need alcohol to help us through the festive season." Her father returned to the table and drank his coffee. "I hope you're well stocked, Jenny. More important than fairy lights."

Jenny wondered if Hayley, who had never experienced a family Christmas, might find their family a little too much.

She thought about what Jamie had told her in his excited phone call. *She has no one, Mum. This is going to be her first-ever family Christmas.*

Her heart had ached imagining Hayley as a little girl, envying all the family Christmases she imagined everyone else was enjoying. And it ached now for the grown woman who still craved the joy of spending the festive season with family, even though they weren't her own. Was she going to be bitterly disappointed by the reality? Was the whole thing going to be a giant letdown compared to her fantasies?

It seemed it was Jenny's responsibility to conjure up an atmosphere worthy of the movies.

She needed to work out exactly what that looked like, but first the basics. She needed to persuade Martin to get dressed and help fix the bathroom door.

And that wasn't going to be easy.

Merry Christmas, Jenny.

4
Hayley

Hayley clutched the seat of the car, wishing Jamie would slow down. The roads were narrow and windy, and at lunchtime they'd stopped for a romantic crab sandwich in a pretty seaside village, a decision she was now regretting. Not that there had been anything wrong with the sandwich. Far from it. It was possibly one of the most delicious things she'd ever eaten (she'd been convinced she could taste the sea), but unless Jamie stopped taking corners as if he was on a racing track, the whole episode was going to lose its romantic edges (and she would lose her lunch).

"Could you slow down? I've never been to this part of England before and I'd like to not die and maybe have time to admire the scenery."

"You'll have plenty of time to admire the scenery when we're home."

Home. It was an alien word to her, but she liked the way it sounded.

"You still call it home, even though you have your own home in Edinburgh?"

"Yes." He smiled. "I suppose I have two homes. The place I grew up, and the place I live now. And by the way, Edinburgh is your home too now. I just hope you don't get bored giving up your nomadic lifestyle."

"I won't." She smiled and gazed at the view. It was dizzying to think that when Christmas was over, she'd be going back to his (she still couldn't quite think of it as "their") apartment in Edinburgh. She was used to moving. Always moving. "It's beautiful here. Wild. I can't believe it's snowing. It's magical."

"You're not missing Thailand?"

"I don't care where I am as long as I'm with you."

"Northumberland is a special place, and I can't wait to show it to you." He reached across and took her hand, which normally she would have loved. She'd spent so much of her childhood starved of affection she now soaked up every morsel in the same way she soaked up sunshine, but right now she wanted him to keep both hands on the wheel.

The thing about whirlwind relationships, as she was discovering, was that every day you learned something new about each other. Take today for example. She'd known from the first day she'd met him that Jamie loved cars, mostly because she'd been standing next to her jeep, which had broken down again, and he'd stopped and said *let me take a look*, and he'd stared down at the engine, muttered something, tweaked something, covered himself in oil, and then the next moment the engine of her jeep was purring happily again. And she'd been so relieved that when she'd asked what she owed him and he'd looked at her and said *how about dinner*, she hadn't objected. Coming from anyone else that might have sounded creepy, but Jamie was incapable of appearing to be anything other than what he was— good-natured and honest.

She'd known that from the first day.

What she hadn't known was that he loved driving cars fast down narrow country roads (he also liked running marathons, watching old movies, playing video games and eating very dark chocolate, but she found those obsessions less terrifying).

"What if your family don't like me? What if I say, or do, the wrong thing?"

"They're going to love you."

He took their support and affection for granted, but that was because he'd never been without love in his life. And he'd never had to earn that love. He didn't live with the fear that people might walk away from him. He had no idea what it was like to be rejected.

"I'm nervous. It feels like an interview. Or maybe an audition." She remembered a time more than two decades earlier when she'd been sitting on a hard chair wearing a new dress that scratched her skin, trying to look like a poster child. She wasn't sure what people were looking for but it turned out it wasn't her. *It happens*, she was told. *It isn't about you.* Hayley had wondered who else it could be about as she was the only child in the room.

"You need to relax." Jamie slowed down as they approached a sharp bend. "Everything is going to be fine. My parents are relaxed, fun, good people."

"I'm sure they are, but it feels like a lot going from never meeting someone to spending Christmas with them. Let me just check my facts again." She'd been memorizing as much as she could to lessen the chances of her doing or saying something wrong. "You're the oldest. Then there are the twins, Rosie and Becky. They both live in London. Becky is a computer whiz and Rosie makes costumes for the ballet. Rosie is madly in love with Declan, who she married in February, and Becky is single. Not dating anyone, but I'm not going to mention that because she isn't the type who likes to talk about feelings." She glanced at him. "How am I doing so far?"

"A star student." He grinned. "What's our dog called?"

"Percy, and he's an English setter. You've had him six years.

58

He loves being stroked, but I'm not to let him jump up or he'll take advantage. He's not allowed in the bedrooms, but Rosie usually ignores that and sneaks him onto the bed when everyone is asleep."

"Full marks, but Hayley, you really don't need to study this as if it's an exam."

"The more I know, the easier it will be. I want to fit in." She filed all the information away carefully. "Ask me something else."

"What's the name of our guinea pig?"

She looked at him. "You have a guinea pig?"

"No. I was testing you." He was laughing. "No guinea pig."

"Have I told you that you're annoying? You need to take this more seriously." She eyed the side of the road, thinking that the snow seemed to be deeper here.

"You're taking it seriously enough for both of us."

"Maybe." She was determined to finish the conversation. "Your mother used to be a nurse. She's an excellent cook. Your dad has recently retired, and he is very excited about that because although he loved his job, it was all-consuming. He's the life and soul of any party and he will always be offering me a drink, but it's fine to refuse. You're sure? That won't sound rude?"

He sighed. "Hayley—"

"I know you think I'm being ridiculous, but these things matter. I don't want to do the wrong thing."

"There is no wrong thing. My mother just wants happy people around her."

"Happy people. Right. I can do that." She mustn't show that she was nervous or she'd make everyone else uncomfortable. "And your parents have been happily married for—forty years?"

"Don't ask me how long it is. I don't pay attention to anniversaries, and neither does Becky." He shrugged. "Rosie might know. She's the romantic among us."

"But they've been together since they were twenty-one, so yes, a long time. What else do I need to know?"

"Nothing. You know more than I do. And it isn't necessary." He gave her a brief glance, understanding in his eyes. "You don't need to study my family, Hayley."

"I want to fit in."

"Just be yourself. Christmas will be chaos. It always is. I doubt anyone will take much notice of you to be honest."

She hoped he was right, because the idea of so many people, all of whom loved Jamie but didn't know her, was daunting. Would they like her? She tried hard not to think that way but her brain was hardwired to ask those questions. It was her default position on every social situation. *No one will want me.*

Because there had been a time when no one had wanted her. Not her mother who had left her in a supermarket bag in a park an hour after she was born, and not the couple who'd thought they might adopt her but then changed their minds.

"Tell me more about your family Christmas. I want to know what you all do. Traditions, that kind of thing."

"I've already told you everything there is to know. You can't possibly want to hear it again."

"I do." This part was magical, so close to her childish dreams. She never tired of hearing about it. "There must be loads of things you haven't shared. For example, when you were little, did you hang your stockings at the end of the bed?"

"No. Downstairs on the fireplace because my mother always wanted us to open presents together."

Together.

She was used to *alone*. *Together* wasn't a word that had played much of a part in her life. She'd been close to some of the staff in the residential home where she'd lived for much of her childhood, but at the end of the day they'd gone home to their own families.

She focused on him. "And what kind of things would be in your stocking?"

"What do you mean?"

"Gifts. What sort of gifts?"

"Oh. I don't know." He gave a shrug. "The usual kind of stuff."

Usual for him.

She felt a twinge of envy that his childhood meant he took things like that for granted.

"Like what?"

"You want specifics? I'm not sure I can even remember—" He slowed down as they reached a junction and then turned right onto an even narrower road. "When I was young it was usually toys. Lego. Model airplanes. Things I could make and build."

"And you made those by yourself?"

"No. Usually with my dad or grandad. Sometimes with Becky because she loved building things too. My mother was good at choosing things that interested us. So Rosie would have dolls and dressing-up clothes, or fabric so she could make her own clothes for the dolls, but Becky and I would have puzzles and mechanical cars that needed building, and one year we had a train set between us."

She could picture the wonder on their faces as they'd opened their gifts.

"What else?"

"There was one year I had racing cars. That was fun, until the dog stepped on the track and broke it."

Thoughtful gifts. Gifts that each child would enjoy.

"Chocolate?"

"Oh yes." He grinned. "Becky and I always ate that before breakfast, but Rosie would hide hers away and save it for later. One year I found it and ate it. Not our finest sibling moment."

She imagined them, sprawled on the floor in front of the Christmas tree in their pyjamas, chocolate smudged on their faces.

"Do you know how lucky you are?"

"Because I could steal my sister's chocolate?"

"Because you have this great family. Because you're loved. You've always been loved."

He pulled over without warning and switched off the engine. Then he unclipped his seat belt and turned to face her.

He cupped her face in his hands and kissed her gently. "Stop worrying." His mouth lingered on hers. "I love you so much."

Every time he said those words she wanted to record them so that she could play them back over and over again.

It should have been freezing without the heating, but she felt nothing but warmth. "I love you too."

He sat back, his gaze fixed on hers. "I know Christmas was always tough for you. It hurts to think about it."

"It's the past. It's done. I prefer to think about now. And I'm excited about now."

He brushed her cheek with his fingers. "You're always so positive."

"Not always. I have low moments like everyone, but that's just life, isn't it? Full of ups and downs. I've learned to ride out the bad moments and when a good thing happens, I'm not going to ruin it by thinking about the bad things. I just grab it and enjoy." Like now. This was one of those good moments.

"But you never had family. Never had someone leave a stocking full of gifts for you."

"People donated things, so I had presents. Except for the year I was moved from one foster home to another a few days before Christmas." She caught his shocked expression and shrugged. "It happens. But it's a particularly bad time to be moved because of the emphasis on family that seems to be part of Christmas. It makes the feeling of isolation all the more acute."

"What presents did you have?"

She was grateful for the change of subject.

"Oh, various things—" She snuggled deeper into her scarf. "A new toothbrush and toothpaste. One year I had a shower gel and the bottle was the shape of a mermaid. A new flannel. Chocolate—that was nice. Crayons and paper. Gel pens. Notebooks to draw in. I loved those. Oh and knickers. Days-of-the-week knickers."

"Days-of-the-week knickers? For Christmas?"

"Yes, and here's the funny thing—they were all Friday."

"Are you telling me you only wore knickers on a Friday? I'm shocked!"

She giggled. "I was so confused. Took me years to figure out it was probably faulty stock that was being sold off."

He was laughing too, but there was something else in his eyes. Something that wasn't laughter, and after a moment he reached out and stroked his thumb over her cheek.

"I'm going to make sure that this Christmas makes up for the last thirty. And this year you will need to hang up your stocking, because Santa is going to pay you a visit."

"Santa?"

"Don't tell me you don't believe in Santa." His cheeks creased into a smile that made her stomach flip. It was his smile that had first caught her attention.

"He's never visited me before. I always assumed that was because he didn't exist, but I suppose it's possible he didn't have my address. Which might have been a good thing. It would have freaked me out to wake up and see a morbidly obese man in a red suit creeping around my bedroom in the middle of the night."

"You wouldn't see him," Jamie said. "He's stealthy."

"Even creepier."

Jamie grinned. "I posted him a letter from you so I'm confident that this year he is going to find you."

"Wait—you wrote to Santa for me?"

"No, *you* did. That night in Thailand when we were up all night telling each other everything. You said you'd never written a letter to Santa. Don't you remember?"

"I remember." She remembered everything about that night. They'd talked and talked. "You made me write one. I threw it in the bin."

"And I took it out of the bin and mailed it."

"You *mailed* it? Where exactly did you mail it to? What address?"

Jamie looked innocent. "To the North Pole, of course, where Santa lives."

"Of course." She reached out and put her hand on his face, feeling the roughness of his jaw against her palm. "You're a wonderful man, Jamie. How did I end up with you? I feel so lucky."

She still couldn't believe he wasn't going to vanish.

"I'm the lucky one. And Santa has worked hard at choosing things you'll love so I think you're going to have a happy Christmas."

"You mean you worked hard."

"Don't kill the magic."

Right now she was so happy, she'd take all and any magic that came her way.

She wanted to say that it wasn't the contents of the stocking that mattered (although she was touched that he'd given so much thought to it because it was another sign of how much he loved her). For her it was spending time with him and his family. Being part of something.

But still the niggle of anxiety remained.

His family were all so close. What if they thought she was the wrong person for Jamie? What if Christmas wasn't dreamy, but stressful?

"You're absolutely sure we shouldn't have told them our news before we arrive? Won't they be shocked?"

64

"No." He fastened his seat belt. "They know we have something to tell them, so they won't be that shocked. I asked them to arrange a party—a small one—just family and close friends. That should have given them some clues."

Her stomach rolled slightly. A party, especially for them. She would be the centre of attention. People would be judging her.

"But what do you think they're expecting us to say?"

"They probably think we're getting engaged."

"But—"

"It's going to be fine. Why are you frowning?"

"Because I'm worried this is all going to be a giant shock for them." Still, she had to trust that he knew what he was doing. "I suppose I always assumed that close families tell each other everything."

"Not always. And not everything. Sharing is optional. We still have some secrets." He shrugged and started the engine. "Let's go. Before I take you to meet my family, we're going for a long walk on the beach and I'm going to show you the most spectacular ruined castle. Wear all your layers. It's going to be cold."

It wasn't the cold that worried her.

She tried to ignore the feeling of disquiet. He knew his own family. If he thought everything would be fine, then he was probably right.

She should stop worrying.

Her first-ever proper family Christmas. This was what she'd always wanted, wasn't it?

Merry Christmas, Hayley.

5

Becky

S he raised an eyebrow when she saw the car.

Sporty. Deep midnight blue. She tried to look casual and uninterested but inside she was as excited as a child waiting for Santa to pop down the chimney. She wanted to crawl underneath its sleek, perfectly engineered body and take a closer look at the engine. She wanted to find an open road and put it through its paces.

For the first time since she'd walked into the airport, she was relieved that nothing was flying.

But she kept her expression blank. "Midlife crisis, Will?"

He dealt with their luggage.

"It's all about the engine. I love engines, you know that."

She did know that. He and her brother had spent hours tinkering with cars when they were growing up and she'd hung around, handing them whatever they asked her to hand then, fascinated by the mechanics and wanting to be part of it all. In that way, and in so many other ways, she was different to her sister.

When Rosie had been playing with dolls and going to bal-

66

let classes, Becky had been playing with train sets and racing cars. When Rosie had gone to ballet camp, Becky had gone to coding camp. She'd built her first game at the age of ten. She'd been the only girl in a group of fifteen boys, but that hadn't bothered her. It had been good preparation for life. When she'd gone to university to study computer engineering, she'd been one of ten girls in an intake of a hundred and fifty, and that hadn't bothered her either. By the time she'd graduated it had been six girls because four of them had switched courses. Becky hadn't understood why they would do that. Didn't they love it? She loved it. Loved it too much to care what other people thought of her or her skills. Programming was a way of solving complex problems, and she loved solving complex problems. And if she was surrounded by people who sneered and mocked her abilities, she ignored them just as she ignored the jibes that she'd only been given a place at what was considered one of the best universities in the world because she was a woman and they needed more women. Let them think what they wanted to think. Tell themselves what they needed to tell themselves.

From day one she'd focused on the work. She was insatiably curious. She wasn't afraid to ask questions, however stupid they might seem. She studied. If she didn't understand something she studied harder. She learned. Her marks were the best in her group. She had a natural talent, but there were other things she wasn't so good at. Small talk. Being sociable with strangers. Making friends. None of that happened easily. She didn't have the knack and didn't know how to develop those skills, probably because she hadn't had to. At school she'd had the same circle of friends as Rosie and her sister, sociable, friendly and good-natured, had done all the work. And Becky had let her.

In her first year of college she'd been on her own. She had a room on a long corridor and shared a kitchen with other students, but she usually grabbed sandwiches or ate cereal from a box that she kept under her bed so that she didn't have to venture into that terrifying space.

In her second year she'd moved out of college accommodation and into a small apartment with Rosie.

Living with her twin was easy because it was familiar.

They understood and accommodated each other's differences (although not without significant grumbling on occasion). Rosie wore short skirts and makeup and loved parties. Becky wore jeans and hoodies and clumpy boots and never understood the point of parties. She didn't like the noise, she didn't have much interest in talking to strangers and she was hopeless at flirting. She preferred being with people she knew. People she was comfortable with. People like Will, although she was a lot less comfortable with him since the wedding.

Still, this car reminded her why she and Will were friends, and it wasn't just because he was close to her brother.

She prowled around the car, trying not to drool on it. She couldn't criticize him for spending his money on it because she would have done the same if she hadn't lived in London. Traffic didn't move much so it would have been cruel and frustrating on both her and the car. And then there was the fact that she didn't have the money. Neither seemed to be a problem for him.

She touched the paintwork reverentially. "Why were you flying up north?"

"You mean when I could have driven this?" The amusement on his face told her he knew exactly how much she loved the car. "Same reason as you. I thought flying would be the fastest way to get home. I had to see a couple of patients first thing so I couldn't make a quick getaway." He loaded the last of their luggage into the car.

"You've seen patients this morning?"

"A couple of complicated cases I wanted to check on before going away." He slid into the car and she did the same, resisting the urge to ask if she could drive it.

68

She almost had to sit on her hands. "Jamie told me you'd got a new job. Congratulations."

"Thanks. He told me you got a new job too." He hesitated. "Do you want to drive? I know you hate being driven."

She laughed. Was there anything he didn't know about her? "That's true, but oddly enough you're the exception."

"I'll take that as a compliment, but if you want to drive at any point just let me know." He reversed out of the space and headed out of the car park. "So how's that going? The job I mean. I haven't seen so much of you this year so I assume it's keeping you busy."

"It's great."

"Mm." He paused while the barrier lifted. "So which part specifically do you hate? Or do you hate all of it?"

She sighed. "Am I that bad an actor?"

"No, but I know you. I've known you since you were—I don't know how old you were. I don't even remember a time when I didn't know you." He emerged from the car park and joined the flow of traffic leaving the airport. Snow swirled in front of them, reducing visibility. "Let's just say that I've known you long enough to be able to tell when you're lying."

He was right. She loathed everything about her new job. She missed her old colleagues and the fun they'd had together. Missed the familiarity and ease of it all. She'd been with the same company since college, and she was known and respected there. Starting somewhere new had proved to be a massive culture shift. And her boss was a problem. The fact that she was a woman should have been a positive in theory, but in practice it wasn't turning out that way. But the thing she found hardest of all was something she couldn't talk about.

But Will was waiting for her to share details, so she gave him the only detail she was willing to share.

"My boss doesn't seem to care about the quality of anyone's work," she said, "it's all about who is present in the office. Who joined in the team lunch. Who went on the team awayday to an escape room. It's just not me. I hate that kind of thing."

He shot her a sympathetic look. "I don't blame you. I'd hate it too."

"I had my appraisal recently and she said *there is no problem with Becky's work, but she needs to join in more.*" She snuggled deeper into the seat. It was so comfortable she could have closed her eyes and slept for the whole journey. It made her realise how tired she was. "It's mandatory to work in the office three days a week, so I do that. But I don't see why it should be mandatory to do group activities outside work. I loved going out with my colleagues in my last job, but that was different. That was our choice, because we liked each other. It wasn't compulsory."

Will slowed down to allow a car to pull in front of him. "Sounds as if it's time for you to find another job."

"I haven't even been there for a year."

"So what? You have skills, Becks. You won't have any difficulty finding another job."

Maybe he was right. She had to be able to do better than this. But what if the next place was as bad?

"I probably should have picked it up in the interview, but I'm not great at understanding humans. They're my least favourite animal."

He laughed. "Your favourite animal being a lesser spotted laptop?"

"Something like that. But I also like dogs. And horses. And most cats. Red squirrels. I like red squirrels." But he had her smiling too. And thinking. "So if you're such an expert on the human condition, tell me how I can convince her that I don't have to be partying until dawn to do my job well."

"Not much you can do. It's her problem."

"Sadly that part isn't true. It's very much my problem." The brief lift in her mood dissipated.

"Do you wish you'd never changed jobs?"

How did he always know exactly which questions to ask? And why did they always get her deep in her gut? Yes, she wished that. She wished she'd shoved all those complicated feelings into a box and ignored them.

But it was too late for regrets. There came a point where you just had to live with the decision you'd made. Remind yourself of the reasons you made that decision in the first place.

"I don't wish that."

He glanced at her. "I never thought you'd leave your old job. You loved it. Did you really have to?"

She felt her insides flip over.

"Yes." This was it. This was the moment she'd been dreading. He was going to ask her the one question she didn't want to answer. She dug her fingers hard into her leg and waited.

She wanted the car to somehow swallow her whole, but although it was a masterpiece of engineering she doubted that particular trick was within its specification.

He was silent for a moment. "Are we going to talk about it?"

Her mouth was dry. "About what?"

He smiled. "Right."

That was it? That was all he was going to say?

She waited a few more seconds but when no other words emerged from his mouth, she slowly relaxed her muscles and let out the breath she hadn't even known she was holding.

Most people would have carried on pushing. They would have dug and probed and then sulked when she hadn't told them what they wanted to know. But this was Will, and he knew she hated talking about her feelings. Instead of pushing, he stepped back.

Once, when she was eight and the family dog had died, she'd run away to the beach so that she could be by herself (Rosie had been howling on their mother's lap. Her father and Jamie were also howling). Will had followed her and sat down next to her. He'd said nothing, just kept her company while she stared fiercely out to sea and tried hard not to cry. And she'd been grateful for his company. Even more grateful that he hadn't tried to hug her, or soothe her, or encourage her to cry. He'd just sat there, by her side, and let her be what she needed to be. Do what she needed to do.

And now he was doing it again, and she was so overwhelmed with gratitude and affection for him she almost flung herself across the car and hugged him.

"I did the right thing leaving." She was going to keep telling herself that. And she didn't want to talk about it any longer or she'd start questioning her decision even more than she already was. "Tell me about your job. You're the big cheese now?"

"I try and avoid cheese because of its saturated fat content." He made light of it, but she knew from Jamie that it had been a significant promotion.

"Same hospital. So you don't have to move house, which is good given all those hours I put into helping you paint your kitchen and plant out your garden, I might have to kill you if you moved."

He smiled. "That's what I thought. It's the reason I didn't relocate. I thought, Becky will kill me and it's bad for a house's value if there was a murder there. Also, I like where I live."

"Yes, I get that." She loved his house, and she was in awe of what he'd done. Yes, she'd helped paint walls, sand floors and bring to life the abandoned garden, but he'd done the bulk of the structural work. "I still can't believe you did it all yourself. That must give you a sense of satisfaction."

"Sometimes. And then at other times I ask myself why I didn't just pay a professional to do it."

"You would never have done that."

He shifted his hands on the wheel. "I wouldn't?"

"No. Firstly because you like to fix things. Cars. Houses. People. Hearts. Arteries. And secondly because you love learning new skills. I remember when you helped my dad and Jamie build our tree house. You kept saying 'show me. Show me how to do it.' It was occasionally annoying."

He smiled. "And you say you don't understand people?"

"I've known you forever. It's different." She suppressed a yawn. "Also, you don't behave in a contrary way like most of the people I seem to meet. You always make sense. So you love your job and you love your home. I'm pleased for you, really." And she was. Will was virtually family and she wanted nothing but good things for him.

"How about you? Apart from the job, obviously. I already know about that. How is your new flatmate working out? It must feel strange not to have Rosie there."

Strange wasn't the word she would have chosen, but it worked. The whole of her life felt strange right now.

"It beats walking into the living room and finding them having newly married sex on the sofa. Also it's a nice change not having Rosie's flimsy underwear drying on radiators and all the half-made dresses she happens to be creating. Not to mention the yoga mat with the weights. I was always falling over her weights. Almost broke my toe on one of them." Did she sound convincing? She'd spent a lot of time focusing on the things that drove her mad about her sister. It was an antidote to more complicated and painful feelings.

"What do you miss most about not having her there?"

Everything.

Becky searched for an answer that wouldn't open up a bigger conversation. "I miss her cakes."

"Cakes?"

"You know Rosie. She was always baking. Whenever she felt homesick, she'd bake. Which was good for me—" she glanced at him "—although probably bad for my arteries, right?"

73

"Probably. But it's all about balance. It's not as if you live on cake."

"No, although since I moved jobs my sugar intake is sky-high. They have chocolate and sugary pastries in the office. Right there, every day, spread out where anyone can grab them. Walking past without taking something requires more willpower than I was born with. Probably another strike against them, but at least sinking my teeth into chocolate stops me sinking my teeth into my boss."

"There are other methods of comfort, Becky. Better ones."

"Nothing is better than chocolate."

He considered that. "Dark chocolate is acceptable."

"Dark chocolate is an abomination. It's milk or nothing."

He winced. "I don't want you to show up in one of my clinics in twenty years."

"Twenty years?" She tugged off her boots and flexed her toes. "Right now I'm trying to survive the moment."

"That's what everyone says. Live for now. Drink the wine. Smoke the joint."

She laughed. "I've never smoked in my life, and you know it. I don't drink much, either. I get my five a day. I run in the mornings, work up a sweat. Milk chocolate. That's my vice. And I get a free pass because one of my best friends is a cardiologist."

"Really? Do I know this person?"

She punched his arm lightly. "I'm relying on you to save me from my own lifestyle."

He shook his head in despair. "What about work life balance?"

"What about it?"

"Do you have it? Balance I mean."

"Work's a passion. The only thing that's stressful about my work is the people I'm working with." She sighed. "Maybe I should turn freelance. Sell myself to the highest bidder. Then I could live anywhere."

"You've had enough of London?"

She'd said enough. Probably too much.

"I just wonder if it's time for a big change, that's all. But I'm going to forget about it now. It's Christmas. My gift to myself is to give my brain a rest from worry and stress." She squinted out of the window. "It's snowing hard. Do you think we'll make it?"

"The motorways will be clear, I'm sure. It will be the roads further north that might give us a problem, but let's see how it goes. No point in worrying. It's not as if we have a lot of other options to consider. How's Rosie doing?"

"She's great, I think."

"You think?" He glanced at her sharply and then focused on the road again.

"Figure of speech. I mean she's fine." Was she? Of course she was. Rosie was now happily married and building a new life. "She and Declan are crazy about each other. They're bliss-fully happy."

He kept his eyes fixed on the road ahead. "But you're not seeing much of each other?"

"Not as much as we did, obviously. Declan's apartment isn't that close to mine, and the new job has been taking up a lot of my time." They'd reached the motorway and she was relieved to see that it was running pretty smoothly, although the snow continued to fall heavily. "Also she's married, and she doesn't need her sister hanging around like a spare wheel."

He was silent for a moment and the only sound in the car was the soft swish of the wipers clearing snowflakes. "That's a big adjustment for you."

Becky felt an ache in her chest. "That's life, isn't it? It requires constant adjustment. Nothing stays the same."

Although if she was honest she'd thought her relationship

with her sister would. She'd never anticipated this. She'd assumed that she and Rosie would always be close, whatever their life situations.

But now she could see that she hadn't thought it through. That she hadn't considered the impact of having a significant other in their lives.

He adjusted his grip on the wheel. "I know you don't really like talking about things—"

"You're right, I don't."

"That's fine, but I just wanted you to know that if you need someone to listen, I'm here. And if there's anything I can do, let me know."

She kept her gaze fixed firmly ahead.

He knew.

He knew all of it. How she was feeling and why she was feeling it. But he wasn't pushing her.

There was a strange pressure in her chest. "There isn't anything anyone can do, but thanks. I appreciate the offer."

She was touched that he'd asked. Even if the rest of her life was a disaster, she still had Will as a friend.

She was relieved that what happened at the wedding hadn't changed that. He could have judged her. She was certainly judging herself.

He reached out and briefly squeezed her hand. "It's going to be okay, Becks. Christmas, I mean. The party. You're going to be fine."

She knew that she wasn't going to be fine at all, but her superpower was hiding her feelings so no one was going to know.

Except Will.

6

Jennifer

She drove home via the forest. It was a detour, but she was worried that the single tree she'd already bought and decorated for the living room wouldn't be enough. Not with Hayley's expectations riding higher than Santa's sleigh.

She'd asked her mother to describe the key elements of a Christmas movie and had made a few notes on her phone. She intended to print it out when she got home so that she could use it as a checklist, but for now she needed to buy more Christmas trees.

She parked alongside a couple of other cars and stepped out into the clearing that had been decorated for Christmas. She had to admit it was charming, particularly today with snow dusting the trees and the scent of the forest in the air.

For the whole of December they opened a special Alpine-style Christmas cabin that sold hot drinks, decorations and various speciality foods. When the children were living at home it was where they'd always gone to choose their tree. They'd made an expedition of it, combined it with a walk along one of the forest trails and a warming mug of hot chocolate.

Her spirits lifted and for a brief moment she felt the same rush of excitement she'd felt as a child when Christmas approached. It was a shame Jamie hadn't brought Hayley home a week or two earlier so that they could bring her here and include her in the preparations. Anticipation was such a big part of Christmas.

It was a slightly strange feeling to contemplate that her son was possibly about to announce his engagement to a woman Jenny had never even met. No matter how old her children were she still worried about them, which was a waste of time, of course, because they were adults and she had no control over their decisions. And although she enjoyed them as adults, there were still times when she thought wistfully back to those days when they were very young.

Christmas was one of those times.

She stooped and picked up a pinecone, remembering a time when Rosie had stuffed her pockets full of them and then taken them home and sprayed them silver. Jenny had loved those impromptu decoration-making sessions, watching her daughter giving free rein to her creative talents. Rosie had often felt left behind by her brother and sister and Jenny had made a point of displaying prominently everything Rosie made.

She hesitated and slipped the pinecone into her pocket, feeling an ache of nostalgia in her chest.

Perhaps it had been a mistake to come to the forest on her own. It was filled with too many memories.

She wished now that she'd brought Martin. He always loved the Christmas preparations and had complained that he'd often missed trips like this because he was working. But even as she had the thought she dismissed it. He would have said no, the way he said no to everything at the moment. A few weeks before they'd been invited to early Christmas drinks with friends, but Martin had said that he was just too tired and she'd felt too awkward and embarrassed to tell them the truth, so she'd muttered some excuse about life being crazy with all three children about to descend.

And she hadn't really wanted to go either because being with them would have made her feel worse about her own life. These particular friends seemed to have retirement sorted. They volunteered, they took long cruises to warm places, they saw their children and babysat for their grandchildren when needed. Their schedule was so packed it was hard to find time to see them. They weren't sitting on the sofa staring out of the window. They certainly didn't feel that life was over.

She felt guilty for making the comparison, even fleetingly. She needed to work out what had happened to Martin to suddenly change his view on retirement but wasn't sure how to approach it. She was dealing with a whole new version of her husband. The man she knew well and had shared most of her life with was capable and sensible. Whenever she had a problem, he was the one she went to for advice. There was a reason his patients had been willing to wait weeks for an appointment to see him when they could have seen a different doctor on the same day. This new version of Martin was a mystery to her, and she wasn't sure how to handle him.

Still, right now her priority wasn't Martin—it was to turn their home into something resembling a Christmas grotto.

With her mother's words wedged in her brain, she bought one more large tree for the hallway, and chose several medium-sized trees in pots, reasoning that they could go in the garden after Christmas and hopefully be used again next year.

Having loaded those into the car, she went back to the log cabin that had been converted into a shop for the Christmas season. She bought extra sets of fairy lights and garlands for the stairs. Extra trees required extra decorations, so she bought those too. Trying not to think about the cost of it all, she loaded all her purchases into the car and checked her list once more.

Outdoor lights.

Before she could change her mind, she called the man who had fixed a leak in their roof the winter before. She spoke to his wife, who began the conversation by saying he was completely booked with only a few days to go until Christmas, but then changed her mind when she realised who she was talking to.

"Roy will be over this afternoon, Jenny, and he'll sort you out. And don't worry about buying lights, we have plenty here so I'll pack them all into his van and you can discuss it with him. There's nothing we wouldn't do for you and Dr. Balfour. He's the reason our Milly is still alive. Virus, that first doctor we saw said, but Dr. Balfour wasn't having any of it. He had one of his feelings, he said, and we're all grateful for that. If he hadn't given her that injection when he did—"

It was something she heard a lot. Everywhere she went, it seemed people had a reason to be grateful to Martin. It made her proud, but also reminded her of how all-consuming his job had been and the difference he'd made.

Maybe the challenge of giving it up was greater than either of them had anticipated.

Thanking the woman, she ended the call and decided she needed to get back if she was going to unload all her new purchases before Roy arrived to decorate the house.

There were a couple of families with young children choosing their tree, and she felt a twinge of envy. She felt an urge to tell them to hold on to these moments because before you knew it, the children would have flown the nest, and gathering them together again would be rare and precious and never the same as when they were young. But she said nothing, because she knew that right now their focus was on the moment and the challenge of preventing those inquisitive children from breaking baubles or pulling berries from branches of mistletoe. If she told them how fast it was all going to go and that pretty soon they'd be looking back and wondering how time had passed so quickly, they'd look at her blankly.

Of course they would. She would have done the same at their stage of life.

She arrived home just before lunch and found Martin still on the sofa where she'd left him. His shoulders drooped. The mug of tea on the table in front of him was untouched. He was staring at the television screen at some daytime quiz show, but she knew he wasn't paying attention. He'd never watched daytime TV in his life before retiring. In fact, he'd barely turned on the TV at all—he'd always been too busy with other things. She'd been unable to persuade him to sit down even for five minutes.

She felt a pang of love and sympathy.

"Martin? How was your morning? I bought a few extra things for Christmas. I could do with some help getting it all in from the car." Hopefully the prospect of Christmas would galvanize him into action. He'd always loved this time of year and was known as a genial host.

"I'm a bit tired. Maybe later."

He didn't even look at her.

She had never felt so helpless. Normally when they were facing a big change, she anticipated the potential challenges. When the children were born, when they left home and the two of them became empty nesters—she always had a plan to help cope with each new phase. But Martin had been looking forward to retirement, talking about it constantly, and when people had asked her if she thought he'd struggle to adjust she'd laughed.

This new reality had come from nowhere and caught her by surprise.

On impulse she sat down next to him. Her Christmas haul could wait.

"I'm worried about you."

He stared at the screen that he wasn't watching. "Why?"

"Because you're not yourself."

"I'm just tired. I'm an old man now, didn't you know?" He glanced at her briefly, with a glimmer of a smile. "I need to rest more."

"You're not old, Martin. You're the same man who was working a stupid number of hours just a couple of months ago."

"Maybe I'm paying the price for that. I really am tired, Jen. Let's leave it at that. I'll be fine."

But she couldn't leave it at that. How could she?

"Has something happened that I don't know about? You were looking forward to retiring."

"I was. And with reason. Finally I don't have to set the alarm in the morning. I can sleep until midday if I want to."

The old Martin wouldn't have wanted to. The old Martin would have thought that was a waste of a life and would have been pressing ahead with a thousand tasks that would have had her head spinning.

She took a different approach. "I took the tree to my parents this morning."

"I'm sure they were pleased. They love a tree, don't they? Was everything okay?"

"Yes, although I think my dad was hoping you might help him."

"With what?"

"His book."

Finally Martin looked at her. "He's been talking about this book forever. Are you telling me he has actually written something down?"

"I'm not sure he's actually written anything, but he's on the verge of it." She saw Martin smile and that small win felt like a triumph. "He wants to talk to you about what he has in mind. He's worried he has been retired for too long, and he wants to make sure what he is planning is current and relevant."

The smile disappeared and his gaze shifted back to the TV. "How would I know? I'm retired too, remember?"

She managed to rein in her frustration. "It's a matter of months since you were the busiest doctor in the area. I don't think you've lost all your knowledge in such a short time."

"Maybe not, but I don't feel up to writing a book."

"My father is the one writing the book." *Or not.* "You're just going to help him untangle his thoughts. I know he'd appreciate it, Martin."

He sighed. "Fine. I'll talk about it with him when he's here for Christmas, but I don't really see what I can contribute." He reached for the remote control and changed the channels. "He did the same job I did."

"But he has been retired for decades. Everything has changed. Priorities change." She paused. "I'd appreciate help unloading the car, and decorating the trees."

"Trees?" He flicked to a nature series. "We already have a tree."

"I bought a few more. To make the house extra Christmassy for Hayley."

"Hayley?"

"Jamie's girlfriend! We're having a party tomorrow night. They have something to tell us. Please tell me you haven't forgotten all this."

"No, of course I haven't forgotten. I just forgot her name was Hayley, that's all. And you can't blame me for that. It's not as if we've ever met her. He has only been with her five minutes."

"It has been a couple of months."

"Exactly. A couple of months. I've had colds that have lasted longer."

"Oh Martin!" She shook her head in despair. "If you're going to be this grumpy when the children arrive then you'll worry them." *And ruin Christmas.*

"I promise to pull myself together and be my usual jolly self."

"Good." She leaned in to give him a kiss. "And you should be pleased Jamie is serious about someone. After that disastrous relationship with Poppy I wasn't sure he'd trust anyone again. I'm relieved he's happy."

"Early days."

"True, but maybe it only took a short time for them to know they were in love. I fell in love with you that very first day I saw you on the ward."

"You did not." He switched the TV off and looked at her. There was a hint of laughter in his eyes. A hint of the old Martin. "I seem to recall you shouted at me for taking bloods from one of your patients without checking with you first. You terrified me."

"If I remember correctly that patient was due for an X-ray at the same time. And I most certainly did not shout. I may have spoken to you firmly." She shifted closer to him. "It feels like yesterday. How has time passed so quickly?"

"I don't know." He rubbed his hand across his jaw and she noticed that he hadn't shaved.

He always shaved.

She took his hand. "You're my best friend. You've always been my best friend. You do know that?"

He hesitated. "Yes."

"Then tell me what's in your head. Tell me what you're thinking. You were looking forward to retirement but it's clear you're not enjoying it so far. You're not yourself. Are you missing it?"

"No. The pressure over the past couple of years have been enormous as you know. It's hard to please anyone these days."

And yet he had pleased them, she knew that, and she hadn't needed to have that conversation with Roy's wife to remind herself of that fact. His patients had loved him. During his last few weeks at work he'd been showered with gifts and cards. They had more scented candles than they would ever use, and if they'd eaten all the chocolates he'd been given and drunk all the wine they would have needed medical help themselves. But she knew how touched he'd been by the outpouring of affection. Had that made him question his decision to retire?

"You were very busy. Although in one way it must be a relief to no longer have the pressure, it's a big adjustment not going to work every day." She was stabbing in the dark but he wasn't offering up any clues so she didn't know what else to do but make some guesses. "Do you wish you were back there?"

"No. Definitely not." He said it so emphatically she knew he was telling the truth.

So it wasn't that he was missing work.

"Martin—"

"I'll be all right. Don't fuss."

Frustration mingled with sympathy. "I can't help if I don't understand."

"There's nothing you can do, Jen."

"I can listen."

"That won't change anything."

"Try."

He paused and then looked at her. "I feel old, that's all."

"Martin, you're not old!"

"I'm retired, Jenny. Put out to pasture." His voice was dry. "Of course I'm old. And the thing about not being busy is that you have plenty of time to think about it. I'm noticing aches and pains that I never would have paid attention to in my working day. I feel as if it's all downhill from now."

She felt a flash of alarm. She'd never heard him talk like this before. "It's a new phase of life, that's all. It will take some adjustment, just like the first day of school or your first day of medical school."

"Not really like that. In both those examples I had a purpose. And the future was exciting. Now the future is—" He paused. "I don't know."

And now she saw the problem. His work had been so demanding, so all-consuming, that there had never been any question of how he was going to spend his day. He went where he was needed and did what needed to be done. He had no time to think. But now whole days stretched ahead and he had no idea how to fill his time.

The problem, she decided, was that he'd let many of his interests and passions slide because he'd been too busy to pursue them.

Maybe what was needed wasn't sympathy, but some frank talking.

"Then we need to explore projects and hobbies that you'll enjoy and find rewarding, but in the meantime your purpose is to stop me being overwhelmed by all the Christmas preparations. By the way, I spoke to Roy's wife. Roy is coming here this afternoon."

"Roy the roofer?" Martin looked alarmed. "Why? Is the roof leaking again?"

"No. He's going to put Christmas lights on the outside of the house. That family think you're a hero, by the way."

He ignored that comment. "Why do we need lights on the house?"

"To make it look festive. I just hope he can get it done before Hayley and Jamie arrive."

"I don't understand why we need to decorate the outside when our nearest neighbours are across the field. Who exactly is going to see these lights?"

"Don't be a grump. It will look lovely. Just like the movies."

At least she hoped it would be just like the movies.

A message pinged on her phone and she instinctively reached for it, because that was what mothers did even when their children were adults, but then she moved her hand away.

"Check it," Martin said gruffly. "It's snowing. One of the kids might have a problem."

She lifted her phone and scanned the message. "It's Becky. On the family group chat. All flights are grounded so she is driving, but there has been a bad accident on the motorway and nothing is moving so they're checking into a hotel tonight and they'll join us tomorrow. That's a shame. There goes my big family welcome-home dinner."

"There will be plenty of people willing to eat Becky's share. You said 'they.'" Martin reached out and took the phone from her. "Who is 'they'? Does Becky have a boyfriend? Is yet another of our offspring bringing a stranger to spend Christmas with us?"

"I wish she would." Jenny retrieved her phone. "I worry about Becky."

"You worry about all of them."

"Becky the most." She could see that Becky was typing so she waited to see what the next message said. "Oh, she's with Will. They're driving up together. That's a relief. I'll worry less about her if I know Will is with her. I'll ring Audrey and let her know, although Will has probably already called her."

She and Audrey had met at a mother-and-baby group when Jamie and Will were both six months old and the two families had been friends ever since.

"Why are Becky and Will together? That wasn't planned, was it?"

"She said that they bumped into each other at the airport and Will offered to drive her."

"That's kind. And he's a good driver."

"So's Becky. She has always been good at driving in snow."

"True. Still, you're probably disappointed there isn't another romance in the air. Come on." He levered himself off the sofa. "I'll get dressed and help you haul the spoils of your forest trip in from the car."

She was relieved to see him finally display some energy.

"Great. I'll call Audrey while you're getting dressed, just

in case Will hasn't had the chance because he's driving." She waited for him to leave the room and then called her friend. "It's me! Guess what?"

"What? Why are you talking in a hushed voice? Have they arrived? Do you like her? Has Jamie confirmed he is engaged?"

"I haven't heard from Jamie. They haven't arrived yet, but they're only coming from Edinburgh and I think he hoped to stop and show Hayley Holy Island and a few other places on the way as she hasn't visited these parts before. They should be here for dinner. No, I had a message from Becky." She glanced at the door, checking there was no sign of Martin. "She and Will are driving up together from London."

"Ooh. Hold on while I go somewhere quiet." In other words, her husband was within earshot. There was the sound of a door closing and then footsteps as Audrey walked to a different room. "Tell me all."

"He hasn't messaged you?"

"Not yet. Why?"

"Because he and Becky are stuck in traffic and they are checking into a hotel for the night." She heard Audrey's muffled shriek of excitement.

"What do you think that means?"

Jenny checked the door again. "Well, the ever-practical Martin would say it means they need somewhere to sleep."

"I hope it's more than that. We've waited long enough, Jen. If ever two people were made for each other it's those two. Let's hope there is no room at the inn, or at least so little room that they have to share a bed. Do you know the name of the hotel? I could call them and reserve every available room but the honeymoon suite."

She could just imagine how Becky would respond to that, and it wouldn't be good.

"You're a wicked, interfering woman, Audrey Patterson."

But she was smiling because even though she was reluctant to admit it, the same thought had crossed her mind.

"I'm not interfering. But sometimes you have to give life a nudge, that's all. And talking of nudges, how is Martin?"

Audrey was the only person she'd confided in.

"Oh, you know—not great—" She let her voice trail off and heard Audrey sigh.

"We're going to have a proper catch-up in the New Year. Walk on the beach. Heart-to-heart and a hot chocolate in that gorgeous new café."

"I'll look forward to it. You'll be at the party tomorrow?"

"Of course, but we won't be able to talk properly there. And we definitely shouldn't talk about you-know-what because Paul would kill me if he knew about our plotting. Will would probably kill me too."

"We've been plotting forever and they've never found out. We should offer our services to MI5. No one would ever suspect us of misdeeds."

"We haven't actually committed a misdeed yet. How are your Christmas preparations going? Are you ready?"

Jenny thought about everything waiting in her car. All the things she still had to do. "I'd be closer to ready if I stopped talking to you." And as she said that, Martin appeared in the doorway with his coat on. "I'll talk to you later, Audrey. I need to help Martin unload the car. Just wanted to let you know about Will." She ended the call and Martin looked at her.

"Where are all these trees going? Do we have enough rooms in the house?"

"In the bedrooms. And if you could string some fairy lights around the room, that would be great."

"Since when did we have trees and fairy lights in the bedrooms?"

"Since my mother gave me a list of all the key elements of

Christmas movies. Lights are key. You can never have too many twinkly lights."

"Are we hosting a film crew or something? What am I missing?"

"Jamie's girlfriend loves Christmas movies. I'm trying to create the perfect Christmas."

He rubbed his forehead. "The perfect Christmas? Isn't that a bit unrealistic?"

"Nothing wrong with aiming high." She handed him the car keys. "If you could bring everything in, that would be great."

If he was feeling that his life had no purpose then the answer was to fill his life with purpose. And right now that purpose was Christmas.

7

Rosie

A re we lost?" Declan peered at his phone. "There's no signal."
They'd been driving all day with just one brief stop
to eat the sandwiches Rosie had packed. Now it was dark and
both of them were tired.

"We're not lost." Rosie was driving, navigating her way
more through instinct than knowledge.

They'd made surprisingly good time driving up north but
then the weather had worsened and so had the traffic. With visibility reduced, the road conditions deteriorating and too much
traffic, accidents had been inevitable. The fields and trees were
coated with snow, the landscape ghostly in the pale winter light.

"Isn't it beautiful? Don't you just love this time of year? The
snow is luminous." Rosie sighed as she scanned the frosted
landscape. "It transforms everything. It even makes ugly things
beautiful. Like that building over there in that field."

Declan squinted. "You mean that abandoned cow shed?"

"Is that what it is? Doesn't it look magical?"

"Um—it looks like an abandoned cow shed. Are you sure
you know where we are?"

"Well, not *exactly* where we are, but roughly. I know we're going in the right direction. We're not far from home. An hour maybe?"

Declan put his phone down. "There is a lot of snow."

"I know. Isn't it fantastic? It makes me think of winter fairy tales and carol singers and tramping across snowy fields with my mother to get to school because the bus wasn't running." She allowed herself a dreamy moment of nostalgia and then glanced at him and saw that he was frowning. "What does it make you think of?"

"Train delays. Frozen pipes. Dangerous roads and multiple accidents."

"Oh." She came back to earth. "That's very pessimistic. Is my driving making you nervous?"

"No. You're a good driver."

It wasn't the compliment she would have chosen, but she'd take it. "Thank you. My brother taught me. And Will."

"Who is Will?"

"Jamie's closest friend. He was at our wedding."

"I remember. Tall guy. Glasses. He sat next to Becky."

"That's him. He's mad about cars, and he took me out in snow a few times after I passed my test. Either he has nerves of steel, or he thought I was a good driver." Rosie slowed down at a junction and saw a signpost. "I know where we are! We're about forty minutes from home. It's going to be fine. There's a great pub near here. They make the most incredible cauliflower cheese. It has this crunchy topping and it's so delicious and creamy it should probably be illegal."

"Sounds good. I'm starving."

"Me too, but we're not stopping. In under an hour you will be facing more food than you know how to eat."

"That's hard to imagine. You're sure your mother will have cooked a meal, even though she doesn't know what time we're arriving?"

"Of course. My mother is relaxed about that kind of thing. Probably because my father was always being called to see a patient just as she was about to serve a meal. She's very flexible and there's always masses because she over-caters. You will be fed until you beg for mercy."

"I remember Becky saying food was a big thing in your house. She told me you ate breakfast and dinner together, sitting at the table, although your dad wasn't always there if he was working."

Occasionally he'd say things like that and she'd be reminded that his friendship with Becky predated their relationship by several years. She'd wonder how he could possibly know something so personal when she hadn't shared it, and then it would occur to her that he must have talked about it with Becky. In some ways Becky probably knew him better than she did.

It was an unsettling thought.

"We ate together when we could. Dad was rarely there for breakfast but tried to make dinner. That was when we talked."

"Talked? About what?"

"About everything. About our day. It was our family time. You didn't do that?"

He stared straight ahead. "No. We lived pretty independent lives. We mostly did our own thing."

She glanced at him briefly although she couldn't see his expression in the darkness. "Your stepmother isn't a keen cook?"

"No. In our house it's more casual. Everyone fends for themselves."

She couldn't imagine it, and now she was worried that he'd find her close family dynamics uncomfortable. Would he feel stifled?

Apart from the wedding, he'd never spent time at her family home. Her parents had visited them in London a few times since the wedding, and there had been a week in the summer when they'd planned to go to Northumberland, but then Declan had been given an urgent work project to deal with so Rosie had gone home alone.

"I'm sure it was nice to have that freedom." She didn't think it sounded that nice, but it felt rude to say so and she didn't want to do anything to shake this new truce between them. She was relieved that they were speaking again and that the atmosphere in the car had warmed a little over the journey.

Still, she would be glad to get home. They'd been lucky to be able to leave the motorway just before the traffic started backing up. Not long now and she'd be hugging her parents and Percy and warming herself in the big cosy kitchen of the Mill House. And with luck Jamie would already be there, which would give her a chance to have a quiet word with him before the party.

"Thank you for coming with me. And I'm sorry about your party." It felt like the right time to say it. "I didn't understand how much it meant to you but now I do."

He shifted in the seat, as if he'd forgotten she was there. "What?"

"Your Christmas party. I thought it was work for you. Duty. Why didn't you tell me how much it meant to you? If I'd known, I would have gone."

"But you made it clear you would have hated it."

"That was when I thought it was just a work obligation."

He kept his eyes on the road. "It is work, but they're also my friends. Good friends. It doesn't matter. Let's forget it, Rosie. Move on."

How could he say it didn't matter when it obviously did?

"It's unusual, the bond you all have. Normally colleagues come and go. It's rare to be working with the same people for five years." The people she worked with changed regularly, and many of them were freelancers.

"It's a great company, we work well together and we all like it there. And people do leave sometimes." He paused as they approached a tight bend. "Like Becky. She left."

Becky.

Becky had been part of his close group of friends. Becky would have gone happily with him to his Christmas party and they wouldn't have ignored her. She would have joined in the conversation because she spoke their language.

Long-suppressed emotions bubbled up inside her, and Rosie kept her eyes fixed on the road ahead, trying to control her thoughts. Growing up, she had often felt inferior to her sister. No matter how hard she tried, maths and spreadsheets just didn't make sense to her. It was all very well for her parents to reassure her that everyone had different talents but it was a fact of life that some talents seemed to be more highly valued than others. What had she excelled at? Making clothes for her dolls.

Because she and Becky were twins, there had been the inevitable comparisons, particularly at school.

They look identical, but she's nothing like her sister.

To be fair, her parents had never made that comment and had always encouraged her creative side. But every time she'd heard a teacher say those words, she'd shrunk a little because they were true. And no matter how hard she worked, she was never going to be her sister.

She'd scraped through the exams she'd been forced to take and then dropped those subjects in favour of the arts, which suited her better.

She'd been thrilled when she'd graduated and immediately landed a job with the ballet company, and hadn't cared that she was probably paid a fraction of what her sister earned.

And she knew she was good at what she did. There was skill involved in creating costumes for the dancers, but most people never thought about that. They watched the performance on-stage and had no concept of the work that had gone into making sure everything was perfect. With costumes there were so many elements to consider. The dancer had to be able to move fluidly, to feel good in the costume and forget about it completely when they were dancing.

Recently she'd been working on *The Nutcracker*, one of her favourite ballets and a staple of the festive season. It always made her feel Christmassy. It used over a hundred costumes and this time she'd made a new tutu for the Sugar Plum Fairy, spending hours sewing together multiple layers of tulle and embedding crystals that would sparkle and gleam under the lights. That costume had inspired the dress she'd made for herself to wear on Christmas Day.

She'd been excited about wearing it, but now she wondered if Declan would just think it was over the top. She was conscious that she dressed very differently from all the people he mixed with during his working day.

She hated the idea that he wasn't looking forward to Christmas. But maybe that was because his own Christmases hadn't been that special. Perhaps he didn't know what to expect.

"I think you'll like spending Christmas at the Mill House. It's always festive and my mother is an incredible cook. Her turkey will be the best thing you've ever eaten, I guarantee it." Was she being too cheery? Trying too hard? "All the other Christmas lunches you've ever had will fade in comparison."

"I've never had a particularly memorable Christmas lunch so that won't be hard. Not that I'm suggesting your mother's cooking is anything other than sublime," he said. "It's just not a meal that has ever made much of an impression on me."

She didn't know what she was supposed to say to that. "Oh."

"You're so transparent." But there was warmth in his voice. "You're worried because this is your favourite time of year and you're afraid I'm going to ruin it. You can relax. I know you love it, and I promise not to spoil it for you."

It wasn't only about her. She wanted him to enjoy it too, but maybe that was asking too much.

She stopped at a junction. "We're only twenty minutes from

home now. Could you message my mother and give her a twenty-minute warning?"

"You want me to message your mother?"

"Yes. Why not? You're her son-in-law."

"I know, but—fine." He picked up her phone and sent a message. "I made it clear it was from you."

It hadn't occurred to her that he might feel uncomfortable with her family. Her friends had always loved sleepovers with Rosie and Becky because their parents were so warm and welcoming. There was always cake and milkshakes and no one ever cared if they built forts in the living room or covered the kitchen table with their artwork.

"Did you never have a family Christmas? Not once?"

He put her phone back in her bag. "Define 'family Christmas.'"

"The whole family together. Doing traditional stuff."

"No. From the age of seven it was just Dad and me, and he wasn't cooking a turkey." He gave a short laugh. "He couldn't even boil an egg, so we ate whatever tins he had in the cupboard."

"Oh." And now she felt extra grateful for all the wonderful Christmases she'd had in her life. "Sorry. I probably shouldn't have asked."

"It's okay to ask." He paused. "I suppose there's a lot we still don't know about each other."

That was becoming clear to her. And she had questions. Questions she was afraid to ask in case she didn't like the answers.

Did we rush this?

Do you wish you'd never married me?

She kept her focus on the road. Of course he didn't wish that (did he?). Becky always said that she overthought things and she was definitely overthinking this. It was true that they were still discovering things about each other, but that was fine. She needed to adjust to that reality, that was all. When they'd met their connection had been so powerful she'd felt as if he'd always been in her life. As if she knew him instinctively, and as if he knew her. But that was her romantic side taking over. She saw now that there were a million tiny details that they hadn't shared.

"If you find our family Christmas too much you are allowed to escape to your room at any point. Or to the pub down the road. Jamie will go with you. And no one will mind." Everyone would probably ask where he was and if he was all right, and her grandmother would probably ask him directly because she wasn't known for her tact, but he didn't need to know that in advance.

"Stop worrying. I know you're close to your family, Rosie. You don't have to apologise for it."

"I don't want you to feel overwhelmed, that's all."

"I won't. There are plenty of things I'm looking forward to."

"You are?"

"Yes. Work has been hard so I'm ready for a rest. And I'm looking forward to walks on the beach and seeing more of the area. We didn't have much time for that last time we were here. I want to do a tour of ruined castles."

"There are plenty of those around here."

"And I'm looking forward to seeing Becky." He glanced at her and smiled. "It has been a while."

He was looking forward to seeing her twin.

That was good, wasn't it? It was good that the two of them got on well. It would have been awkward if a sibling didn't like your partner, even more so when that sibling was a twin and her closest friend.

"I'm looking forward to seeing her properly too. It feels like ages since we had a proper chat. But I suppose a new job is always tough and time-consuming."

"Yes, although it shouldn't be for Becky. She's a genius. To be honest I was surprised she chose that particular company. She would have been snapped up by any number of places. It seemed like a strange choice."

"Maybe they paid more."

"That wouldn't be it. Becky doesn't care that much about money. She's more interested in intellectual challenge."

She swallowed. "You know my sister as well as I do."

"Well, I've known her for a long time. More than five years."

"Yes." She kept her attention fixed on the road and told herself not to overthink things. "So if it's not a better job, why did she move?"

"That's what I don't understand. You move jobs for one of three reasons. One, you've been fired or there are no prospects where you are—that's not Becky. Two, someone makes you an offer you can't refuse, but that's not Becky either. Three, you want a bigger challenge."

"Well, there you go. It's obviously number three on your list."

"But that job really wouldn't challenge Becky. She could do it in her sleep."

It was like being back at school again. *Your sister is a genius.*

"Well, she must have had a reason for leaving, and no doubt she'll tell you about it."

"Yeah, it will be good to catch up. Everyone at the party was saying how much they missed her. We were disappointed that she didn't join us."

"You invited Becky?" Why didn't she know that? "But she didn't go?"

"No, she said she was busy."

Rosie was gripping the wheel so tightly her hands had started to hurt. "You didn't mention that you'd invited her."

"I didn't think of it. I assumed she might have mentioned it as you're in touch all the time."

"Not all the time. Not since she started the job." The road conditions were worsening and Rosie slowed her pace. "I've seen her a lot less since we were married."

He shifted in his seat, his long legs cramped by luggage and limited space. "She's probably been giving us time to ourselves. She's thoughtful like that."

Every time he opened his mouth, he seemed to be praising her sister, which would have been nice had it not been for the fact that he didn't seem to be similarly impressed by Rosie.

All she needed was for him to say *you're nothing like your sister.*

"It sounds as if you miss her."

"Yes. She's good fun. And brilliant, obviously."

"Obviously." Rosie stared straight ahead, her creative mind spinning scenarios that hadn't occurred to her before.

Fun. Brilliant. Friends for years.

She was so distracted by her own thoughts she almost missed the final turn, but at the last moment she registered where she was and turned the wheel sharply.

"We're here."

She drove along the lane that led to the house, thinking about Becky and Declan. Becky had talked about him for years before Rosie had finally met him, and it was usually when she was laughing about something. It had been Declan this and Declan that. Rosie had been so used to hearing his name that by the time she met him she felt as if she'd known him forever.

Becky and Declan.

No. No way. They liked each other and they'd been colleagues, but it was nothing more than that. She was definitely letting her imagination run away with her.

Trying to clear her head, she pulled into the driveaway of the house and blinked, dazzled.

For a brief moment she wondered if she'd taken the wrong road because her family home didn't usually look like this.

The whole house glowed and twinkled against the snowy

landscape, its roof and windows highlighted by a profusion of tiny lights. A large wreath hung on the front door, which was framed by lanterns and two sparkling Christmas trees. The path leading up to the house had been cleared of snow, but the trees that surrounded the house shimmered white and silver in the darkness.

The place radiated Christmas warmth and Rosie gazed at it in wonder, momentarily distracted from her less-than-comfortable thoughts.

"Okay, that's—unexpected."

"What is?"

"Lights on the house. My dad was always too busy to do the outside and my mother gets dizzy on ladders. Usually we have a wreath and that's it."

"It looks good. Welcoming." Even Declan stared. "Your house looks like something out of a Christmas movie."

"I know. And I love it."

She did love it, but it didn't erase the niggling worry that had taken hold in her head.

Declan and Becky. Declan and Becky.

Was Declan wishing he'd married her sister?

8

Becky

"D o you think this place even has room for us?" Seeing the number of cars in the car park, Becky didn't feel optimistic. "We might be sleeping in the car."

"We're not sleeping in the car." Will pulled into a space and switched off the engine. "Did your mother respond?"

"Yes, she said not to worry about turning up a day late and not to take any risks on the road."

"That sounds like a typical maternal response. Let's go and check out the room situation before we unload our luggage."

She glanced at the hotel. Smoke curled from the chimney, tiny lights shimmered around the eaves and a large Christmas tree was visible in the foyer. "This would be Rosie's dream hotel." She undid her seat belt. "You don't want to call your mother before we go in?"

"We both know that your mother will have been on the phone to my mother within two minutes of receiving your message."

"True. Okay, let's go and see if there is room at the inn."

"I don't mind sleeping in a corridor if I have to, but I hope they have a restaurant because I'm starving. I wonder if Rosie and Declan are stuck in the same traffic."

"They're not. According to my mother they're almost home. Declan messaged her half an hour ago. They were ahead of the accident apparently. Lucky them."

"Maybe. Or maybe we're the lucky ones." Will locked the car. "I remember reading a review about this place or something. Brilliant restaurant."

"Great. Anywhere that will feed me gets a full five stars from me. Although it's probably less good for us if everyone wants to stay here."

She dragged on her coat and walked with him across the snow-covered car park to the main entrance of the hotel.

He held the door open for her. "You don't mind stopping? Your entire journey up north has been disrupted."

"I don't mind." Part of her was relieved. The further up north they'd driven, the more her stress levels had risen.

But she'd been granted a reprieve, until tomorrow at least. She was happy about that.

They stepped through the doors into a foyer warmed by a blazing log fire. A large Christmas tree sparkled in one corner.

"That's a good start," Will said and smiled at the woman who approached. "We don't have a reservation, but we were hoping for dinner and a couple of rooms?"

"Dinner I can do—I have one more table if you don't mind sitting down in half an hour. But I only have one room left and it's up in the eaves. Restricted headroom, although you should be able to stand up in the centre of the room." She eyed Will's height. "Maybe. Just one bed, but it's a big bed and there's also a very comfy armchair."

Just one bed? Becky frowned. It sounded like a bad romcom.

"You don't have a second room?"

"No." The woman glanced briefly at a couple who had walked in behind Will and Becky. "And in fact we won't have that one for long, so—"

"We'll take it, thanks." Will handed over his credit card in exchange for a key, which he handed to Becky. "You go up to the room and I'll unload the car."

"We'll do it together, that way you won't have to make multiple journeys."

He didn't argue with her, probably because he knew better than to do so, and they managed to grab everything and staggered back across the now icy car park without mishap.

Then they negotiated the challenges of an old winding staircase that grew narrower as they reached the top of the hotel.

Becky opened the door and laughed.

"She wasn't kidding about the ceiling height. It's definitely a mind-your-head situation, Dr. Patterson. You might want to crawl in on all fours."

He followed her in, ducking his head to avoid the low beams. "This building is sixteenth century. Were people shorter then?"

"No idea, but this was probably the maid's room." She pushed her suitcase into a corner and deposited her coat on top. "You can have the bed. I'll sleep in the chair."

"I'll sleep in the chair. I can sleep anywhere. One of the benefits of a medical training." He hung up his coat and opened his suitcase. "We have twenty minutes before dinner. Do you want to shower? There probably won't be time for both of us to use it."

"Of course there will. I'm not Rosie. I don't need an hour in the bathroom and then another hour to dry my hair. I'll be out in five minutes." She grabbed a few things from her suitcase and headed into the en suite bathroom. True to her word, she emerged in under five minutes wearing one of the luxurious dressing gowns provided by the hotel.

Will was on the phone. "No, we're fine. We'll see how the

weather is in the morning and send you a message. We should be with you by lunchtime so there will still be plenty of time before the party." He listened for a moment and then smiled. "She's fine. Yes, they had two spare rooms. Lucky for us. Anyway I need to go because we have the last available dinner reservation and we don't want to lose the table, because we're both starving. See you tomorrow." He put his phone down on the bed.

She tightened the belt on her robe. "You told your mother we have two rooms?"

"Yes. It avoids speculation."

Becky opened her suitcase. "She doesn't think we can share a room without jumping on each other?"

"She has an active imagination, and she thinks I spend too much time at work. She likes to point out that I have a job, and a home, and that the only thing missing from my life is romance."

"Yeah, I get that, but not with me. I mean, I'm virtually family. That would be a bit gross, right?"

He hesitated briefly and then smiled. "Totally gross. Have you finished in the bathroom?"

"Yes, I've—"

"You have five minutes to get dressed." He disappeared into the bathroom and a moment later she heard the sound of the shower running.

She stared at the door and frowned, wondering why that exchange had seemed odd.

He was probably just embarrassed. Or even appalled at the thought of his mother pairing the two of them off.

He was probably trying to wash away the image.

And talking of washing, was he really going to manage in the tiny bathroom?

The shower was nestled under a sloping roof. Would he even fit?

She pictured him trying to wedge his wide shoulders under the jets of water and then imagined him naked. Naked. Will?

The trajectory of her thoughts left her feeling hot and flustered and she was relieved there was a door between them. He'd been in there for a minute which meant she had approximately two minutes to calm herself down.

What was wrong with her? Since when had she started imagining Will naked?

It was that comment about his mother wanting romance for him, obviously. Why had he told her they had two rooms? Why hadn't he just laughed and told her it was one room but hey, this was Becky so that wasn't exactly a problem.

The two of them together was a ridiculous thought. She and Will had known each other forever. She loved him of course—absolutely, but in the same way she loved her brother. In many ways Will was her second brother, which made imagining him naked both weird and unsettling.

That was definitely *not* something to dwell on.

Trying to delete that image from her brain, she rummaged through her suitcase looking for something suitable to wear. Not jeans presumably. And definitely not her hoodie. The place had looked romantic. Dressy. She wasn't good at either of those things, but she didn't want them to be refused a table, so she dug out the red dress she'd borrowed from Rosie and never returned and pulled it on together with thick black tights and boots. She so rarely wore dresses the whole experience felt weirdly unfamiliar, but at least no one would throw them out of the restaurant.

She dried her hair in less than a minute, glanced in the mirror to check she didn't look as flustered as she felt and saw Will emerge from the bathroom.

His chest was bare and he had a towel looped around his waist. It came rather too close to the image she'd had only moments earlier and she opened her mouth to ask why he hadn't used one of the robes when she realised there had only been one and she'd used it and then left it in a heap on the floor.

She hung up the robe and then repacked her suitcase. "I'll wait for you downstairs."

"Why would you do that? Wait for me here. It will only take me a moment to dress."

He was true to his word, and moments later they were heading down to the restaurant.

The place was crowded, and the atmosphere lively. Candles flickered on tables and festive garlands studded with tiny lights were strung along the beams. Their table was nestled in one corner, close to the crackling fire and slightly apart from the other tables.

They ordered their food and Will smiled at her. "This is cosy."

"It is." It was also intimate. Normally she wouldn't have noticed but now she was noticing.

She took a sip of the wine that had been delivered to the table and was relieved when the food arrived. At least it gave her something else to focus on.

Dinner was delicious, and the conversation should have been easy because this was Will, but for the first time in her life she felt self-conscious with him and it made her skin prickle. The dress didn't help. She wasn't used to sitting across from him wearing a dress. Also there were candles, and fairy lights, and the atmosphere was unashamedly romantic.

The couple closest to them were holding hands across the table, clearly on a festive date.

Becky ran her fingers round the neckline of the dress, wishing she'd worn something different. She was hot, and not just because she was sitting close to the fire.

It was Will. Or rather, it was that conversation she'd overheard him having with his mother.

She was struggling to act normally. "So is your mother in full-on matchmaking mode? Are you likely to find lots of single women invited for Christmas?" She decided that the best thing was to make a joke of it. Get it out in the open.

"I hope not. I prefer to choose my own dates."

"And how is that going?"

He helped himself to bread. "Evidently not well enough for my mother."

"Which is why you didn't tell her we were sharing a room. I get it. But she'd be scraping the barrel if the only woman she could think of to match you up with was me."

"Why is that? I happened to notice that more than one person stared at us when we walked in." He lifted his gaze to hers and she noticed that behind his glasses his eyes were a mesmerizing glacial blue.

Why hadn't she noticed how blue his eyes were before? If someone had asked her what colour his eyes were, she wouldn't have had a clue.

She swallowed. "They were probably thinking *that woman is wearing her sister's dress*. Or else *what is a man like that doing with a girl like her?*"

He reached for his wine. "Or maybe they were thinking that we make a beautiful couple."

She put her fork down. "Will, I know you're teasing me, but could you stop? You're freaking me out."

"Why am I freaking you out?"

"Because we don't think of each other like that, and we never have." Enough. *Enough!* "This duck is delicious. How is your fish?"

"It's good." He put his glass down. "Doesn't your mother interrogate you about your love life?"

"No. She knows better than to waste her time. I'm not one for spilling my innermost feelings, you know that." Except that she had, hadn't she? With him. She could feel him looking at her and suspected her cheeks were as red as her dress. "Not usually, anyway. And definitely not to my mother. So have you dated anyone since—" She rummaged in her mind for the name of the last person he'd introduced her to. "Elsie?"

"No. There has been no one since Elsie."

"She seemed—nice." She tried her hardest to sound convincing, although if she was honest she hadn't warmed to Elsie at all. "And she was totally crazy about you. When we all went to that wine bar for your birthday last year, she seemed very into you." Which had been annoying if she was honest because she hadn't seen Will for a few months and had been trying to have a proper conversation with him, which hadn't been easy with Elsie draped over him like another layer of clothing. Elsie had been friendly enough on the surface, but Becky had sensed an underlying hostility that hadn't made sense to her. "What went wrong there?"

He finished his fish. "She ended it."

"Oh." Becky wasn't sure how to respond to that. Was he sad? "I'm sorry. And you even introduced her to your parents."

"Yes. That was a mistake." He put his fork down. "That was delicious. I assume you have room for dessert?"

"Of course." She grinned at him. "You don't really need to ask, do you? Why was it a mistake to introduce her to your parents?"

"Because it complicated everything."

"Relationships are always complicated. It's the reason I avoid them. I like things to be ordered and logical, and there is nothing ordered or logical about emotions." She waited while their plates were removed. "Did she break your heart?" She felt fiercely protective all of a sudden. What was wrong with Elsie? Who would want to break up with Will?

He picked up his wineglass. "No."

"Good. But now I see why your mother is matchmaking. She wants to get you out there again."

The waiter appeared with dessert menus but Will shook his head and gave him a quick smile.

"We don't need the menu, thanks. Just bring us anything that has chocolate. And a couple of spoons."

"We have several—"

"Great. Bring them all. Thank you."

Becky leaned forward. "Will Patterson, did you just order all that saturated fat and sugar? Is the god of cardiologists about to strike you down?"

"Probably. But I'm sure there are worse ways to go."

The desserts arrived and were placed in the centre of the table. Three plates showcased different chocolate confections.

"Yum. Why did I bother with a main course? I could live on dessert. This is amazing." Becky dug her spoon into a miniature sponge that oozed hot chocolate sauce. "I didn't think you were a chocolate addict."

"I'm not. But I know you are."

"For a moment there I thought I was learning something new about you. I can't eat all of this by myself or I'll never fit through the door of our room, so you'd better help me."

He picked up a spoon and tasted the chocolate tart. "So how about you? Have you been dating?"

"No. Too busy." She saw him raise an eyebrow and sighed because she knew why he was asking. "Okay, not too busy. Too crap at dating would be more accurate. It's like job hunting. You have to project your best self the whole time and it's exhausting. All that small talk and smiling and trying to be interesting and magnetic when all you really want to do is head home and watch a good movie in bed with a massive bowl of popcorn."

"You could put that on your dating profile."

She ate half the chocolate mousse. "You don't think mentioning bed at that point would attract the wrong sort?"

"Maybe. I don't know. I don't think I'm any better at dating than you are."

"Why is it so hard?" She thought about Elsie, who she'd thought had been madly in love with Will. "Life has a weird sense of humour, doesn't it? You'd think humans should be designed to only fall in love with people who love them back. It should be programmed into us somehow."

"It would certainly make life more convenient."

"And less painful. Still, at least we have chocolate."

"True." He cut another slice of chocolate tart. "This is good."

"It is. This was a great idea. You have great ideas." She finished the mousse. "This is how I want to die. Are you going to finish that tart?"

"No, you go ahead." He shook his head in wonder as she took the last slice. "I've never been able to figure out how someone so small can eat so much and remain small."

"I burn it all off in nervous energy."

They finished their meal, headed upstairs and Becky rooted around in her bag for the key. Why was he standing so close to her? She couldn't concentrate. And then she realised he didn't have much choice about it because here in the eaves of the hotel the corridor was barely wide enough for two people. Her heart was pumping, and she felt a tightness low in her stomach.

Desperate, she fumbled with the key, but she couldn't get it to turn in the lock. "Stupid thing—"

"Let me." He covered her hand with his, calmly jiggled the key and the door opened. The contact lasted only a few seconds but left her feeling as if she'd touched a live wire.

"Great. At least we're not sleeping in the corridor." She walked into the room, but it brought her little relief because he was right behind her. "Here we are. Our spacious suite. With one bed. It's like a romcom, isn't it?"

"Is it?" He closed the door and turned the key, ensuring their privacy.

She swallowed. So now they were locked in together. It was a sensible, precautionary measure. She would have done the same thing herself if her key-turning skills weren't so bad.

"Yes. Rosie is addicted to stories with just one bed. Hero

and heroine forced together, that kind of thing."

"Okay." He put the key down on the table near the door. "I'm trying to see the romantic potential in that. I'm assuming that in a romcom, one bed doesn't mean someone has to sleep on the floor."

"No. One bed is supposed to be a shortcut to romance. You're forced to share. It's a cold night. Things happen. Will, you have to know this."

"Why would I? I'm more of a crime guy. In the books I read, if there is one bed then there's usually a dead body tied to it. But I'm enjoying the education. Don't stop."

"That's pretty much all I know. I'm not exactly a romance expert. That's more my sister's area." And now she wished she hadn't started babbling about romantic comedies. The last thing she wanted to think about was romance. And there was nothing remotely amusing about this situation.

With the door closed she was conscious of just how small the room was. Conscious of him. She never thought of Will that way and now, thanks to that phone call with his mother, she was thinking of it. And it was uncomfortable. She wanted to reboot her brain and start over.

She felt horribly jumpy and on edge. He, on the other hand, seemed maddeningly relaxed.

"Are you all right?" He undid the buttons of his shirt. "You seem tense."

"Just tired. We should get some sleep." Not exactly a reboot but the closest thing. "If the weather improves, we could make an early start."

"No point in rushing. It will be icy first thing, and we need to give them time to clear the snow."

She felt boiling hot and wanted to strip off a layer of clothing, but you couldn't exactly strip off a dress. Why did Rosie love dresses so much? It made no sense to her. They were okay for a couple of hours, but then she just wanted to tug it off and pull on something more comfortable.

She rummaged in her suitcase and found what she was looking for.

"I don't sleep naked so you needn't worry that I'll give you an eyeful in the night."

He stared at what she was holding in her hand. "Reindeer pyjamas?"

"It's Christmas, in case you'd forgotten."

"You have nightwear for each season?"

"Just Christmas. They were a gift from Granny. Rosie's are covered in snowmen. I wear them pretty much all winter because they're comfy and they keep me warm if I thrash around in the bed and lose the covers."

"You do a lot of thrashing?" His smile caused her heart to skip a few beats.

"It has been known. I also talk in my sleep and walk in my sleep. If that happens just steer me back to the bed. No need to wake me up."

"I had no idea the night ahead was going to be so exciting." Casually, he reached for the buckle of his belt, and she froze for a moment and then fled to the bathroom.

"I won't be long."

"Becks—"

"I just need the bathroom."

"Are you all right? Did you eat too much chocolate?"

"Yes, something like that." She closed the door between them and leaned against it. Would he actually have undressed with her standing right there? Had he forgotten she was in the room? No, it wasn't that. It was just that they'd known each other forever and he didn't see her that way. "Probably shouldn't have drunk that wine."

This was *not* going the way she'd hoped. She should have

felt relieved that they'd been forced to stay overnight because it gave her a reprieve from the family reunion she was dreading, but right now she wasn't feeling relieved.

Frustrated with the workings of her mind, she turned on the cold water and splashed her face.

She wished Will had never called his mother, or at least that they hadn't had that conversation.

Now she kept imagining him naked. And she kept thinking he was looking at her in a different way which was *definitely* her imagination going into overdrive.

She took a deep breath and then yanked the dress over her head.

This was insane. She had to stop thinking this way. Will didn't have those sorts of feelings for her and she didn't have those sorts of feelings for him, either. They had a long friendship and yes there was love, of course there was, but not that sort of love. Not the heart-racing, rip-each-other's-clothes-off, explosive type of love. The love she felt for Will was warm and safe and quiet. There was nothing explosive about it.

She wasn't like Rosie, who fell in love quickly and then fell out of love at approximately the same rate.

Becky had only ever been in love with one man in her life.

And he'd married her sister.

9

Hayley

It was snowing steadily now, soft flakes of white spinning and swirling in front of the car, sparkling in the headlights like frozen confetti.

Jamie drove confidently, followed a narrow lane for a short distance and then turned through a set of open gates. "We're here. This is home. Someone has cleared the worst of the snow so that's good."

"This is it? I don't see a house."

"You will in a minute."

"You don't have any houses near you?"

"Nearest neighbours are across the field. The Pattersons. Family friends. She's a retired dentist. He's a historian. Written books about this area. We're on the borders with Scotland so it's all battles and conflict. Pick a time in history and someone was probably invading us. We have more castles than any other county, most of them in ruins of course but that just adds to the interest. My closest friend, Will, is their son. You'll meet him at the party."

"He is the one driving up with Becky?"

"Yes, although I've no idea how that happened. I don't think it was planned. Then along from them are the Freemans. Geoff and Rita. I was at school with their youngest daughter, Beth. We kissed once."

"You kissed her?"

"Technically she kissed me. We were seventeen. School play." He grinned and she resisted the temptation to punch him on the arm.

She loved these little insights into his past. It was like slotting another piece into a large jigsaw puzzle.

"Are you trying to make me jealous?"

"I don't know. If I was, would it be working?"

"Annoyingly, it might be. Have you seen her since?"

"Of course. She always comes to my parents' New Year's Eve party if she's home. And brings her husband and her three cute, but very noisy, children."

He always made her laugh, and right now she needed that because now that the reality of meeting his family was only moments away, she felt increasingly nervous. Her hands were a little shaky and it puzzled and annoyed her because she'd been taking care of herself for her whole life. Her childhood had been an emotional wasteland and she'd learned to rely on herself. She was fiercely independent. She'd built a life and taught herself not to need people. Which made her feelings for him all the more surprising and unsettling.

She gazed at his profile. How had she ended up here? Somehow this man had sneaked under her defences, and he'd done it without her even noticing. She'd gone from being self-reliant and never needing anyone to being unable to imagine a life without him, and that was terrifying. She felt vulnerable, and she wasn't used to feeling vulnerable. It made her a little unsteady, and that unsteadiness grew as they approached his home.

They'd had such a happy day and now she felt almost afraid. Nervous and a little sick.

She curved her fingers into her palms and immediately felt his hand cover hers.

"You're going to be fine." He spoke softly. "I'll be right there with you. The whole time."

The fact that he seemed to sense everything she was feeling was something she was still getting used to.

What shook her was the depth of feeling she had for him. It was like standing on a cliff edge, a breath away from falling.

She tried to lighten her mood. "What if I need the bathroom? Are you going to follow me there?"

"If it's the downstairs bathroom it will be a tight squeeze—" he glanced at her briefly "—but I never mind being squashed into tight spaces with you."

Her stomach flipped.

They couldn't get enough of each other, and for a wild moment she wished they'd gone away somewhere, just the two of them, but she'd been seduced by the idea of a family Christmas, and also she knew how much it meant to him to be with his family at this time of year. She would never have asked him to skip it.

And it was too late for regrets because she saw a gleam of lights through the snowy trees and then the driveway curved and opened up and there, right in front of her, was the house.

It had the most perfect dimensions, and she felt a lump form in her throat because if she'd been asked to design her dream family home this would have been it. Soft light glowed and through one of the downstairs windows she could see the sparkling outline of a large Christmas tree.

She felt as if she'd landed in one of her own festive illustrations.

"It's so pretty."

"Yes. Normally we just have a wreath on the door, so my parents have clearly upped their game." Jamie parked next to two other cars, swinging into the space with ease. "Looks as if

Rosie and Declan are already here. That's good. It will be less overwhelming for you if you meet people in stages."

She couldn't stop looking at the house. She'd drawn so many Christmassy images, imagined so many festive houses, and yet none had looked quite like this. Because this was real. Whatever she drew, she was always on the outside. An observer. But now she was going to be part of it.

And with that realisation came another flash of disquiet.

"Are you sure we shouldn't tell them our news right away?"

"No. We'll wait until this evening. Make a big announcement."

"Okay."

They were his family. He knew them, surely? And what did she know about family dynamics. Nothing at all.

He leaned in and kissed her. "I love you. You are the best thing that has ever happened in my life and nothing is going to change that."

She'd never been the best thing in anyone's life before and she still couldn't totally believe it or trust it. It was like taking a step onto ice, not sure if it was going to hold your weight.

"I love you too." And she hoped this whole thing wasn't going to backfire. She and Jamie felt as if they'd been together forever but for his family their relationship was new.

Would it all be too much? What if they disapproved? *What if they didn't like her?*

She wished she didn't care so much what other people thought, but she did care. She cared a lot.

She gathered herself and opened the car door. The cold bit into her and she shivered and grabbed her coat.

Jamie gathered together their bags and he'd barely closed the car door when the front door opened and a pool of golden light spilled across the snowy pathway that led to the house.

A group of people appeared in the doorway, all talking at once and a large dog bounded across the snow to greet Jamie.

"Hey, Percy—" He stooped and made a fuss of the dog and Hayley did the same, relieved to have something to focus on because this whole meeting felt so awkward.

"He's adorable." She rubbed his back and cupped his sweet face in her hands and then laughed when Percy leaped on her, planting snowy paws in the middle of her chest.

"Now you've done it." Jamie closed a hand on his collar and pulled the dog down. "No jumping."

"It was my fault for encouraging him." And she didn't mind. It was a relief to find that at least one family member seemed to approve of her. "He's gorgeous."

"He'll take advantage. Hi, Mum—" He stepped forward to hug the woman who had picked her way across the snow to greet them.

"I'm so happy you're home. I missed you." She was tall—almost as tall as Jamie—and slim, with dark hair swept up casually and secured by a clip at the back of her head.

"Yeah, me too. It's good to be here. I'm looking forward to Christmas."

"So are we."

"The house looks amazing! Did you and Dad do that?"

"No—we have Roy the roofer to thank for our next-level light show."

Hayley stood awkwardly, waiting, watching the way they hugged. Tightly. Like two people with a long and unbreakable connection. Family.

Eventually the woman stepped back and gazed at Jamie. "How was the journey? Did you manage a trip to Holy Island?"

"Yes. And we stopped for lunch and had a walk on the beach at Embleton."

"Good choice. It's beautiful there." She turned with a smile. "And you must be Hayley. I've been so excited to meet you."

"I—oh—" Hayley found herself wrapped in a warm hug, and she stood for a moment, caught off balance by the sheer warmth of the greeting. She wasn't used to it. She didn't know how she was supposed to respond so she hugged the woman right back, and when she finally let go she discovered that her nerves had receded and she no longer felt sick.

Jamie was grinning. "This is my mother."

"I assumed as much." And she could see instantly where he got his warmth and kind nature. "It's good to meet you, Mrs Balfour."

"Call me Jenny." Jamie's mother stood back and beamed at both of them, a gleam of emotion in her eyes. Then she shivered and glanced up at the sky. "This is all very pretty and festive, but if it doesn't stop snowing Will and Becky will be stranded for the whole of Christmas. Come inside. It's freezing out here. Rosie has been standing with her nose pressed to the window, waiting for you to arrive."

"Woohoo Jamie!" A young woman sprinted across the snow, her long hair flying. She flung her arms around Jamie. "I'm glad I arrived before you. I've hidden all the chocolate. There is no way you're finding it this year."

"You think?" He hugged her tightly and then let her go. "We both know I'll find it."

"You won't. It's good to see you." She stood on tiptoe to kiss his cheek, her voice lowered. "Tomorrow we are going for a long walk on the beach. Just us. I need to talk to you. It's important."

It was only because she was standing close by that she heard those words. Hayley wondered what Rosie needed to say to Jamie that she didn't want anyone else to know.

And then Rosie turned, her eyes sparkling and her cheeks dimpled in a friendly smile. "You must be Hayley! I'm Rosie. I've been dying to meet you. Welcome to our Christmas grotto. We only arrived about ten minutes ago so we haven't even unpacked. We're ruined Mum's beautiful hallway with our chaos."

She vibrated with energy, and Hayley wondered whether she

went to bed exhausted every night or whether she was blessed with superhuman stamina.

"Let's go indoors—" Jenny ushered them all inside and Hayley stepped cautiously over the threshold of Jamie's family home.

If the outside of the house looked welcoming and festive, the inside was even more so. A large Christmas tree dominated the hallway, and candles glowed and flickered on every surface alongside garlands of greenery. Through an open door she could see a log fire blazing, and Percy immediately padded into the room and helped himself to the warmest spot.

Hayley had never been anywhere like this. She wanted to curl up by the fire with Percy and never leave.

Jamie dumped their bags in the hall next to his sister's and glanced around him. "Wow. Did you leave any decorations for anyone else?"

Rosie grinned. "I know! Isn't it brilliant? Mum has gone totally overboard. Probably because of Hayley, in which case thank you, Hayley, you're welcome any time."

Hayley had no idea how to respond to that, and fortunately she didn't have to because at that moment Jamie's father stepped forward to introduce himself, and so did Declan, Rosie's husband.

She noticed immediately that Declan was far more reserved than his wife. Or maybe he was just tired. She knew they'd driven up from London in pretty bad weather.

He stood in silence, his dark eyes watchful, and Hayley knew instantly that he was a listener, not a talker.

Rosie, on the other hand, was very much a talker.

"This bag can stay down here." Rosie pushed an overstuffed bag into a corner with her foot and her mother tutted.

"You're not to leave things lying around, Rosie. We have a house full of people and they don't want to be tripping over your belongings."

"But they're presents. They're going to go under the tree!"

"Then put them under the tree." Jenny shook her head and turned to Hayley. "I hope you'll make yourself at home. If there's anything at all you need, you're to let me know."

"How come Hayley is allowed to make herself at home and I have to be unnaturally tidy?" Grumbling away, Rosie dragged the bag into the living room and then emerged again. "That's unfair. It isn't Christmas if you're not tripping over presents."

She was pretty, Hayley thought. Really pretty, with hair the colour of polished oak that tumbled over her shoulders in bouncy waves, and eyes the same green as Jamie's.

Jenny didn't seem to be interested in her daughter's appearance at that moment.

"If your grandmother trips and breaks a hip you'll be cooking the turkey."

Hayley stood quietly by the Christmas tree, her head buzzing. She wanted to join in and be part of the banter, but those types of exchanges could only happen between people who knew each other well. They were normal family dynamics, something she knew nothing about.

"I can cook a turkey," Rosie said. "Whether anyone would want to eat it is another matter. I always panic it won't be cooked and I'll poison everyone."

"You'd ruin it on purpose," Jamie said, "just to make us all eat your boring vegetarian option."

"I wouldn't share my mushroom Wellington with you if you were starving and begging me. If you want to eat a sweet, kind little turkey who never did you or anyone any harm, then go ahead."

"I've seen the turkey. Trust me, it's not little."

"Ignore them," Jenny advised Hayley, "I've never understood why my otherwise adult children, all of whom have responsible jobs, revert to childhood when they're home."

Jamie grinned at Declan. "She hasn't turned you vegetarian yet?"

"Declan eats fish," Rosie said, "but he also loves vegetarian food. Adores it."

"Either he's lying to you or you've been brainwashed." Jamie gave Declan a sympathetic slap on the shoulder. "How do you stand living with her?"

Rosie glanced at Declan, and Hayley thought she saw a flash of anxiety in that look.

Before Declan could answer, Rosie turned away and gathered up a couple more bags.

Her shoulders were stiff and Hayley knew then that she hadn't imagined anything. She sensed that the brightness Rosie exuded was false. That it was taking a supreme effort that had just proved too tiring. Perhaps because she so often adopted a false face herself, she was able to detect it in other people.

She felt a wave of sympathy. She didn't even know Rosie, so why did she have a sudden urge to follow her, pull her to one side and check she was all right?

She remembered Rosie quietly telling Jamie that she wanted to talk to him. Maybe it was related.

Or maybe nothing was wrong, and she was misreading everything. She didn't know these people, so that was entirely possible.

"You must all be tired and ready for some food," Jenny said, "so why don't you get settled in your rooms and then we'll all enjoy a drink before dinner."

"Let's do this. The sooner we unpack, the sooner we can eat." Rosie clomped her way up the stairs and Declan followed with the rest of their bags.

"You and Hayley are in your room, Jamie." Jenny didn't seem to notice anything amiss, and Hayley decided that if Rosie's own mother didn't think anything was wrong then there probably wasn't anything wrong.

She picked up bags and Jamie's father appeared by her shoulder.

"Let me take those for you. You don't seem to have brought as much stuff as my daughter."

"I travel light." She could have told them that she didn't own much stuff. That she pretty much took what she had everywhere she went. But that was definitely too much information, so she simply smiled her thanks and followed Jamie's father up the stairs.

He eyed the garland, twisted around the stair rail. "I hope no one needs to grab that thing or they'll probably get a rash or stab themselves on holly. Jenny has gone a bit over the top I'm afraid."

"I can hear you, Martin!" Jenny's voice floated up the stairs. "And it's called decorating for Christmas. Something the whole family used to help with before they left home and you filled your days being retired. Now I'm a one-woman festive machine. Jamie? When you've taken up your luggage, will you help me bring in more logs from the shed? It's freezing and we're going to need them if this snow doesn't stop. I don't want anyone wading through snowdrifts to top up the fire."

Hayley followed Jamie and his father along a wide landing and then through a door right at the end of the house.

"This is my room." Jamie dropped their bags in one corner. "And we have our own Christmas tree! Nice touch. Thanks Mum."

His mother appeared in the doorway. "I saw it when I went to buy some extra decorations and I thought it would be perfect in this room. I've put out fresh towels. The window rattles a bit in the wind but I've put extra layers on the bed so hopefully you won't be cold."

"I won't be cold," Hayley said. "I'm never cold."

Jamie frowned. "You're often cold."

"No, I'm not. And anyway this room is warm," Hayley said quickly, mortified. "It's very snug."

Jenny gave Hayley another hug. "Well, if you *are* cold, you'll find extra blankets in the cupboard just outside your room. It's so good to have you here. Now I must go and check on dinner and we'll see you downstairs for a celebratory, welcome-home drink whenever you're ready." She left the room and closed the door behind her, giving them privacy.

Hayley walked to the window and sat down on the cushioned seat that spanned the width of the glass. She stroked her hand over the dark green fabric and glanced around her. It was a beautiful room, made even more so by the sparkle of lights from the Christmas tree. The walls were painted the colour of pale moss, which gave the room a warm elegance. One entire wall was covered in bookshelves, and another in black-and-white photographs. The large bed in the middle of the room was piled with cushions and several warm throws, and lamps placed either side sent soft light across the room. "This was your room when you were growing up?"

"Yes. It looks over the garden, not that you can see anything now when it's dark." Jamie opened a suitcase and started putting clothes away. "Why did you say you're never cold?"

"I don't want to be a nuisance. I'll be fine."

"Okay, but if something isn't right you have to say so." He glanced at her. "To me, at least. Don't be polite."

"I'm fine, Jamie." She stood up and went to take a closer look at the photographs. She saw images of vast, windswept beaches and ruined castles. The photographs showed the landscape's wild beauty, but also hinted at its stark, unforgiving nature. "They're stunning. Who took them?"

"Me. I went through a photography phase. Dad indulged me and let me turn the cellar into a darkroom."

"You have talent."

"Thanks, I'm nowhere near as creative as Rosie, though." He abandoned what he was doing and stepped closer. "Are you okay? Was it all too overwhelming?"

"Meeting everyone? Not so far. Your family are charming.

Friendly." She looked around the room again. "And I can't believe your mother bought us our own Christmas tree."

"She did that for you. Because I told her you loved Christmas."

She remembered the hug. The warm smile. The genuine welcome. Something stirred inside her. "She's kind."

"Yes." He studied her face. "Do you want to freshen up or anything or shall we go straight downstairs? I know this is a lot, so I'll take my lead from you and if it all feels like too much you're to tell me."

It was a lot, but she was determined to join in. To be part of things. She didn't want his family to think she was anti-social or skulking in her room.

She reached out and touched his face. "I'll change, as I've been walking on wild beaches today. But I'll be quick."

"No hurry. Bathroom is there—" He waved a hand and she walked into the bathroom and closed the door.

She leaned against it and breathed, eyes closed. She could still feel the hug his mother had given her. Only people who had never felt the need to protect themselves hugged like that. Without reservation.

Pulling herself together, she turned and stared into the mirror and tried to see herself as other people might.

It was funny how the outside of a person told you little about the inside. She probably looked normal to them. They didn't know that she was a seething mass of insecurities, held together by willpower and determination.

She finished in the bathroom and changed out of her jeans into a short dress in a shade of rich violet blue which she teamed with boots.

Jamie immediately tugged her against him. "You look so good in that dress I just want to take it off. On second thought, let's not go downstairs." He cupped her face in his hands and kissed her. "Let's order room service."

"I'm not sure you can order room service in your own home, can you?"

"I'll tell them I have this urge to lie down on the bed." He muttered the words against her mouth. "It's true."

"Then they'll come looking for us and that would be embarrassing." She eased away from him regretfully and reached for her bag.

She quickly replenished her makeup. A touch of blush. A swipe of lipstick. Not too much, but just enough to give her confidence.

Then she was ready.

She heard the sound of laughter from somewhere in the house and Jamie closed his hand over hers.

"Sounds as if they're all in the living room. Daunting, I know. But let's do this."

Let's do this.

She knew he wasn't talking about joining the family for drinks. This was the moment. He was going to tell them. She'd wanted him to tell them, but now the time had come she wished she could postpone the moment. She wanted to dig her heels in and buy herself some time, but she forced herself to walk with him down the stairs.

Her heart was hammering. This was the part she'd been dreading, and for that reason it was probably best that they got it out of the way. If Jamie was right, then everyone would be happy for them. If he was wrong—well, whatever happened it wasn't going to be her worst Christmas. She'd had plenty of those in the past.

Delicious smells wafted from the kitchen and she could hear the rumble of conversation from the living room.

She took a breath and followed him into the room.

"And I said to your grandmother, I really don't think—" Jenny broke off as she saw them. "Here they are! We decided champagne as it has been so long since we've been together.

This bottle was a gift from some of Martin's patients. We were waiting for you before opening it. Martin, give Hayley a glass, unless you'd rather have something nonalcoholic, Hayley? No pressure."

No pressure? The whole thing was pressure.

"Thank you. Champagne would be lovely."

Jamie frowned at her. "You don't drink."

"It's fine!" She felt heat pour into her cheeks.

"But—"

"I have sparkling elderflower in my left hand and champagne in my right," Jamie's father said, proffering two glasses. "Pick whichever you prefer."

She didn't want to inconvenience anyone, but as he was holding both she gave a smile of thanks and took the elderflower gratefully.

"Great. And come closer to the fire," Jenny said. "There's so much snow coming down outside that window it's making me cold just looking at it. I'm going to be awake all night worrying about Becky and Will."

Martin handed a glass to Jamie. "Given that they messaged to say they'd booked into a cosy hotel, you're going to be losing a night's sleep for nothing. And if you're losing a night's sleep then no doubt so will I."

Jenny raised her glass. "I thought we'd all be here to do this together tonight, but that's an excuse to do it all again tomorrow when Becky is here. And anyway tomorrow we'll be too busy with the party to have a family moment so let's make the most of it—" She smiled at Rosie and then at Jamie. "Welcome home. It's going to be a special Christmas."

Hayley took a sip of her drink, wishing for a moment that she'd chosen the champagne. At least it might have numbed the terror of what was to come.

She watched as Rosie crouched down to make a fuss of Percy. It felt surreal, to be standing around a fireplace with this perfect family. But of course she was the outsider. No matter how welcoming they were, she was always the outsider. Would she ever feel comfortable here?

She glanced at Declan, wondering if he felt the same way but he was watching Rosie.

"And now, I cannot wait a moment longer." Jenny looked expectantly at her son. "I've ordered the drink and invited the guests. The food is all planned and the celebration is tomorrow. The only thing left is for you to tell us what we're celebrating."

Jamie put his glass down on the nearest surface and reached for Hayley's hand.

His fingers were warm and the strength of his grip was the only thing preventing her from bolting from the room.

"Hayley and I have something to tell you."

"And we can't wait to hear what it is!" Jenny glanced at Martin and back at Jamie. "Although we've already guessed, obviously."

Jamie paused. "You have?"

"Of course. You're going to tell us you're engaged." She looked at Hayley's finger. "Or getting engaged. That's what this party is, I assume? A celebration of your engagement?"

If she hadn't been clamped by Jamie's side, Hayley definitely would have run.

"Well, you're on the right track, but we sort of skipped the engagement stage." Jamie drew Hayley closer. "The party is a wedding celebration. Hayley and I are married. We got married a few weeks ago."

10

Jenny

Married! And he didn't tell any of us. Not even his sisters?" Jenny paced across the room and back again. Emotion was coiled inside her, desperate to escape.

"Keep your voice down, Jen." Martin glanced at the bedroom door. "Hold it together."

"I've been holding it together all evening. I feel as if I'm going to burst. Why didn't he tell us? Warn us? She wasn't even wearing a ring so there was no way we would have guessed." She sat down hard on the edge of the bed, trying to calm herself. She didn't want to feel this way. "Our Jamie. He got married and he didn't even tell us and maybe that shouldn't upset me, but it does." She felt the bed dip as Martin sat down next to her.

"Of course it does. But the reality is he's not a child anymore. He's a grown man able to make his own decisions."

"I know. And I don't want to influence his decisions. But who decides to get married without telling his family?" She was upset and hurt. And she didn't understand. Couldn't make sense of it. This was Jamie. Jamie, who had always been so thoughtful. Who had talked to them about anything and everything. "Did we do something? Say something? We've always been support-ive and accepting of his choices. I thought we were close. We've always made it clear that he can talk to us about anything, so why wouldn't he have shared this with us?"

"I don't think this is about us." Martin put his arm around her. "It's about him."

"And her. Do you think Hayley is the reason he did it this way? Do you think she insisted?" There had to be something, because this wasn't like Jamie.

"I don't know, but he doesn't seem like a man being coerced. He seems happy."

She thought about the way Jamie had been since he arrived home. Yes, happy, but also relaxed and with a definite bounce in his step. She thought about the smile and the way he'd looked at Hayley. The way he'd gripped her hand. The gesture hadn't just been loving, it had been protective. It had said *I'm right here and I've got your back.* And she thought of the way Hayley looked at him. As if her world began and ended with Jamie.

"He did seem happy," she said. "And so did she. They seemed happy together."

"And that's good. In the end, that's all that matters."

"It is." She turned to look at him, her vision blurred with tears. "So why do I feel so bad?"

He took her hand. "Probably because the news was unex-pected. You need time to get used to it, that's all. Time to ad-just."

His words made her feel a little better. "It's not that I don't want him to be with her, just that I would have liked him to have shared it with us. Is that wrong?"

"No. It's human. I suspect a small part of you is worried be-cause this is his first serious relationship since Poppy. It's natural to be concerned about the speed of it."

She nodded. "I don't want to see him hurt again."

"I know—" his fingers tightened on hers "—and the two

of you have always been close, so the fact that he didn't share this with you is bound to sting a little."

She couldn't argue with that. "He was our first. And he was always so easy to be around."

"Funny how time erases memories of sleepless nights and temper tantrums. I have a vivid memory of him throwing pasta at the wall on one occasion, but we'll let that go."

She smiled, remembering the same incident and thinking how easy it was to smudge out the past. "There were difficult moments, but that's parenting. There are stages, and you move through them. Babyhood, the toddler years, teenage years—"

"Let's not linger on that particular period in our family history."

"There were plenty of slammed doors, that's for sure, although more so with Rosie." She rubbed her fingers across her forehead. "And then empty nest. I was dreading it. Whole articles are written about it. I remember that day we dropped him off at medical school and I was all prepared to be brave and fight back tears but he was so excited to be there, introducing himself to everyone else in his corridor, propping his door open and looking so happy as he anticipated everything that lay ahead, I didn't feel like crying. How can you cry when your child is happy? It's all a parent wants, isn't it?" She leaned her head against his shoulder, the memories playing through her mind like a movie.

"Yes. We were relieved to see him settle so fast, but that doesn't mean it wasn't difficult. As a parent your job is to let go, even when your instinct is to hold on." He stroked his thumb across her palm. "I suppose no one really knows how each stage will affect them, and it depends a lot on what else is going on. We were busy. Preoccupied with our own lives."

"So you're saying this is another stage."

"Well, isn't it?" He lifted his hand and stroked her hair. "He's still our child, even though he's a man and has been for a long time. And when a man says 'this is the woman I want to share my life with' that's another stage. And it's a big one. Someone else is the priority in his life. It requires everyone to step into a new role. It's another change, and handling change is never easy. I used to see the impact of change all the time at work. People struggling with changes to their health, their family, their work. Parenthood, divorce, redundancy, menopause—the list is endless."

And retirement, she thought. Some people struggled with that too, and Martin was one of them. But maybe it was easier to see things clearly when they weren't happening to you.

And right now her focus was on Jamie.

"I feel guilty. If I was that good a mother, I'd have simply hugged him and offered congratulations."

"Unless my memory is playing tricks, you did exactly that."

"But it was a struggle. An act."

"That part didn't show. You said the right things, Jen. You did the right things. And if it's going to take your insides a little while to catch up—well, no one needs to know."

He was always so calm and logical. And insightful. Just talking it through with him made her feel better. It wasn't hard to see why so many patients had been willing to wait weeks for an appointment with him rather than taking the first available slot with whoever happened to be free.

She kept her head against his shoulder and felt his arm tighten. "You're wise."

"It comes with age." His tone was dry but she ignored that.

"It comes from spending years dealing with people. Understanding them. And from having good instincts." She breathed. "I actually like Hayley."

"Me too. She seems like a smart, sensible young woman. And she looked worried about Jamie's big announcement. I have a strong suspicion she didn't want to spring it on us."

"I don't want her to feel uncomfortable. I want her to know she's welcome. Tomorrow I'm going to make that clear. But right now—" She lifted her fingers to her forehead and rubbed. "My head is throbbing."

"That's the champagne. You don't usually drink."

"I think it's the stress of keeping up an act." And she was still worried they might have sensed her reaction. "Do you think they could tell I was shocked? I don't want Jamie to think I disapprove of the relationship, because I don't. And I wouldn't hurt him for the world." She hated the idea that she'd been anything less than fully supportive. That was the person she wanted to be, but this evening that ambition was being severely challenged.

"You were warm and welcoming. You spent ages looking at their photos." His arm was still round her. "Stop worrying."

"Rosie was quiet when they made their surprise announcement. Do you think something is wrong?"

"Was she quiet? She made a big fuss of them."

"Yes, but after only after a pause. Initially she looked shocked and a bit horrified, I thought."

"I was too busy gaping at Jamie to notice. She was probably taken by surprise, like the rest of us."

"Maybe. Although you know what Rosie is like—she wears all her emotions on the outside so she's not hard to read. Something felt off. From the moment she arrived home she has been very hyper. Excited."

"That's our Rosie. It's Christmas," Martin said. "She loves Christmas."

"It felt as if she was trying a little too hard. And Declan barely said a word. Did you notice that?"

"He's a guy who speaks when he has something to say. An admirable quality in my opinion. And it's not as if he knows us that well. Rosie was probably worried that he might be overwhelmed by a family Christmas. And then came Jamie's announcement. It was all a bit intense. She was probably anxious." He gave a half laugh. "It feels like too much to me and they're my family."

"You love having everyone home."

He hesitated. "Normally, yes."

She waited. Was he finally going to talk about himself and his own feelings?

"But not this time?"

"It just all feels—I don't know, Jen. Different. Sad? I suppose I'm increasingly conscious of the passage of time. It seems only yesterday the kids were young and at Christmas we'd be setting up train sets and putting together bicycles and they'd be cannoning into our room before the sun was up wanting to start the day. And now they're all married—well, not Becky, but no doubt that will come soon enough, and then there will be grandchildren and I just want to stop time because it's going so fast and—"

She put her hand on his. He saw everything when it was someone else, but not when it was him. "It's a new phase. It takes time to adjust—isn't that what you're always telling everyone else?"

He sighed. "Easy to say, not so easy to do. Although you seem to handle it all easily. Apart from surprise weddings, obviously."

Was that really what he thought?

She stared at the photographs on her bedside table. "When I dropped Jamie at medical school I cried all day for a week."

"What?" He frowned. "You were happy for him. You just said that a moment ago."

"Yes, I was happy at the time, but when we got home, I cried and cried."

He turned to look at her. "I don't remember that."

"You weren't here. You were working. I dropped the girls at school and then came home and cried."

"Why didn't you tell me?"

"You were busy at work and you didn't need to come home to me complaining. And anyway, I felt a bit silly to be honest.

What was there to complain about? Our son was doing something he loved. That was a cause for celebration."

"But you were struggling."

"Yes. There are so many parenting milestones. Like the day your child starts school, and leaving them there looking so tiny and vulnerable and lost with a hoard of other children feels so wrong and unnatural and you go home to an empty house for the first time and you keep watching the clock, counting the hours until you can pick them up." She thought back to that day she'd taken Jamie, remembering how tightly he'd held her hand in the moments before she'd taken him into the building. "And if you're lucky they love it and want to go back the next day, but if they're miserable and unsettled then you feel like the worst mother in the world and taking them back the next day breaks your heart. But at least they come home."

"But when you drop them at college, it's different," Martin said.

"Yes. You drive home with that empty car, feeling as if part of your life has been torn away. And you know it's never coming back. 'Empty nest' is a mild term for what's essentially a bereavement of sorts. You try and see it as a new beginning but that doesn't change the fact it's an ending."

There was a long silence and then he cleared his throat. "So how did you deal with it? I mean apart from crying."

"That only lasted a week." She thought back to that time. "And I did what I usually do when struggling with change. I forced myself to focus on all the good things. I reminded myself how lucky we were to have a healthy son who had made it adulthood and was excited about his choice of career. I thought about all the patients I looked after when I was a nurse who didn't have that option. People whose lives had taken an unpredictable, often brutal course. I reminded myself that children leaving home and becoming independent is the natural order of things."

"That's true."

She put her hand on his leg. "And I reminded myself that what I was feeling was normal, and that humans are remarkably adept at handling change. I just had to keep going and re-shape my life a little. I had more time with the girls. More time to explore my own interests. And then I went through it all again when the twins left home, but by then I'd learned what I needed to do. Did I feel the loss sometimes? Yes. I still do. I felt it when I went to the forest to get the tree, but I focus on how lucky I am to have all those happy memories stored away. I miss those days because those days were good, and I'm grateful for that time."

"I don't remember it hitting me that hard." He slipped off his shoes. "I felt a bit strange when I walked into Jamie's room after he'd left for medical school, but I didn't dwell on it."

"You didn't have time to dwell on it. You were so tied up in work—and of course your life didn't change that much. I was usually the one who took them to school, who helped them navigate friendship challenges, and exam stress."

He was silent for a moment. "So you're saying this is the first time I've been in a position where I have time to think about change."

"Yes. And don't underestimate the impact of that. You've been a doctor for your entire adult life. Retiring is a big thing. You're bound to have conflicted feelings, and this time you can't block it out with work. As you just said to me, it takes time to adjust. You have to give it that time. Be patient."

"I'm discovering that giving advice is easier than taking it." He rubbed his hand over his face. "It's tough on you and I feel frustrated with myself. I should be able to do better than this."

She laughed, because it was such a Martin comment. "This isn't an exam. You don't pass or fail. It's an ongoing thing. There are going to be moments when you feel fine, and then moments when you don't, and hopefully those moments become fewer as time passes."

"It's not fair on you. I feel bad."

"Don't. We're a team, we always have been." And she felt better than she had because now she had a much clearer understanding of the problem.

"Dad will be here tomorrow. You should talk to him."

"Nothing to talk about. I'm not depressed, Jen. You're right, it's just a big adjustment and I wasn't expecting it because I was looking forward to retirement. Talking to your dad isn't going to change anything."

"I wasn't suggesting a consultation. And I wasn't suggesting that you need his help." Although she suspected that maybe he did. But what he also needed was something else to focus on. "I was thinking that what you're dealing with might make a perfect chapter for his book. It's something we all struggle with, isn't it? Change? As you say, you saw it all the time when you were working. People navigating changes to their family circumstances, which impacts on health. Changes in health generally. Your body lets you down sometimes, and learning to live with that reality is an adjustment. Life is one big adjustment. And you might not need Dad's help, but he definitely needs yours. Mum thinks that if you don't help it will never get off the ground."

He stood up and put his shoes away. "I'm not sure there's an audience for this book if I'm honest, but I don't want to kill your dad's enthusiasm." He unbuttoned his shirt. "There is so much health advice on the internet."

"But that's the point! There's too much, and if you don't have knowledge, where do you start? You know what it's like when someone searches their symptoms on the internet. It's a nightmare. You imagine the worst. The book my father wants to write is the type of advice you might get from your family doctor, but also focusing on prevention."

"I don't know, Jen—"

"It would give him a boost to make some progress with it, but he can't do that without your help. You've only recently retired. You'd be able to guide him. Help him." *And he'd be helping you, too*, she thought, but she didn't say that part aloud. "Will you at least think about it? Ask him about it tomorrow? Will you do it for me?"

Let him think that. Let him think he was doing it for her. For her father. For anyone other than himself.

"All right." He tugged off his shirt and leaned down to kiss her. "I'm going to take a shower. It's been a long day."

She'd never known a day to pass so quickly, but she guessed that in the world he was living in right now time passed slowly. She was going to do what she could to help with that.

But first she had to get her head around Jamie's news.

Hayley was his wife now. A member of the family. A new phase.

Martin's reminder that they'd adjust to this and that it would soon feel normal had been helpful.

"I feel better than I did, but I still wish they'd told us."

He dropped his shirt into the laundry basket. "Would it help if I reminded you that there were things we did and told our parents about afterwards?"

"Like what?"

"Buying this house for a start. You were worried your parents would tell you that it was old and expensive and too far away from the village and schools and that you'd spend your life in the car, so we put in our offer and told them afterwards."

She felt a flash of guilt. "That's true, but it's not quite the same thing."

"The principle is the same. We wanted to do what we wanted to do, and we didn't want to be influenced by them."

"That's true. And I remember being terrified when I called to tell them because I thought they'd list all the reasons we'd regret it. Which is, of course, why we didn't tell them until it was too late." She sighed. "Okay, fine, you've made your point. I'll try and remember how it felt to be young and independent."

She stood up, overwhelmed by everything. Christmas wasn't supposed to feel this way. It was supposed to be lighthearted and fun and filled with silly moments. It wasn't supposed to be this serious. It wasn't supposed to be filled with anxiety.

"I need fresh air. I'll take Percy out while you're in the shower."

"Now? Jen, it's after midnight and it has been snowing all day."

"The dog still needs to go outside. I'll be fine. I'll wear boots and plenty of layers. I've lived here all my life. You don't have to tell me how to dress for the weather." She tugged open a drawer and pulled out her thermal underwear and fleece-lined trekking pants.

"Do you want me to come?"

"No. Go to bed. You look tired." Normally she would have relished his company, but not right now. She wanted to be on her own. She needed to give her emotions a rest and try to replenish some of her energy for the next day.

She tiptoed downstairs and grabbed her thick jacket. Percy trotted to the door in anticipation, tail wagging.

At least someone was behaving normally, she thought.

She opened the front door and shivered as a blast of freezing air entered the hallway.

Percy bounded ahead, sniffing the ground, his paws leaving prints in the snow.

Jenny followed him, feeling better for being outdoors. It had stopped snowing and the crisp clean air cleared her head. The solitude and the sense of space was calming.

She tilted her head back and breathed the icy winter air.

Usually this was one of the best places in the country for

stargazing but tonight the sky was black, most of the stars obscured by clouds. Was there more snow coming?

She hoped the weather wouldn't stop Becky and Will making it home tomorrow.

She was looking forward to seeing her—particularly now, when the emotional landscape around her felt so unstable. Becky was her steady one. There was never any drama with her. Especially no romantic drama, at least none that she talked about. No doubt she'd shrug off the news that Jamie and Hayley were married, and if she felt that Rosie was upset about something it would take her a matter of seconds to tease it out of her sister. And calm her down. Becky always calmed Rosie down. They had each other's backs and always had. Knowing that Becky would soon be home lessened the worry about Rosie.

Jenny thought about her daughter sharing a car with Will. She smiled as she imagined Audrey, just a short distance away, spinning romantic scenarios.

If she'd learned one thing lately it was that your children's romantic relationships rarely followed a predictable path.

It was fun to speculate, but over the years she'd forced herself to accept that Becky and Will didn't have those sorts of feelings for each other. You could wish for it, and both she and Audrey had wished for it, but wishing for it didn't make it real.

And it didn't really matter. Friendship was important, too, and she liked knowing that Will and Becky were good friends. In the end that was probably more sustainable.

Right now all she cared about was that Becky's life wasn't complicated. She was already handling all the change she could cope with.

11

Rosie

Rosie pulled on her clothes and crept out of the bedroom without waking Declan. They'd slept side by side but had managed not to touch once in the night. Normally she liked to sleep wrapped around him, but for her the emotional distances made it impossible to connect physically. She was afraid to reach for him, and he didn't reach for her.

Despite the very late night and the exhaustion of the journey, she hadn't slept at all, which wasn't so surprising because she could never sleep when she was upset.

She needed to talk to someone, preferably her mother. She could always talk to her mother about everything. But if she knew Rosie was worried then she'd worry, and Rosie didn't want to give her extra stress at Christmas when she already had more than enough. More than usual, thanks to Jamie. After his shock announcement the night before, Rosie had no doubt her mother had spent most of the night awake worrying.

Maybe she could talk to her dad. He always had something wise and sensible to say, even if he did have a tendency to turn everything into a consultation and give her his "doctor" look. Also, he was always up early, which meant there was a reasonable chance they'd be able to talk before anyone else was awake.

She crept into the kitchen, expecting to smell coffee and see her father reading the news on his phone while doing his morning exercises.

The kitchen was empty. Usually her father was up and around at six and it was now eight o'clock. Maybe she'd missed him. Maybe he'd already gone for a walk.

She frowned and checked by the back door. His coat was on the peg, so he hadn't gone for a walk. Presumably he was having a lie-in after their late night. Or maybe he'd been up all night soothing her mother's anxiety.

A moment later Percy nosed his way into the room, tail wagging.

"Where's Dad?" She bent to make a fuss of him. "Has no one taken you out this morning yet? We'll go together." Perhaps her father had gone out much earlier with the dog and had now gone back to bed.

Squashing down the disappointment that she wasn't going to be able to talk to him by herself, she grabbed her coat, pushed her feet into her boots and headed outdoors.

The snow had stopped falling and the sky was bright blue, the sun dazzling. The landscape was frosted white and silver, the surface of the snow sparkling in the sunshine.

She pulled on her hat and her sunglasses, zipped up her coat and headed away from the house to the footpath that led to the beach. The path itself was buried under a layer of snow but she knew the route so well she could have walked it with her eyes closed.

The air was icy and she settled her scarf over her mouth and nose and stamped her feet to warm them.

Percy bounded ahead, occasionally pausing to thrust his nose into an interesting looking mound of snow.

She'd been walking for ten minutes when she heard someone call her name.

"Hey, Rosie!" The voice came from behind her, and she turned to see her brother approaching.

This wasn't good. She would have talked to either one of her parents, but in the circumstances, she didn't know what to say to Jamie.

"I came downstairs to make coffee and heard you creeping out of the house."

"I was trying to be quiet. I didn't want to wake everyone."

"I was already awake. I brought the coffee with me, and cups. Thought you might want one." He gestured and she saw now that he'd slung a backpack over his shoulders. "Where are we going? The beach?"

He was assuming that wherever she was going, he'd be going too.

"Shouldn't you be taking that coffee up to Hayley?"

"She's still asleep." He crouched down to rub Percy's back. "Where's Declan?"

"Still asleep." Or was he? She didn't know if he was asleep or pretending to be asleep so that he could avoid interaction with her. Her mind was going in all sorts of directions she'd rather it didn't.

"I'm surprised Dad isn't up. He is usually obsessed with getting his early-morning light."

She was surprised too. For her entire childhood, her father had been the first out of the house. "He's retired now. Maybe he's having a lie-in."

"Doesn't sound like Dad, but maybe it's a good thing he isn't here. It gives us a chance to have that chat you wanted." Jamie straightened and headed to the beach. "It's freezing. The roads will be lethal. I don't suppose Will and Becky will be here before this afternoon so I might take Hayley into town. I want to show her our brilliant secondhand bookshop. Do they still serve that amazing hot chocolate at Christmas?"

"I think so. Sounds like a fun trip." They'd spent so many hours there as children that it had almost felt like a second home.

"You and Declan are welcome to join us."

"Oh—" She tugged her hat further over her ears. "Thanks, but we'll probably stay home. Granny and Grandad are coming over for a family breakfast and then staying. I promised to help Granny with her dress. There's a tear in it that needs mending. I haven't seen them for ages so I don't really want to go out. Maybe another time."

"No worries. I didn't know Granny and Grandad were coming this morning. In which case we might postpone our book trip. I want Hayley to meet them." They'd reached the edge of the beach now, and Jamie stopped for a moment and breathed deeply. "It's beautiful. Just look at it. That huge stretch of sand and just us. It's incredible. We were so lucky growing up in this place."

She looked at him, bemused. "Are you feeling okay?"

He glanced at her. "Never better. Why?"

"Because you've seen this beach at least a thousand times in your life and I don't remember you ever getting poetic about it before. I seem to remember last year you were griping that the place was so cold and inhospitable you didn't understand why all those people in the Middle Ages didn't choose to invade somewhere warmer."

"That was last year. This year I'm appreciating it."

"Right." Wondering what had happened to her brother, she turned and stared at the miles of windswept sand and the choppy sea. "Hayley seems nice."

"She's incredible." He thrust his hands into his pockets. "I know it's early days and you've only just met her, but when you've spent some time with her I think you'll find she really *is* nice. Special." He turned back to the ocean. "We connected instantly. After five minutes I felt as if I'd known her forever. She's had a tough life, and yet she's turned into this amazing, warm and funny person. There's no bitterness, or resentment about the past. No complaining about what she didn't have or doesn't have now. She really believes in doing whatever you can with whatever life throws at you. I've never known anyone to look on the bright side the way she does. Most people I know are always moaning about something, but not Hayley. She appreciates every little thing. She has made me see the world differently."

Rosie waited for him to draw breath. "So you like her, then."

He laughed. "Sorry. Am I horribly boring?"

"Not yet. I'll tell you when you are because that's what sisters do." And if she was honest, she was envious. What would Declan say about her if someone asked him? Would he admire her the way Jamie seemed to admire Hayley? Certainly, she'd been the same way after they'd first met. She'd used Declan's name so many times in one conversation that Becky had threatened to move out. "I'm pleased you're happy."

"I am. I honestly never thought it was possible to feel this way about another person. I always used to look at couples and wonder how they knew they were right for each other. Marriage is such a huge step, I couldn't figure out how they had the confidence to go for it, especially after Poppy. How could they be sure enough that it wouldn't go wrong? That one of you wouldn't just wake up one day and wonder if you'd made a mistake."

Rosie's mouth was dry. "Mm."

"Honestly, I didn't really get it, but now I do. It took a few hours for me to realise I wanted to spend the rest of my life with her."

"Okay, now you're on the verge of making me nauseous, and I'm generally considered a romantic person. Coffee might help. Are you planning on drinking it at any point or did you just add it to the backpack for weight training?"

"Coffee! How could I have forgotten?"

"I think you had other things on your mind." She watched as he swung the backpack off his shoulders and pulled out the flask and mugs. Percy bounded across to them, nosed the backpack hopefully and then trotted away again when he found nothing more interesting than a flask.

Jamie handed her the mugs to hold. "So what did you want to talk to me about?"

"Oh, nothing." She held the mugs steady while he poured the coffee. "That smells good."

"But yesterday you said you wanted to talk to me about something. You said it was important."

"Did I? I can't even remember now. Probably something to do with Christmas. Good idea to bring coffee. I wouldn't have thought of this."

"That's because you were sneaking out in a hurry, trying to leave the rest of us behind."

"I wasn't sneaking." She waited for him to put the flask back in the bag and then handed him one of the brimming cups. "I was trying not to wake the household. We all had a late night and we're going to have another late night tonight with your party."

"Ah yes, the party." He took a sip of coffee. "When I said we had something to celebrate, what was everyone expecting?"

"Engagement, obviously, like Mum said."

He watched the steam rise from the mug. "So how much did I shock everyone?"

"A lot, but you must know that." She pulled off a glove and let the warmth of the cup seep into her fingers. "Why didn't you tell us before? Why the big secret?"

"I thought it was better done face-to-face. I assumed that saying 'by the way, I just got married' wouldn't have come across well in a phone call."

It hadn't come across particularly well when delivered in person, but she didn't say that. She didn't want to spoil his moment. "I'm sure you're right." She blew on her coffee to cool it.

"I was a bit worried Mum might be upset, but she seemed very relaxed about it all, and excited."

Seriously? He thought their mother had been relaxed and excited?

She adored her brother, but was he really that emotionally clueless? Or maybe love had clouded his brain. It had been obvious to her that their mother had been making a supreme effort to cover her shock and hurt. She'd made an admirable attempt, but Rosie hadn't thought anyone had been fooled by her enthusiastic response. Clearly she'd been wrong about that. And perhaps that was a good thing. There was no way Jamie would have wanted to hurt their mother.

"Was there some reason why you decided to get married quickly and in secret?" She sipped her coffee, which was cooling rapidly in the freezing air. "What's wrong with having your family there? Are we particularly embarrassing?"

"Yes, horribly." He grinned and finished his coffee before shaking the drips from the mug onto the snow. "Just kidding. I love my family, you know that. But I thought it would make the whole thing easier for Hayley if we did it quietly, just the two of us. No fuss."

"Easier? Are we difficult?"

"It wasn't so much the people as the principle." He took her empty mug and tucked it back inside the rucksack with the flask and the other mug. "She doesn't have family. If we'd had a big wedding—or even a small, family-only wedding—she would have had no one there. Not that she would have said anything, because that isn't how she is. But I wanted it to be about the two of us and nothing else. Doing it the way we did felt more—I don't know—" he shrugged "—equal, I suppose. It was about us, and no one else."

"She has no family at all?"

"No. She grew up in care. She had no one encouraging her to do her homework. No one clapping for her in a school play. No one stealing her chocolate at Christmas. She has been her own cheerleader for her whole life. But now she has me."

Rosie felt a lump form in her throat. "That makes me want to cry."

"Because she has me? You feel sorry for her?"

"No, you idiot." She gave him a push. "Because she has never had anyone in her corner."

"I know. It makes me sad too, although she hates it when I say so. She prefers to think about now. And now she has me in her corner. I'm there for her, through thick and thin no matter what."

Rosie felt herself well up. She wanted Declan to feel that way about her.

Jamie peered at her. "Are you crying?"

"No, it's the cold air—" She brushed at her eyes. "And I might be a bit emotional today."

"You always are. Especially at Christmas. You love this time of year. And it's snowing. This must be your dream."

"Absolutely." She blinked back tears and forced a smile. "My dream."

He hooked the backpack onto his shoulder. "Do you want to walk a bit more?"

"Yes." She needed to shake off the thoughts she was having. She needed to stop asking herself questions about her own relationship.

They walked along the beach together, wrapped up warmly against the winter cold. Miles of sand stretched ahead and they were the only people walking.

Everyone else was probably snuggled up in the warm kitchen drinking hot chocolate and feelings Christmassy.

She zipped her coat a little higher to keep out the icy air.

Instead of feeling sorry for herself, she forced herself to focus on Jamie. And that wasn't so hard because she wanted to know more. She could never resist hearing someone's romantic story. "So you met her in Thailand and wham, that was it. You decided to marry her."

"When you know, you know. You're one of the few people who will understand that because the same thing happened with you and Declan." He paused for a moment, watching as Percy raced across the sand. "You were married quickly and that has turned out well, hasn't it?"

She'd thought so at the time, but now she wasn't so sure. But there was no point in voicing that as he was already married. It was too late for her experience to make a difference, and the last thing he needed was to hear about her marital problems.

"Yes, it was quick for us too."

She was embarrassed. She felt like a failure. Who had marital problems after less than a year?

He gave her a searching look. "What's wrong?"

"Nothing. I'm just worried about you, that's all. You're my big brother. I want you to be happy."

"You can stop worrying because I've never been happier."

"Good." She slipped her arm into his. "Let's go home. We can help Mum prepare breakfast so she doesn't get overwhelmed."

"You still can't remember what it was you wanted to say to me?"

"No. Which just proves it couldn't have been important." It wasn't her brother she needed to talk to, she realised, nor her parents. It was Declan. She needed to tell him how she was feeling. She needed to find out how he was feeling. They needed to try to work out where and when their relationship had started to unravel.

Jamie checked his phone. "Nothing from Hayley. I need to

check she's okay. I wonder if Becky and Will are on their way. Have you heard from them this morning?"

"No." Thinking of her sister brought back all her anxieties about Declan. He was obviously looking forward to seeing Becky. Was her sister feeling the same way? Becky and Declan had been friends for years before Rosie had arrived on the scene. It hadn't crossed her mind that there might be anything more between them than friendship. Becky would have told her, surely?

But she knew that wasn't true. She shared everything with Becky—every feeling, every date, every kiss. Becky rarely shared her innermost self, even with her sister.

Rosie tried to think back to that first night when Becky had invited her to join them. The night she'd met Declan for the first time. He and Becky had already been at the table, drinks in front of them. They were laughing about something, but not sitting particularly close together. Not touching. She'd seen friendship, not romance.

"I can't wait to hear all about Becky's new job," Jamie said. "How's it going?"

Rosie pulled herself back to the present. "I don't know. I'm looking forward to finding out more."

"But you and she talk all the time—"

"Not so much lately. I think she's been giving us space because we were newly married. And she has been busy, I've been busy—you know how it is—" She quickened her pace. "It's freezing out here. Let's get back in the warm."

She didn't really know how it was, but she intended to find out.

But before then there was something she had to do.

Smiling, she bent down, scooped up a large ball of snow and threw it at her brother.

12

Hayley

She could hear laughter and conversation coming from the kitchen and she wasn't sure what to do. Should she stay in her room? Join them? It was her first-ever family Christmas and she had no idea what was expected of her. Yes, she was married to Jamie, which technically made her part of the family, but she didn't feel like part of anything.

Maybe it was her. Maybe she wasn't capable of feeling as if she was part of something.

She'd slept badly, her mind replaying the moment Jamie had made the announcement. Everyone had said all the right things but there had been a split second, a moment that she would have missed had she not been looking at Jamie's mother, when she'd seen something less than delight. She'd seen shock and wished now that she'd pushed harder to persuade Jamie to tell them in advance. The knowledge that they were now adjusting to this major piece of news hadn't done anything to help her relax.

She'd eventually fallen asleep in the early hours and woken to find the bed empty and a sweet note on the pillow from Jamie.

Taking the dog out for a walk. Back soon. I love you xx

She'd folded the note and put it in her bag along with the others (she kept every note he'd ever written her and sometimes reread them to check this was all real) but she couldn't help wishing that instead of writing her a note, he'd woken her up and taken her with him. She wanted to get this right. She wanted to do the right thing and say the right thing, and she didn't know what those were.

She'd showered, dressed and then stood by the window watching for him, wondering when exactly she'd become so insecure and pathetic that she needed a man by her side before she left the room. In the distance near the sea she could see two figures and assumed that if one of them was Jamie then the other was presumably Rosie, or maybe his mother.

Were they talking about her? Wondering what on earth he'd been thinking marrying her with no warning?

She sighed and sat down on the window seat.

She glanced down at the rings on her finger, the ones they'd agreed she wouldn't wear until after they made their announcement. The diamond had come first, then the thin gold band just a few weeks later. Part of her still couldn't quite believe it. Not the rings, but the feelings she had for him. She hadn't known it was possible to feel this way.

Correction. She hadn't known it was possible for *her* to feel this way. This kind of life happened to other people, not her, and nothing in her past experience had prepared her for it.

She'd learned to take care of herself, to give herself praise, encouragement and nurture. Sharp words, when necessary. When it came to leaning on someone, trusting someone, she was a novice. By rights she should have taken her time over it, taking it step by cautious step. But from the moment she'd met Jamie caution had been left by the roadside. She had no idea why or how she trusted him, but she did. She had no doubts about her own feelings, and no doubts about his. But this—

this family gathering and being all together for Christmas—was something else.

Watching Christmas movies gave you atmosphere and fairy lights but it didn't teach you anything useful about how to navigate family dynamics. They were a unit, knitted together by shared history and love. How did an outsider become part of that?

Impatient with herself, she was about to force herself to join them downstairs when there was a tap on the door.

Hoping it was Jamie, Hayley opened it.

Rosie stood there, her cheeks pink from her walk outside, her hair long and loose and tumbling. "Hey there. I came to lure you down for breakfast. Mum has sent Jamie to bring in more logs, even though I pointed out I'm more than capable of hauling a few logs." She pretended to flex her muscles. "He won't be long, and in the meantime I make an excellent cappuccino if I can tempt you. Or I can make tea, if you're not a coffee drinker. English Breakfast, green, peppermint—you must state your preferences, and don't be polite otherwise you'll be eating and drinking things you hate for the rest of your life."

"Coffee is great, thank you."

At least Rosie was friendly. Hayley hadn't been sure what reaction she'd get this morning after their announcement the night before.

She quietly scanned Rosie's outfit. Thick leggings and a pretty Fair Isle sweater. She breathed a sigh of relief. She'd been unsure what to wear (was she supposed to dress up? Look festive?) and in the end she'd put on black jeans with a cream cable-knit sweater that she loved.

"While it's just the two of us, let me see the ring." Rosie grabbed her hand and peered closely. "Oooh, it's beautiful. I didn't know Jamie had such good taste. Was it a surprise? Tell me how he proposed."

Hayley wasn't used to divulging private information. And

she definitely couldn't share that particular anecdote. They'd been in bed, naked, and Jamie had pulled her close and said *this is how I want to spend the rest of my life*, and she'd said *so do I*, and that had been it. A moment of delicious intimacy, binding them forever. Surely that was supposed to be private, even from family? "It was—he—"

"I can see I shouldn't have asked." Rosie gave her a naughty grin. "Better keep it to yourself. There are some things a girl doesn't want to know about her brother. Come on. It's Christmas Eve Eve, which always means pancakes."

Hayley followed her into the kitchen that looked over the garden and from there to the sea. The room was warm and inviting, and surprisingly cosy given its generous size. A vase of winter foliage sat in the middle of the large kitchen island, pale eucalyptus mingling with stems clustered with scarlet berries.

Jenny was standing at the kitchen island mixing something in a bowl. Delicious smells wafted from the oven, and rows of freshly baked gingerbread men lay cooling on a rack.

"Ah, there you are, Hayley." She paused what she was doing. "I hope you slept well. Sit down. Take five minutes because it will be chaotic soon. We have so much to do for the party later. My parents will be here shortly, and then Becky. And Will, of course, although I expect he'll be going home and coming back later tonight. It must all be a bit overwhelming for you, all these names and people that you don't know, but Rosie can tell you who everyone is, so don't feel daunted."

At least Jamie's mother was speaking to her, which was a relief. More than speaking. She was warm and welcoming, as if Hayley was a treasured guest and not someone who had been sprung on her.

Hayley smiled gratefully as Rosie put a cappuccino in front of her. "Thank you."

Declan appeared, his hair damp from the shower.

He greeted them politely, and Hayley remembered Jamie

telling her it was Declan's first Christmas with the family too. It was almost a comfort to think that someone else felt as awkward as she did.

Rosie walked across the kitchen and gave him a quick kiss on the cheek. "Nice shower? I hope Jamie didn't steal all the water. I took Percy out for a walk, but I left you to sleep because you looked so comfortable—"

"Rosie, breathe," Jenny said. "Are you a morning person, Declan? Rosie has too much energy for most of us in the morning, but of course you're used to her by now. Breakfast won't be long, but in the meantime I suspect what you need is strong coffee."

Declan gave a faint smile. "Strong coffee would be good, thank you."

"I'll make it." Rosie headed back to the coffee machine, keeping her back to them.

Hayley watched her, taking in the slight slump in her shoulders. Last night she'd suspected something wasn't right between them and she had the same feeling this morning. They were tiptoeing, being careful around each other. She could almost feel the yearning in Rosie, as if she was longing for something she couldn't have.

She glanced back at Jenny, but Rosie's mother was rinsing berries and either hadn't noticed or didn't seem to think anything was wrong.

Rosie waited while coffee dripped into the cup. The aroma of fresh coffee drifted across the kitchen. "Hayley, did Jamie remember to give you the Wi-Fi password? It's *dontdrinkanddrive234*. All lowercase. It was Dad's not-very-subtle way of getting that message home to us, and all our friends, when we were growing up."

Hayley typed it into her phone. "That doesn't work."

Declan frowned. "You haven't changed your password for ten years?"

"Oh, it's been far longer than ten years," Rosie said cheerfully, handing him his coffee. "Declan will now have a minor heart attack."

"Becky hasn't changed it?"

"Now you mention it, she did, but Dad changed it back again. They compromised and *Drive* has a capital letter. Try that."

Hayley did and it instantly connected. "Perfect."

Declan's expression suggested he didn't think it was perfect but was too well-mannered to argue.

"Talking of Dad, where is he?" Rosie glanced at her mother. "I expected him to be up hours ago."

"He's been sleeping a little later since he retired." Jenny tipped the berries into a bowl. "He probably needs the rest."

"Rest? Dad?" Rosie laughed. "That's funny."

Hayley looked at Jenny to see if she was laughing.

She wasn't.

"He's getting older," she said, adding a spoon to the bowl of berries. "And this has been a tiring year for him. Did you and Jamie enjoy your walk on the beach?"

Why had she changed the subject?

Hayley waited for Rosie to question her mother further, but she didn't.

"The walk was gorgeous. Freezing, obviously, but Jamie brought coffee, which was exactly what we needed. And we had a small snowball fight, so it was like old times."

"That sounds like a good start to the day." Jenny was relaxed again, moving around the kitchen gathering napkins and cutlery and placing them on the table.

Hayley had assumed that close families communicated all the time—what she hadn't known was that so much of it would be unspoken.

She had to stop overthinking. She didn't know these people. She didn't know who they were underneath the warmth and good manners, so how could she possibly understand the more subtle dynamics? Experience had taught her that the only way to really know someone was to spend time with them and see them in different situations, particularly stressful ones. That was when people tended to show their true selves.

Maybe Declan was an introvert who was as uncomfortable as she was with this mass family gathering. Maybe Jamie's father was exhausted from all the Christmas preparations.

The back door opened and Jamie walked in, bringing with him cold air and armfuls of logs.

"I put the rest in the garage, so at least they're close by, but these should keep us going for a while. Dad has another lot. He's just coming."

"Your dad was out there with you?" Jenny smiled. "That's good."

"He showed up after the hard work was done." Jamie dumped the logs into the large basket by the door and pulled off his coat. "I don't smell bacon. I was promised bacon. Tantrum incoming."

"Save your tantrum," Jenny said. "It's next on Rosie's list now she has finished coffee."

"Why me?" Rosie grumbled. "Why is it always me who ends up cooking bacon? I'm the vegetarian of the family."

Percy trotted to the kitchen door and barked.

Hayley decided this whole thing would be easier if she had something to do. "Why don't I cook the bacon?" She stood up and Rosie handed her a pan.

"That would be appreciated. Stop barking, Percy!"

Jenny frowned. "Hayley is a guest."

"No, she's not." Rosie pulled a packet of bacon from the fridge, holding it away from herself between finger and thumb before passing it to Hayley with a shudder. "She's family now, and if she doesn't mind cooking bacon, that's going to make her my favourite sister-in-law."

Hayley took the bacon. "How long have you been vegetarian?"

"Ever since I realised that roast chicken was actually a chicken."

"She was seven years old," Jenny said. "She cried. We had to have a funeral for the carcass. And all she ate for the next three years was margarita pizza. That's Rosie for you." She handed Hayley an apron. "Wear that, honey. Your jumper is too pretty to spoil. Percy, please stop barking. Next time we decide to get a pet it's going to be a goldfish."

Jamie walked across to Hayley and curved a hand over her shoulder. "Did you miss me?"

Yes, she'd missed him, which was unsettling given that he'd been gone for only just over an hour. She wanted to turn into him and press her lips to his, but she was conscious of all the other people in the room. Keeping her hands off him in public might be the biggest challenge of the holidays.

"Yuck. Enough." Rosie smacked her brother on the shoulder. "I know you're newlyweds, but if you want to slobber, do it outside. Percy! What is *wrong* with the dog? Jamie and I took him out an hour ago." She opened the door between the kitchen and the hallway and Percy shot out of the room, tail wagging. "Oh, a car is arriving. That's why he was barking. He's such a good guard dog and we ignored him. Sorry, Percy. You are a clever, wonderful dog and you deserve better humans in your life. I'm going to spend the rest of Christmas making it up to you."

"A car? That will be Granny and Grandad." Jenny put down the plates she was holding and started rushing around the kitchen, clearing the surfaces. "They're early. And I'm not ready."

"They're family," Rosie said logically. "How ready do you need to be?"

"Readier than I am. I need to look relaxed and in control, otherwise your grandmother will worry that having them here is all too much. The first thing she'll say is 'are we too early?

I'm worried we're making too much work for you. We don't have to stay for Christmas. We could come over for the day.' You know what they're like." She whisked off her apron and smoothed her hair. "Do I look relaxed?"

Rosie stole a berry from the bowl and studied her. "Honestly? No. You look stressed out of your mind."

"Really?" Jenny looked even more stressed. "Jamie, can you go and help with their luggage? Delay them if you can. My parents live close by," she told Hayley, "but at Christmas they always come to us, although I did expect us to have a little more time to prepare before they arrived. Still, at least we're dressed. There was one year when I was still in my nightdress. We started doing it when the children were little, and it has become something of a family tradition."

Family tradition. Something she knew nothing about.

Hayley waited for the bacon to sizzle and brown, feeling nothing but admiration for Jenny. She was clearly stressed by the early arrival, but she didn't want her parents to know. She wanted them to feel welcome and wanted. It made her wonder again what Jenny really thought about Jamie's shock announcement. She was obviously a master at hiding her true feelings. Was that what she'd done last night?

But that wasn't her main worry right now. She'd barely got used to the family she'd already met and now she was about to meet more. It was daunting, mostly because she didn't know what her role was. She wished there was an instruction manual for new family members.

The effort to appear relaxed and at home was exhausting.

"Did you tell Granny about Jamie and Hayley?" Rosie took a final gulp of her coffee before putting it back down on the countertop. "I mean because she's eighty-five and probably shouldn't be subjected to big shocks at her stage of life. It isn't kind."

There was another blast of cold air as Jamie's father came into the kitchen.

"Do not say things like 'her stage of life' when your grandmother is within hearing. Eighty-five is the new fifty," her mother said, "and yes, I called her this morning to share the exciting news. I thought it was better that way. Come to think of it, that's probably why she's early."

Exciting news.

Feeling her cheeks flush, Hayley flipped the bacon.

Jamie definitely should have told his family in advance of their arrival.

"If Granny is tactless, don't be offended," Rosie warned Hayley. "She says it's her age, but Mum says she has always been like that."

"She did have a habit of speaking her mind, that's true. This isn't the time, but when we're on our own ask me to tell you the story of the school Christmas baking competition when I was twelve." Jenny pulled two loaves of fresh bread out of the oven and put them on a wooden board in the middle of the table. "Rosie, could you grab some of that strawberry jam I made in the summer, please? It's on the top shelf. And slice the bread. Whatever people don't eat for breakfast we'll have for lunch. I made a spicy parsnip soup yesterday."

"I'm going to say hello to Granny. I'll slice the bread in a minute." Rosie vanished from the room.

"What exciting news are you talking about?" Jamie's father stamped the snow off his boots and left them by the back door.

"About Hayley and Jamie." Jenny put a slab of butter next to the bread. "Have you finished outside?"

"Yes. We should have enough logs for the next couple of days." He hung his coat on the peg and then headed across the kitchen in his socks.

"I was thinking that we ought to check on Edna Murren at

some point. With this much snow, she might have a problem getting out of her drive."

He nodded. "I'll give her a call. Jamie and I can go across and clear her driveaway if necessary."

"Good idea. I'll get you a plate for that bacon, Hayley," Jenny said. "Martin, can you cook these pancakes, please? You always do a good job."

"You don't need to praise me to get me to do it. I'm not six years old."

"The praise was genuine. You always cook them perfectly. But I need you to hurry up." Jenny handed her husband the bowl of freshly made batter and took a warm plate from the oven for Hayley's bacon. "Thank you for doing that, Hayley. You're a lifesaver."

It was like a relay race, Hayley thought. Each family member handing something on to someone else. A team.

There was a flurry of activity in the hallway and then a slim woman with short white hair walked into the room, loaded down with bags.

She wore a soft wool dress in a shade of pale caramel that flattered her features. Hayley decided that if she looked half as elegant at the age of eighty-five, she would be satisfied.

Jenny swapped stress for a smile and opened her arms. "Happy Christmas! It's probably a bit early to say that but it always feels as if Christmas has started when you and Dad appear."

"You're sure we're not too early? I'm worried we're making too much work for you. We don't have to stay for Christmas. We could come over for the day. But if that's what you'd like, speak now, because your father is already upstairs unpacking. You must be stressed. I'm worried we're making a lot more work for you by being here."

"And that wouldn't be anywhere near as much fun." Jenny ignored Rosie's and Jamie's grinning faces and hugged her mother. "With this number of people in the house, two more is no more work at all. And we're not stressed. We're all totally relaxed here, aren't we, Rosie?"

"Totally relaxed," Rosie parroted. "Never been more relaxed in my life."

Jenny was barely listening. "Jamie, did you take the luggage upstairs? Oh, Rosie, what *have* you done to the dog?"

Percy ambled into the room wearing a pair of brown velvet antlers.

"I'm training him to be a reindeer." Rosie bent down and straightened the antlers. "Everyone else in this family has to multitask, so I don't see why Percy should be the exception."

"He looks rather confused," Jenny said.

The whole family is mad, Hayley thought, intrigued that the antlers didn't seem to be bothering the dog. But the chaos of it all helped her to relax. Nothing was perfect here.

"Jamie has already taken our luggage upstairs, and Brian is pottering up there. You know what he's like. These are presents." Rosie's grandmother waved the bags. "They're to go under the tree, but not too close to the fire. Why is Rosie laughing?"

"Because you said exactly what we knew you'd say about it all being too much work and how you should come for the day and it's funny." Rosie wrapped her arms round her grandmother and kissed her. "I love you, Granny. You're adorable."

"Well, that's nice. I can't believe it's Christmas again already. It seems like yesterday since the last one. So much fuss and bother and work and then it's over in a flash. Are you going to play the piano and sing for me later?"

Rosie pulled a face. "I don't think—"

"No, she is not." Jamie retrieved the antlers that had fallen off under the table and slipped them back onto Percy's head. "Rosie, I'll pay you not to sing."

"I'd *love* to sing, Granny," Rosie said. "Anything to make you happy. I shall sing morning, noon and night. I will even serenade Hayley and Jamie in their bedroom. *Deck the halls with boughs of holly*—" she sang loudly, beaming at her wincing brother, and then grabbed her grandmother by the hand and led her to Hayley. "This is our newest family member, Hayley. Hayley, this is our grandmother, Phyllis. You should probably just call her Granny."

Slightly overwhelmed by the sibling interplay, Hayley extended her hand and found herself being hugged again. This was less surprising than it had been when Jenny and Rosie had hugged her. Maybe she was getting used to it.

"It's good to meet you."

"Jenny told me your wonderful news," Phyllis said. "So exciting. A real whirlwind, which is romantic. Or maybe you're pregnant? Which would be delightful by the way, so don't worry that there will be any judgement from me."

"Agh!" Rosie covered her face with her hands. "You cannot ask people that, Granny. Boundaries, remember?"

"Oh, don't be ridiculous, Rosie." Her grandmother settled herself at the table. "This is family."

"All the more reason to have boundaries," Rosie muttered, shooting Hayley a look of apology.

Her grandmother hadn't finished. "I could ask you the same question, Rosie."

"You could, but you're not going to," Jenny said quickly, looking more stressed than ever. "How were the roads when you drove over here? Were they clear?"

"The roads were fine, although what that has to do with being pregnant I have no idea." Phyllis unfolded a napkin. "Don't give me that look, Jenny. All I'm saying is that I approve of Jamie and Hayley just going ahead and getting married, whatever the reason. There's too much fuss these days. And the money people spend! I always wanted to elope, but Brian wouldn't hear of it."

"Is that true, Granny? Tell us more." Rosie sat down next to her grandmother, her focused expression suggesting she was taking personal responsibility for the conversation topics for the remainder of the season.

"I didn't want all that fuss, and my parents couldn't afford it. If we'd lived in Regency times, I would have gone straight to Gretna Green, particularly as your grandfather wanted us to get married before having sex. He was very old-fashioned. Fortunately I put an end to that thinking and successfully seduced him."

"Granny!" Rosie screwed up her face in appalled horror at the image. "Too much information."

"Stop being prudish. I was young once too, you know." She gestured to Hayley to sit next to her and Hayley dutifully sat, braced for whatever was coming next.

She'd asked Jamie on more than one occasion if he thought his family would assume she was pregnant. He'd replied that if they did, they would be far too polite to ask. Clearly he hadn't factored in his grandmother.

"I thought you did live in Regency times." Rosie was still trying to steer the focus of the conversation away from her and Hayley. "Just kidding. You're a spring chicken, Granny. And if you had lived in Regency times you would have looked gorgeous in the dresses."

"Except that I would have been cleaning the kitchens, not wafting around the manor house. And anyway, I'm not sure I would have looked good in Empire Line. Do you have photos, Hayley? An album? I'd love to look at it."

"I have lots on my phone but it's upstairs charging," Hayley said. "I'd love to show you later."

"I look forward to it. I should have known the photos would be on your phone. These days everything is up in the sky, isn't it."

Rosie grinned. "It's the cloud, Granny."

"Same thing. Basically it's not real. Not the same as having a lovely old-fashioned album that you can flick through. Now tell me, Rosie, how was *The Nutcracker*?" She reached into her bag and pulled out her glasses and a cutting from a newspaper. "I saw this review and cut it out for you. I wish I could have seen it." She turned to Hayley. "I used to take Rosie to the ballet when she was little. It was something we did, just the two of us. Being a twin wasn't always easy, and those girls were so different from each other. I like to think I contributed to Rosie's career choice."

Hayley imagined Rosie and her grandmother seated side by side in the darkness, enchanted by the shimmer and twirl of dancers onstage.

"I've never been to the ballet, but I've seen it on TV and I once illustrated a book about a dancer."

"I'd love to see those illustrations. You must show us later. I've seen some of your drawings on your website. Wonderful. Rosie loved ballet as a child," Phyllis told her. "She was a very talented dancer but she also loved making things and in the end that passion won."

The tension around the table eased as the conversation shifted onto safer ground.

"I did love dancing, but I was a bit clumsy. Remember that performance when I tripped over that boy who was a tree trunk?" Rosie reached down to stroke Percy, who had settled himself by her chair, hopeful of being given a treat.

"I seem to remember he couldn't keep still, which was why you tripped. Now tell me about *The Nutcracker*. Was it as good as that performance we saw together in Edinburgh when you were sixteen?"

This is what a family is, Hayley thought, *a group of individuals knitted together by shared moments and memories.* How did you become part of that? It wasn't about doing or saying the right thing. It was so much more than that.

"No, but that might have been because that time we were in the audience," Rosie said. "This time I was backstage and in full-blown panic mode. It was the first time I've made a costume for the Sugar Plum Fairy. I have photos to show you. The tulle was a bit of a nightmare to work with and I never want to see another sequin in my life, but it looked fabulous under the lights. I wish I could have sneaked you in to see the performance."

"London is too far away. Why can't you work closer to home?"

"Because London is my home." Rosie reached out and stole another couple of berries.

Jenny pulled the bowl away from her. "Stop snacking on berries! Or at least serve yourself a proper portion in the bowl."

"I like grazing."

"You're not a horse, and we're trying to make a pretence of being civilized here. What is Hayley going to think of us? Martin, how are those pancakes coming?" Jenny bustled around, checking for missing items on the table and encouraging everyone to sit down. "Isn't this a treat? All together, apart from Becky, and she thinks they should be with us just after lunch. Oh there you are, Dad!" She crossed the kitchen and hugged the man who had just walked into the room.

Phyllis put her hand on Hayley's arm. "Brian, this is Hayley."

He turned to her, eyes twinkling. "Ah, Jamie's new girl-friend."

"Wife," Phyllis reminded him, "not girlfriend. And you need to behave yourself."

"That's right, wife." He winked at Hayley. "And as she is already a member of the family, I don't see that the way I behave matters. It's too late for her to change her mind." He gave a generic wave to everyone at the table and headed straight for Martin, who was flipping pancakes. "I could use your input into my chapter on the impact of cold weather on the heart."

"Right. Well, we'll get to that after breakfast, Brian." Martin handed his father-in-law a plate of pancakes and gestured to the table. "Let's eat, shall we? And you can tell us how it's going. The writing I mean."

"Never ask a writer how the writing is going."

Phyllis rolled her eyes. "If he's tetchy, it's because he's not actually writing."

"I am writing."

"Writers write, Brian, whereas you spend most of the day staring out of the window."

"I'm sure Shakespeare had moments of staring out of the window. I'm thinking. Planning." Brian put the pancakes in the middle of the table. "I assume these aren't all for me, so tuck in."

"I'm sure thinking is the most important part of planning a book." Soothing and conciliatory, Jenny moved the bowl of berries next to her mother. "Help yourselves. I know how much you love them."

"They're a wanton extravagance at this time of year." Despite that, Phyllis heaped berries onto her plate, and Jenny caught Hayley's eye and struggled not to smile.

"Well, if you can't be wantonly extravagant at Christmas, I don't know when you can be. Hayley, do you have everything you need? Don't be polite or you'll starve. Help yourself."

"I'll keep an eye on her." Phyllis eyed Hayley's empty plate. "Eat, dear, or Jenny will worry that you don't like the food."

Hayley helped herself to pancakes and bacon.

"Have a few berries too. Vitamins." Phyllis spooned them onto her plate. "Now tell us everything. I especially want to know about that first moment when you knew you were in love with Jamie."

"I apologise for my wife's intrusive questioning." Brian sighed. "Give the girl space, Phyllis."

"It's not being intrusive, it's showing interest. And I'm sure there are things she's happy to share now she's part of the family."

"What if she isn't happy to share them? You're putting her in a very awkward position."

Jamie sat down next to Hayley and she felt his hand on her leg, under the table.

He leaned closer to her. "Ignore them. They're always like this. You did say you wanted to experience a family Christmas." He was openly laughing. "Welcome to my family. A gathering of dysfunctional misfits."

"Speak for yourself! And I don't know why you're whispering, Jamie," Rosie said, "because we can all hear you. I'd like to know everything about Hayley too."

"Maybe she could eat her breakfast before the inquisition starts." Jamie heaped pancakes onto his plate and covered them in maple syrup. "This, by the way, is one of the reasons we got married on a beach by ourselves. I thought if we waited until she'd met you all, she might back out."

"Charming." Rosie shot her brother a look. "And Percy is very hurt because he would have enjoyed being Dog of Honour."

"Okay, that's enough." Jenny sat down in a vacant chair. "Can we please at least pretend to be normal for the duration of one short meal? Hayley, I'd like to say they're not usually like this, but it would be a lie. Answer any question you feel like answering and ignore the rest. Now let's eat, because there is a lot to do in preparation for tonight." She helped herself to bacon. "And *please* would someone take those antlers off the poor dog."

13

Becky

"I can't believe they're already married." Becky stared at her phone, reading the message for the hundredth time. "What is *wrong* with my family? They meet someone and wham, suddenly they're in love. There must be something faulty in our DNA. Does it really happen that way? Has that ever happened to you?"

"No." Will's attention was focused on the road. "It hasn't."

"So generally speaking, you find you need to know someone before you fall in love."

There was a pause. "Generally speaking, I do find that, yes."

"Good to know. I'm glad I know at least one normal person."

They'd been driving for a few hours and hadn't said much to each other until the message had come in from Rosie.

She sneaked a glance at him, aware that something had changed.

Yesterday it had been relaxed and—well—normal. Today everything felt tense. *He* seemed tense. She was pretty tense herself, but that was mostly because she kept reliving the moment when he'd walked out of the shower with only a towel around his hips (she'd known him for her whole life and suddenly she couldn't stop thinking about his shoulders). But he couldn't possibly know that. He couldn't possibly know what was going on in her head so he must have his own reasons for behaving strangely.

Maybe he was bored with her family drama. Or maybe he was just tired.

She wanted to ask if he was okay, which was definitely something Rosie would have done, but she hated being asked that question herself so she kept it to herself and focused on the latest drama emanating from her family.

"I'm glad Rosie warned me. At least now I can practice rearranging my features into a delighted expression."

"You're not delighted?"

"I don't know. My emotions about things tend to be more neutral, you know that. I'm not like Rosie. Roller Coaster Rosie. Up one minute and down the next."

He smiled. "I remember you calling her that. It was an apt name."

"You've known Jamie forever. Does this seem weird to you? Suddenly getting married? I'm sure Granny will immediately assume she's pregnant. I hope she doesn't say it out loud. But I doubt it's that. What do you think?"

He didn't answer immediately. "I suppose if you know you've met the right person, then it's not weird."

"But people don't know, do they? Not really. It's not an exact science. If it was, no one would ever get it wrong. People think they're in love and then suddenly they're not. Or they think they're not in love, and suddenly discover they are."

Like her, for example. She'd had no clue she was in love with Declan until Rosie's wedding. She'd seen him almost every day for the five years they'd worked together. They'd sat side by side. Worked on projects together. Brought each other coffee and chocolate from the snack bar that the company made available to employees. Ranted to each other in the corridor when no one was listening. Gone for the occasional drink and pizza after work. They were friends. And she hadn't known she'd wanted anything more than that until the day he'd married her sister. Her feelings had crept up on her and she hadn't even noticed.

How did that happen? *Why* did that happen?

She stared at the road, pondering.

The snow had been cleared and lay in soft piles along the side of the road, the surface glinting in the sunlight.

Will slowed down as they approached a sharp bend. "That's a very Becky thing to say."

She turned to look at him. "What? What do you mean?"

"You want a logical explanation for everything. Evidence. You always have. You don't let feelings influence your decisions."

"Because feelings are weird, unpredictable things that come and go, and change, which is why I try not to pay attention to them."

"So if you feel something strongly—"

"I wait until the feeling passes. I certainly don't use it as a basis for decision making. And what's wrong with that? If you're doing a trial into a new treatment for some medical condition you look for evidence that it works, don't you? You don't rely on gut instinct."

"No. As you say, evidence. Lots of evidence, from different sources."

"Exactly. Because you don't want to get it wrong and risk damaging the patient. And yet time and time again people rely on gut instinct to make the biggest decision of their lives and yes, when it goes wrong, they're damaged. There has to be a better way."

"You've never made a decision based on feelings?"

She shrugged. "I suppose choosing what to eat is driven

by my feelings. Burger or pizza. Which am I in the mood for. Does that count?"

"Yes. And chocolate. Eating chocolate is always an emotional decision."

"True. But that's the limit to which I let feelings dictate my actions. Feelings are unregulated and unreliable. And that's probably why I'm dreading Christmas. I'm going to be drowning in everyone's feelings. Jamie's, Rosie's, definitely my mother's because I can't imagine she isn't hurt that she didn't get invited to the wedding—" And her own. She'd be drowning in her own feelings too.

This was going to be the first time she'd seen Declan in months and she was dreading it. She'd made it easier for herself by never being in the same room as him, but that was about to change.

However she felt about seeing Declan and Rosie together, she had to hide it. She adored her sister and she would never do anything to hurt her. But Rosie was intuitive, and that was one of the other reasons Becky had been avoiding her. She was terrified she might not be able to hide the way she felt.

She'd tried to push it out of her mind, but they were going to be home in an hour and there would be no more avoiding it.

She groaned. "My Christmas is going to be full of other people's romances. Lots of kissing and cuddling. Kill me now." She should have made an excuse. It would have been awful, but better than this alternative. "I can't do this. Can we just drive straight to Scotland and find a cute bothy in the middle of nowhere to hide out? Tell everything we were snowed in on the journey?"

"Sure." His tone was light. "If that's what you'd like."

She slid lower in her seat, imagining it. "Right now, it's exactly what I'd like."

"You're just tired, Becks. You're always cranky when you're tired."

"I'm not cranky." She stared ahead and then looked at him. He knew her too well, that was the problem. "Okay, maybe I'm a little cranky. But I'm not tired. That bed was comfortable. Like sleeping on a cloud. I slept brilliantly."

There was a pause. "Really?"

"Ten hours straight. Which is so unusual for me. Normally I'm like a meercat, on full alert for most of the night. You?"

"I didn't sleep that well." He adjusted his grip on the wheel. "I had things on my mind."

Things? What things? Was she supposed to ask?

"You probably slept more than you think."

She knew for a fact she'd woken up before him. In the end they'd agreed that Will sleeping in the chair was just too stupid for words. The bed was big enough for both of them and they'd known each other forever, so it made perfect sense for him to lie down on one half of the bed and get a proper night's sleep so that they would both be fresh for the journey.

To begin with it had felt strange and she'd lain there rigid, afraid to move in case she accidently touched him, but then finally she'd drifted off and had the best night's sleep she could remember having in years.

She'd woken feeling warm and comfortable and it had taken a moment for her to realise she was snuggled against him with her head on his chest. Turned out those shoulders of his made a very satisfactory pillow.

She'd unpeeled herself carefully, trying not to wake him because she didn't want to risk an awkward moment, but luckily for her he hadn't stirred. Which was how she knew he'd slept for at least part of the night.

But his sleep pattern wasn't her main problem right now.

"So how am I supposed to handle this?"

"Handle what?" He slowed down as a car pulled out in front of them. "You need to be specific. Is it Declan? Seeing your family? Their feelings? Your feelings?"

"All of the above."

"I'm sure it will be easier than you think."

"Maybe, but what if it isn't. We're friends, right?"

"Yes. We're friends."

She frowned. "You hesitated."

"I did not hesitate."

"You definitely hesitated."

"What is it you want from me, Becky?"

He sounded tired. Maybe he really hadn't slept the night before. After all she wouldn't have known, would she? She'd been asleep.

"Friends help each other out. Isn't that what you said?"

He paused. "Yes. That's the general idea. What help do you need?"

"I need help working out how I handle the meeting. Those first few moments. I walk into the room and—" She glanced at him. "And what? What do I do?"

"What would you normally do?"

"I'd hug everyone. Generally I'm not much of a hugger, but if you don't hug family they just hug you anyway so you might as well go along with it and get it done." She narrowed her eyes as she looked at him. "Are you laughing?"

"No. Definitely not laughing."

"Are you sure? Because your eyes have gone crinkly at the corners."

"It's the sun."

"Oh."

"So what exactly are you asking me?"

"Do I hug Hayley? I've never met her before. Seems a bit much. Will she think it's a bit much or will she expect it?"

"I don't know. Why don't you take the lead from her."

"Wait to see if she grabs me, you mean? Good plan. Okay, so that's Hayley sorted out. The others are obvious, so that just leaves Declan. Am I supposed to hug Declan? I've been avoiding him for so long I have no idea what a normal greeting would be."

He kept his eyes on the road. "Did you used to hug him?"

"Never. He was a colleague. If I'd hugged him we both would have been hauled up in front of management. And when we were outside work he was just a friend so hugging would have been weird. Trust me, he would have found it weird too. But now? We're related. It's different. It's going to be awkward."

"Does it have to be awkward? It's not as if anyone knows you have feelings for him." He took the road that ran adjacent to the coast.

"*You* know."

"I don't count. There are plenty of things I know about you that other people don't."

"That's true."

In the distance she could see the jagged outline of a castle. They were almost home. She felt slightly sick.

"Will you come in with me?" She blurted the words out. "I mean, you're Jamie's closest friend. It would be entirely normal for you to want to say hi right away and roast him about the fact he didn't ask you to be best man and all those male bonding type of insults."

He glanced at her briefly. "You want me to come in with you?"

"Yes. That's pathetic, isn't it?" She slumped slightly in her seat. "I'm pathetic. Since when have I needed to ask a man to hold my hand through something difficult? I hate myself."

"But you're not asking me because I'm a man, are you? You're asking me because I'm a friend." His attention was back on the road, so she could no longer see his expression.

"Yeah, you're right. A friend." And when you thought of it like that it sounded different. Better. "And it would mean I'd owe you. So you can call in the favour any time. If your printer breaks, or you click on a link you shouldn't have clicked on and download a virus—whatever. I'm your woman."

A faint smile touched his mouth. "You don't owe me, Becks. A friendship isn't transactional."

"Maybe not, but I won't forget." She studied him, wondering if she was asking too much. "So will you do it?"

He turned into the lane that led to the house.

"Will I come in with you and hold your hand?"

"Yes. Well, not literally. Metaphorically. Obviously I don't expect us to walk in there clinging to each other. I just—it would be nice if you were by my side, that's all. It would take some of the heat off me."

Becky held her breath as she waited for his answer.

He followed the curve of the driveaway and parked alongside Jamie's car.

He sat for a moment and turned off the engine. "You want me by your side. As a friend."

"Yes, of course as a friend."

But now she was thinking of the way he'd looked when he'd walked out of the shower. The width of his shoulders. The swell of hard muscle. The intense blue of his eyes.

Her mouth went dry.

She sneaked a look at him and saw him nod.

"Of course I'll come in with you. No problem."

She should have felt instant relief and she did, but that relief was threaded with something else. Something she didn't recognize or understand.

Something that made her wonder if, maybe, his presence wasn't going to make things easier after all.

14

Jenny

Jenny pulled a tray of mince pies from the oven and put them on the rack to cool. She and her mother, with help from Rosie, had been cooking since breakfast for the party, while Jamie and Declan had balanced on ladders stringing lights around the trees in the back garden that Roy the roofer hadn't had time to do.

It was a cosy family moment, or would have been if it hadn't been for Hayley, who was fiddling self-consciously with a half-drunk cup of coffee as she watched Jenny and Rosie roll out pastry and assemble mince pies. When Jenny had asked earlier if she'd like to help, Hayley had shaken her head. *I'm not much of a cook. I'll probably ruin them and poison everyone.*

Jenny had carried on chatting, keeping the conversation neutral, but now she made a decision. No matter that she occasionally wished secretly that everything could just stay the same for five minutes and not change, that was never going to happen. And she was honest enough with herself to know that if that did happen, she'd be worried because she wanted her children to have love in their lives, even if it changed the shape of their family.

She'd always considered herself to be the glue that held them all together. She was the conductor of the family orchestra, drawing all the individuals together, making them aware of each other. When the children were young, she'd refereed their fights, taught them to listen and pay attention to each other, and help each other when they could. That had continued to a lesser extent even after they'd left home. She knew they were busy and sometimes the effort of keeping connections going slipped to the bottom of the priority list, so she sent them small reminders.

Have you remembered Granny's birthday?

Don't forget to wish Rosie luck for the performance tonight.

She'd once sent Rosie across London to check on Jamie, who had been ill with flu and wasn't answering his phone. Rosie had ended up looking after him for three days and she'd never let her brother forget it.

And now it was time for her to draw Hayley in.

It was up to her to accommodate this new version of her family.

Yes, she was upset that Hayley and Jamie had married in secret, but that was history. Even she could see this was one of those moments when you had to step over your own feelings and move on. And she had to admit she'd never seen Jamie so relaxed and happy. Watching him smiling at Hayley and exchanging anecdotes had gone a long way to healing the hurt in her chest.

For better or worse, Hayley was now part of the family, and Jenny could see she was anxious about it. She kept glancing out of the window at Jamie, as if wondering when he was going to rescue her.

Jenny thought back to the Christmas movie she'd watched (admittedly on fast-forward, because she'd been very short on time). It had included a scene just like this one, where three generations of the same family were baking together in the

179

kitchen, so she'd been hoping this would tick one of the boxes on Hayley's "Dream Christmas" bucket list. But that wouldn't happen if Hayley was a spectator. Being on the fringes of something was awkward. It gave you time to focus on all the things you were anxious about. It was important that she felt included.

"Hayley?" She decided to be more proactive. "It would be a great help if you could make cinnamon spice biscuits? They're a family favourite." She saw a flicker of panic in Hayley's eyes.

"I have no idea how. I've never baked anything."

"Never?" Rosie looked intrigued. "What do you do when you're stressed?"

"I do a workout. I run." Hayley's cheeks were pink. "I use exercise, basically."

"Well, that's a lot healthier, but nothing beats the comfort of baking," Rosie said.

Hayley shook her head. "I'd ruin them."

"You wouldn't." Jenny intervened. "And it wouldn't matter if you did. We've all had disasters in the kitchen. Like the time Rosie forgot to put sugar in my birthday cake. Remember that?"

Rosie sniffed. "I was distracted, that's all. And it wasn't as bad as that year you used a new method to cook the turkey and it was raw inside. I was glad to be vegetarian."

Jenny's mother glanced up from the sandwiches she was making. "I remember that year. Chaos. There was much screaming coming from the kitchen. We didn't eat lunch until five o'clock."

"That was awful, I admit it. And I learned a lesson there. If something works, don't change it." Jenny put a clean bowl on the table and removed flour and sugar from the shelves. "You'll need mixed spice, ground ginger and cinnamon, Hayley. You'll find them in the tiny jars in the cupboard near the fridge."

Hayley gave up arguing and hunted for the jars. "You have hundreds of jars."

"I like to cook. They're in alphabetical order."

"In my flat they're just crammed into a cupboard in total disarray and half of them have gone out of date," Rosie said. "I aspire to have a kitchen like my mother's. Maybe one day, when I finally concede to being a grown-up. Mince pies are done. I'm moving on to mini quiches."

Hayley brought the spice jars back to the table.

"Great. Now we need to find the recipe." Jenny rooted around in the drawer and found the recipe she'd scribbled out years before. She didn't need to look at it, but she wanted Hayley to have a sense of ownership. "This recipe is easy to follow. I've been making these for years. The children love them and they make great gifts."

"Gifts?"

"Yes. Sometimes we put them in jars with a pretty label and give them to friends." She put the digital scales next to Hayley. "First weigh your dry ingredients. That's right." She hovered over Hayley's shoulder, offering tips and encouragement, as she had when her own children were young.

"This is scary," Hayley said as she measured spices and added them to the bowl. "You only get once chance to get it right. In my job, if I make a mistake, I can just delete it and start again."

"You do the same with baking," Rosie said. "I once threw away an entire batch of cupcakes because I reached a really good part of my book, lost track of time and burned the lot. It happens."

Hayley laughed and then turned back to the bowl in front of her.

She studied the menu carefully, running her finger along the writing and then she measured and sifted and mixed, asking Jenny questions as she did.

She's never done this, Jenny thought. *She's never cooked with family.*

And suddenly she realised how hard this must be for her. How alien.

A lump of emotion formed in her chest and she cleared her throat.

"That's it. Now bring it all together in a ball and we're going to put it in the fridge to chill."

"The fridge?"

"It makes it easier to work with. While it's chilling, we can choose our shapes." She grabbed the tin where she kept the cookie cutters.

"Stars and snowmen," Rosie said, returning her attention to the quiches she'd been making. She sliced through a piece of smoked salmon. "No sense in breaking with tradition."

Hayley picked them out. "How about a Christmas tree?"

"Good idea."

Less than an hour later three trays of cookies were in the oven and Hayley was flushed with satisfaction.

"How long do we cook them for? Having made it this far, I don't want to burn them."

"We'll set a timer so we don't forget about them and check them after ten minutes. This is where we reward ourselves with a drink. Coffee? Or I could make a festive hot chocolate with a touch of cream and cinnamon?"

"Go for it," Rosie said. "Hayley needs a crash course in comfort food. And we can run off the calories on the beach later."

Jenny whipped up four hot chocolates and put them on the table.

In an attempt to create a festive atmosphere, she'd lit a couple of orange-and-clove-scented candles and turned on the fairy lights that she'd persuaded Martin to string around the room the day before. She'd stopped short of having a Christmas tree in the kitchen, but she'd filled a large earthenware jug with holly, eucalyptus and pine and placed it at the end of the kitchen island.

Hayley seemed enchanted. She kept glancing around her as if she couldn't quite believe what she was seeing.

"It's gorgeous in here." She slid her hands around the mug, her gaze lingering on the fairy lights and the pinecones. "So Christmassy. It's like a movie set. And the room smells delicious."

"That's your cookies baking. They always smell divine." Jenny felt a hum of satisfaction. So far, so good. And she had to admit it *did* look pretty. She wouldn't normally have bothered turning on fairy lights or lighting candles in the morning but maybe she'd rethink that in future. Hayley was right. It *was* Christmassy.

"It's important to make the indoors as comfortable and welcoming as possible in the winter," she said. "Of course we try and be outdoors as much as we can, but there's too much to do right now, which is why we're all in the kitchen."

"I feel terrible that Jamie and I have made things complicated for you with this party." Hayley took a sip of hot chocolate. "Everyone has extra work to do because of us."

Jenny felt a stab of guilt. Had her own feelings showed? "We couldn't be more excited," she said firmly.

"That's true. We're very excited. I love a party. Any excuse to dress up," Rosie said. "And don't feel terrible—that's what families are for!"

Hayley glanced up briefly. "Is it?"

Jenny wondered if Rosie's comment had been tactless in the circumstances.

Flustered, she took the plate of sandwiches her mother had made, covered them and slid them into the fridge. "Even if you hadn't got married, we still would have been celebrating something tonight."

"Mum's right," Rosie said. "You'll soon get used to the fact that we celebrate at every possible opportunity. It's Dad's fault. He used to say to us 'you have to celebrate each moment because you never know what tomorrow will bring.' And then he'd get called out to see a patient and wouldn't be there for the moment we were celebrating. But we carried on without him anyway."

That was the story of her life, Jenny thought, glancing through the window to the garden. She'd become used to carrying on without him, but she'd thought that once he retired that would change.

Apparently not.

She frowned through the window. She'd assumed he was outside with Jamie, but there was no sign of him.

Where was he?

Hayley was still in conversation with Rosie. "Jamie says the same thing. He says all we can be sure of is this moment, so we should make the most of it."

"He gets it from his father and also from his grandfather," Phyllis said. "Brian was the same. It comes from being a doctor, I think. Being faced with all the different ways in which life can throw you a curve through no fault of your own. It teaches you to live in the moment."

Jenny turned away from the window. "I suppose it's not a bad way to live, although I did point out to the children that one does have to plan for the future too, just in case this particular moment doesn't turn out to be your last."

Hayley laughed. "It certainly does seem like justification for extravagance. Jamie is better at it than I am. He's more relaxed. More impulsive, I suppose. I'm trying to be a bit more like him. Not to be so careful all the time." She sounded a little wistful, as if maybe it was a fault in her to be more cautious about life.

"Jamie always had a safety net," Jenny said quietly. "Which would have made it easier to take risks." She couldn't imagine what it must be like to grow up without a web of family ready to catch you when you fell.

Hayley looked at her and something passed between them. An understanding.

Jenny glanced at her mother and felt a rush of gratitude.

Here they were, three generations together, preparing for a family celebration.

She remembered being ten years old, preparing for Christmas with her mother, her aunt and her grandmother.

Did she take it for granted? Yes, she did sometimes. Despite her own experiences as a nurse, she took her family for granted. And it was a privilege to be able to do that. To not have to think about it or doubt it. They were just *there*.

The timer beeped and Jenny gestured to Hayley. "Come and check your handiwork, Hayley. Let's see if they're cooked."

She opened the oven and peered inside. She'd made them so many times she knew they'd be cooked but she said nothing as Hayley crouched down and studied them.

"How can you tell?"

"They're a lovely pale brown. Perfect. We don't want to overcook them or they'll be hard." She handed Hayley oven gloves. "Pull the trays out and we'll put them to cool. Then we can leave them plain or ice them."

While Hayley was tending to her baking, Jenny slid the quiches into the oven and set the timer again.

She washed her hands. "What are Declan's family doing this Christmas, Rosie? Do they mind him not being there?"

"No. Christmas isn't that big a deal to him—I mean to them. So he was okay about coming here with me. More than okay, obviously." She tripped over her words. "He was excited. *Is* excited. It's going to be great. Especially as Dad won't be running off to heal the sick."

Jenny saw her mother glance at Rosie with a faint frown.

There was no doubt that Rosie wasn't quite herself. It wasn't what she was saying as much as the way she was saying it. With slightly too much energy, as if she was making a supreme effort to be jolly and convince everyone she was fine.

She hoped her mother wasn't about to ask a tactless question, but fortunately Phyllis turned her attention back to the mince pies.

But now Jenny was worrying about Rosie again. She'd

thought last night that something wasn't quite right, and although Martin had dismissed her concerns she still felt that. She made a mental note to find a way of getting Rosie on her own later.

In the meantime she kept her own response warm and neutral. "Well, we're very happy you were all able to come home."

Rosie glanced at the door. "Talking of Dad, where is he? Normally he's trying to persuade us all to play Scrabble or go for a family walk. I haven't seen him since breakfast, and that was only briefly. And he wasn't around when Jamie and I took Percy out this morning."

Jenny wiped the kitchen table. "I think he's outside helping Jamie and Declan."

She hoped being vague might work, but Rosie squinted through the windows.

"I don't see him. Jamie is out there with Declan stringing up lights, but no sign of Dad."

Jenny met her mother's gaze briefly and knew she had to do something about it before it became a focus.

"I'm sure he's somewhere around. I'm just going to remind Jamie to cut some more holly for me." She removed her apron. Where was Martin? And was he expecting her to cover for him? Was the whole of Christmas going to be this way? "Rosie, perhaps you and Hayley could carry the glasses through to the living room ready for tonight."

She headed for the back door, grabbed her coat, pushed her feet into her boots and joined her son outside.

Jamie was laughing at something Declan had said and Jenny was pleased to see the easy comradeship between them.

It was freezing and she slid her hands into her pockets.

"That's looking good."

"I cut the holly you wanted." Jamie was balanced on top of the ladder, trying to string the last length of lights around the tree. "It's by the back door in a bucket of water. It jabbed me a million times when I was trying to cut it, and Declan is actually bleeding. Worse than owning a cat."

"I should have given you gloves. But thank you."

"And while I'm up this apple tree, I cut some mistletoe. For the party. In case anyone wants an excuse to kiss." He gestured to a bunch of it on the ground. "And on that topic, can you ask Granny to stop asking people if they're pregnant?"

"You say that as if I have some control over her, which you know I don't. Anyway, it's a bit late. She has already asked Hayley and Rosie. There's only Becky left, and as she's single I'm hoping she'll escape. Have you seen your dad?" She kept her smile bright and the question casual. She didn't want the children knowing something was wrong.

"Not since breakfast." Jamie reached and secured the final loop of lights then descended the ladder with an alarming lack of care. "I assumed you had him on kitchen duty."

"No. He's probably helping Grandad with his book. Don't fall, will you?"

"Obviously falling isn't my intention." Jamie helped Declan move the ladder. "Is this the book that doesn't exist?"

"It exists in your grandfather's head." But it wasn't her father's book, or lack of it, that was worrying her right now. She needed to find Martin. "I need to get back inside. Thanks, both of you."

"Is Hayley okay? Granny isn't interrogating her, is she? I don't want her to be overwhelmed and she is far too polite to tell her to mind her own business."

"She's been helping us cook," Jenny said. "She has been a great help."

"Good. She'll like that. We just need to check these lights work and then I'll come back in and help her." Jamie stood back to survey their handiwork. "Any news from Becky and Will?"

"Not since that message first thing saying that they expected to be here early afternoon."

And she was looking forward to Becky's arrival. Becky would at least be able to work out what was wrong with her sister and hopefully fix it. That would be one less thing for Jenny to worry about.

"Where is Dad?" Jamie glanced at the house. "I really want to talk to him about work before they arrive and it gets busy. I need his advice."

"About what?"

"Job. I have to do some work with the primary care team next year." He shrugged. "Don't worry. I'll talk to Dad when I'm finished here."

Only if Martin deigned to make an appearance.

Jamie slapped Declan on the shoulder. "We've earned ourselves a drink. What's for lunch, Mum?"

"There's soup on the stove, a fresh loaf and stack of sandwiches in the fridge, courtesy of your grandmother, who has been buttering bread all morning. Help yourselves." She refrained from pointing out it wasn't that long since breakfast. It was always the same at Christmas and if she was honest, she enjoyed it. Not only because it felt delightfully normal and like the old days when she could never keep her fridge full, but also because it made her feel needed.

She went back indoors and hunted for her father. She found him in Martin's study, listening to music through headphones. There was no sign of Martin.

He pulled off the headphones when he saw her. "Palestrina motets. Always puts me in a festive mood. Remember that concert we went to in Durham Cathedral?"

She felt a rush of love for him. "I do. It was wonderful, although I seem to remember having freezing hands. Have you seen Martin? I thought you might be working on the book."

"No, but don't tell your mother that or I'll never hear the last of it." He shook his head. "Martin said he had to do some jobs this morning, but suggested we take an afternoon walk and discuss some ideas then."

"Right."

"Are you still worrying about him?" He reached out and gave her arm an awkward pat, and she felt a ridiculous urge to put her head on his shoulder and let him solve her problems as she had when she was little. She was sixty and today she wanted to be a child again, letting older and wiser heads fix the things that needed fixing.

"I'm too busy with Christmas and tonight's party to worry about Martin," she lied. "I'm sure he's fine."

Her father gave her a keen look. "It's a life change. Give him time. He'll adjust."

"Of course he will. Absolutely." *But how much time?* She had things of her own to adjust to. Like the fact that her son had married without telling them, and there was a new family member standing in her kitchen who was clearly struggling. It was Jenny's responsibility to make her feel welcome and comfortable within the family. Also, there was the niggling feeling that something wasn't right with Rosie. She needed Martin's support, not his absence. "I love you, Dad." It suddenly seemed important to her that she say the words.

She saw her father's gaze soften.

"I love you too. And I'm going to talk to Martin, so don't you worry."

"That would be good. But do it discreetly. I'm trying to hide it from the kids. I don't want them to worry. I'll let you get back to your Palestrina." She kissed him on the cheek, eased the headphones back onto his ears and headed upstairs.

It was all very well her father promising that he'd talk to Martin, but first someone had to find him. And then he had to be prepared to listen.

Frustration shifted to concern.

She checked their bedroom, but it was empty. She glanced through the window to the beach but saw no one.

Her anxiety deepened. He wouldn't have left the house without telling her, would he? Where could he possibly be?

She pulled out her phone. She felt faintly ridiculous calling him when they were all at home together, but it was worth a try. A moment later heard the sound of his phone ringing. She followed the sound to Becky's room, pushed open the door and there was Martin. He was fully clothed and lying on top of the bed with his eyes closed.

"Martin?"

He opened his eyes. "Why are you phoning me when I'm in the house? Is this a new thing?"

"No, it's what I do when I can't find you. What are you doing in here?"

"It seemed like somewhere no one would look." He sat up and ran his hand over his face. "Seems I was wrong. What's up?"

What's up? Seriously?

"It's Christmas, and everyone is downstairs working hard. Why are you hiding?"

"I'm not hiding. I was listening to a podcast." He pressed something on his phone to pause it. "I'm taking some personal time. That's allowed at Christmas when you have a house full. Everyone needs space occasionally."

She didn't point out that their house had been full for less than twenty-four hours and Christmas hadn't even started yet so he couldn't possibly be in need of quiet time.

She thought about her mother, Rosie and Hayley working side by side in the kitchen, Jamie and Declan hanging lights in the garden. The only person not contributing was her father, who was given a free pass because of his age and health.

Everyone was busy except Martin, who was hiding.

Jamie and Rosie had noticed his absence. Her mother had

given her a look. Her father knew things weren't right. This wasn't the atmosphere she wanted over Christmas.

She wanted everything to be normal. She wanted to enjoy a family Christmas. She wanted to make the most of it because who knew when they'd all be together again? It was supposed to be a special time. It wasn't supposed to be riddled with anxiety.

"People are wondering where you are. I couldn't find you. You scared me!" She sat down hard on the edge of the bed, giving herself a moment to digest the fact that he was fine. "I've been looking everywhere for you."

"Well, not everywhere, because here I am."

She straightened the throw on the end of Becky's bed. "Obviously I wouldn't have thought to look in Becky's room."

"Which is why I chose it." He removed his earbuds. "What's the matter?"

Thinking about everyone downstairs working and his kids wanting to spend time with him, she was about to erupt with frustration when she glanced at his phone and saw the title of the podcast he'd been listening to.

How to Survive Life After Retirement.

Her frustration vanished and she felt a little flicker of optimism. He was trying. That had to be good.

"Is it an interesting podcast?"

"No, it's useless. Apparently I should now be relishing having more time to spend on the garden. I should be deadheading roses and mowing the lawn."

She was relieved to see a glimmer of the old Martin. "You hate gardening."

"Exactly."

"Anyway, it's winter and the garden is under a foot of snow, so I don't think this is the time to explore that interest."

"It's not an interest. Never has been." He swung his legs off the bed. "What do you need me to do?"

"I need you to be your old self."

"My old self was a busy doctor, so I can't exactly be that, can I?"

"That was your job, Martin, not who you were." But plenty of people were defined by their jobs, she knew that. She'd done some research on it during the night when she'd been unable to sleep. *How people react to retirement.* "Or at least, pretend to be your old self. Just so people don't ask questions."

He fiddled with his phone. "I never really had to plan my day, did you know that? From the moment I walked through the door, I knew what was expected of me, and any variation on that came from responding to other people's requests."

"If you're saying that you need help structuring your day then I can help with that. Jamie is waiting to talk to you about his job, although I don't know the details. After you've talked to Jamie, you could give Rosie a hug because she has been talking about you all morning and seems in need of something, although I'm not sure what. And then you can talk to Dad, who really would appreciate a conversation." She paused, watching his expression. "It's Christmas, Martin. I don't want the kids to know anything is wrong. They'll worry. They work hard and they get so little time off. They deserve to relax."

She hated herself for using guilt as a weapon but right now she'd do whatever it took to enlist his help.

He sighed and stood up. "All right, let's do this. The doctor is in the house."

"No, Martin, not the doctor. The father. The son-in-law." She hesitated. "And the husband."

She said it softly and he looked at her for a long moment.

"Yes." He gave her a thoughtful look. "Yes."

She thought he was about to say something else but instead he headed downstairs to join everyone.

It was a start.

15

Rosie

If there was one thing guaranteed to make you aware of the cracks in your own relationship it was being in the same room as a happy couple.

Rosie rescued a decoration that Percy had managed to knock onto the floor and hung it on a higher branch of the tree. The living room was ready for the small invasion of people later, the food was all prepared and the house looked like a Christmas grotto. This was normally her favourite part of the season, with Christmas still ahead and all the family gathering together.

Today she felt tired. Keeping up her happy act was draining. Her grandmother had already asked her twice if she was sure she was okay (*being pregnant can make you emotional, you know*), and it had taken all her willpower not to sob on her shoulder.

She would have talked to her dad if she could have found a moment alone with him, but he hadn't been around earlier and now he was in the study with her grandfather, supposedly working on the famous book that no one in the family believed would ever really be finished.

Her mother was in the kitchen again, putting the finishing touches to an elaborate cake.

Jamie and Hayley were sprawled together on the sofa, scrolling through photos on his phone, occasionally laughing at something. Her head was on his shoulder and her fingers were entwined with his.

Rosie felt a shaft of envy, remembering when she would have done exactly that with Declan.

She rearranged the presents under the tree and sneaked a glance at him. He was reading, settled in an armchair close to the fire.

Had he chosen that chair on purpose so that Rosie couldn't join him?

And would she have wanted to?

Why was she such an overthinker? It was *exhausting*. All she really wanted for Christmas was a personality transplant.

"Rosie?"

She glanced up to see her grandmother standing in the doorway clutching her dress.

"Granny."

"You said you'd help me fix this, dear, but if you're busy—"

"I'm not busy." She was relieved to have something else to think about. "Show me the problem."

"I was planning to wear it for the party tonight but there's a little tear in the fabric. I'm worried that if I wear it, it might get worse."

Rosie took the dress and examined it. "I can fix that easily. I'll put a little tuck in it, so the repair will vanish into the folds."

"The fabric isn't easy to work with."

"It's fine. Easier than all the tulle I used for the Sugar Plum Fairy. The repair won't show, I promise." She turned it inside out and smoothed the fabric, working out how best to do it.

"I love this dress," her grandmother said. "It's the best thing I've ever owned."

Jamie glanced up and grinned. "Nothing to do with the fact that your granddaughter made it?"

Phyllis lifted her chin. "Actually, no. This dress makes me feel special. When I'm wearing it I feel like my best self. I know it suits me, and that's because it is well designed and well made. Left to my own devices I would have chosen something safe. Probably black, navy or caramel because at my age I don't have the confidence to wear a colour, but Rosie insisted on gold. I've never worn gold in my life before." She reached out and touched the dress almost reverentially. "Rosie has such a talent. She's very gifted, but all you science and mathematically minded people don't notice. Declan? Do you realise how extraordinary your wife is?"

There was a silence, and Rosie saw Declan lift his gaze from the book and look at her.

"Yes," he said softly. "Yes, I do."

Rosie's cheeks caught fire. She couldn't believe her grandmother had put him in that position. What was he supposed to say? *My wife can barely turn on her own laptop*, or *it would be nice if she could hold an intelligent conversation with my colleagues*?

"You're embarrassing me, Granny." She grabbed her mother's sewing box from its hiding place on the lower shelf of the bookcase and settled down on the empty sofa. Percy immediately sprang onto the sofa next to her, settling himself against her leg. "Don't come too close, darling. I'm using needles. I don't want to turn you into a pincushion."

"You shouldn't be embarrassed. You should be proud. When she was young, she had no confidence." She was still addressing Declan, who had closed his book and was listening politely. "Thought she wasn't as clever as her sister and brother."

What was her grandmother trying to do?

"That's because I wasn't. It's time for peace on earth, Granny. Or at least, peace in this living room." Rosie was tempted to grab one of the Christmas stockings hanging near the fire and tie it over her grandmother's mouth.

"I used to tell her, there is more than one way of being smart," her grandmother said. "Some people are quick with numbers, some people are good with words, and others are creative. That's Rosie."

"Okay, Granny. Enough." She threaded the needle and settled the dress on her lap.

"She was the prettiest dancer. If she hadn't grown those extra few inches, I swear she'd be the talk of the ballet world by now. Have you seen her dance, Declan?"

Only after several glasses of wine, Rosie thought. She caught Declan's eye and saw a glimmer of laughter there. He knew how uncomfortable she was.

"She's a great dancer," he said, the look in his eyes suggesting he was remembering the same evening she was, when she'd danced around their living room, removing her clothes layer by layer.

That memory connected them, and for a moment their tensions evaporated and the invisible barrier between them melted away.

He held her gaze and if there hadn't been other people in the room she would have gone to him then, curled up on his lap and pressed her mouth to his. It would have been okay. Everything would have been okay. She felt as if a few well-placed stitches would pull together whatever rift had appeared. All they needed was some time together.

"You're not concentrating," her grandmother said. "You're going to stab yourself with that needle, and I don't want blood on my dress."

She'd been looking at Declan, thinking of how it felt when he kissed her. No one kissed the way Declan did. No one had made her feel the way he did.

Her stomach flipped and she saw his eyes narrow as he registered the look in her eyes.

She cleared her throat.

"That's what happens when you embarrass me, Granny." She focused on the dress on her lap, mending it carefully. Given that her grandmother was her biggest supporter, she didn't want to ruin her dress. Also there was the matter of personal pride.

Her stitches were tiny, her work accurate, but she could feel Declan's gaze on her and the whole thing took far longer than it should have done.

"There." She handed it back to her grandmother and closed her mother's sewing box. "Good as new."

"Thank you. I can't wait for tonight when I can wear it."

Rosie smiled. "It will be fun."

Percy sprang from the sofa, barking, and Rosie winced as his tail smacked her in the face.

"Great. Thanks, Percy. Now I'll have a black eye for the party."

"He heard a car." Jamie stood up and walked to the window. "It's Will and Becky. They're here! Now Christmas can really begin. I can't wait to introduce you to Becky, Hayley. She's great. I'm looking forward to catching up with her properly."

"Me too. We've hardly seen her this year." Declan put his book down and stood up. "I'll see if I can help with luggage."

He'd barely spoken this morning but now her sister was here he was on his feet and heading to the door, showing almost as much enthusiasm as Percy.

And just like that, the fragile thread that had briefly connected them snapped again.

Jamie followed him out of the room and Rosie stood up and gave herself a stern talking-to.

She was imagining things. Just because they'd hit a rough patch didn't mean Declan was regretting marrying her. And it certainly didn't mean he would have preferred to be with Becky.

She was about to follow her brother and Declan out of the room when she noticed Hayley perched on the edge of the sofa as if she didn't know whether to follow everyone or stay out of the way.

Rosie glanced at the door but Jamie had walked off with Declan.

Men! Why were they so clueless? It didn't seem to have occurred to Jamie that Hayley might feel awkward and self-conscious.

"This must be a bit overwhelming for you," she said. "You're meeting someone new every few minutes. Exhausting."

Hayley gave an awkward smile. "I want to do the right thing, but I don't know what that is. Like now, for instance. Do I stay out of the way, or do I help unload the car? I don't want to get in the way and I don't want to be rude. Advice welcome."

Advice? It was a family Christmas. Her advice would be to enjoy. But then she put herself in Hayley's position and imagined spending Christmas with a close-knit family of whom she knew precisely one person. And that person seemed oblivious to the stress Hayley was feeling. Why hadn't Hayley said something to him?

And then she thought of all the things she hadn't said to Declan. It wasn't always as easy as it sounded.

"You're not supposed to be doing anything at all," she said firmly. "It's Christmas. Your Christmas. Sure, we all help out, but there is no pressure on anyone. Do what feels right."

But there was pressure on Hayley, she could see that now. She didn't know how she was supposed to behave. And Jamie had just abandoned her without any thought about how awkward Hayley might find it. Rosie made a mental note to keep an eye on Hayley, and also to have a few sharp words with her brother. Maybe she wasn't finding it easy to talk to Declan, but she was more than able to reprimand her brother. It was what sisters were for.

"Let's go together—" Rosie held out her hand. "I'll introduce you to my twin. She's not at all scary and also she would never ask if you were pregnant. So there's that."

Hayley laughed and stood up.

On impulse, Rosie took her hand and gave it a squeeze.

"I'm so pleased you've joined our family. I'm happy for you and Jamie."

At least someone's relationship was working out, she thought as she and Hayley headed outside.

Rosie saw Becky laughing with Will as they unloaded luggage and parcels from the car.

Jamie was saying something to both of them and then Becky glanced up and saw Rosie.

Without hesitating, Rosie sprinted across to wrap her in a big hug.

"I missed you."

"Yeah—missed you too—" Becky hugged her back, but Rosie sensed a certain reserve that wasn't normally there.

Maybe it was because she was in a sensitive mood. Or maybe it was because they were all gathered outside in the freezing cold.

"You had an interesting journey." She let go of her sister and gave Will a hug. "Good to see you."

"You too. You and Declan did better than we did with all that snow."

"We were ahead of you. We missed the accident."

Rosie introduced her to Hayley, and while they were talking she tugged her brother to one side.

"You know something, Jamie? If you want to be in her corner then you need to be there in her corner—it's easy to say and not so easy to do! She needs to feel as if you've got her back."

He hauled another bag out of the car. "What are you talking about?"

"Hayley." She spoke in a whisper. "You keep abandoning her."

"Abandoning?"

"Yes! Like now. You shot out to see Becky and Will without giving a second thought as to whether meeting yet another person might be stressful for her. She didn't know whether she was supposed to follow you or hang back."

He looked stunned. "I was going to welcome them. I intended to introduce them to Hayley, obviously."

"But this is awkward for her. Difficult. All these new people. Even you have to see that, surely."

He raised an eyebrow. "*Even* me? What's that supposed to mean?"

"Well, you're sometimes a bit clueless. But fortunately, you have me." She patted her brother's arm. "You're welcome."

"I—"

Rosie scooped up a piece of luggage and headed back to the house without giving Jamie time to think of a suitable brotherly retort. Her own relationship might be under pressure, but at least she could help Hayley and Jamie.

Soon everyone was back inside, along with Becky's luggage.

Her father and grandfather had emerged from the study, and everyone seemed to be talking at once.

Rosie felt a moment of satisfaction as she saw Jamie put his arm round Hayley and introduce her to Becky.

"Hey there." Becky was about to shake hands but Hayley stepped forward and hugged her.

Rosie grinned. Obviously, their family had already had an impact on Hayley.

"Good to meet you." Becky smiled awkwardly. "And this is Will, er—family friend."

Their mother hugged Will. "It's good to see you. Thank you for driving Becky."

"Hey, I drove us half the way." Becky bent to make a fuss of Percy. "I'm in love with Will's car. It's the same one that Finn bought, Declan. Remember?"

Declan smiled. "Yes. As I recall, he was too afraid to drive it so it spent most of its life in the garage."

"And someone bumped into it when they were parking." Becky winced at the memory. "Remember when he came into work with red eyes and you thought someone in the family must have died?"

"Yes." Declan was laughing too. "We couldn't stand his misery, so we all clubbed together to get the paintwork fixed."

"And he chose a bright yellow, so that everyone would see the car."

"It looked like a psychedelic banana."

They were both laughing so hard they could hardly stand up.

Watching them, Rosie was again reminded of how much history they shared. Far more than she and Declan shared.

Jamie clearly noticed too. "I forget that you and Declan know each other really well, Becks."

"Yeah." Becky made a fuss of Percy. "We worked together for five years. I was the one who introduced him to Rosie, re-member? I was his work wife."

Work wife.

Rosie looked at her sister, her attention caught by her tone and facial expression. And suddenly she knew. It all fell into place.

It wasn't only Declan she needed to worry about. It was Becky.

Becky had feelings for Declan. Strong feelings.

The ground shifted beneath her feet and she reached out to grab the back of the nearest chair for support.

Her sister hadn't stayed away from them because she wanted to give them space—she'd stayed away because she found it dif-ficult being around them.

Why hadn't it occurred to her before? This was what Becky did. When she found something difficult, she avoided it. As a child she would hide behind the sofa rather than talk about what was bothering her. She shut everyone out, including Rosie.

The last few months had been the equivalent of Becky hid-ing behind the sofa. Not because she was giving her sister space, but because she was hurt.

Rosie had fallen crazily in love with Declan and she hadn't even paused to wonder if her sister might have feelings for him too. To be fair, she'd been given no reason to suspect it.

But in the end it didn't matter that it hadn't been intentional. It had happened. She'd married the man Becky was in love with.

This was why Becky had changed jobs. Not because she wanted more money or a bigger challenge. But to put distance between herself and Declan. It was the reason she'd refused to share their apartment and had instead chosen to live with a stranger.

"You're in love with him." The words spilled out of her with no filter.

The room fell silent. Her grandmother's teacup rattled as she turned to put it on the table.

Jamie stopped stroking Percy.

Her father frowned.

Her mother cleared her throat. "Rosie, dear—"

Becky was staring at her, her expression pinched and shocked. "What did you say?"

"You're in love with Declan." She knew instinctively that it was true, and her heart ached. What a mess. What a total mess. "You've been in love with him this whole time. It didn't occur to me before now, but it should have done. I should have recognised the signs."

"What signs?" Becky's hands were clenched into fists by her side. "What are you talking about?"

"You've been avoiding me. Us." It might as well have been just the two of them. All her focus was on her sister.

And her sister looked panicked.

"Yeah, because you two were slobbering all over each other."

"And that must have been difficult for you." Rosie swallowed. She felt terrible. She shouldn't have blurted it out, but it was too late to change that so she carried on. "Why didn't you tell me? And why didn't I see it? That night you introduced us—I thought then how comfortable you were with him, how you chatted and laughed and didn't squirm or look at the door or want to be somewhere else."

"Of course I was comfortable with him. We were work colleagues forever." Becky turned to look at Declan, her expression fierce. "Say something."

He'd been frozen to the spot but now he stepped forward. "Rosie—"

She ignored him, her gaze still fixed on her sister. "You talked about him as a colleague, but you never said you had deeper feelings—Becky, *why*?" What had she done? What had she done to her sister? "I didn't see it. And then you were weird at the wedding, and I knew something was wrong but I couldn't work out what—how could I not have known?"

Becky glanced at the door, as if she was judging the distance. "I was not weird at the wedding."

"You rushed out of the room and spent an hour in the toilet."

"I ate shellfish."

"We all ate shellfish."

"You didn't all eat the shellfish I ate. One bad prawn is all it takes. I was unlucky. And you are wrong." Becky's voice was shaking. "You couldn't be more wrong."

"Becky—"

"Stop! We weren't going to do this now but I see we have no choice. We were going to keep it a secret," she stumbled slightly, "because of Jamie and Hayley and this being their special moment, and because of Christmas and everything else that is going on, but given what you're saying, and what you're thinking, which by the way is *totally* wrong, you need to know that—well—" she sucked in a shaky breath "—I'm in love with Will."

Rosie heard their mother gasp.

"*Will?* You mean—our Will?"

Thrown by that totally unexpected announcement, Rosie

dragged her gaze from her sister to Will. He was looking directly at Becky and his expression gave nothing away. How did people do that? she wondered. How did people manage to keep their feelings inside? No matter how hard she tried, she couldn't manage it.

Their mother put her hand to her chest, her eyes shiny.

"Oh Becky! Will!" There was surprise and delight in her voice. "Is this true?"

"Of course it isn't true." Rosie wasn't buying it. She knew her sister. She *knew* her. "Will? Seriously? You expect us to believe you're in love with Will?"

"Yes." Becky stepped closer to Will and slid her hand into his. "And he's in love with me. Why do you think we spent last night at a hotel?"

Jamie cleared his throat. "Er—because it was snowing and there was a ten-car pileup and you always get impatient if you're forced to sit still in traffic for more than three minutes?"

"That was just the excuse we used, but what we really wanted was a romantic night together before having to be apart for Christmas. We had this gorgeous room right up in the eaves of the hotel over snowy fields. We woke to the sound of church bells."

Rosie heard her dad mutter *there seem to be a lot of those ringing around here at the moment* and her grandmother say *surely one of them is going to be pregnant soon*, and then her mother hurried forward and hugged Becky and then Will.

"Audrey was hoping you'd end up in one room. I don't believe this!"

Rosie didn't believe it either. Will? It didn't make sense to her. Will was gorgeous of course, but he and Becky had been friends forever. If something was going to happen, it would have happened long ago.

"The one thing you'll learn about being part of a family," Jamie muttered to Hayley, "is that there is no end to the drama."

Will finally reacted. "You talked to my mother?"

"We were exchanging messages because we were worried about the two of you being snowbound. You told her you had separate rooms, Will. You were obviously being discreet, which was very thoughtful of you. It's selfless of you both to keep your happy news to yourselves, but I'm sure Jamie and Hayley won't mind sharing the attention, will you?"

Jamie shook his head and then stepped forward and gave Will a brotherly hug.

"Took you long enough." He gave Will a slap on the back. "You're a brave man, taking on my sister. But at least she'll be able to solve all your tech issues."

Rosie's head was spinning. This didn't feel right. Why was everyone just accepting this?

"Wait!" She blurted the word out and everyone looked at her. "Will? You haven't said anything at all." She saw Becky glance up at him.

She's nervous, Rosie thought, her suspicions solidifying. *She's afraid he's going to say the wrong thing.*

The two of them shared a long look, loaded with unspoken communication.

And then Will curved his arm around Becky and pulled her close. There was something unmistakably protective about the gesture, and Rosie felt the first flickers of doubt.

She wouldn't put it past Becky to lie if it meant disguising her emotions, but Will? Will wouldn't do that. And there was something in his eyes when he looked at her sister that made her breath catch. Will had feelings for Becky. Strong feelings. You couldn't fake that.

Maybe they *were* together. She really wanted to believe it. Not that it changed the fact that Declan seemed to be regretting marrying her, but at least she wouldn't have her sister's broken heart on her conscience.

"As Becky said, we didn't intend to go public with our news

yet. It didn't feel like the right time." Will's voice was steady, his arm firm around Becky's shoulders. "But maybe it is the right time." He smiled down at her and something in that smile killed the last of Rosie's doubts.

He loved her, she could see it. He really did love her. Warmth flooded through her, followed by relief and also hurt.

Why hadn't her sister told her? True, Becky kept her feelings to herself, but there was no way she wouldn't have shared something this big with Rosie when they'd been living together. Before Declan. Before marriage had changed everything.

For the whole of their lives she'd known what Becky was thinking before anyone else did, and now she was standing here feeling the same surprise and shock as everyone else.

Becky still looked a little unsettled but that wasn't surprising. Rosie knew her sister would hate all this attention. That was probably another reason that she hadn't announced it sooner.

"Oh this is wonderful!" Their mother couldn't contain herself a moment longer. "We couldn't be happier, isn't that right, Martin? This is going to be the perfect Christmas."

Rosie didn't share her mother's optimism.

She'd obviously been wrong about Becky's feelings for Declan, but what about Declan's feelings for Becky?

All it took was a quick glance at Declan to know that her own relationship issues were far from solved.

Her family may have decided to ignore her outburst, but not Declan.

She could feel him looking at her and knew they had a difficult conversation coming. She could see he had questions. And why wouldn't he? She'd just thrown a hand grenade into her marriage, and it hadn't been in great shape before that.

She wondered if it was too early to ask for a strong Christmas drink.

16

Becky

Her sister had guessed! How had she suddenly guessed? And why had she blurted that out about Will? What had she been *thinking*?

If she'd felt awkward before, she felt even more awkward now.

After the chaos of the last hour she should have felt relieved to finally be alone with Will, but she'd never felt more uncomfortable and embarrassed. She wanted to hide under a rock and never come out again.

Instead Becky huddled deeper into her coat and braced herself for the fallout of her actions.

How much worse could it get?

She'd just endured the most excruciating hour of her life, accepting everyone's congratulations, even raising a glass in a toast, and then fielding questions about her "relationship," and generally being overwhelmed by other people's excitement (if this was how it felt to actually announce one's engagement, she was never doing it. The *fuss*!). She'd reached the point where she was so overwhelmed and frantic she was about to scream out a confession and tell everyone to leave her alone when Will had taken her hand firmly and steered her to the door.

We've been trapped in a car and we need fresh air. This is all a little overwhelming for both of us, I'm sure you understand, he'd said with a calm smile as he'd urged her gently out of the room and grabbed both their coats, extracting her from her family before they could bombard her with more questions and before she could open her mouth and confess to her terrible lies.

Outside the house he'd put his arm around her, and when she'd jumped in shock he'd pulled her closer, holding her firmly.

"They're watching us out of the window," he'd said, "so if you want this little charade of yours to last more than a couple of minutes you'd better play along."

Charade.

And now here they were, alone, still playing out that charade.

She groaned and turned her face into his shoulder. What had she *done*?

She couldn't believe he was taking it so well. When he'd suggested a "walk" she'd assumed he was going to tug her behind the nearest tree and demand to know what she was playing at. And she wouldn't have blamed him.

But so far he hadn't done that. Which was very Will.

He'd always been a decent person. And a good friend.

And for a moment she wished she could just stay where she was, safe in the curve of his arm.

"It's snowing again," she mumbled. "Are you sure you want a walk? I mean, we could just find a quiet spot in the garden and you could yell at me there."

"Why would you think I'm going to yell at you?"

"Er—I assumed that was why you suggested fresh air. So you could vent your anger without everyone hearing."

"I suggested fresh air because I could see you were so stressed you were about to say something you'd probably regret."

"We are *way* past that point. Were you even listening to the words that came out of my mouth?"

"I was listening. It was—interesting. I've never seen you so emotional before."

"I'm sorry. So sorry." She kept her face hidden in his coat. "I'm going to dig a hole and lie down in it until Christmas is over."

"That sounds both cold and uncomfortable. I'm sure we can find an alternative option."

"You could just lend me your coat. I like your coat." She could have sworn he was laughing, but why on earth would he be laughing? And when she glanced up at him his expression was serious.

"Let's walk."

"You seriously want to walk? You're not freezing?"

"I was born here, just like you. I'm used to the weather. And a walk is the only way we're going to be able to have the talk we urgently need to have."

"I think I've done more than enough talking for one day."

"No, you haven't."

He kept his arm around her, his broad shoulders protecting her from the worst of the wind as they headed along the narrow path that led from the house to the beach.

Snow lay underfoot, softening every footstep and blurring the edges of the trail.

Eventually the path reached the sand and she stopped.

This was far enough, surely. No one would overhear them here.

And she just wanted to get the conversation over with.

"Will—"

"Can you believe there is snow on the beach? It's magical."

"Yes, but—"

"It's not the first time. It happened a few years ago. People were stranded in holiday cottages, unable to leave. Created havoc."

"I remember."

She wondered how long they were going to carry on talking about nothing at all, when they had something far more important to talk about.

And then finally he turned her to face him.

"Why are you looking so devastated?"

"You really need to ask? This is a total disaster, but I'll fix it, I promise. I'm sorry. I'm sure you're very angry. I don't know what came over me but I wasn't expecting Rosie to put me on the spot like that. I didn't even know she suspected! And then she just blurted it out in front of everyone and frankly I wanted to die right there, but—" She stopped as he pressed his fingers to her lips.

"I know. It's okay, Becks. I'm not angry. A little surprised, maybe. Generally when I'm in a relationship with someone, I know about it."

Mortified, she leaned her head into his chest again and felt him shaking. She glanced up. "Are you *laughing*?"

"Yes." His eyes were brimming with it. "You have to admit it's funny."

He had such blue eyes. And he had a way of looking at you that made you feel—

No! She wasn't going to think about that now.

"It isn't at all funny. How can you laugh?" She covered her face with her hands. "Why did I say all that? Why didn't I just tell Rosie she was wrong?"

"You did tell her she was wrong." His voice was steady. "She didn't believe you."

"Still, I should have found a different way to convince her. I didn't think. It was a hideous situation, and I didn't know what to do. And having said all that I've made everything a thousand times more complicated. How am I going to undo this? Forget burying myself in a hole. I think I just want to die."

"That seems a little extreme." Gently, he eased her hands away from her face. "I'm sure we can find a less dramatic alternative."

"You're still laughing."

"Because it really was funny. I keep seeing your dad's face. And your mother's face. I've never seen your mother so happy."

"I know! She was almost dancing on the spot. I'm amazed she believed me. I'm obviously a better actress than I thought." And because he was laughing and didn't seem at all angry, she started to laugh too. "What a mess. I did warn you I was terrible at relationships."

"I had no idea that included pretend relationships. You're shivering." He unwrapped the scarf from his neck and put it around hers instead. "Time to plan, before you get frostbite."

"I already have a plan. I'm going to march back in there, confess that I was so stunned by Rosie's ridiculous statement that I panicked and blurted it out without thinking. I'll tell them everything I said was rubbish. What has really shocked me is the fact that they believed that we're together. I mean, it was as if they'd been waiting for it. That's insane, isn't it? We've known each other forever. Your mother might be trying to match you up with any woman who comes your way, but mine doesn't do that. Why would she even think us being together was a possibility?"

His gaze was steady on hers. "I don't know. I suppose you were convincing."

"Maybe." It occurred to her that no one in her acquaintance would have treated this situation as calmly as Will. "Anyway, let's go back inside and I'll execute my plan and take what's coming to me."

"Your plan is flawed."

"It is?"

"Yes, because your objective was to stop Rosie thinking you're in love with Declan. If you backtrack now, you won't have solved your problem. You'll have to spend the whole of Christmas trying to convince your sister and it will be stressful and exhausting."

Her mood slumped. "That's true." And deep down she was mortified. She'd stayed away, she'd done everything she could to keep her distance. And she was so good at hiding her feelings she'd been confident that her sister would never find out. "You're right, I really don't want Rosie to suspect she was right all along."

"And presumably it will make things awkward with Declan too."

"I wasn't looking at Declan. I have no idea what his reaction was."

"He looked shocked."

"Yeah, I can imagine." She groaned again. "I am never going to be able to look the man in the face again. What on earth must he be thinking?"

"How did it feel when you saw him?" The question was casual. "Are you still in love with him?"

Declan.

The strange thing was that until Will had mentioned him just now, she hadn't given him a single thought since leaving the house. Which was odd, because for the past few days she'd thought of nothing else. She'd been dreading the moment they came face-to-face in case she gave herself away.

How could she have forgotten him so easily?

"Becks?" Will prompted her gently.

"I don't know." She frowned. "You know I'm not good at expressing my feelings and that's mostly because I'm not very good at understanding what I'm feeling. My emotions are a total mystery to me. Declan has been part of the fabric of my life for so long I'm having trouble figuring out what I feel or where he fits. I can't even work out where my sister fits, and that used to be simple. I'm going to spend the whole of Christmas avoiding half my family. Yay. Fun times ahead."

"If your sister thinks you're with me then it won't be difficult at all. You won't need to avoid anyone."

"What are you suggesting? That we stay 'together'? Well, you did say that if there was anything you could do to help . . ." As jokes went it was pretty lame, but he smiled anyway.

"I seem to remember telling you to let me know." He adjusted her hat, tucking a strand of hair inside so that it didn't blow across her face. "Maybe next time our relationship status is going to change you could warn me, so that I don't blow it."

"You didn't blow it. You were amazing. You could have stood there and said 'I don't know what she's talking about' but instead you rescued me from my own mess. You're a good friend, Will. The best. And now I'm going to be a good friend back by fixing this before it goes any further."

"Why? There's no hurry. I don't have some girlfriend waiting in the wings who is going to be distraught by the discovery that I'm in a relationship with someone else. The easiest thing for everyone is probably to let this ride."

"Let it ride?" She stared at him, sure she must have misunderstood. "You mean keep the pretence going?"

"Why not? Seems like the best solution to me. It would stop you feeling awkward around your sister, and around Declan. You could relax. You might even enjoy Christmas."

She thought about it. He was right. It would make everything so much easier if everyone believed they were together.

"I can't believe you'd do that for me."

"I know. I'm a total hero." He was teasing her, but the way he was looking at her made her feel decidedly strange.

It was probably lack of food. They'd both skipped lunch.

"Don't get arrogant or you'll stop being my hero." She quickly thought it through, examining the idea for holes. "So, you're suggesting that for Christmas we carry on the pretence—and that might work because all the attention is going to be on Jamie and Hayley anyway, and you'll be with your family for most of it—and then what? In the New Year we tell them that we broke up? What reason would we give?"

He shrugged. "You didn't like my Christmas gift? I could get you something you'd truly hate to make it more plausible. Everyone would feel sorry for you and completely understand your reaction."

She laughed. "What would you get me?"

"Er—a lifetime membership to the noisiest night club in London?"

"Ouch. That would definitely be enough to ruin the relationship."

"Or maybe a stack of romance novels."

"That's my sister's addiction."

"I know. You read crime and nonfiction. But I'm trying to give you a bad gift, remember?"

"Right. You're good at this. Bad gifts, I mean."

"I know you."

That was true. In fact, it was a little unsettling just how well he knew her.

His hands were thrust deep into his pockets. He was standing close to her.

"It's Christmas in two days," she said. "You don't have time to buy a gift so that isn't going to work. You can just say you got tired of seeing me in a hoodie, or that you were appalled by my chocolate habit, or I wouldn't go to big noisy parties with you—there are endless reasons."

"I happen to like your hoodie. It makes me smile. And I'm not a lover of big noisy parties, either, and the people closest to me will know that, so neither of those excuses are going to work."

"We'll think of something else." She paused. "Do you have

any bad habits I don't know about that might provide useful material in a breakup?"

"Several."

"And they are—?"

"I'll disclose them at the appropriate moment. As we are supposed to be displaying togetherness, this isn't that moment. Put your arms around me."

"Excuse me?"

"Your sister is about to join us."

"What?" Her heart rate doubled. She couldn't deal with Rosie now. "I can't do this."

"Yes, you can. Put your arms around me." He pulled her against him and she wrapped her arms around his neck.

Her heart was thudding.

"Thank you, Will."

His gaze dropped to her mouth. "For what?"

"For not raising your eyebrows when I announced we were together. For not yelling 'you have to be kidding me' or 'do you really think I want to spend the rest of my life with Becky?' For being such a good sport and not saying the wrong thing. When we get back, we'll announce that you're going to be spending Christmas with your parents as planned because it isn't as if you get back up north to see them that often, and that after the party tonight, we won't be seeing much of each other until we're back in London."

"All right. Although I'll have to think what I'm going to say to my parents."

That was a complication she hadn't considered. "Do your parents have to know?"

"Your mother will be on the phone to my mother before Santa squeezes his extra-large self down the chimney."

"I'll tell her not to say anything. I'll emphasise that we never meant for this to come out this way and we want to do it together, at the proper time. I'll say this is Jamie's moment, or

215

we think everyone should focus on Christmas—I don't know. Something."

They heard Rosie calling their names but they both ignored her.

Becky shivered as a few flakes of snow landed on her hair.

Will brushed them away and then he cupped her face in his hands, studied her for a long moment and then lowered his head and kissed her.

It was so unexpected she almost jumped, but his mouth was warm and skilled, his kiss slow and deliberate, and instead of jumping she kissed him back, her fingers curling into the front of his coat as she tried to balance herself. Kissing didn't normally make her head spin, but today her head was spinning.

Keeping one hand locked behind her head, he used the other to hold her against him and she found herself pressed against the hardness of his thighs, anchored in place by the solid strength of his body. She forgot that it was snowing and she was freezing, she forgot that he was doing this to convince her sister, she forgot everything except the exquisite intimacy of his kiss.

When he finally lifted his head she was glad he was still holding her because she felt dizzy and slightly disconnected. Also disappointed that he'd stopped.

Will. *Will?* Never in a million years would she ever have suspected he would kiss like that. Not that she'd thought about it. She hadn't thought about *him*, not in that way (until the night before when for some reason she'd started thinking about little else).

She knew exactly why he'd kissed her. He was helping her. Because that was what friends did. If she'd known he was that good at kissing she would have suggested they do it sooner. And more often. As a hobby, obviously. Like enjoying a drink, or a movie. Not because it meant anything.

"Will! Becky!" Rosie's voice drifted across to them. "I've been yelling, but you couldn't hear me."

Becky waited for Will to release her but for some reason he didn't seem to be in a hurry.

"Sorry, Rosie. We were—preoccupied." He was talking to her sister but still looking at Becky and she found she couldn't look away.

He really did have the bluest eyes.

She swallowed. "That was—"

"Yes," he said softly, brushing her cheek with the tips of his fingers. "It was."

She kept telling herself that this was Will, just Will, but her heart rate wasn't paying attention. There was a delicious squirmy feeling low in her belly which refused to die down.

"You're surprisingly good at this—" she felt her cheeks go pink "—pretending I mean, obviously."

There was a hint of laughter in his eyes. "Obviously."

"But we have a plan."

He hesitated. "We have a plan."

"You two! I've been yelling and you didn't even hear me." Rosie arrived, breathless. "And I thought it was bad watching Jamie and Hayley slobbering all over each other, and now you two are doing it too?" She gave Becky a keen look and Becky wondered if the words *big fat liar* were tattooed on her forehead.

"You'll have to forgive us—" Will kept his arm around Becky "—we've kept it a secret for so long it's a relief to finally be able to be honest about our feelings."

"Right—I—" Rosie gave a helpless shrug. "I can't believe you didn't tell me! And I'm sorry. I don't know what made me say what I said. It's been crazy lately and Declan and I—well, that doesn't matter. I'm so happy for you, really. And I know you probably hate me for making you the focus of attention, but if it's any consolation I embarrassed myself far more than you." She gave Will a big hug and then did the same to Becky.

Becky felt Rosie's hair brush her cheek and she felt her arms squeezing her tightly. Something swelled in her chest. *She'd missed her sister. She'd missed her so badly.*

They held each other and it took a moment for it to dawn on Becky that Rosie hadn't finished her sentence.

She'd said *Declan and I . . .*

Was something wrong between the two of them? No, surely not. She'd never seen two people more wrapped up in each other than those two. But something must be wrong. Why else would Rosie be feeling so insecure about her relationship?

But Rosie wasn't one to bottle up a problem. If she was worried, she would have talked to Becky before now surely?

She ignored the little voice in her head reminding her that she hadn't exactly made herself accessible to her sister. She tried not to think about the number of times Rosie had invited her over and she'd refused.

Guilt shimmered through her.

She had no idea how she was going to handle this. She needed to sort things out with Will and fix things with her sister.

But this wasn't the time.

"Forget it. No harm done. We should get back." Her head was throbbing. She hated emotional chaos. "Will needs to get home and see his parents."

"Oh, no need for that. They're here." Rosie adjusted her hat to stop her hair blowing across her face. "That's what I came to tell you."

"Here?" Becky's stomach lurched. "You mean here at our house?"

"Yes." Rosie linked arms with her as they headed back to the house. "Our mother called your mother, Will."

"Right." Will's stride didn't falter. "Of course she did."

Crap. *Crap.*

Drowning in guilt and mortification, Becky glanced at him but his face revealed nothing.

She told herself that this wasn't the end of the world. They'd make it through Christmas and then end it. He'd had relationships that had ended before. This was simply going to be another one of those. They'd say it was amicable. They'd realised they just weren't compatible. That way it wouldn't impact on their parents' friendship.

Her confidence in her plan lasted until they walked back inside the house.

There, standing in the hallway, were Will's parents, his mother's eyes glistening with tears of joy and his father beaming.

His mother rushed over to them and wrapped Becky in her arms, hugging her tightly.

"Oh Becky, Becky, my dearest girl."

Becky stood rigid. This was her worst nightmare. Also, was it possible to break ribs with a hug? Who knew Will's mother was so strong.

"Jenny called us, and we came straight over! Why didn't you tell us! Oh, I'm so excited I'm all over the place. Don't be upset—I'm sure you wanted to tell us yourselves, but we couldn't wait. We're so happy! This is the best Christmas gift you could have given us." She gave Becky another squeeze and then turned to her son. "I don't know whether to scold you or hug you—"

Becky wanted to say *go for the scold—it hurts less* but Will had already stepped forward to give his mother a warm hug.

"Hi, Mum."

"That's all you're going to say?" His mother sniffed. "Why didn't you say anything to us before now?"

"Well, because I—" Will met Becky's horrified gaze across the top of his mother's head. "We hadn't really planned to announce it yet. It wasn't the right time."

"But what better time is there than Christmas, when the whole family is here to celebrate together? Your sister is going to be thrilled. What time is it in Canada? When can I call her?

She has been worried you've been spending far too much time working." His mother turned and reached out a hand to Becky. The tears were now streaming down her cheeks. "You're so right for him. I've always known it."

Becky opened her mouth but no words emerged so she closed it again. Had Will's mother been drinking? She was talking as if they were a match made in heaven, not a match made in desperation.

"Mum." Will was calm. "You're embarrassing Becky."

"Don't be embarrassed!" She squeezed Becky's hands. "You'll give him a reason to come home in the evenings instead of spending all those hours in the hospital. Perhaps you can even persuade him to take a lunch break. He's very good at his job of course, and we're proud, but in the end there is more to life than work no matter how important that work is. Family should come first, every time."

Becky couldn't breathe. She was swamped by panic. She'd kidded herself that this was controllable but it was already bigger than she could handle. She wanted to hide behind the Christmas tree the way she had when she was very young.

This was terrible. Awful. What had she done?

Not only was this not what they thought it was, but it was clear that she wasn't who they thought she was either. They saw her as some stay at home siren who would lure her son back from the hospital with the promise of lunch and lingerie.

Becky thought about the hours she spent in front of her laptop. "Work is important to both of us." She finally croaked out some words but no one was listening to her.

His mother seemed to have gone into some sort of excited trance and her own mother was almost as bad, looking on with a happy smile.

"I always knew," Will's mother said. "I always knew the two of you shared something special. I said it years ago, didn't I, Paul?" She looked at Will's father, who nodded dutifully.

"You did say it. On more than one occasion."

"I said, *those two are perfect together and they don't even know it*." She was beaming. "How did the two of you finally get together? I want all the details."

It was like a very bad sitcom.

Becky was reeling. "Er—it was—" Her voice tailed off. She didn't know what to say. She hadn't anticipated having to answer questions. What had she started here? Panic tickled the back of her throat. She needed to tell them. Right now. Before this became more complicated than it already was. This just wasn't fair on them. Or on Will. "Look, all of you—I need to—"

"It was sudden," Will said smoothly, interrupting her before she could finish her sentence. "It crept up on both of us. And now this is all a bit overwhelming for Becky so I think we should all try and relax and tone it down. No more questions. She doesn't love being the centre of attention."

Thank goodness for Will. Thank goodness he knew her so well.

But he'd just made everything a hundred times more difficult for himself. Couldn't he see that?

"No, of course. Forgive us, Becky," Will's mother said, but she exchanged a quick delighted smile with Jenny that clearly said *I can't wait to talk about this with you.*

"Why don't we all go back to the living room and have a drink next to that beautiful tree," Jenny said. "Jamie, take an order from everyone. It's the party tonight so if people want to stick with tea that's fine. I have a beautiful blend of spiced Christmas tea that was a gift from one of Martin's patients. It's delicious."

She urged everyone across the hallway and through the door where the fire was flickering and fairy lights were twinkling. So many fairy lights.

Becky had never seen so many lights in one place in her life. She blinked, dazzled. It was like being inside Santa's grotto or on a movie set. Her mother had clearly gone mad. Either that or there had been a sale in the local lighting store.

"I love this room." Hayley gazed around her with something close to wonder. "It's everything I imagined Christmas would be. Just perfect."

So that explained it. Her mother had done it for Hayley. Making the place extra Christmassy.

Becky felt a burst of love for her mother but made a mental note not to come into this room with a hangover.

Percy was curled up behind the tree and Becky contemplated joining him.

"Well." Her mother sat down, perched on the edge of the sofa. She looked happier than Becky had seen her look in a long time.

Her father, however, looked distracted.

Becky frowned as she studied him properly. He looked tired. Now that he was retired she'd expected him to look refreshed and energetic.

Was something wrong? Was it the stress of having everyone home or was it something else?

Making a mental note to find some time alone with him later, she sat down on the sofa next to Will.

He took her hand and she gave his a grateful squeeze.

She owed him. And she'd find a way to repay his kindness, and she could start by giving him an immediate escape.

"This is all very exciting, but I'm sure Will needs to get home," she said, watching as Jamie walked into the room carrying a tray rattling with cups. "It has been a long journey and—"

"We were talking about that." Will's mother exchanged looks with Jenny. "We agreed it makes no sense for the two of you to be separated over Christmas now that we know your secret. So Jenny and Martin have kindly invited Will to stay over the holidays, and we're coming over to join you for Christmas lunch. I'm bringing extra turkey and pigs in blankets! After being friends for all these years I can't believe our two families are going to be officially joined together. All together for Christmas."

Stay?

Officially joined? *All together for Christmas?* Somehow they'd gone from fake dating to fake forever.

Becky closed her eyes. She couldn't handle this. She wasn't built to tell lies. She was hopeless at it.

And she had no idea how to untangle the mess she'd made.

17

Rosie

Declan closed the door of their bedroom and stood with his back to it. "You and I need a conversation."

Rosie swallowed. "I've been saying the same thing for days, but this isn't a good time. People will be arriving soon. We should be getting ready for the party, and—"

"Now, Rosie. We need to talk right now."

She sat down on the edge of the bed. Never had she found talking about her feelings so difficult. "Fine. What did you want to say?"

He shot her a look of raw incredulity. "Is that a joke? You declare in front of everyone that your sister is in love with me, and then you ask me what we need to talk about?"

She fiddled with the fabric of her dress. "Obviously I was wrong about that. And I'm embarrassed. But it's good news about Becky and Will, isn't it? I think they'll make a great couple."

"I don't want to talk about Becky and Will. I want to talk about us." He spoke in a low voice that wouldn't carry beyond their bedroom, but his tone was no less forceful for that. "What made you think Becky was in love with me?"

"It didn't cross my mind until she walked through the door today. I just had an instinct." But it turned out that this time at least, her instincts had been wrong. Which was a huge relief. She'd been feeling dreadful that she'd unwittingly ruined her sister's life by marrying Declan, but obviously not.

Later, she'd think about how hurt she was that Becky hadn't told her what was happening with Will, but right now her mind wouldn't let her think about anything except Declan.

"But why?" He stepped closer to her, bemused. "Why would that thought even cross your mind?"

She wished he would stop talking, but clearly that wasn't going to happen so she resigned herself to having the conversation they probably should have had a few days ago.

"I suppose because it was something I'd been thinking about," she mumbled. "The two of you are very well suited."

"Well suited?" Declan was looking at her as if she was speaking a language he didn't understand. "Becky? Seriously?"

"Why not?" She felt compelled to defend herself. Maybe she'd been wrong, but there had been a strong foundation for her fears. "The two of you get on really well. You've known each other a long time."

"As colleagues. Friends."

She shrugged. "Friends is a good starting point for a relationship." And she realised that even though she'd been wrong about Becky's feelings, she wasn't necessarily wrong about Declan's. Maybe he had feelings for Becky but they weren't returned. "I just—lately I've started thinking that maybe you'd be happier with her than you are with me."

"*What?* Wait—you think I'm in love with your sister?" His voice was hoarse. "Why would you think that?"

Wasn't it obvious?

"Because she's everything I'm not."

He was still staring at her, struggling to absorb what she was saying. "I can't believe this is what you've been thinking. And you didn't say anything." He ran his hand over the back of his neck. "How long?"

"How long, what?"

"How long have you been thinking it?"

"That perhaps you would have preferred to be with Becky? I don't know. Since your Christmas event I suppose. Or maybe after that evening you took me to meet your friends. It occurred to me that Becky would have fitted in perfectly. She would have understood the conversation. She would have joined in." She twisted her wedding ring. "You and Becky know each other well. I realised the other day that most of what you know about me, and my family, you know from Becky. You stand there and say 'do you remember when,' and that isn't something you ever say to me. The two of you have this whole history."

He stood still, stunned into silence. Then he shook his head.

"Because we worked together for five years. You learn a lot about a person when you work side by side with them for that length of time."

"I know." She knew it was logical, but it didn't change the way she felt. "I suppose I'm thinking that Becky is more your type, that's all."

"Becky and I have never so much as flirted together."

"Becky doesn't really know how to flirt so that doesn't mean anything."

"Enough." His tone was raw and he walked across and tugged her to her feet. "I do not have feelings for your sister. Not those sorts of feelings. I have never had those feelings for your sister. I'm shocked that you would even think it. What have I done to make you think it?"

His eyes were stormy, and he'd dragged his hands through his hair leaving it rumpled and unruly.

She wasn't used to seeing him show this much emotion and she was mesmerized by it. He was always calm and level-headed, his emotions steady and restrained, so much so that those occasions when he seemed to struggle with emotional control stood out in her mind. The night she'd proposed. Their wedding.

And now. The fact that he was definitely struggling for control was an indication of how much he cared. Something stirred inside her. Finally she didn't need to ask herself what he was thinking and feeling, because she could see it on his face, and she knew that if he just kissed her right now everything would be fine. It was what they needed. What they both needed to bridge that distance that had formed between them.

They could be late to the party. There was so much drama erupting in the family she doubted anyone would even notice.

"Rosie?"

She realised she'd lost the thread of the conversation. He'd asked her a question. "Sorry?"

She could see the shadow on his jaw and the thickness of his eyelashes. Underneath his half-buttoned shirt she caught a glimpse of his body, lean and strong. He applied the same disciplined approach to exercise that he demonstrated in every other aspect of his life.

She was painfully aware of him. She wanted to touch him. She wanted to reach out and release the rest of those buttons. She wanted to—

"Rosie?" The change in his voice told her that he was feeling it too.

They probably needed to talk more about Becky. About her insecurities. About her feelings and his, but the level of attraction between them made it a struggle to focus.

His gaze dropped to her mouth. She felt her heart thud harder.

He was going to kiss her. At last he was going to kiss her and everything would be okay.

She felt his hands close over her shoulders, saw the passion blaze in his eyes as she slid her arms around his shoulders.

And then there was a loud knock at the door.

They froze, their mouths so close they were almost touching. Neither of them moved.

Rosie wanted to ignore the knock. There was no way she was answering the door. No way.

The knock came again and Declan let his hands drop to his sides and turned away, his breathing unsteady.

"You'd better answer that." He walked to the window, keeping his back to the door.

Engulfed by frustration, Rosie glanced briefly at him and then hurried across the room. Whichever member of her annoying family was disturbing her at this delicate point in her life, they were about to regret it. She was going to kill them slowly. No, on second thought, she was going to kill them quickly so that she could get back to what she was doing.

She dragged open the door.

Jamie stood there, looking handsome in a midnight-blue shirt and chinos.

"Sorry to disturb you. Hayley has a dress emergency."

She felt like telling her brother that thanks to him she had a sexual frustration emergency and that took priority. But this was about Hayley. Hayley, who was already feeling nervous and out of place. Hayley, who was now family. She couldn't say no to Hayley.

She cleared her throat and tried to focus. "A dress emergency?"

He pulled a face. "Hayley bought a dress for tonight and the hem isn't straight, or something. I don't know. This is your area of expertise, not mine. Any chance you could save the day? You're flushed. Are you feeling okay?"

No, she wasn't feeling okay. "I'm fine."

He glanced down at her. "Why aren't you dressed?"

"Because—" Because she was having marriage crisis talks and for a short time she'd actually forgotten about the party. "It takes me a while to get ready, you know that."

"Well, if you could hurry up and find time to help Hayley, that would be appreciated. She's worried the dress is all wrong, and before you accuse me of not having paid her enough compliments, I definitely have. I've already told her I think she looks great. Apparently that's not enough."

Because Hayley was on edge. Hayley was overthinking everything.

As someone who had turned overthinking into an art form, Rosie had nothing but sympathy.

"Of course." She forced a smile. "This is her evening after all. I'll be there right away. I'll sort her out and then get dressed myself. Just let me grab my emergency repair kit."

She walked across her bedroom, conscious of Declan watching her. The tension between them was so thick she was surprised her brother didn't sense it but he appeared clueless to the atmosphere in the room.

Instead he gave Declan a sheepish smile. "Sorry to steal her away."

Declan managed a brief nod. "No problem."

If Rosie hadn't known better she might have thought he was in pain.

She picked up her repair kit and paused. "This won't take me more than a few minutes, I'm sure."

"Take your time." His tone was rough. "I'll use the shower."

Clearly he was as frustrated as she was.

"Right." She wanted to say something else but she couldn't with her brother standing there, so she followed him out of the room and focused on Hayley's dress.

It took her less than twenty minutes to assess the problem and fix it, but by the time she walked back into their bedroom braced to finish the conversation the room was empty.

There was a note on her pillow.

Your dad needed me to move furniture so that people can dance. I'll see you downstairs when you're ready.

She turned it over in case he'd scribbled something on the back but there was nothing.

No *I love you*. No *I'll meet you up here later*.

Nothing.

She scrunched up the note and threw it in the bin.

She was expected to get through the evening without finishing what they'd started. Had their conversation fixed things? She didn't know, and she hated unresolved conflict. Hated it, and they'd already been at odds for days.

And now she was expected to smile through a whole evening and celebrate romance. What an irony.

She grabbed her dress and slid it on. She wished now that she'd chosen something less eye-catching. Black or navy maybe, not petal pink even though she knew she looked good in petal pink. She'd fallen in love with the fabric and designed the dress herself, but now she was worried it was too girly. It was the sort of dress that would have made Declan's friends stare at her with their mouths agape and normally she wouldn't have thought about it, but she was thinking of it now.

She checked her reflection in the mirror and sighed. She did love the dress. It was gorgeous. It fitted perfectly and the colour alone lifted her mood. The truth was she didn't want to wear black or navy. Black made her feel gloomy. She wanted to wear this sparkly pink dress.

This was who she was. This was the woman Declan had dated and then married.

Whether he was regretting that decision, she still had no idea.

18

Jenny

It has certainly been an interesting Christmas so far. Jamie married, Becky declaring undying love for Will." Martin reached for the clean shirt he was wearing for the party. "Are you sure putting them in the same room was that the right thing to do?"

Jennifer scooped her hair into an elegant knot and started on her makeup. The first guests would be arriving in an hour but she was satisfied that almost everything was done. "Are you turning puritanical on me all of a sudden?"

"That's not what I meant, and you know it." He buttoned the shirt. "I've known you a lot of years, Jenny. I know the way your mind works. You don't really believe that Will and Becky are together, do you?"

"Not for a moment." Smiling, she met his gaze in the mirror and saw him shake his head. "What?"

"I thought we agreed a long time ago not to interfere in our children's lives once they reached adulthood."

"I wouldn't call it interfering exactly." She rummaged in her makeup bag and dug out her mascara.

"Inviting Will to stay and putting them in the same room isn't interfering? What would you call it?"

"Making the most of circumstances." Jennifer picked up her mascara and stroked it onto her lashes. "Believe me, it's the right thing to do."

"Go along with their fake relationship? Why?"

"Because they did it for a reason, Martin."

"Now you've lost me."

She finished her lashes and put the mascara back in her makeup bag. He saw more than most men would, but still not all of it.

"Didn't you see Rosie's face? She really believed that Becky was in love with Declan." And it explained why Rosie had been behaving strangely. They'd had a fight about something. Or hit a rough patch. Something that had made Rosie question Declan's feelings for her. "That's why Becky said what she said. I don't believe she intended to say it, but having said it she decided to keep it going to make it easier for them. For Rosie and Becky, I mean."

He pulled on the shirt. "Easier? You don't really believe Becky is in love with Declan, do you?" He watched her face and raised his eyebrows. "You *do* believe that."

"I think she probably believes it, and that's what matters right now. And Rosie believes it." Her heart broke for her daughter. For both her daughters because she knew how hard the emotional upset would be for Becky to handle. She probably wanted to hide behind the Christmas tree and never come out.

"You don't think Rosie saw through Becky's sudden declaration?"

"I think she was shocked, as were we all, but Becky's response was instantaneous. She blurted it out as if it was a secret she'd been keeping. I thought she was convincing."

"Yes." He fastened the buttons of his shirt. "Funny really. I never thought our Becky was much of an actress. Remember her clomping around the stage in *Alice in Wonderland* when she was nine?"

"It was a ridiculous production, and they never should have forced her to take part." Jenny frowned. "I should have gone into school and insisted she be allowed to work behind the scenes or something. It's a regret of mine."

"You have regrets?"

"Plenty, but mostly about Rosie. I regret not looking carefully at alternative schools, when it became obvious that it wasn't the right place for her. The school should accommodate the child, shouldn't it, not the other way round. Individuality should be encouraged, not stamped out."

"We thought the girls would do better in the same school. Support each other."

"And to some extent that was true, but Rosie still compares herself to her sister and feels less somehow. The school played a part in that. They didn't really value the arts the way they did science and technology."

"We made the decisions we felt were right at the time, and that's all anyone can do. You can't be sure something else would have been better. It might not have been. Unfortunately you can't take two paths at the same time."

"I know."

"She has done well. Made a good life for herself. Your mother is floating round in the dress Rosie made her telling everyone her granddaughter is a genius."

Jenny felt a rush of love for her mother. "She has always made them feel valued. Treated them as individuals."

"So did we."

"I know. But Rosie doesn't have Becky's confidence."

"Socially, she has far more confidence." He tucked his shirt in and checked his reflection in the mirror. "And I don't understand what any of this has to do with Declan and Rosie?"

"I'm not sure." Jenny stood up. "But you know Becky isn't

as comfortable with strangers as Rosie is. She probably wouldn't even have talked to Declan if she hadn't worked side by side with him for all those years. She got to know him by default. She grew comfortable with him. And then along comes Rosie with her chat and her charm."

She thought back to their childhood, to the countless times she'd taken the twins to parties and watched with relief as Rosie had played the role of both friend and bodyguard to her more socially awkward sister.

And the support hadn't been one-sided. When Rosie had struggled with physics, maths and chemistry it had been Becky who had helped her, spending hours patiently explaining equations and probabilities as Rosie sat there getting more and more upset by her inability to understand any of the concepts.

Martin reached for his shoes. "So you're saying Becky realised she was in love with him after he started dating Rosie."

"I don't know for sure, but I think it's possible."

"But she didn't say anything."

"This is Becky," Jenny said. "Of course she wouldn't say anything."

"So when did Rosie figure all this out?"

"Today, I think, judging from her reaction. When Becky walked through the door. Although I would guess that maybe it had been playing on her mind for a little longer than that. And she was right about the wedding. Becky did disappear for an hour."

"And you don't think it was shellfish?"

"At the time I didn't question that explanation, but now? I don't think it was shellfish. I was caught up with wedding madness, but I remember Will went to check on her and they were gone for ages."

He sat down on the edge of the bed and breathed out heavily. "So what was Will's role in all this? You think he knew Becky had feelings for Declan?"

"Oh, I'm sure he knows. They're great friends. Either way, by playing along with this we're allowing them all to save face and we might stand some chance of salvaging Christmas. So you're to go downstairs and behave as if this is all real." She looked at him and he shook his head.

"I don't know, Jen. This feels like one of those ridiculous Shakespearean comedies where everyone swallows magic mushrooms and ends up with the wrong person. Where does this end? What if we play along and I end up walking Becky down the aisle next summer?"

She noticed that he seemed more energized and engaged since Becky's shock announcement earlier.

"Forget next summer and focus on Christmas. Rosie feels bad, and hopefully seeing Will and Becky together will change that. Becky feels bad, and hopefully this will give her some space to get herself under control and figure out her own feelings. You could talk to both of them. You've always been good at getting them to open up." And maybe doing so would make him realise he was needed. That retirement didn't mean he couldn't be useful and wanted.

"And what about Will's parents? We've known Audrey and Paul forever. I'd rather this wasn't the end of a beautiful friendship."

"They adore Becky. You saw their reaction downstairs."

"Yes, that's my concern. They think it's real. What's going to happen when they find out it's not?"

Jenny selected a pair of earrings. "We'll worry about that when it happens. You look handsome, by the way. I intend to test your theory that your best years are behind you. Just warning you."

He laughed. "You're changing the subject." He reached down and secured a strand of hair that had escaped from the twist at the back of her head. "You look good too. You haven't changed at all."

"I wish." She smiled at him in the mirror. "But thank you. Did you find time to talk to Jamie about his job?"

"We're going to talk properly tomorrow. And yes, before you ask, I also had a brief chat with your father about the book and we were going to talk more this afternoon, but that was before Becky turned up and shocked everyone with her announcement. I feel as if I should start making appointments for people."

"Not a bad idea. You're certainly in demand. But I'm sure there will be plenty of time for you and Dad to talk properly over Christmas."

Earlier she'd been worried that he just wasn't going to be able to shake himself out of his state of gloom, but now she was feeling more optimistic.

"You're still changing the subject. You're seriously not worried that putting Will and Becky together in a room is unfair on both of them?"

"Not at all." If she was right, and she really hoped she was, it might be just what the pair of them needed. "They shared a room last night and still seem to be speaking to each other so I'm sure they'll be just fine."

"But what do you think is going to happen?"

"I don't know, but it's going to be interesting." Unwilling to voice her hopes, she stepped into her dress and turned her back to him. "Would you zip me up, please? We have a great deal to celebrate."

"You're not still upset with Jamie then?"

"No. As you wisely pointed out, it wasn't to do with us. I like Hayley. And from the little I've learned about her since she arrived, I'm sure it would have been overwhelming for her to have a big family wedding. She so obviously wants to fit in and do the right thing. Having to worry about all that would have stressed her on her special day."

"There's a right thing to do? Maybe she should tell our children that. Between Jamie announcing that he's married, Becky saying she's with Will—even if that's fake—Rosie and Declan having issues and Will moving in with us for Christmas, everything feels chaotic. No one is behaving the way I expected them to. Apart from the dog. So far he is the only predictable one. Christmas is supposed to bring surprises, but not usually ones that give you ulcers and raised blood pressure."

"That's life, isn't it?" She leaned in and kissed him. "Not much turns out the way we expect it to."

"That's true." He gazed at her for a moment and she knew he was thinking of his own situation.

"And sometimes the only thing we can control about a situation is our own feelings."

He gave a half smile. "Are you telling me I need to sort myself out?"

"No. You already know that. I'm reminding you that these things can take time." She held out her hand. "Let's go and see what other surprises our children are about to spring on us."

"You think there will be more? In that case I'm going to need a drink."

"Don't drink too much. I want you conscious later."

19

Hayley

"Everything okay? You're a little quiet. Is meeting all these new people stressful?" Jamie steered Hayley closer to the Christmas tree, slightly away from their guests, who were grouped in various places around the living room, hallway and kitchen. "Are you wishing I'd never suggested a party?"

"No. I want to meet your friends and family. And they're interesting. Nice people." She felt as if she'd met a million new people although in fact there were probably fewer than twenty. She'd met a couple of Jamie's friends who were home for Christmas, family friends, neighbors and of course Will's parents. And every conversation she had taught her more about Jamie. "And the place looks so Christmassy. Your mother has worked hard."

"She loves this time of year. She loves having the whole family together." He studied her. "If it's too much we can escape back to our room. Whatever you need, I'm here for you."

"Jamie, this party is for us!"

"Exactly. It's for us. And if you're finding it stressful, then we should leave. If anything feels awkward, you're to tell me. I'm going to be right here."

She studied him closely. "Why are you suddenly treating me as if I'm fragile?"

"I'm not."

She raised an eyebrow. "Jamie?"

He sighed. "How is it you can read me so well? Rosie might have pointed out that I wasn't being supportive enough, and I intend to rectify that."

"You're supportive, Jamie."

"No, I thought about what she said and she's right. Because I'm so comfortable with my family I assumed you would be too. I keep forgetting they're strangers to you. I'm sorry I abandoned you when Becky and Will arrived."

So that was what had prompted Rosie to have words with him.

Hayley was touched that she'd noticed and touched that she'd taken the time to try to make the situation easier.

"I don't need protecting. You don't need to worry." She hesitated. "I just don't want to do, or say, the wrong thing, that's all."

"Is that why you're quiet? Because you're worried about doing or saying the wrong thing? Say what you like. Do what you like. In fact, if you need to sneak upstairs, just whisper in my ear." He curved his arm around her and pulled her closer. "And if you could do that sooner rather than later, I wouldn't object. Why did I want a party? I must have been mad. All I want is to be alone with you. What do you think? Shall we do it?"

She felt the warmth of his hand on her back and for a moment she even considered it. Then she dismissed the idea. This was his family. These were the people he'd known all his life. She wanted to know them too.

Also it would upset his mother, who had gone to so much trouble.

"I don't want to leave. I like watching everyone. I like learning new things about you. Did you really lock your teacher in the classroom when you were ten or was that something your friend said to embarrass you?"

"Sadly, it's true. I showed a distinct lack of judgement, although in my defence I should say that the snow was the best ever and the whole class wanted to build a snowman. I tried to make it happen."

"The goals of a ten-year-old. Did he ever forgive you? The teacher?"

"It was she, and yes, she did. You met her earlier. Mrs Everly. Standing over by the fireplace talking to Becky. Slightly scary looking."

Hayley looked across the room and recognised the woman deep in conversation with his sister and Will. "She didn't mention it."

"She told me once that she believes it's important to let a person move on from their mistakes."

"Good for her."

She shifted her gaze from Mrs Everly to Jamie's parents, who were standing near the piano. Jenny was wearing a fitted dress in a deep shade of plum. She looked both elegant and festive, her hair swept up in a casual updo, secured by a sparkly clip. She and Martin were chatting to Will's parents, and laughing so hard it made you want to laugh with them. The affection between them was visible for all to see.

As she watched, Jamie's mother gestured for Will and Becky to join them.

Hayley felt wistful and a little sick.

"Your parents are so happy about Becky and Will."

"Yes." His gaze rested on her face. "What? What are you thinking?"

"Nothing."

"We agreed never to do that." His voice softened. "We agreed that we were always going to share what we were feeling."

She hesitated.

"I keep thinking of the expression on your mother's face when Becky announced that she was in love with Will."

"You mean the shock?"

"No," she said quietly. "Not that." The moment was imprinted on her brain.

"What then? I didn't notice anything. But I was probably too busy gaping at Rosie and wondering what was going on."

Hayley put her drink down on the nearest table. "She looked as if all her dreams had come true. She was thrilled. Her expression was pure joy."

"That isn't so surprising. My parents and Will's parents have been friends since before they had kids. They went to antenatal classes together. Dad delivered Will when he was born because the weather was terrible and they couldn't get to the hospital. My mother loves Will like a son."

Hayley nodded. She knew she shouldn't care so much, but she couldn't help it. "I'm sure that's it. It's great to see them happy."

He frowned. "Why is my mother's response to Becky's announcement making you look as if your dog died?"

Should she tell him? Yes, maybe she should.

"Because she didn't look like that when you told her we were married." The moment the words left her mouth she regretted them. "Forget it. I know I'm being oversensitive." She knew she was hardwired to expect rejection and she tried hard to fight against that.

"I think you've got it wrong. She was pleased." He took her hand. "She said all the right things."

"Yes, she did."

"But?"

She hesitated. "But I don't think she meant them. She was making a supreme effort, for your sake and because she's a kind person. She said what she knew needed to be said because she loves you and the fact that we're married is a done deal. But was she happy about it? Did she look as if her dreams had come true? No." And it added to her growing admiration for his mother. To be warm and welcoming while also feeling hurt took immense strength of character.

"Hayley—"

"We should have told them, Jamie." She looked up at him, wishing they could wind back time. "Instead of springing it on them. We should have told them right after we got married, or even before. And then they would have had a chance to get used to the idea. And maybe they wouldn't have loved it or been thrilled, because they don't know me and I'm sure they would have wanted to be there with you—I get that—but they wouldn't have been as shocked. I want them to accept me, and I think by not telling them in advance we've made that harder."

Jamie listened then glanced at his mother, who was deep in conversation with Will's mother.

"Honestly?" He turned back to look at her. "I wasn't really thinking about my family. I was thinking about you."

"Me?" The look in his eyes made her heart turn over.

"Yes. Getting married was about us. The two of us. I wanted to focus on that and looking at the way you are right now, I think I made the right decision."

"Am I doing something wrong?"

"No," he said quietly, "but you're thinking of everyone but yourself. And that wasn't what I wanted. We could have told them before we got married and maybe they would have been fine about it, but if they weren't then you would have been worried, and I would have felt guilty. I wanted the day to be about us, and I didn't want anything intruding on that. And we could have told them before we arrived yesterday, but again, that might have ended up being a stressful conversation."

"What are you saying? That by surprising them with our news the way we did they were forced to be polite?"

"Not really. I'm saying that my family, much as I love them, have never been the priority here. This has always been about you. Us. Your needs come first for me. You come first."

She was touched, but still she wondered if it would have been less stressful if they'd announced it before.

"I just hope one day your mother will be happy you married me."

Jamie pulled her close and kissed her briefly. "She already is. Now come and meet Angela. She's the woman standing by the fireplace."

"Your college friend?"

"Yes, we shared a house along with four others, Will included. Angie is the reason we can all cook. She insisted we do a night each and she wasn't willing to eat bolognaise every time." He led her across the room and for the next hour Hayley chatted to people and got to know more about Jamie.

They were helping themselves to another drink when she happened to notice Becky hovering by the doorway. "Your sister looks as if she'd like to escape."

"Which sister?" He followed her gaze and laughed. "Yes, Becky hates big gatherings. Any moment now you'll look round and she will have vanished. She'll be in her room with headphones on, doing something on her laptop."

"She's beautiful. I've never met identical twins before. It's a little unnerving. It's a good thing Rosie has long hair and dresses differently or it wouldn't be easy to tell them apart."

"Becky's hair was long too until she was about sixteen. They played all kinds of tricks on us when they were young. And occasionally at school."

She was intrigued. "Pretending to be each other? As a joke?"

"No, usually one of them was saving the other. I remember one occasion when Rosie was being bullied and so Becky pretended to be her and sorted them out." He caught her questioning look. "You don't want to know, but it got Becky suspended. Except she was suspended as Rosie, which got complicated."

Hayley laughed. "I can imagine."

"It worked the other way round too. Becky had to stand on-stage and recite a poem at some end-of-school event or other—I don't remember exactly. It was her idea of hell."

"So Rosie did it?"'

"Yes. And she did it perfectly, by which I mean she was just good enough but not outstanding." He shrugged. "She was Becky."

Hayley felt a shaft of envy. "So they've always been close. In each other's corner."

"Always."

She thought about what had happened earlier. The distress on Rosie's face when she'd blurted out her belief that Becky was in love with Declan.

"Did you know Becky and Will were together?"

"No, but it makes sense to me. Far more sense than Becky and Declan." He finished his drink and frowned. "I don't know what made Rosie say that. Although she has always had an active imagination."

But a statement like that had to come from somewhere, didn't it?

"When she came to our room to help me with my dress, did she seem like herself to you?"

"Now you mention it, I did think she was looking strange when I knocked on her door to ask for help, but I assumed she was feeling awkward because she'd made a fool of herself. You might have picked up on that."

Hayley hesitated. He was the one who knew his sister, not her. One day, maybe, she'd know them well enough to be able to form her own judgement. To know when to offer help and when to stand back.

"You're probably right. Your sister is very kind."

"Rosie? Yes, she is, providing you haven't stolen her Christmas chocolate. Then she's ruthless. Have you tried those mini quiches my mother made? They're delicious."

"I have. And they are. Your mother is a great cook. And so good at making people feel welcome."

"So apart from the fallout of shocking my family with our announcement, what do you think of your first family Christmas?"

She glanced around the room, at the groups of people enjoying each other's company.

"It has been interesting. And a lot more complicated than I imagined."

"I did warn you that your vision of family life was a long way from reality. Chaos, isn't it?"

Yes, elements of it were chaotic, but it was so much more than that. There was a warmth about the gathering, a lightness and air of anticipation as if everyone had left their complicated lives at the door with their coats and were just enjoying the moment.

She could have watched them forever, the interactions, the way they knew each other. They all looked so comfortable and happy.

And then she noticed that there was no sign of Rosie.

20

Rosie

She'd made a total fool of herself. She could feel everyone looking at her and speculating.

Rosie leaned against the locked door of the downstairs cloakroom, trying to calm herself.

Through the door she could hear the muffled sounds of music, conversation and laughter—people enjoying the party. She should be out there too, celebrating her brother and Hayley's exciting news, but she felt too embarrassed.

Why was she always so emotional? Why couldn't she be calm and contained like her sister? She should have hit a pause button instead of blurting out her thoughts.

But she'd never mastered pausing, and now, thanks to her big mouth and lack of filter, her marriage to Declan was under a spotlight. Everyone was watching them and speculating. And she knew Declan would hate that. Like Becky, he didn't love being the focus of attention. And they were definitely the focus of everyone's attention.

The moment she'd walked down the stairs to join everyone her mother had pulled her aside to check everything was okay, and she'd wriggled her way out of that encounter only to have to go through the same thing again with her grandmother. She'd braced herself to have the same conversation with Becky, but there had been no sign of her—presumably because she was with Will somewhere. She was still getting her head around the fact that Becky was now with Will, and also that her twin hadn't shared something so monumental with her. There had never been a time when she'd been surprised by something that had happened in her sister's life, because she always knew. But not this time. Was that why Becky had kept her distance? Because she'd been pursuing her own romantic relationship?

She stared at herself in the mirror and removed a smudge of mascara with the tip of her finger. She couldn't spend the evening hiding in the cloakroom. Eventually people would come looking for her. But she wasn't in the mood to smile and be sociable. The one person she really did need to talk to, preferably without interruptions, was Declan.

She couldn't forget the stunned expression on his face when he'd confronted her in the privacy of their bedroom. He evidently wasn't in love with Becky. She hadn't inadvertently disrupted a romance. Which was a relief, although she wished she'd ascertained that fact in a less public and humiliating way. Also it didn't soothe her anxiety that maybe she was the wrong person for him.

The door handle rattled as someone tried the door and she tensed.

"Rosie?" It was Jamie. "Are you in there?"

"Give me a minute." If her brother hadn't knocked on the bedroom door when he did, would she and Declan have fixed things? "Can't you go and use one of the upstairs bathrooms?"

"No, I want to talk to you."

Oh for—

"If you could just go away, that would be great."

"I'm not going away until you come out. And given that I'm

247

missing my own party, it would be good if that could happen sooner rather than later. Also, I know how to open this door from the outside so if you don't open it I will."

Brothers! Who needed them?

She yanked open the door and glared at him. "What? Can't a girl use the bathroom without interruption?"

"Yes, but you weren't using the bathroom. You were hiding."

"I hate you."

"No, you don't. You hate yourself. That's why I'm here." He pulled her behind the large Christmas tree that their mother had put in the hallway. "Stop chewing over what happened."

"Chewing? I'm not chewing."

"Yes, you are. You were standing in there promising yourself you are never going to open your mouth and speak again. And don't bother denying it, because I've been your brother long enough to know what goes on in your head."

"If you're going to tell me that people barely noticed and I didn't humiliate myself—"

"I'm not going to tell you that. People *did* notice and you definitely humiliated yourself." He grinned. "The moment will probably be talked about for at least the next forty years."

"Thanks."

"But it doesn't matter." He moved a decoration that was hanging perilously close to the end of a branch. "You gave me some good advice about Hayley, so now I'm going to do the same for you."

"I hate advice."

"Well, tough." But this time his voice was gentle. "We all say and do things we regret from time to time. But move on. You're using up energy reliving that moment when your emotions got the better of you, when what you should be doing is using that energy to solve whatever problem you and Declan have. Nothing else matters. No one else matters."

"Says the man who knocked on my door just as we were trying to sort it out."

"Ah." Understanding dawned and he pulled an apologetic face. "I thought things were a bit tense. Sorry about that."

"It's okay. I suppose it was all in a good cause. Hayley looks stunning in her dress."

"She does. And so do you." He gave her shoulder a squeeze. "It's a shame to hide that dress in the bathroom and behind a Christmas tree."

She sighed and stroked the fabric. "This dress deserved to have a memorable evening, but it's memorable for all the wrong reasons."

"Still plenty of the evening left. And yes, you're excused."

"Excused from what?"

"From the rest of my party."

She looked at him, uncertain. "I need to talk to Becky."

"That can wait. And anyway, she's wrapped up with Will." He flashed her a wicked smile. "Go and sort things out with Declan. He's your priority. But remember there's no lock on your door so you'd better wedge a chair under the handle or something."

She felt her throat sting. "Jamie—"

"Hey, it's okay." He pulled her into a hug. "And one thing I can guarantee is that in this family everyone is going to find something new to talk about by tomorrow."

She sniffed. "I don't suppose you could announce a pregnancy or something? That would take the heat off me."

He laughed and handed her a tissue. "That would give Granny way too much excitement for one Christmas. You might want to replenish your makeup before you rejoin the party—your nose is so red you could audition to be Rudolph."

"Thanks a lot."

He walked away from her, picking pine needles from his sleeve.

Rosie stood for a moment. He was right of course. This wasn't the best time to talk to Becky. And her priority had to be Declan. Her marriage.

She took a deep breath, nipped back into the cloakroom and did a minor repair job on her makeup and then followed Jamie. She might be overemotional, but she wasn't a coward.

She walked back into the living room and joined Declan, who was deep in conversation with her grandmother, his head tilted as he listened. The room was noisy with much laughter as everyone enjoyed catching up.

Normally she loved a party, but right now she wanted to grab Declan's hand, slide away and finish the conversation they'd started.

"Rosie mentioned that you usually go skiing at this time of year?" Her grandmother was an expert at getting people to talk about themselves.

"Yes. With my friends. A group of eight of us."

"What fun." Her grandmother beamed. "Have you all known each other a long time?"

Rosie hoped this wasn't going to turn into one of her grandmother's embarrassing interrogations. She'd done the same thing when Rosie was a teenager and had brought friends home. Often her grandmother had been there but instead of leaving them to raid the kitchen for food, she'd whip up delicious milk shakes, produce plates of freshly baked cookies and join them at the table. Her friends had all adored her. *Call me Phyllis*, she'd said, and had proceeded to encourage them to discuss all their problems with her. They'd all thought it was brilliant that Rosie's grandmother was interested in the detail of their lives and was never judgmental, but Rosie had been mortified and Becky had refused to be part of it. More often than not she'd retreated to her room with her laptop.

The years hadn't subdued her grandmother. Here she was, her warmth and interest drawing information from Declan with surprising ease.

"More than a decade," he told her. "We were at college together and six of us work in the same company. We hire a chalet or an apartment every year."

"That must be magical—all that snow. But how do you divide up the jobs? Christmas is so busy! You don't fall out over who is doing the cooking?"

"No. We have a rota, and whoever doesn't cook clears up. Someone is in charge of bringing Christmas decorations and we all do a Secret Santa." He paused. "It started by accident, the first year we were in college. Most people were going home for Christmas and a group of us—we were all living on the same corridor—well, none of us had that kind of family gathering to go home to. We got talking, and we thought why not create our own version of Christmas? So we all wrote down which parts of Christmas we'd like to see happen. For someone it was the tree, for someone else the presents, someone else the food. One of my friends had always dreamed of a white Christmas, which is when we decided to go skiing. Sorry, this is too much detail—" he hesitated "—but you get the idea."

"I like details. Details help you to see the whole picture, and now I see it. You incorporated all those things that each of you craved—" her grandmother touched his arm "—and you made your own Christmas. How clever of you. And how wonderful."

"It wasn't all wonderful," Declan made a joke, "Maya's dream was to sing Christmas carols—don't ask me why—so we all had to sing. The people in the apartment next door complained."

Phyllis laughed. "I would have loved to have been there. I would have joined in."

"I'm sure you would." Declan gave a brief smile. "It was just to get us through that first Christmas. And it worked so well and we had such a good time we did it the next Christmas too. And the Christmas after that. We've been doing it for the past ten years, although not everyone makes it every year of course, particularly as we've got older. Pat didn't make it last year because he had work travel. Shona was pregnant and didn't want to risk it. There is usually someone missing."

Rosie swallowed. And this year he was the one who was missing, because he was with her.

He'd told her he spent his Christmas "skiing with friends." He'd never shared this level of detail. She hadn't known any of this.

Her grandmother was smiling. "That sounds like an excellent way to spend Christmas."

Rosie hadn't thought it sounded excellent at all until she'd heard him describe it. And now she could picture it.

For him, his friends weren't just friends. They were his family. They'd all supported each other through tough times. They supported each other as her family did. They did their best to meet each other's needs, whether that meant singing carols or walking in the snow. The reason he'd been so upset about her skipping his work Christmas party was because it seemed to him that she was rejecting his friends.

And finally she understood. And she was frantic to continue the conversation they'd started earlier.

"Do you mind if I steal Declan, Granny?" She reached for his hand and saw her grandmother smile.

"Steal away." Her grandmother gave her a conspiratorial wink. "I shall cover for you if anyone asks."

"Knowing you, the cover story will be more salacious than the truth." Rosie leaned down and kissed her grandmother briefly and then led Declan out of the room.

"Where are we going?"

"Somewhere we can talk. Somewhere we can be alone." She was determined now, and sure it was the right time to have the conversation they needed to have. "This gathering must be a bit of a strain on you."

"It's not." He seemed oddly reluctant to leave. "It's good to have the chance to get to know your family a little better. Your dad was telling me that it feels weird being retired."

Her father had said that? Rosie was surprised, both by the fact that he'd confided in Declan but also that he felt that way. He'd been stressed out and exhausted for the past few years so she'd assumed he would be relishing his new life.

"Weird how?"

"Just that his new life is an adjustment, that's all."

"It seems strange that he would mention that to you, out of the blue."

"It wasn't out of the blue. I asked him how he was finding being retired. I assumed for someone like him, whose whole life was dedicated to helping people, stepping back must be difficult."

He'd asked. And her father had told him.

Rosie should have asked him the same question, but there had barely been time to breathe since she'd arrived home and she'd had no time alone with him. She felt a pang. She didn't want to think about her parents growing older. To her they were always there, always the same, providing the solid foundation for her life. She realised with a flush of shame that she more often than not thought of them as her parents, and not as individuals with the same problems and challenges as everyone else.

"I'm glad you talked to him."

"He's an interesting man. And your grandmother is a real character."

"She is. And she loves you. I hope she didn't embarrass you too much,' Rosie said. "She does have a tendency to put people on the spot and she is never tactful."

"I think she's brilliant."

"You do?" She was surprised. Declan rarely talked about

himself, and the one thing her grandmother excelled at was persuading people to tell her all their innermost secrets. "I worried you might find her questions intrusive."

"Far from it. She seemed genuinely interested. I never knew my grandparents." He hesitated. "You have so many layers of family. Grandparents. Parents. Siblings."

"Is it overwhelming?"

"No, it's—" He paused, searching for the word. "It's enviable. You're lucky. I can see why you love coming home for Christmas. You're part of something."

"You're part of it too now, but that doesn't mean we can't still be alone sometimes."

Still holding his hand, she headed up the stairs to their bedroom and closed the door firmly behind them.

He raised an eyebrow and she shrugged.

"Last time we tried to have a conversation we were interrupted. That's not going to happen this time. It's too important. Unless smoke and flames start appearing under that door, we're not opening it." She walked to the window, suddenly nervous. They had so much to talk about it was hard to know where to start. "That story you told my grandmother—I didn't know any of that."

"I told you I spent Christmas with friends."

"But not the detail." She turned to face him. "Detail is everything. Your friends are your family, I see that now."

He stared back at her. "I hadn't thought of it that way but yes, I suppose that's true."

"It explains a lot. It explains why you were so upset that I didn't come to your Christmas party. That was wrong of me. I didn't understand, but I do now. I'm sorry."

"I should be the one saying sorry." He crossed the room to join her. "We made you feel uncomfortable. We know each other so well it's always an adjustment when something changes."

"They were surprised you were with someone like me." She touched the fabric of her dress. "I was right about that."

"You were right they were surprised, but wrong about their reasons." He gave a faint smile. "They weren't wondering why I'd chosen to be with you, Rosie—that was pretty clear to everyone. They were wondering why someone like you would choose to spend an evening with them."

"What do you mean?"

He gave an awkward shrug, as if it was obvious. "You're dazzling, Rosie. You light up every room you walk into with your warmth and energy. They knew I was crazy about you, which added extra pressure. They didn't know what to say to you. Maggie confessed afterwards that you made her want to give up wearing hoodies and wear a dress instead, but she didn't have your confidence. She wanted to ask you to go shopping with her. Finn admitted he was too scared to speak to you directly in case he made a fool of himself and you dumped me because of my terrible taste in friends. And when Harry said you weren't my usual type, he was gazing at you with awe. I think you missed that part because you were feeling self-conscious."

She gave a shocked laugh. "I thought—I didn't understand any of the conversation."

"They talked about the one and only thing they're confident talking about. Probably hoping to impress you," he said and then gave that slightly lopsided smile that always made her stomach flip. "That backfired, didn't it?"

The possibility that they might have felt insecure too hadn't crossed her mind.

"I felt stupid. I assumed they thought I was stupid. You get frustrated that I don't use a password manager, and that I hate two-factor authentication almost as much as I hate spreadsheets and that you're always having to connect my headphones because my Bluetooth doesn't work and they're undiscoverable."

"No one thought you were stupid. And I didn't know you

were thinking it, because it's only recently I discovered that you've always compared yourself to your sister. Knowing that, your insecurities about my friends and colleagues make more sense. I just assumed you were regretting marrying me."

He was standing close to her. So close. And the words he was speaking seemed to bring him closer still.

There was a tightness in her throat. A pressure in her chest.

"I thought the same about you. I thought you were regretting marrying me. When we were in the car and I asked you, you hesitated."

"Not because I regretted it, but because you were so upset I thought we needed to pause the conversation."

"That's the worst thing to do when I'm upset."

He touched her cheek with his fingers. "I'm starting to understand that."

"I was the one who urged everything forward. I was the one who proposed to you. I started wondering what would have happened if I hadn't done that. Maybe I wasn't right for you and I hadn't given you a chance to discover that. That's when I started thinking you might have been happier with Becky."

"Why didn't you tell me what you were thinking?"

"Because I was too scared I might be right." She gave a shrug, embarrassed. "I have an overactive imagination. It's a curse."

"Your imagination isn't a curse, it's a gift. Being with you is a gift."

She put her hand on his chest, curling her fingers into the front of his shirt. "We see the world so differently."

"That's true." He cupped her face with his hands, stroking her cheeks with his thumbs. "And I love that. I'm grateful for it every day. I treasure our differences. I like seeing the world through your eyes."

"You do?"

"Yes. You notice things I don't. You see things I don't. I

look at snow and I see traffic issues and grounded planes. You see something magical."

He lowered his head and kissed her, gently at first and then more deeply, and she felt that kiss right through her body, shimmering across her skin and sinking deep into her bones and her soul. If they'd ever had a more intimate connection she couldn't think of it. Her mouth and body were locked against his and in that moment he was all hers and she was all his.

His hands were gentle as he eased her dress away from her shoulders, her name on his lips as he moved aside the silken waterfall of her hair with gentle fingers and kissed his way down her neck. She felt the roughness of his jaw, teasing sensitive flesh and then his mouth returned to hers, as if he was unable to resist that most intimate contact. She melted under the skilled slide of his tongue and the erotic brush of his fingers, her eyes closing against the twinkling Christmas lights. There should have been darkness but everything inside her was lit up and sparkling, her senses alive and on fire.

Without easing her mouth from his she stripped away his shirt and fumbled with his belt, urgency making her uncoordinated.

She opened her eyes, needing to see as well as feel and she gave a shiver of delicious anticipation as she met the dark intensity of his gaze. For a moment she felt shy, which was ridiculous of course because it was Declan and it was far from their first time, but somehow it had never felt quite like *this*.

The Christmas tree bathed the room in a warm glow and they sank to the floor next to the soft heap of their abandoned clothing, locked together in a pool of shimmering light, too desperate for each other to take the few steps to the comfort of the bed that awaited them.

She slid her fingers through the gleaming layers of his hair, then stroked her hands over his shoulders, her palms lingering on the swell of muscle, a gasp on her lips as he teased the sensitive tip of her breast with his tongue and then moved slowly down her body, each teasing stroke making her breath come a little faster.

None of it was enough. Whatever he did, she wanted more and she writhed and arched, urging him on because this was what she wanted and she wanted it now. His mouth found hers again, his kiss deep and hungry and she felt the pleasure shoot through her body in tiny shivers and flares of heat. He closed his hands over her hips and shifted her and she felt the familiar weight of him, the delicious heaviness, and then the intimate pressure as he finally surged into her, his desperation every bit as great as hers. He silenced her soft gasp with his mouth, his breath mingling with hers as they moved, and he kept kissing her all the way through the wild adventure, occasionally lifting his mouth just enough to tell her how much he loved her, how beautiful she was, and how perfect.

And she knew she wasn't perfect but he made her feel perfect and when the pleasure raced over them she held him and he held her and it felt like nothing she'd ever experienced before. It was a new level of intimacy, their connection deepened by new discoveries, by curiosity, by acceptance, and she knew in her heart that this relationship was so right that no matter what challenges came their way in the future, they'd deal with them together.

Later, much later, she lay with her head on his chest and her limbs wound around his, feeling closer to him than she ever had before.

She felt sated and satisfied and overwhelmed with happiness.

"I was wondering—" she stroked her hand over his abdomen, her fingers lingering, "how is your first family Christmas going so far?"

He gave a soft laugh. "I'm enjoying it more than I thought was possible." He shifted slightly. "Although this floor is hard."

She smiled against his shoulder. "I'm very comfortable."

"That's because you're lying on me, not the floor." He pulled her closer and kissed the top of her head. "But it's okay. And given that you're virtually lying under the tree, does that make you my Christmas gift?"

"I'm already yours. You can't gift the same thing twice."

They heard the faint sound of footsteps somewhere beyond the door and both of them froze.

She covered her mouth with her hand to stifle a giggle. "I feel like a naughty teenager."

He pressed his lips to her hair. "If you did those things when you were a teenager then you were definitely naughty."

They were talking in whispers, the words for them alone, the exchange as intimate as everything else they'd shared.

"You're cold." He smoothed his hands over her skin and eased himself upright, pulling her with him to the bed.

They snuggled under cosy layers, adopting the same position they had on the floor.

She kissed the corner of his mouth. "I've actually never had sex in my parents' house before."

"Did we even remember to lock the door?"

"I don't have a lock on my door. My mother has been nagging my dad to do something about that for ten years."

"I'm glad I didn't know that before. It might have given me performance anxiety."

She gave a gurgle of laughter and buried her face in his chest to smother it. She could have stayed like this for the rest of Christmas. "The sex was amazing, but so was the talking. I'm glad we finally had a proper conversation."

"So am I and it's my fault that we didn't do it sooner. You kept trying to get me to talk about it."

She snuggled closer. "You have to get to things in your own time. I understand that. You're like Becky. You prefer to ignore your feelings."

"That's true to an extent and I definitely need to work on

that because I understand now that if I don't tell you how I'm feeling, your imagination will simply fill in the gaps and I'd rather we worked with the facts." He stroked her back, his hand lingering on the curve of her hip. "But on this occasion, that wasn't why I didn't want to talk."

She lifted herself on her elbow and looked down at him. "Why then?"

"Because I was afraid you were regretting marrying me, and I didn't want to give you the chance to tell me that. I wanted to hang on to what we had for as long as possible. I'm not sure if that's avoidance or cowardice. Both, probably."

She gazed down at him and then lowered her head and kissed him gently. "I suppose there are still a lot of things we don't know about each other."

"That seems to be true." He shifted her so that she was underneath him. "We should do more talking and less guessing. Spend more time getting to know each other."

She looked up at him, breathless. "That sounds like fun. I suppose we should have done that part before I proposed."

"It wouldn't have made a difference to my feelings, but while we're on that topic I have a confession—that night you proposed—you beat me to it by seconds."

"I did?" It took a moment for her to absorb that, and when she did she felt a thrill of delight. "You were going to propose to me?"

"Yes. I decided when we were at dinner that you were the best thing that had ever happened to me. I didn't want to wait another moment to ask you. It was a spur-of-the-moment impulse thing."

"But—" She listened to him, her heart thumping. "You don't do spur of the moment. You don't act on impulse. You think everything through."

"Not this. This time I just knew. And yes, part of me wanted to wait, and choose you a special ring, and find the perfect place and the perfect time because I'm a planner, but then I saw the snow and the look in your eyes as you watched it and I knew the moment was perfect."

She swallowed. Maybe they didn't know everything about each other but he knew her much, much better than she'd thought. "So you were going to do it?"

"Yes. I had a paperclip in my pocket and I fashioned it into a ring."

She stared at him, astonished. "Declan?!"

He pulled a face. "Not very romantic, I know. It should have been a sparkly diamond or something."

Her heart softened. "I think it's the most romantic thing I've ever heard."

"I wish I'd gone ahead and bought that diamond, but I kept telling myself that it was too soon, and I didn't want to freak you out. And I was standing there watching you, seeing how happy you were, wondering if I'd mess it up if I gave you a paperclip and then you turned and kissed me and proposed, and I felt like the luckiest guy on the planet," he said softly, "because you were looking at me exactly the same way as you looked at the snow."

She smiled, her vision blurred by tears. "And you say you're not poetic."

"I'm not. I was stating a fact." He stroked her cheek with his fingers. "Don't cry. Please don't cry."

"These are happy tears." She sniffed and caught his hand in hers. "What colour was it?"

"The snow?"

"The paperclip."

He kissed the palm of her hand and then kissed her. "It was green. Not right for you. It should have been pink."

"Green would have been just fine." She murmured the words against his lips. "I love you."

"And I love you. And if you could stop crying that would be great."

They heard the sound of laughter coming from downstairs and the slam of the front door.

Declan eased his mouth away from hers and raised an eyebrow in question. "Do you think someone will come looking for us? Should we go back downstairs?"

"I doubt anyone will notice we've left, and I don't care if they do." She pulled his mouth to hers again. "Tonight I'm right where I want to be. Tell me more about how you were going to propose."

21

Jenny

Downstairs, where the party was in full swing, the focus wasn't on Rosie's absence.

"Stop staring." Jenny nudged Audrey in the ribs, almost spilling her drink in the process.

"Staring? I'm not staring, I'm observing. I'm feasting my eyes on a picture I've imagined in my head a million times."

"I wish you'd keep your thoughts in your head, alongside those images." Jenny stepped in front of Audrey, blocking her view of Will and Becky, who were chatting on the other side of the room, heads close together.

"You're no fun at all." Audrey tried to peep round the side of her. "They look so right together. Just look at the expression in her eyes. The way she's looking at him. And Will is so protective, did you notice that? He's not leaving her on her own for a moment. And his hand has never left her back."

"Audrey—"

"It *has* to be serious. There is no way those two would finally take the plunge and announce they're together unless they were sure that this is it."

Or unless such an announcement diverted attention from something else entirely.

Jenny decided that this wasn't the moment to voice her suspicions.

She'd naively assumed that worrying about your children would end when they grew up and left home but she'd discovered that as soon as the well emptied itself of the worries of childhood it was immediately refilled with other worries.

Like now.

She had no idea what was going on with her daughters, but at least Rosie and Declan had left the room together. That was a start. But it did nothing to alleviate her unease about Becky.

She was tempted to pull her aside and ask her directly, but Becky never liked talking about her relationships and Jenny had always been careful to respect that.

The best thing she could do for her daughter would be to somehow shift Audrey's attention elsewhere. She felt guilty for not being able to protect Becky from the speculation.

She focused on her friend. "Will you and Paul be going to France next summer?"

"What? Yes, probably." Audrey's gaze was fixed beyond Jenny's shoulder. "Although we're obviously not going to book anything at the moment."

"You're not?" Jenny knew that her friend usually organized her holidays right after Christmas because she liked to have something to look forward to in the dark days of January. "Why?"

"Because there might be a wedding."

"Audrey!"

"What? It's not as if this is a whirlwind courtship, Jen. Not like your Jamie, or even Rosie. Will and Becky have known each other forever. They don't exactly need time to discover if they're right for each other. They've had their whole lives. They know. And don't pretend you're not scheming too because I seem to remember that you were the one who invited Will to stay for Christmas."

Jenny was beginning to regret her actions. "You don't think you're jumping ahead?"

"Who is jumping ahead?" Phyllis appeared. "Don't Will and Becky look adorable together? Becky looks so happy. I think this could be *it*."

Jenny gave up her valiant attempts to divert attention. If her mother was joining in, then the battle to protect Becky was truly lost.

She turned her head, allowing herself to look at her daughter. Becky *did* look happy. And now she was starting to doubt herself. She'd been so sure that their relationship wasn't real— that Will was somehow protecting Becky.

But looking at the two of them now, she started to wonder.

Maybe it was real. Maybe she was wrong. Or maybe she was right and the whole thing was about to come crashing down.

With that thought hovering at the front of her mind, she went to find Martin.

"Do you know what I want for Christmas?"

His look was one of alarm. "I'm not sure I want to know given that it's too late for me to deliver on it."

She shook her head. "It's not a thing. Nothing you can buy."

"Our bank account thanks you."

"What I really want for Christmas is one hour, just one hour, where it feels as if everything in the family is steady. One hour where everyone is happy, and nothing is complicated, and I can leave maternal anxiety at the door and just enjoy the moment instead of worrying about how we're going to handle the next crisis." She stared out of the window, at the snow that was drifting slowly through the darkness. "Do you think people without children worry less?"

"No. They just worry about different things."

"You don't worry as much as I do."

"I don't need to, because I know you're doing the worrying for both of us. You've got that covered. No sense in duplicating."

After all these years he still made her laugh.

"How did I end up being responsible for worry?"

"Hey, I got bins and clearing the gutters. Serious stuff."

"You pay someone else to clean the gutters."

"Nothing wrong with delegating."

"I wish I could delegate my anxiety. Just hand it over."

He leaned closer. "I tell you what, for Christmas this year I'll take half your worries. You can just hand them over and forget about them."

"You won't take them seriously. You'll dismiss them."

"You mean I won't nurture them, feed them until they grow and grow and gradually take over? What I do with my half is my responsibility. Stop micromanaging." He put his arm around her. "Which worry in particular is at the top of your mind?"

"I have a few fighting it out for top place."

He gave her the same thoughtful look she'd seen him wear when he was checking a patient's test results and was trying to figure out what they meant.

"One thing I learned when I was working was that it usually takes something big to go wrong for people to understand how worry-free their lives were before. Over and over again, I'd hear people say 'I worried about stuff that just wasn't important,' or 'my life was pretty perfect and I never even noticed.'"

"You're saying that the answer to my worry is to give me something bigger to worry about?"

"I'm saying it's all about perspective." He glanced across the room to where Will and Becky were standing together. "We have healthy children, living their lives, and yes, those lives are full of ups and downs and drama, but that is normal."

"Stop being so reasonable and logical." She saw Becky smile

at Will. "Do you think the kids know how much we worry about them?"

"No. We're their parents. We're the solid, dependable foundation of their lives. We're like a charging unit—forgotten most of the time, until we're needed and then they plug into us and hope we still work. They don't think about us as individuals. They see us only in relation to them. They don't know that we're mere mortals with vulnerabilities and worries, capable of making decisions every bit as dubious as the ones they make."

"Maybe we should tell them."

"No. Best to allow the illusion to continue for as long as possible."

And she realised she felt the same way about her parents, often seeing them in relation to her, rather than thinking of them as individuals with their own hopes and fears. She felt a pang of guilt and made a promise to herself to encourage them to talk more about their lives when they were growing up. To listen more. And she was going to tell the kids to do the same.

More often they teased them, or corrected and educated them, telling them that they *just couldn't say things like that now.* There was a casual assumption that they were too old to understand, but maybe it was more that the kids were too young to appreciate just how much their grandparents *did* understand. The world changed, technology advanced, but people's emotions didn't change. Fear, excitement, hope, grief—those things were experienced by everyone, whichever generation you were born into.

She reached for Martin's hand, doing it sneakily in case one of the children noticed and said *yuck, Mum, please!*

"I'm glad I married you."

His fingers tightened on hers. "Even now when I'm driving you insane, moping around and feeling sorry for myself?"

"Especially now, and you're not moping. You're adjusting."

"Adjusting." He nodded. "I'm going to use that as an excuse every time you try and get me to do something I don't feel like doing. 'I can't do it right now, I'm adjusting.'"

There was so much they'd shared together, so many struggles they'd helped each other through. And she didn't need something bad to happen to know she was lucky to have him.

And although she knew he couldn't take the anxiety from her, it made her feel better to know she wasn't alone with it.

22

Becky

She felt as if she was in a goldfish bowl. If they didn't stop staring at her, she was going to leave as her sister had just done.

Becky had watched them slip out of the room without a word to anyone. They'd been hand in hand, which had to be a good sign, surely.

Hopefully they were fixing whatever was wrong, and she felt relief that she felt nothing but warm, sisterly feelings for both of them, and also a pang of guilt because in normal circumstances she would have known something was wrong in Rosie's life and she would have been there for her.

It hadn't crossed her mind that while she was staying away, her sister had been in trouble. Her sister had needed her. She'd assumed that she and Declan were living in wedded bliss.

Still, that was for later. Right now she had problems of her own.

Her own spontaneous announcement had led to consequences she hadn't foreseen. Fixing the mess she'd got herself into wasn't going to be easy, and would involve hurting people

269

she loved, including Will's mother, whose unbridled delight in the situation was uncomfortable to witness.

She could see her, huddled with her own mother and grandmother and she had no doubt who they were talking about.

Becky hated being the focus of attention and right now she and Will were definitely the focus.

"You're tense," Will said and she flicked her gaze to their parents.

"Can you blame me? They're gossiping. I can see it from here. What are we going to do?"

He took her hand and squeezed it. "We're going to join them."

"Are you mad?"

"No. The way I see it, if we join them, at least they can't talk about us behind our backs."

They crossed the room and Will kept a firm hold on Becky's hand.

"You two look as if you're having fun." Audrey beamed at them and Becky decided that Will's mother was the one person who might give her grandmother a run for her money in terms of tactlessness. They'd obviously been dipped in the same gene pool.

"It's good to have a chance to catch up with everyone," Will said calmly and his mother smiled.

"I'm just glad it's all finally out in the open."

Out in the open?

Will sighed. "Mum—"

"We used to talk about it," Audrey was saying, "Didn't we, Jenny?"

"Talk about what?" Her mother sent Becky an apologetic glance. She looked distinctly uncomfortable.

"Becky and Will. When they were growing up, we used to say how perfect they'd be together."

What?

270

Becky gaped at her mother in disbelief and saw her blush furiously.

"Well, obviously we were only having fun. We weren't serious."

"I was serious! So were you!" Audrey laughed and nudged her. "You were worried that the two of them were such close friends and so comfortable together they might not notice that they had deeper feelings."

Her mother had thought that?

She'd never said a word to Becky. Never tried to matchmake or encourage their relationship in any way. She'd never commented on Becky's relationships at all, and Becky had always been grateful for that because her relationships had mostly been brief and unsatisfactory and definitely not something she wanted to put under the spotlight.

But it seemed that hadn't stopped her mother from conjuring up her own scenarios.

The thought of her mother and Audrey enjoying a coffee together while discussing her and Will made her want to bolt from the room.

She was contemplating doing just that when she felt Will's hand rest on her back, firm and reassuring.

"We'll leave you to your reminiscing," he said. "It's Christmas. Becky and I are going to dance."

Dance? Was he kidding? And what did Christmas have to do with anything?

True, other people were dancing (and she might never forget the sight of Mrs Everly using tinsel in place of a feather boa), but Becky didn't dance.

"I don't—"

"Tonight you do."

"Off you go, the pair of you!" Audrey waved them away, not even pretending to be subtle in her approach. "We can see you're struggling to keep your hands off each other."

Becky chose the lesser of two evils and let Will tug her into the middle of the room.

"I hope this idea of yours turns out better than the last one," she muttered. "Joining them was *not* a good idea."

"Agreed. Sorry about that."

"I'm not sure if dancing is the frying pan or the fire," she said, "but just remember I really don't dance, so if you're not careful you might spend Christmas wishing you'd specialized in broken bones rather than hearts."

He smiled and pulled her against him, picking up the rhythm of the music. "I know you don't like dancing. But I thought you'd prefer this option to listening to my mother planning our wedding."

She looked up at him in despair. "I had no idea my stupid announcement would escalate in this way. They're unstoppable. It's horrific. *Now* can I dig a hole and lie down in it?"

"No." He steered her to the left to avoid colliding with someone. "It's below freezing out there and the ground is too hard to dig. Do you know how many people have heart attacks from clearing snow in low temperatures?"

In other circumstances she would have laughed and they would have had a fun conversation about statistics, but she was beyond smiling. "This is *awful*. Do you think they've really been talking about us for all these years?"

"I don't know, and it doesn't matter. It doesn't change anything." His hold on her tightened. "What they want, or don't want, is of no relevance to us."

"Easy for you to say. When I break up with you, they're going to hate me."

"That's not going to happen."

What was he talking about? Of course it was going to happen.

"Also they'll assume I've gone crazy." She rested her hand on his shoulder and felt the curve of hard muscle under her palm.

She kept thinking of the moment the night before when he'd emerged from the shower and the image was so distracting she missed his next question. "Sorry? Did you say something?"

"Why will they think you're crazy?"

"Isn't it obvious? Because no woman with a brain would—" She stopped, and felt her cheeks heat.

He raised an eyebrow, waiting. "No woman with a brain would—?"

"Be in a relationship one minute, and break up the next," she said lamely.

"Right."

He watched her for a moment, his gaze lingering on her flushed face, and she kept thinking about that kiss and hoping deep down that he might find a reason to do it again. And thinking about the kiss made her think of other things and suddenly she could picture them together, and she knew exactly how it would feel.

She had a horrible feeling he could read her mind and to cover the awkward moment she tried to spin him closer to the Christmas tree. Unfortunately Percy chose that same moment to join them on the dance floor, and he had less of a clue about dancing than she did. He inserted himself between them and Becky stumbled. She would have lost her balance if Will hadn't anchored her firmly against him.

She dug her fingers into his shoulder, conscious of the hard press of his body against hers. "Oops, sorry."

"No problem. You caught me by surprise."

She couldn't catch her breath. "I did warn you about my dancing."

"You did." He held her tightly. "Although I think Percy takes the blame for that particular move. He seems to think it's his turn to dance with you."

"The dogtrot is his favourite dance, didn't you know? It's

the canine version of the foxtrot." She was desperately trying to ease the tension and maybe she succeeded a little because Will laughed.

"I'd like to see that, but I claimed you first so he's going to have to wait in line."

I claimed you first.

She felt a surge of heat and a delicious tightening low in her pelvis, all of which was inappropriate given the reality of their situation. Pretending to lust after each other was one thing. Actually lusting was something else entirely. She felt as if she'd broken an unspoken rule. Crossed a line.

Aware of just how physically close they were, she tried to ease away from him, but he pulled her back, anchoring her body to his.

Why was he holding her so tightly? And then she realised that he was behaving like her lover, which was the role she'd cast him in. He was playing his part. He was doing it to help her. She should be grateful. Instead she felt hot and unsettled. This was a romantic thing to do and she didn't think of herself as a romantic person. She felt like someone who had been given a part she hadn't auditioned for.

Normally she hated dancing because it highlighted how uncoordinated she was, but with Will for some reason she had no problems. His movements were smooth and assured, his hold on her secure. It was probably because he kept her welded against him that she had no opportunity to take a wrong step or move in the wrong direction.

She was aware of the hard pressure of his body against hers and she realised that she wasn't the only one who was aroused.

The hum of conversation and the notes of the music slid into the background and for a moment it was just the two of them, everything around them forgotten except for the twinkle of fairy lights and the soft glow of the Christmas tree.

She was painfully conscious of the warmth of his hand on her back and the hot flare of desire low in her belly.

She'd never thought of dancing as particularly erotic (at least not when she was doing it), but with Will it felt less like a dance and more like a prelude to something. And she wanted that something more than she'd ever wanted anything. She wanted *him*.

The realisation slammed into her, leaving her breathless.

Will.

When he'd agreed to go along with her spontaneous announcement, she'd been grateful. She'd failed to anticipate how well he'd play the part, or the depth of her response.

How could she feel this way about him? They'd been friends for all their lives. She'd spent so much time with him. She'd helped paint his kitchen. She'd planted up half his garden. They'd met up in wine bars and restaurants. They'd walked along the river together in sunshine and rain. They'd kissed hundreds of times over the years, but they'd never *kissed* until today. She'd known him forever and yet right now she felt as if she didn't know him at all. Her body and mind were reshaping everything she knew and felt.

Deeply unsettled, she tried to rationalize the way she was feeling. Will was attractive, there was no doubt about that. She saw the way women looked at him when he walked into a room. The lingering glances when they went for long walks together.

Her reaction was just a logical, physical response, that was all, and no doubt so was his.

"So how are you feeling?" He murmured the words into her ear. "We haven't had a chance to talk properly. Are you finding it difficult?"

"Difficult?" Yes, it was difficult. She couldn't think when he was this close. Her usually sharp mind had softened and blurred. Her concentration was severely impaired.

"Seeing Declan after all this time. You were dreading this moment. You've been avoiding family gatherings."

Declan?

He was asking her about Declan?

She'd barely given Declan a second thought since the moment Will had kissed her, and hearing his name now was disorientating.

What did that say about her? Ever since the day of the wedding she'd believed she was in love with Declan, but now she couldn't access those feelings. Where had they gone? What had happened?

"I—it hasn't been difficult. Thanks to you." She lifted her gaze to his, expecting him to smile and say *no problem*, or something similar. Instead he held her gaze and they exchanged a long look, the attraction between them a palpable, living thing.

And she was engulfed in a delicious confusion. Was he still pretending? Was that intense look in his eyes for the benefit of the people watching? She had no idea.

Her heart was thudding so hard she was sure he must be able to feel every beat. She hoped her reaction wasn't obvious. She didn't want to give their parents any more fodder for their gossip.

"I don't suppose you feel like getting out of here?" His voice was rough and soft. "I'm finding the scrutiny a little wearing. I'm sure you are too."

She glanced across the room and saw her grandmother and Audrey watching them.

And she had a feeling that this time she'd really given them something to talk about. They'd probably been able to feel the heat and chemistry from across the room.

Over by the door her mother was in deep conversation with her father, both of them smiling, as if they were celebrating something.

Were they talking about her? Thinking about her? Planning her future?

She wasn't looking forward to the conversations that were no doubt going to come her way.

"You're right, we should get out of here. Should we tell people we're leaving?"

"No." His answer was clipped. Brief. As if other people were the last thing on his mind. Without letting go of her hand, he led her out of the room to the stairs and this time she didn't look left or right because she didn't want to know who was watching them leave or imagine the level of speculation.

And anyway now she had something else to think about, something more immediate and pressing. Sharing a room.

She kept telling herself that this was no different from the night before, when they'd shared a bed in the hotel. But it felt different. It felt as if everything had ratcheted up several notches.

Earlier in the day when she'd been unpacking and wrapping presents, Will had disappeared home for an hour and returned with a small suitcase which he'd stowed in her bedroom. She stared at that case while she was getting ready for the party, its presence in her bedroom a glaring reminder of the mess she'd managed to create.

And she no longer knew what was fake and what was real, and she truly had no idea how Will was feeling so when they reached the door of her bedroom she stopped.

The moment they stepped through that doorway the pretence would end. No more dancing. No more long looks. No more people watching. Stepping through the door meant stepping back into reality. Which was maybe why she hesitated.

She had her hand on the door handle when she heard voices on the stairs.

Before she even had time to react, Will turned her to face

him, slid his hand behind her head and lowered his mouth to hers.

Excitement engulfed her in a whoosh, and she melted against him, grateful to whoever it was who had chosen to use the stairs at that moment.

She heard the slam of a door in the distance and understood dimly that he was doing this for someone else's benefit, but she didn't care about that. She only cared that he was kissing her again and that it felt every bit as good as it had the first time.

She clung to the front of his shirt and he nudged her gently into the bedroom and shouldered the door closed behind them.

She expected him to immediately release her, but he didn't. He kept kissing her, his hand in her hair, locking her mouth against his and she thought that if all she did for the rest of her life was kiss Will then it would have been a life well spent.

He shifted his hold on her and she wrapped her arms around his neck, off balance both physically and emotionally. She'd learned how to keep her emotions and senses under control, locked inside, but now there was no containing them.

But then she remembered that he was doing this for her. To help her out.

Harnessing all her willpower she eased her mouth away from his.

"Do you think they've put a camera in this room? Are they watching through the keyhole?"

"I don't know, and I don't care."

She closed her eyes as his mouth brushed the tender skin of her jaw and then her neck. "All I'm saying is, you don't have to do this."

He paused long enough to speak. "Do I look as if I'm being coerced?"

"Will—"

"Forget them, Becks. Forget all of them. What do you want?

Should we stop?" His mouth was so close to hers she couldn't focus. "Is that what you want?"

He was asking her to make a choice. To decide. No more acting. No more fake.

"No. I don't want to stop." Of course she should be asking herself why. A tiny part of her knew that this was just going to make a complicated situation even more complicated, but she didn't care. Her need for him overwhelmed everything.

She'd known him her whole life, but this was a different Will. He felt familiar and yet at the same time deliciously un-familiar. His kiss was hot and hungry, the brush of his fingers slow and deliberate as he touched her jaw and then her throat.

She was consumed by a raw and visceral longing and so was he. She felt it in his touch and tasted it on his kisses. Her knees felt wobbly as he urged her back to the bed and gave up sup-porting her altogether as he stripped off her clothes.

She tumbled back onto the soft covers of her bed, her fingers divesting him of his shirt and then his belt, his hands removing their underwear, their movements uneven and urgent. And then there was nothing but heat and urgency and an intimacy that she knew was going to change everything. With every brush of his fingers and touch of his mouth he reshaped their relationship and she did the same, and during those secret steamy moments in the semidarkness of her room she discovered new things about him but also new things about herself.

And afterwards, when all the lines between them had been blurred or redrawn, she lay with her eyes closed, reluctant to open them because her eyelids formed the only barrier between her and the real world. She didn't want to step back into reality. The real world meant confronting what had happened, making decisions, thinking about other people, thinking about what was right. The real world meant stress and pressure and expectation.

For a short time she'd done what had felt right, and she'd done it just because it had felt right and for no other reason.

What had started as fake had become real, or maybe it had always been real but she'd refused to see it. She'd slotted him firmly into the friend box because he was an important part of her life and she wanted it to stay that way. Friendship had a longevity that didn't always come with romantic relationships.

How could she ever have thought she was in love with Declan? Her feelings for him were a pale, insignificant shadow of what she felt for Will.

She *loved* Will, and this time there was no doubt. No confusion. No question about what she was feeling. She'd never been so sure of anything in her life. And understanding that made everything clearer.

She could see now that it had never been about Declan. It wasn't losing Declan that had shaken her that day of the wedding, it was losing Rosie. Her twin. The entire emotional landscape of her life had changed and she hadn't been able to decipher her feelings.

But she was clear about her feelings now.

Her heart, her soul, all of her belonged to the man lying next to her.

She didn't regret what they'd shared. Not for a moment was she regretting her choices, but she was under no illusion as to what had just happened under the soft sparkle of Christmas lights. Yes, they were lovers, but she knew that for him at least it changed nothing. It was complicated, but in some ways not at all complicated. For him their night together had been no more than a surrender to physical chemistry, a union of two people who'd made a choice and knew exactly what they were doing. What they were giving. And she wasn't going to pretend otherwise. She wasn't going to let herself think of fairy tales or happy endings, because in the delicious blur of memory, which she knew she'd relive over and over again, there was one thing she couldn't ignore. He hadn't said *I love you*. Through the whole wild, desperate encounter where he'd whispered words against her mouth, he hadn't said anything that might indicate that his feelings had changed. The chemistry between them was honest and real, but he hadn't pretended even for a moment that it was anything more. In their moments of deepest intimacy, he hadn't spoken those words even though at one point she'd willed him to.

And now what?

She wanted to stay here, pressed against his warmth, wrapped tightly by the memories of the love they'd shared.

Tomorrow was Christmas Eve, but for once she didn't want Christmas to come. It was going to be hard to pretend that nothing had changed, and yet that was what she had to do.

She'd play the game, hold his hand, smile into his eyes and act like a woman in love, and that part would be easy because it was real.

And when the time came to let him go, she'd play her part as agreed. She'd let her heart break privately, and hope that all his experience with that particular part of the human body didn't give him extra insight into her feelings.

The irony of the situation hadn't escaped her.

She'd pretended that she was with Will to avoid complication. She hadn't anticipated that it would make things a thousand times worse.

But she wasn't going to think about that now.

She was going to keep her eyes closed for a little longer.

23

Jenny

Jenny was up early on Christmas Eve. Despite her reassuring conversation with Martin she'd barely slept, anxious thoughts racing through her mind. Jamie (had he rushed into this marriage and was it going to crumble in time?). Becky (was it real?). Rosie (what exactly was the problem between her and Declan?). Martin (would he be able to adjust to retirement and what if he couldn't?). Why was it that worries seemed to grow and feel insurmountable in the depths of the night? A problem that niggled at two in the afternoon could feel like the end of the world at two in the morning. And why was it that she still worried about her children even though they were adults and had been making their own decisions for a long time?

Martin had reminded her that he shared the worry with her but that statement had provided little comfort in the dregs of the night when she was wide awake and worrying and he was fast asleep and clearly not worrying at all. Then, at least, she'd held the weight of it and it had pressed on her until she was hardly able to breathe.

She'd almost kicked him awake and said *it's your turn to worry now, I'm done*, but she wasn't selfish enough to do that, and anyway she didn't trust him to worry properly and give all the problems and potential problems his full attention.

And now it was Christmas Eve. This was usually her favourite day, when all the fun of Christmas still lay ahead. Normally they bundled up after breakfast and all went for a family walk on the beach, but after the chaos of the night before she wasn't sure that would happen.

She checked the living room, grateful to Audrey, who had stayed to help her clear up after the rest of the guests had left. Thanks to her friend, and also to Hayley, the place was immaculate and ready for them to enjoy Christmas.

She walked into the kitchen and flicked on the lights. Not just the main lights, but the fairy lights and the tiny glowing Christmas trees she'd bought, and the pinecone garland that she'd strung along the tops of the cupboards, and which Martin had already managed to pull off twice by opening the doors too violently. He'd muttered *there's too much Christmas in this house* as he'd untangled himself from fake greenery, but she didn't agree with him.

The room looked cosy, and she stood for a moment and absorbed the warmth of it, feeling it lighten her mood. Maybe at night she should wrap herself in fairy lights and switch them on whenever she had dark thoughts. It made her think of the nightlight she'd bought Jamie when he was three years old and going through a phase of being afraid of the dark. It had projected stars onto the ceiling and she'd lain on her back on the bed next to Jamie and together they'd watched the stars swirl above them and he'd forgotten about monsters and dark corners and menace and focused instead on the light.

That was what she needed to do.

Maybe she wouldn't take everything down after Christmas. Maybe she'd leave a few lights to brighten the dark days of January.

She made herself a cup of coffee and drank it while gazing at the snow-covered garden. The fresh fall of snow overnight had smoothed out footprints and provided the perfect winter backdrop, dazzling under bright sunshine and blue skies. She knew it would be cold out there. The sort of cold that would numb faces and fingers within minutes. The sort of cold that made you want to rush back to the house for hot chocolate or homemade soup.

A white Christmas. That was the one part of her planning for the perfect Christmas that she hadn't been able to control, but for once the weather had delivered.

She heard footsteps and turned, the mug clasped in her hands.

"Hey, Mum." Jamie wandered in, sleepy eyed, his hair damp from the shower and his feet bare.

He was a grown man and a respected doctor but sometimes she caught a glimpse of the teenager he'd once been and, weirdly, the toddler. It was as if the whole of his life was stored in her head like a photo album for her to flick through. Jamie, aged two, with ice cream on his face. Aged six, covered in mud where he'd ridden his bike through a puddle. Aged fifteen, with red eyes because he liked a girl who didn't like him back.

And now. A man. Married.

"It's freezing, Jamie. Don't you own socks?"

"I couldn't find any and didn't want to wake Hayley. And it's toasty warm in here." He gave her a quick hug. "Brilliant party last night. Thanks for arranging that. You're the best."

"I enjoyed it. It was fun getting everyone together. I didn't expect to see you this early."

He shrugged and yawned. "I knew you'd be down here. Thought we could have a chat. Christmas has been a bit chaotic so far."

Chaotic? That was one word for it. She had others in mind but she kept them to herself because she sensed he wanted to talk about something. Unlike Becky, who never wanted to talk about anything, and Rosie, who wanted to talk about everything all the time, Jamie often liked to talk things through but did so at his own pace. He picked his moment, and she was expected to recognize the moment.

And now she was glad she'd chosen to come downstairs early. "Coffee?"

"Yes, but I'll make it. You've worked hard enough." He grabbed a mug and made himself a coffee while she watched and waited.

"Hayley seemed to be enjoying herself last night."

"Yeah." He wiped up the mess he'd made. "She finally relaxed a bit. She's been trying so hard to do and say the right thing. It's a relief to finally see her being more herself."

Jenny felt a pang of sympathy for Hayley. "It must be difficult being parachuted into someone's big, noisy family. Particularly if you're not used to it."

"Yes. I underestimated how stressful it would be. And I made the whole thing worse."

"In what way?"

"Because I should have told you before, instead of making a dramatic announcement. I feel bad." He sent her a sheepish look and put his coffee down on the side. "I'm glad to catch you on your own because I wanted to say sorry."

"To me? For what?"

"For not telling you we were married. I thought it was best, but I can see now it was the wrong decision. And Hayley really wanted to tell you, so don't blame her. I was the one who wanted to wait until we were face-to-face. And that made it hurtful for you and even more stressful for her."

He'd always owned his actions. At eight years old when he'd broken one of her vases while throwing a ball to his sisters in the living room, he'd never tried to pass the blame.

"I'm not blaming Hayley. I'm not blaming anyone."

"But I hurt your feelings. Will you forgive me?"

She looked at him and her chest ached. Didn't he know that when it was your child, you'd forgive anything? Every transgression. Every thoughtless act.

She put her coffee down, wrapped her arms around him and gave him a hug, as she had when he was six years old. "There's nothing to forgive. You did what you felt was right and I understand. Don't think about it again."

"I love her, Mum."

There was a pressure in her throat and she held him close. "I know you do. I can see that. And she loves you right back. And I'm glad." And she was glad. She cleared her throat and stepped back, retrieving her coffee from the side.

"I wasn't expecting it to happen. Wasn't expecting to meet anyone. To fall in love. I've been careful since—" He broke off and she nodded.

"I know. I was worried you might be a little too careful and miss out."

He took his coffee to the table and sat down, legs outstretched. "She's brave. Every single person in her life has let her down, but for some reason she has chosen to trust me."

"She's obviously a good judge of character."

And a lucky woman.

Did every mother think that? Yes, probably, but in this case she knew it to be true.

He rubbed his finger over a dent in the table.

She thought of all the times she'd seen him sitting in that exact spot. As a toddler, chomping on fingers of toast. As a teenager, doing his homework. A medical student, studying for his finals.

That table had witnessed all the different stages of their family life.

She felt a wave of nostalgia but pushed it away.

Instead of feeling sad for the years that had passed, you had to be excited for the years that hopefully lay ahead. You had to keep moving forward.

She pushed aside the emotion and kept the conversation factual. "Will you stay in Edinburgh?"

"Yes. I've turned our spare bedroom into a studio/office for her so she can work from there."

"She won't mind being in one place?"

"No. It's what she wants. Her choice." He smiled and finished his coffee. "We'll stay in my apartment for now and then maybe move to something bigger at some point. We'd love a garden. We both want a dog, and that should work as Hayley will be able to work from home."

She imagined the two of them planning together, whispering into the night as they plotted out their future and she remembered that she and Martin had done the same when they were first married.

They'd expected life to accommodate their plans, and for the most part they'd been lucky.

By the time she was Jamie's age she'd already had three children. She'd looked at her parents and been unable to imagine ever being that age, and now here she was—close to the age they'd been back then. Was it strange that on the inside she felt no more than her thirtysomething self? She'd aged on the outside, but not on the inside.

Occasionally she felt a twinge of anxiety about growing older and the challenges that might bring, but then she remembered all the patients she'd cared for whose lives had been cut short, people whose life plans had been dented or decimated, and it reminded her to feel grateful that she was still here.

Occasionally you had to ignore the thoughts in your head or at least refuse to engage with them. It was like having biscuits in the house. Just because they were there didn't mean you had to eat them. Unpleasant thoughts were the same.

They could be there, but you could choose to ignore them. Instead she focused on enjoying the things that made her happy. Seeing family, cooking, walking Percy on the beach, chatting with friends, and reading. Some people might have considered those to be small things, but Jenny knew they were the big things.

And right now her focus was on enjoying this family Christmas, in whatever shape her family presented itself.

"Have you had a chance to have a proper catch up with your sisters?" She asked the question casually, feeling guilty for trying to extract information about his siblings.

"Which one in particular are you worried about?"

She sighed. He knew her as well as she knew him. "Both of them. Did you know about Becky and Will?"

"No, but that doesn't mean anything. Haven't seen either of them in a while. We're at opposite ends of the country and our paths haven't collided. But it makes sense."

Did it? She wanted to ask if he thought the whole thing was a pretence, but she decided that wouldn't be wise. "You think it's serious?"

"I'm sure it is. There is no way they would have announced it if not. You know what Becky is like. I always thought they'd be good together. Wasn't sure they'd ever see it themselves though. Neither of them seemed able to look beyond friendship. You must be pleased—" He stood up and grabbed the tin where she'd stored the mince pies. "You always used to say that Will spent so much time here when we were kids that he felt like another member of the family."

"Yes." She had said that. And now she didn't know what to think.

She'd been so sure that Will and Becky had been faking their relationship, but watching them on the dance floor the night before she'd almost revised her opinion.

She could still feel the sharp pain as Audrey had dug her in the ribs with her elbow. *Do you see that?*

Jenny had seen it. Everyone had seen it. Even Martin had raised a questioning eyebrow in her direction. And then the pair of them had disappeared.

And so far this morning there had been no sign of them.

Jamie ate a mince pie, the pastry crumbling onto the table. "Maybe they will have a big summer wedding. Compensate for your eldest eloping. I'm kidding. We both know Becky would hate a big wedding."

"Wedding? Even if they are really together, dating is a long way from marriage. Jamie, you're not seriously eating mince pies for breakfast?"

"No. This is an early morning snack." Jamie pulled two more from the tin and sealed the lid again. "What do you mean, if they're together?"

"Nothing. I just wasn't sure how serious it is, that's all. Don't eat any more. I'm making a big Christmas Eve breakfast." Some things never changed, she thought, and one of those things was how much her children could eat.

"Have you ever known me to refuse breakfast?" He glanced up as the door opened. "Morning, Granny."

And that, Jenny thought, was the end of her quiet conversation with Jamie.

"Did you sleep well? Is anyone else awake?" She pulled out a chair for her mother. "Any sign of Rosie or Becky?"

"I'm the only one up. Your dad is still asleep, so I left him. I thought maybe a lie-in might help him structure his thoughts for his book. No sign of Rosie or Declan, and after what I witnessed last night I don't suppose we'll be seeing Becky and Will any time soon."

"What did you see, Granny? Share." Jamie stood up and made his grandmother a cup of tea.

"They were kissing. I didn't know it was possible for two people to kiss for that long without coming up for air. Thank you, dear." She patted Jamie's arm gratefully as he put the tea in front of her.

"Did they know you were there?" Could the kiss have been a performance?

"They were still kissing when the bedroom door shut behind them, so even if it began that way it didn't end that way. They definitely weren't thinking about me."

Jamie sneaked another mince pie. "How do you know what happened once the door closed?"

"I might have paused outside their door as I was passing. Not for long of course. Just long enough to confirm that they were still kissing."

Jamie choked on the mince pie and Jenny thumped him on the back and then fetched him a glass of water.

She sent her mother a silencing look without any real hope that it would silence her. There were some things that were better off not voiced, but her mother had yet to discover that. She was one of those people who thought plain speaking was a virtue, a conviction Jenny had never shared. Sometimes she found herself holding her breath, willing her mother not to speak her mind.

"That's enough, Mum. Unless you were looking through the keyhole, I don't see how you could have drawn that conclusion."

"There are other ways of determining what is happening behind a closed door. Sounds, for a start."

"You're saying you had your ear pressed to Becky's door?"

"No. I just stood close, that's all. If they'd been doing it for my benefit they would have been laughing or whispering the moment the door was closed. At the very least there would have been conversation. There wasn't. Which confirmed that I was wrong in my suspicions."

Jamie finished the water. His eyes were watering but Jenny

wasn't sure if that was the coughing or the attempts to contain his laughter.

"Suspicions?"

"I thought for a short time yesterday that Becky and Will were faking their romance. But I was wrong."

Jenny wondered if her mother had been listening outside her and Martin's bedroom door. From now on she was going to communicate in written notes when her mother was staying.

"What made you think that?"

"Remember that time Becky covered for Rosie when she spilled blackcurrant juice on the sofa? She had the same look on her face yesterday when she announced that she was with Will. I thought to myself *blackcurrant juice*."

Jamie scooped up all the crumbs he'd dropped. "Do you speculate about all of us?"

"Of course, dear. I'm your grandmother." She made it sound as if it was part of the job description rather than a lifestyle choice.

Jamie leaned forward, intrigued. "So when I told you I had something to announce, what did you think it was?"

"I wasn't sure, but imagining the various options made for a very entertaining few days so thank you for that. I was relieved it was a wedding, and not something like an incurable disease or a sudden desire to emigrate to a far-off country, although the fact that you wanted a party to celebrate did offer up a few clues. And it's good that Rosie and Declan have sorted out whatever their problem was."

"That's enough, Mum," Jenny said quickly, removing the mince pie tin before Jamie could consume the lot. "You have to let the children lead their own lives and not interfere."

Her mother tilted her head. "Says the woman who made sure Becky and Will shared a room last night."

Jenny felt heat creep slowly up her neck. "That's because they said they were together. I was being hospitable."

"Of course you were. And so was I when I stopped to listen outside the bedroom. I needed to check they didn't need anything. But I decided they seemed to have everything they needed."

Jamie shook his head, thoroughly entertained. "You're appalling, Granny."

"I want my family to be happy," his grandmother said. "What's appalling about that? And when Becky joins us for breakfast, I'm confident she'll have a big smile on her face. All's well that ends well, as the saying goes."

Jenny made a mental note to be more discreet around her mother because if Becky figured out that everyone had been speculating, all was definitely not going to end well.

24

Rosie

Rosie was lying in bed thinking that if it weren't for the distance she felt from her sister this Christmas might just turn out to be the best ever, when her phone lit up with a message from Becky.

I need you! Meet me outside!

Surprise was followed by relief and she slid out of bed, careful not to wake Declan. Her relationship with her sister was the one black cloud hovering over her happiness. For their whole lives their thoughts had been synchronized, not in a weird, mythical *we're twins and can read each other's minds* way but in a *we know each other completely* way. And then suddenly that wasn't the case anymore and there were things Becky didn't know about her and things she didn't know about Becky. She'd watched helplessly as they'd drifted apart for reasons she didn't understand, then tried not to be hurt when it turned out that Becky was seeing Will and hadn't told her. But now Becky was reaching out to her. Messaging her spontaneously. Finally!

She dressed quickly in her warmest clothes, tiptoeing around the room so she didn't wake Declan, who was still asleep (which was hardly surprising given that they'd managed less than four hours of sleep the night before).

She closed the bedroom door carefully behind her and headed downstairs.

She heard Jamie's voice coming from the kitchen and was surprised he was awake so early after such a late night. He was obviously talking to their mother.

Not wanting to announce her presence, Rosie pulled on her coat and boots and ventured outside.

The cold air hit her in the face, waking her up.

Becky was pacing, her strides creating rows of footprints in the new snow that had fallen overnight. A look of relief crossed her face when she saw her sister.

"Thank goodness. I was afraid you'd be asleep or something."

"What's wrong?" Rosie wrapped her scarf around her neck. "Has something happened?"

"Yes, something has happened and I have no idea what to do." Becky stopped pacing and thrust her hands into her pockets. "What is *wrong* with me?"

Rosie waited, shivering, but Becky was staring across the snow to the beach.

"I—er—I don't know what's wrong with you. You have to give me more. Do you have a temperature? A sore throat?"

Becky shook her head. "I'm not ill. Why would you think I was ill?"

"Because you said—" Rosie shook her head. "Never mind. Why don't you tell me what has happened?" And she wished then that human beings weren't so complicated because if she'd understood that something was wrong earlier then maybe she could somehow have stopped it happening and protected her sister. Because that was what they did, wasn't it? They looked out for each other. When she was young, she'd felt sorry for all her friends who hadn't been put on earth with a twin sister. "Becky?"

Becky gave her a desperate look. "I slept with Will." The words rushed out of her and Rosie stared at her, confused by what her response was supposed to be to that not entirely unexpected revelation.

"Okay." She chose her words carefully, searching her sister's face for clues. "Well, given that you're together, I assume that's not the first time. So why—"

"It was the first time! That's the point. The problem." Becky sucked in air. "It was the first time."

"But you said the two of you were—" Rosie stopped. What was she missing? She was starting to feel her lack of sleep, and also the lack of proper conversations with her sister over the past months. There were gaps, and she was stumbling into them. "I'm so confused."

"So am I. That's why I messaged you. This wasn't supposed to happen."

"What, sex? You were going to have a relationship without sex?"

"No! I mean—yes—" Becky turned scarlet. "Sex wasn't part of the plan, that's all."

"Plan?"

"Agh." Becky covered her face with her hands. "It was supposed to be fake. A pretence. Just to get me through the whole awkwardness of Christmas. And suddenly the whole thing got weird, and now this."

"Fake?"

"Yes, fake." Becky let her hands drop. "Could you stop repeating everything I say?"

"If you could finish a sentence then yes, maybe." Rosie saw the misery in her sister's eyes and felt her frustration melt away. "Are you saying your relationship with Will isn't real?"

"It wasn't supposed to be real, but last night was definitely real. It was as real as it gets. And I thought it would be okay. It's not as if I'm the kind of person who spills her emotions over everyone, anyway. I had this whole plan about behaving as if nothing was wrong, nothing had changed, but it has. And I don't think I can do it." Becky's shoulders drooped. "I'm in love with him. Really in love this time."

"This time? Wait a minute—" Rosie was struggling to keep up. Her brain felt as if it was working in slow motion. "A moment ago you said it was fake. That you were pretending. What do you mean?"

Becky closed her eyes briefly. "I never intended to have this conversation. Promise you won't hate me?"

"You know I could never hate you. Why would you say a thing like that to me?"

"Because this whole thing has been a nightmare, and I've lost my sense of perspective." Becky rubbed her fingers over her forehead, trying to find the words. She shook her head. "This is so awkward."

"Becky—"

"Okay! That thing you said—"

"Thing?"

"About me being in love with Declan. You were sort of right, but also not right. It's true that for a while I thought I was in love with Declan, but—" she lifted a hand "—before you freak out let me assure you that I was wrong about that. There was never a point where I was in love with Declan. Turns out that seeing you get married was a very confusing time for me. Your wedding was like an earthquake in my life. It shook everything. My emotions were a mess. And I wasn't expecting that. I'm a pretty level person as you know and suddenly I was feeling far too many feelings. It was all feelings, feelings, feelings. Nightmare."

Rosie stared at her. "You—"

"Let me say it again just so there is no mistake. I'm not in love with Declan. And I never have been. I just thought I was. And frankly it was awful. The last few months have been awful. No fun at all."

Rosie stood for a moment, digesting everything her sister was saying.

"So that day at the wedding," she said slowly. "It wasn't shellfish."

"No. I had a bit of a meltdown. And you're going to ask me exactly what happened and honestly I don't really know. I was standing there, watching you exchange vows with Declan, and suddenly it was as if someone had dropped a bomb into the middle of my life. I hadn't really thought about it much before that moment, but when I saw him looking at you, and you looking at him, I felt as if I'd lost something. The most important thing in my life. And at that point I was very confused, and I thought it was seeing Declan marrying you. But now I see it wasn't that. It would have been the same whoever you'd married. You and I had always navigated life together, side by side, and suddenly you had someone else by your side, and I was happy for you, honestly, I really was, but I was also—" She swallowed hard. "Bereft. I felt as if part of me had been cut away. For the first time in my life I felt as if I was facing the world alone, and that was terrifying. I didn't know how I was going to get through life with half of me missing. But I only figured most of this out recently. Because I'm emotionally illiterate, as you know." Her voice cracked and Rosie felt her own throat thicken.

"Becky—"

"I panicked. In that moment I really, *really* didn't want him to marry you and it took all my willpower not to stop the whole wedding happening."

Rosie thought back to her wedding, remembering that exact moment Becky had described. Declan had looked at her as they'd said her vows and she'd never felt so close to anyone, so deeply connected. It had been such an intimate moment, she'd forgotten everyone around her, including her sister.

She'd had no idea that her sister had been suffering.

"So you escaped the moment the ceremony was over and locked yourself in the bathroom." There was an ache in her chest. "Why didn't you message me?"

"Because at that point I hadn't deciphered exactly what was wrong. And anyway, it was your wedding day. Also I don't deal with my problems by chatting about them, you know that. That's what you do. I go to the gym, or do some gaming and shoot zombies."

"I hate to think of you on your own." Rosie's vision was blurred and she touched her sister's arm. "I can't bear it."

"I wasn't on my own."

Rosie brushed tears away. "You weren't?"

"Will was there," Becky muttered. "He followed me. He saw how upset I was. Which, obviously, was a very uncomfortable moment. Because when you're feeling feelings, the last thing you need is someone else seeing you feeling feelings."

"Did he know why you were upset?"

"Yes, I told him. Unfortunately. Yet another humiliation to deal with. I told him everything, how seeing you getting married was killing me and how I thought I might be in love with Declan because seeing him marrying you made me feel so ill. And I was mortified by the whole thing. I hated myself for feeling that way."

"And what did Will say?"

"He mostly listened. You know Will—he's good at that. And he gave me a hug and helped wipe mascara off my face. And he said something that at the time I dismissed—" Becky frowned, remembering. "He said 'are you sure this is about Declan?' And I asked him what he meant, and he said that it must be hard seeing your twin sister getting married. And I said, well yes, of course it was, but it was because of Declan. My feelings for him were like a huge wedge between us."

Rosie listened, ignoring the cold air and the shimmer of light on the surface of the snow. "This is why you stayed away from me. From us."

"Yes, although that was a crazy thing to do because I missed you so much."

"And why you changed your job?"

"Yes. Also crazy. I hate my new job."

Rosie thought about it, the pieces gradually falling into place. "Why didn't you talk to me about all this? Instead of staying away, why didn't you talk to me?"

"Because the words *by the way, I think I might love your husband* don't make for an easy conversation starter?"

"And you don't love him? You're sure?"

"Never been more sure of anything."

Rosie groaned and pulled her into a hug. "I'm so relieved. So unbelievably relieved."

"Well, obviously." Becky patted her shoulder, her voice rough. "We're close, but being in love with the same man would definitely cross a line. Although just for the record, even if I did love him, I'd never do anything to stand in the way of your happiness."

Rosie pulled away, thinking for the millionth time how much she'd missed her sister. "That's not why I'm relieved. I'm relieved because for a brief but horrible moment when you walked through the door yesterday and you and Declan were laughing together, I really was afraid that I'd inadvertently got in the way of *your* happiness."

"No. Never thought of him that way until the day of your wedding. We were just great friends, that's all. And as for what happened at the wedding—Will was right. It was never about Declan. It was about watching you get married. I felt as if I was losing you, and it was crushing. I hadn't expected it to affect me that way and I couldn't decipher my own feelings. I love you more than anyone, so how could I begrudge you the happiness I saw on your face that day? What sort of person does that make me?"

"The sort of person who is lucky enough to have a twin sister."

Becky brushed flakes of snow from Rosie's coat. "You have some explaining to do too. Yesterday when you blurted out that I was in love with him—did you really think that?"

Rosie stared across the sea, watching the waves foam as the wind caught the surface of the water. "Not really, but I'd managed to convince myself you were better suited to him than I was."

"Why? Why would you think that?"

"Because you and he have so much in common. Whereas he and I are really different."

Becky looked at her. "Different isn't a problem. You and I are different, and it has never been a problem for us."

"That's true. But you *have* to love me. I'm your twin. It's compulsory."

Becky grinned. "Not true. I don't have to love you, I just do. Because you're brilliant in every way. I've always been your biggest supporter."

Rosie felt the familiar stab of insecurity. "I sometimes wish I was more like you, that's all."

Becky stared at her. "Why would you want to be more like me? I'm not comfortable talking about my emotions. I'm terrible with people I don't know, but you walk into a room and light it up."

"But you're really smart."

"You're really smart too."

"I can't fix a computer when it crashes."

"I can't fix a dress when it tears or make a tutu." Becky's eyes narrowed. "This is why you thought I was in love with him? Because you have some misplaced idea that to be happy people need to be clones of each other?"

"Maybe. A little. Declan and I hit a bit of a difficult patch over the last few weeks—misunderstandings, nothing more, and I started wondering if I was just the wrong person for him. If he was wishing he'd married someone like you instead." Rosie gave Becky a quick summary of everything that had happened. Saying it all aloud, she was suddenly conscious of how many of her problems originated from paying too much attention to her overactive imagination.

Becky shook her head. "I didn't know you were having problems. Why didn't you talk to me? Now I feel even more terrible that I wasn't there for you."

"Don't blame yourself. I probably wouldn't have talked to you about it anyway."

"Of course you would. You talk about everything. I envy that."

"Not this." Rosie swallowed. "I couldn't talk about Declan. It was too—personal. It would have felt disloyal. The person I needed to talk to was him, but I didn't know how to get him to open up." She saw the flash of frustration in her sister's eyes.

"I can't believe Declan went into shutdown mode. When he started dating you, I told him *make sure you talk to her properly*. He assured me he would. Does this mean I have to kill him?"

"Please don't. I really like him." Rosie pushed her hands into her pockets. "And we're figuring out this whole communication challenge. Our different styles. I was at fault too. My creative brain spins scenarios that aren't there. I overthink everything."

"No, really? I didn't know that about you." Becky grinned then reached out and squeezed Rosie's arm. "He adores you. I don't know much, but I know that."

"Yes." Rosie thought about the night before and felt her cheeks grow hot. She couldn't stop thinking about the way he'd touched her. The things he'd said to her in the depths of the night as they'd explored and shared, their intimacy played out under the soft spill of silver light from the Christmas tree. "He does love me."

"And you need to stop thinking you're wrong for him. I can assure you Declan and I would drive each other crazy within two minutes."

"That's probably true." Rosie thought about it. "He squeezes the toothpaste tube from the middle."

Becky shuddered. "That's grounds for divorce in my book."

Rosie grinned. "And he never finishes a cup of tea. By the end of the day there will be six half-drunk cold mugs of tea around the place."

"He did the same thing in the office. Which confirms we would be a match made in hell. Although I think I already knew that."

"Which brings us to the next part of this catch-up," Rosie said. "Will. So your relationship started out fake, and now—?"

Becky groaned. "Now it's a horrible mess. Which sums up my whole romantic life. He stepped in to help me because he's a good friend. He did it for me. He acted a part."

Rosie thought about what she'd witnessed.

"Are you sure that's what it was? Because I saw the way he kissed you yesterday and that didn't look to me like a man who was acting a part. He looked like a man who couldn't keep his hands off you. Are you telling me that wasn't real? Because from where I was standing it looked real."

"The fact that he's a good kisser is real. The chemistry is real enough." Becky huddled deeper inside her coat, hiding her scarlet face. "Nothing else was."

"But last night—"

"We slept together. Blame the chemistry. Or the magic of Christmas. I don't know. It doesn't really matter. We're both consenting adults. It happens. Impulse. Spur of the moment."

Rosie tilted her head. "Will has never struck me as a guy at the mercy of his impulses. He has always been very cool and controlled. Which is actually very sexy."

"Okay, whatever, but we both know sex doesn't have to mean love."

Rosie studied her sister's expression and saw something she'd never seen before. "But you *do* love him." She wondered why she was even asking the question when the answer was so obvious.

"Yes." Becky gave her a helpless look, as if it was something she was just coming to terms with herself. "How did that happen? I've known Will forever. Last year I spent weeks at his place, helping to decorate his house. I didn't feel anything other than friendship. Or maybe I did. I wanted to punch his girlfriend for being—I don't know—his girlfriend, I suppose. That might have been a sign. How can I be so clueless about my own feelings?" She sounded so frustrated Rosie almost smiled.

"When did you work it out?"

"Last night, although I suppose if I'm honest I was having inappropriate thoughts when we shared a room on the way here. And I've never had inappropriate thoughts about Will before. It was unsettling."

"Really?" Rosie was curious. "Never?"

"No. Of course not. Why?"

"Because Will is smoking hot. Surely you noticed that."

"Well, I mean—he—" Becky swallowed. "No, I'm not sure I did. To me he has always just been Will."

Rosie's smile widened. "Will. Our brother's best friend. It's such a classic romance trope."

Becky made an impatient sound. "You do know that's fiction, right?"

"Doesn't mean it can't happen in real life. You are proof that it does. You're in love with him."

"Keep your voice down." Becky glanced nervously towards the house.

"Why so secretive?"

"Because this is all fake, remember? We're pretending. And when Christmas is over, we break up and that's it. At least, that's how it was supposed to be."

"But you don't want that anymore."

"No. But I can't tell him it's suddenly real for me." Becky shrugged. "I have to carry on pretending that I'm pretending. Can you imagine anything more confusing? It's enough to fry your brain. That's why I'm standing out here now. I decided I didn't want to be there when he woke up. It will be easier to keep up this charade if we're surrounded by people."

"Or for once in your life you could not hide your feelings and tell him exactly what you just told me."

"That I love him? That for me it's all real?" Becky looked appalled. "I can just imagine his reaction. He'd freak out and I'd die of embarrassment. I don't think so."

"I've never seen Will freak out about anything, and I can't imagine it happening. He's always cool and calm."

Becky wrapped her arms around herself, stamping her feet against the cold.

"I can't tell him. He's Jamie's best friend. He's my best friend, after you of course but you don't count. I don't want to ruin that. I still want to be able to help decorate his house and meet him for a drink after work. I don't want our relationship to be awkward and if I told him the truth, it would be awkward."

Rosie had never seen her sister so flustered. "So what are you going to do?"

"I'm going to keep doing what I usually do. Hide my feelings, keep going."

"Because that approach has worked so well for you in the past."

Becky ignored that. "And I'm going to get a new job because the one I'm in right now was a mistake. After Christmas I'm going to call some recruiters."

"If you want to give up your job you could always move in with Declan and me while you find another one. It would save on the rent and we have a spare room."

"Thanks. I couldn't do that to you."

"I'd like it. Not having you around has been painful. Strange. Not at all good."

"Really?"

"Yes, really. I missed you so much, and that was unexpected although it probably shouldn't have been. I think I was as shocked as it seems you were."

Becky nodded. "Turns out you and I knew everything about how to be together, and nothing about how to separate."

Rosie slid her arm into her sister's. "Fortunately, we don't have to learn that."

"But I have to get used to not being your number one person. I have to learn how to share you. I've never been that great at sharing."

Rosie grinned. "I know. It's a good thing we had different interests growing up, so you were never that interested in my gifts."

"Except for your chocolate."

"You and Jamie were as bad as each other."

Becky leaned her head on her shoulder. "How do I fall out of love with Will?"

"I don't know, but whatever happens I'm here for you and we're going to figure it out together." Rosie watched as a robin hopped onto the snow-covered hedge, its red breast providing a splash of red in a world that was white. "And for the next couple of days you don't have to worry about it. You're pretending to be in love with each other. No one has to know that for you it's real. It will be easy."

"Except when we're in private." Becky sighed. "He's probably awake by now. What am I going to say to him about last night?"

"You don't have to say anything. Just behave normally."

"Nothing about this situation is normal. And I don't know what to say to him when we're alone. And how do I handle the ending?" Becky gave a whimper of horror. "I don't even want to think about what happens when I break up with him. Both sets of parents will be horrified. I never should have pretended we were together, but I had no idea it was going to escalate like this. It's like a very bad romcom."

"A very good romcom! I can see it now—*A Merry Little Lie*."

"Oh, very festive."

They walked back to the house, arms linked.

"You're still my number one person, by the way." Rosie pushed open the front door. "You always will be. Just don't tell Declan that."

"Don't tell Declan what?" Declan was standing there, wearing his coat. "I was just coming to find you."

Rosie's heart lifted. "You were? Why?"

"Because I woke up and you were gone. I wanted to check everything was okay. In case—well, in case you wanted to talk about anything."

Becky grinned. "Who are you and what have you done with strong, silent Declan?" But she gave his arm a squeeze as she walked past him. "Good for you. Next thing we know you'll be drinking a whole mug of coffee and not leaving half of it."

Declan raised an eyebrow and turned back to Rosie. "What was that about?"

"Nothing. Nothing at all." She stood on tiptoe and kissed him. "Happy Christmas Eve. It's my favourite day."

25

Hayley

Hayley sat on the floor of the living room, helping Jamie to wrap presents.

"I've told everyone they're not allowed to come in until we open the door." He reached for a box and the large bag of wrapping paper that his mother had recycled from the year before. "This is the hard part. My grandmother insists on using the same paper as many times as possible. It gets stored in a bag and reused. Just make sure you've removed any previous tags that say 'from Becky to Rosie' or it gets very confusing. And when you get given a gift try not to rip the paper off in joyous abandon. Peel it carefully and don't tear it."

Hayley, who had been frugal for most of her life, thought that sounded entirely logical.

"I like the fact that you reuse everything. This is another family tradition?"

"One of the more annoying ones." He pulled out a sheet that seemed to have more holes than paper and rolled his eyes. "You see what I mean? What are we supposed to do with this? Wrap a Swiss cheese and hope the holes line up?"

She giggled and took it from him. "It's fine. I can cut round the holes and use it for the makeup we bought for Rosie."

"*You* bought." He watched as she neatly cut and wrapped, trimming edges and discarding old tape. "Okay, you're good at this. I should have predicted that."

"It's not rocket science, Jamie."

"It is if you didn't inherit the wrapping genes."

She placed Rosie's gift in the middle of a piece of newly trimmed paper. "There are genes that dictate your skill at wrapping?"

"I'm convinced of it. Rosie inherited them. Becky and I didn't. We don't need labels for our gifts. Just look at the ones trying to push their way out of their wrapping."

"Could you write a label, or is that another genetic deficiency?"

"Labels I can do." He jumped to his feet as someone opened the door. "Don't come in here! We're wrapping."

"Why couldn't you wrap in the bedroom?" Rosie's voice came through the gap in the door. "You've banned the whole family from the living room."

"I thought it would be festive for Hayley to wrap the presents under the tree."

"While the rest of us stand out in the hallway? Thanks a lot, Jamie. Now I know where your priorities lie."

"You've never been my priority, Rosie. You're the youngest child. Get to the back of the line."

"But I'm supposed to be playing the piano and singing carols with Granny."

"All the more reason for me to keep this door closed."

"*I hate having a sibling.*"

"I know. But you're going to love me when you see your Christmas present." Grinning, he leaned his weight against the door and closed it, ignoring his sister's protests.

"I bet Hayley bought the presents! I bet you didn't choose

a single thing." Rosie's voice was muffled as she banged on the door.

Jamie was laughing. "I chose Hayley, didn't I? She's my gift to me. And a great choice she was too. Now go away and don't try and come in again or I'll eat your chocolate."

Hayley watched this exchange with fascinated amusement. "I never imagined adult siblings could be so juvenile."

"Oh, keep watching. You haven't seen anything yet." He settled down next to her and fished more paper out of the bag. "This is the point where Rosie would normally have run to our parents and said 'Jamie is being mean to me.'"

Hayley trimmed and wrapped. "And what would happen then?"

"My mother would usually come to whichever room I was in and say 'Jamie, stop being mean to your sister.'"

"And did that work?" Hayley deftly tied a ribbon around a book they'd bought for Becky.

"No. But then Becky would come into my room and either thump me or do something to crash my laptop. She was a much more effective disciplinarian." He sat back on his heels. "Are we done?"

"I think so." She pushed the stack of gifts under the tree along with the others. "I wrapped your gifts before we left home."

"And I did the same with yours, although no doubt mine will be considerably less elegant." He leaned forward and kissed her. "How are you doing? Are you enjoying yourself?"

"Very much." And she was, except for the niggling insecurities that she couldn't shake off. What did Jenny think of her, really? She knew that in theory it shouldn't matter because the important relationship was between her and Jamie, but it *did* matter. She wanted to feel like part of the family. But she also knew that couldn't be rushed. It would take time.

"After lunch we usually go for a long family walk on the beach."

"Sounds good. With Percy?"

"Of course. He's the most important family member."

"Jamie?" His father's voice came through the doorway. "When you've finished wrapping, can you join your grandfather and I in the study? We're drafting a chapter on common skin conditions seen in primary care. I need your input."

Jamie glanced at Hayley, and she waved him away.

"Go! I need a cup of coffee after all that wrapping so I'm heading straight to the kitchen after I've cleared up here. I'll be fine."

Jamie kissed her briefly and left the room to join his father.

Having been kept out of the room for the past hour, Percy was delighted to be allowed back to his favorite place in front of the fire.

Hayley played with him for a while and then tidied up and made her way to the kitchen.

Jenny was on her own there, rinsing cranberries.

She glanced across as Hayley walked into the room. "Is the wrapping finished? Where's Jamie?"

"Jamie's working on the book. And the wrapping is done." She hesitated. "Can I do anything?"

"I'm making cranberry sauce for tomorrow." Jenny tipped the cranberries into a pan. "I've already squeezed the oranges. If you could grab the brown sugar from the cupboard over there, that would be great." She gestured and then wiped her hands on her apron.

Hayley opened the cupboard, located the sugar and was about to pass it to Jenny when a piece of paper caught her eye. It was tucked next to a large jar of homemade granola, and it had her name at the top of it.

She picked it up. It was a list, and the heading was *Perfect Christmas for Hayley*.

Jenny gave a little shriek and shot across the kitchen.

"You weren't supposed to see that!" She reached out to take

it and then let her hand drop. "Sorry. I've been keeping it hidden, but I checked it this morning and forgot to put it back."

"You made a list of things that would make a perfect Christmas?"

Jenny made a despairing gesture. "Yes, but—"

"A perfect Christmas for me?" She could see how awkward Jenny felt and maybe she should have let it drop, laughed it off, said something flippant, but she couldn't. Flippant was for small things that didn't matter, and this wasn't small. And it mattered.

"Jamie mentioned it when he called, that's all," Jenny said. "He told me how much you wanted a dream family Christmas. I wasn't sure what that involved so I watched a couple of movies and made notes."

"Notes?"

"I wanted everything to be perfect for you. I wrote down the things I thought we could reproduce, at least in the house. Sadly I can't conjure up shops selling gingerbread and candy canes and snowy villages with cobbled streets, which seems to be a staple of some of the movies I watched, but I managed other things. Extra trees. Extra lights. It was all supposed to look effortless and natural and now I've spoiled the illusion by leaving my scribbling lying around. It was supposed to be like one of Rosie's ballets—a performance where no one sees the workings behind the scenes."

But sometimes the workings were more important than the final performance, because the workings meant something.

Hayley felt a lump in her throat. "You did this for me?"

"Yes. I wanted you to feel at home. I wanted you to feel like part of the family." Jenny's shoulders slumped a little. "I wanted you to like us. Me."

And Hayley realised in that moment that she wasn't the only one who had been worried. Jenny had been worried too. And caring enough to make a list of things to make Hayley feel festive, and at home.

"Thank you. This is amazing. I can't believe you did this."
It was difficult to speak. "You made us—me—so welcome,
and then we gave you such a shock. I'm so sorry we didn't tell
you before we arrived. Don't blame Jamie. He did it for me."

"Don't think about it. I understand."

"But it hurt you—"

"A little maybe, but not for long, and families are full of these
tiny bruises. Cuts and scratches, that's all. They heal. They don't
damage the whole."

"You must think—"

"I think you're perfect, Hayley." Jenny reached out and took
her hands, squeezing them. "Just perfect."

"I'm so far from perfect."

Jenny smiled. "Well, that's good. If you were perfect,
it would be exhausting for the rest of us. Perhaps I should
have said that I think you're perfect for my son. He's a lucky
man. I'm looking forward to spending more time with you
and getting to know you." She hesitated. "We're your family too, now. I know you're both adults, but I'm always on
the end of a phone if you need a listening ear. And I love
Edinburgh. Perhaps I could drive up and meet you for lunch
occasionally."

"I'd love that. Jamie doesn't often have time off in the day
but—"

"I meant you," Jenny said. "You and I. We could spend some
time together. Get to know each other a little better."

"Oh." She imagined taking Jenny to the little café she'd discovered in the backstreets and catching up over coffee. "That
would be lovely."

"I'll try not to be like any of the stereotypes of mother-in-
law."

"I wouldn't even know what those are."

She'd arrived feeling like an outsider, hovering on the edges,
and now here she was gradually being folded into the family.

Any further conversation was interrupted by Martin, who walked into the room carrying another stack of papers.

"Right! I think we finally have a plan. A list of topics and chapters. Jamie helped us with the last part. Take a look and tell me what you think."

"Ah, the book. In this family, everything stops for the book." Jenny exchanged a glance with Hayley and took the papers from him. "Brian's Book." She looked at him. "That's Dad's final decision on the title?"

"No. But if we wait to find the right title, we're never going to write the book. Ignore that. Take a look at the contents." He sat down at the kitchen table and patted the chair next to him. "Think about the stuff we worried about as new parents."

Hayley left them to it and carried the sugar over to the cranberries that Jenny had already tipped into the pan.

"Oh Hayley, thank you!" Jenny glanced up at her. "The recipe is right there because I always forget the amount of sugar. Just throw it in the pan with the orange juice and heat it. I'll be there in a minute."

"Sorry—" Martin looked up. "Just leave it, Hayley. Jenny can do it in a minute. This won't take long."

"Hayley doesn't mind doing it. She's helping, Martin."

"She's a guest."

"She's not a guest, she's family. She can make cranberry sauce. That's what family does." She put her glasses on and read through the chapter list. "You have a chapter on menopause. Good. And what to do if your doctor doesn't take you seriously—I like that—"

Feeling a warmth she'd never felt before, Hayley turned back to the stove, leaving them to it.

She had cranberry sauce to make.

26

Becky

Becky's first encounter with Will was in the kitchen with the whole family gathered for breakfast.

He appeared in the doorway just as everyone was loading the table with food, so any possible awkwardness was lost in the general chaos.

His hair was damp from the shower and he wore jeans and a shirt that seemed to accentuate the blue of his eyes. Meeting his gaze across the room, Becky felt her heart flip and wondered how it had taken her so long to realise she was in love with him. How could she have missed something this big, that seemed to fill every part of her?

Will.

She was tempted to sprint across the room and hurl herself at him, the way Percy did when he saw someone he loved, but she managed to restrain herself. People often told Percy to get down and she didn't want that happening to her, particularly not in public. She was allowed to do it of course because she was supposed to be in love with Will, but now she was actually in love with Will she was confused about how to behave.

She knew her face was red and hoped no one was watching too closely. What was he thinking? Was he regretting last night? Was he wondering if she was reading more into it?

She needed to show him that she was fine with it all. That nothing had changed.

She put down the bowls she'd been holding and crossed the room to greet him, lifting herself onto her toes to kiss his cheek. It turned out to be a mistake because the moment her lips made contact with his freshly shaved jaw it triggered a memory of the night before when she'd done exactly the same, only they'd both been naked at the time. His arm curved round her and he gave her an intense, questioning look but she simply smiled up at him, pretending that she was pretending.

Then they joined the others at the table, their small private exchange eclipsed by multiple simultaneous conversations.

"These buns are fresh from the oven so don't burn yourselves," her mother said, placing them on a large plate in the middle of the table.

Delicious Christmas scents of cinnamon and spice wafted through the kitchen.

"It was a modern interpretation," her grandmother was saying to Rosie, "and I didn't like the costumes."

"One of my friends worked on that production." Rosie helped herself to a bun, blowing on it to cool it. "The choreography was spectacular."

Becky noticed that Rosie and Declan were sitting closer together than they had the day before. She suspected they were holding hands under the table.

On impulse she took Will's hand, allowing herself to touch him while she was still allowed. She wondered if he might pull away but instead he curled his fingers over hers, pressing her hand onto his thigh. The same thigh she'd seen naked the night before. The same thigh that had pressed up against hers.

"But they danced in sacks!" her grandmother said. "And the

set was a single black wall. Ballet is supposed to be beautiful. What's beautiful about a sack and a black wall?"

Rosie nibbled the edge of the bun. "It was edgy, Granny."

Her grandmother made a disparaging sound. "It was ugly, wasn't it, Brian?"

"The clue is 'Not genuine.' Anyone?" Her grandfather was absorbed with his crossword as usual and Phyllis poked him in the ribs.

"Brian?"

"What?" He looked up from the paper. "What did I miss? Oh, cinnamon buns. Now I know it's Christmas. You're wonderful cook, Jenny."

"These came from the supermarket," Jenny said, "but I was wonderful at heating them up."

Becky felt Will's thumb gently stroke her fingers. She didn't dare take a cinnamon bun in case she choked.

"I was telling Rosie about the ballet we saw," Phyllis said. "The one with everyone in sacks."

"Oh. Yes, that was ugly." Brian returned to his crossword. "The clue is 'Not genuine,'" he said to no one in particular, tapping his pencil on the paper.

"Fictitious," Martin said, adding a stack of sourdough toast to the table. "Jamie, are you ready with those eggs? Is there anything else anyone needs? If not, then tuck in."

Her grandfather shook his head. "It's only four letters."

"Mock." Jamie appeared at the table with a pan of freshly scrambled eggs and everyone served themselves. "Sham."

"Phony," Jenny said and then frowned. "No, that's five letters."

"Fake," Will said, and Becky felt her heart stop. Was it her imagination or had he put emphasis on the word? Maybe he was reminding her that none of this was real. As if she needed reminding.

She pulled her hand away from his and helped herself to a cinnamon bun.

Was it her imagination or was her mother looking at her a little too closely?

"Fake! That's it. Good lad." Brian filled in the letters with a flourish, protesting when Phyllis tugged the paper away from him.

"Enough! We have this every day of the week. Do we need to have it at Christmas too?"

"It keeps my brain agile."

"Your brain isn't going to wither away over one meal. And if you really want to exercise your brain you could finish writing your book. You know—that book you've been talking about for the past fifteen years."

"We are not talking about the book at breakfast." Jenny sat down and took a slice of toast and a spoonful of scrambled eggs.

"We've done a plan," her father said. "Haven't we, Martin?"

"We have. It's a good plan."

Percy sat down by Rosie's chair hopefully, tail wagging.

Rosie stroked his head. "Percy should have a Christmas treat."

"He's going for a long walk on the beach soon, with the entire family in attendance," Martin said. "That's a Christmas treat."

Becky was grateful for the chaos, grateful for her family, who were loud and noisy enough to ensure that no one was paying any one individual too much attention.

After breakfast Rosie helped her mother prepare a few dishes for Christmas lunch the following day, while Becky followed tradition and played Scrabble with her father. Will had excused himself to answer a call from the hospital about a complicated patient.

"So how's my girl?" Her dad studied his tiles and then played his first word. "How's the new job working out?"

If her mother had asked the question she might have prevaricated because she didn't want to worry her, but she was always honest with her dad. "It's not. It was a mistake."

"Oh?" He lifted his gaze to hers. "Anything you want to

talk about? Not that I know anything about your line of work of course, so I'm probably not much use to you."

Something in his tone caught her attention. "You're a lot of use, Dad."

He toyed with one of his letters, staring at the board. "It's okay to make a mistake, Becky. Knowing you, you're beating yourself up about it, but it's okay to get something wrong. And it's okay to change your mind. That's all part of life."

"I should have known."

"We don't always know how we're going to feel about something until it happens." He carefully placed his letters on the highest scoring option. "Life requires constant readjustment."

"That's true." She looked at him closely, wondering if he was talking about himself or her. "How's retirement? It must feel strange being able to put yourself first for once. Nice for us, though."

"What do you mean?"

"This is the first Christmas I can remember where you've been here for every meal and not rushing out to see someone in trouble. Also—" she placed her letters around his, her choice of word making him groan "—this is the first game of Scrabble that hasn't been interrupted. It's nice. Although I still maintain that you were using patients as an excuse because you knew that if you stayed, I'd beat you."

He frowned at his letters, concentrating. "I have horrible letters. Horrible. You probably will beat me. And yes, it is nice, although I'm still getting used to the slower pace of things."

She waited while he made his move, wincing at his high score. "So much for horrible letters. Are you and Mum going to travel? What are your plans?"

"We haven't made any yet. I need to do that. It has taken me a while to adjust."

"Well, as you're always telling me, that's okay. It's exciting. Great opportunity to do something new, that isn't medicine. You could do anything. Learn cross-country skiing. Go on a cookery course in Tuscany. Do a computer programming course." She scanned her letters, determined to outdo him.

"I suppose I could. First, I'm going to help Grandad write his book."

"That's good. We could get you both on social media. Two Wise Doctors, or something."

"Mm. Not sure I want to do that. You'd want me to dance or something."

"Dancing is good exercise." She put down her letters and he groaned.

"*Quixotic* on a triple word score? Becky!"

"I know. I'm heartless."

"I wouldn't describe you that way." He stared at his letters dolefully. "So—you and Will."

Oh no. Her dad never asked about her love life but today it seemed he was breaking with tradition for some reason. "Yeah."

"Audrey and your mother got a little overexcited at the party last night."

"Just a little."

"I expect that felt like pressure." He glanced at her. "Ignore them, Becky. You do what feels right for you."

She felt her throat swell with emotion. He wasn't interfering. He was telling her not to let anyone else interfere. "Thanks, Dad."

"I mean it. You don't make a decision to keep other people happy, Becky. And whatever you decide is good with us. We're always here for you, you know that."

She felt a heavy pressure in her chest. Where would she be without her family? She loved them so much, but she never said so. She wasn't like Rosie. Did they know?

"Dad—I—"

"I know." He reached across and patted her hand. "No need to say anything."

She wrestled with her emotions, watching as he made his move. "No! Please tell me you're not putting *wheeze* on a triple letter score."

"And that's me finished." He held up his hands. "What's the total? I think you'll find I've won. But if you want a rematch, that's fine with me."

"No! Playing with you dents my confidence."

"Go on. Just one more game, Becky."

It was all very familiar and comforting, but at that moment Will walked back into the room.

He tucked his phone back into his pocket. "Sorry about that. You know how it is, Martin."

"I do." Martin stood up. "And you're making me realise how good it feels not to constantly be on edge, waiting for those calls. For the first time ever I'm going to help Jenny in the kitchen. You two should relax for a while."

Relax? She'd never felt less relaxed in her life.

"I should probably help Mum, too," Becky said quickly, ignoring Will's raised eyebrow as she shot across the room to the door. "It's not fair for her to have to do everything."

She felt jumpy and nervous because she knew the conversation with Will couldn't be avoided forever.

Or maybe it could. Maybe it was going to be one of those things they'd never mention again.

After lunch, they joined the traditional family walk on the beach, and walked hand in hand, chatting to Jamie and Hayley, and Becky discovered that providing she didn't look at Will directly, it was perfectly possible to maintain the charade.

When Jamie had asked where they were living Becky said cheerfully that they were *mostly at Will's house*, and that they hadn't really given much thought to what their next steps were.

She was conscious of Rosie watching her closely and wondered, given Rosie's general inability to hide what she was feeling, whether telling her the truth might have been a mistake, but at the same time it felt good having her sister in her corner.

And the walk was one of her favorites. The vast empty beaches were something she missed when she was in London, and now she made the most of it, striding out with Will as Percy bounded ahead, enjoying the space.

It was cold, but the sky was a bright blue and the sun dazzling.

Everything was going well until they turned to go back to the house and Will caught her arm.

"You go ahead," he said to the others. "Becky and I want five minutes more to make the most of the fresh air and scenery. Living in London, we've missed this. And there are things we need to talk about."

Becky stiffened. You didn't need to be a genius to work out what those were. He wanted to check how she was feeling about the night before. He wanted to check she knew nothing had changed.

He wanted a conversation that was honest, no longer pretending, and she wasn't sure she could do that.

She gulped. "I should help in the kitchen."

"Everything is under control—" her mother waved her away "—you and Will enjoy yourselves. You both work so hard. You deserve some time together."

Rosie caught her sister's desperate look. "I could use some help wrapping my presents," she said, her lame attempt to help demolished by Jamie.

"What? You're much better at wrapping than Becky. You're the best wrapper in the family."

Out of excuses, Becky resigned herself to the fact that she was going to have to be alone with Will. And to be fair this was a conversation that needed to be had at some point, so that point might as well be now. He probably wanted to talk about how they should handle the breakup. She didn't pretend for a moment that what they'd shared the night before would have changed anything. Unless it had made him want to bring it forward.

"I'll come and find you when I'm back." She gave Rosie a weak smile and Rosie stepped forward and hugged her.

"I love you."

"For goodness' sake, Rosie, your sister is going for a walk, not a trip to the moon. You'll see her in half an hour." Tutting impatiently, her grandmother hustled Rosie away, leaving Becky alone with Will.

She'd never felt awkward with him before, but now she felt awkward. She kept thinking about the night before. The way he'd kissed her. The way he'd touched her.

"You don't need to keep avoiding me, Becks. Whatever is on your mind, you can say it to me."

If she said what was on her mind she was pretty confident that he'd faint with shock, or at least go striding after the rest of her family in a mild state of panic.

"I'm not avoiding you. It's Christmas. Always chaotic, in my house at least."

He watched her for a moment. "So the fact that you were gone when I woke up this morning—that wasn't you avoiding me?"

"No! I was up early and someone needed to walk Percy."

"Walk Percy. Right." He paused. "I'm going to ask you a question, Becks, and I want you to answer honestly. Do you regret last night?"

Regret?

"No, I don't regret it." That was easy to answer. "Don't worry about it. It's all good. Forget it."

He raised an eyebrow. "Forget it?"

"Well, obviously not *forget*, I mean it was great—" she didn't want to insult him "—but no point in making it more than it was. We'll call it what it was. Christmas chemistry."

"Christmas chemistry? And what is that exactly?"

"You know! Festive spirit. Peace and goodwill to all men."

"I don't recall us consuming any spirits, Christmas or otherwise. And I don't recall any other men being involved either."

She gave him a desperate look. "You know what I mean!"

"I don't know what you mean, Becks."

Why was he being like this? She was making it so easy for him to agree that they should just put last night behind them. Why wasn't he helping her?

"It doesn't matter." She'd never been so flustered. "Anyway, moving on from that, we need to talk about our breakup. Tell me how you want me to do it. I was thinking I could just say that the whole thing isn't working out, and it's my fault. What do you think?"

He thrust his hands into his pockets and stared out across the ocean. "I don't like that."

"Okay." She stared at his profile, trying to read him. "What if I say that spending all this time together at Christmas made me realise that I'm not the right person for you. You deserve better. Does that work for you?"

"No." He shook his head. "That doesn't work for me at all."

"Oh." She was thrown. "Okay, well tell me what does work for you, and I'll do it. Anything. You've been so great, Will. You helped me out of a really horrible situation, and I owe you. Whatever you need from me, I'm here for you."

"Is that right?" He turned to look at her, his gaze lingering on her face.

The look in his eyes unnerved her. "Well, yes. Within reason, obviously. You've been so generous. And convincing. No one would ever have guessed you were pretending."

"Why do you think that was, Becks? Why do you think I was convincing?" His tone was soft and she felt her heart thud a little harder.

"I—you're a good actor—"

"You think I was acting last night?"

"No, but—" Images from the night before played in her head like a movie and she swallowed. "We don't have to dissect everything. Just thanks, that's all. We'll talk about it another time." She turned, intending to head back to the house, but he caught her arm.

"You're not going anywhere—not until we've finished this conversation. I know you don't like talking about emotions, but you're going to talk about this. So I'm going to ask you again—" He lifted her chin with his fingers so that she had no choice but to look at him. "Why do you think I was convincing?"

She couldn't find any words and when she didn't answer he took her face in his hands.

"It wasn't hard because I wasn't acting," he said softly. "The hard part has been pretending *not* to love you all these years."

She stared at him. "You—"

"I love you, Becks. After last night you have to know that, surely? I love you, and I've loved you for a long time."

The cold air crept under her coat but she didn't notice. She wasn't aware of anything except him, and she felt joy slowly seep into her, the sheer volume of it pushing aside doubt and anxiety and all the other complicated emotions that had swirled inside her since she'd realised how she felt about Will. It had always been Will. He was her person.

And she was his person.

He loved her. Not only that, but he'd loved her for a long time.

How was that possible? It felt too perfect, and she knew life was rarely perfect.

"You never said anything." Her mouth was dry. "You've never said that word. In all the years we've been friends. All the hours we've spent together. You've never said that word."

"I'm saying it now." He took her face in his hands, his gaze holding hers. "I love you, Becks. And I probably should have said it a long time ago, but I wasn't sure if you felt the same way and I was afraid of damaging what we had. And maybe also damaging my friendship with Jamie. Our parents' friendship. I didn't want things to be awkward."

"A long time ago?" She stared at him, her mind working. "How long?"

"I'm not sure. But at least the last few years." He stroked her cheek gently with his fingers. "Why do you think Elsie broke up with me?"

"I have no idea. I assumed she was a woman with poor decision making skills."

He smiled. "She broke up with me because she knew I was in love with you."

"How could she possibly have known that?"

"She saw us together. And she knew I was a lost cause." He lowered his head and kissed her again before lifting his mouth from hers just enough to enable him to speak. "So are you going to tell me how you feel now?"

She flung her arms round his neck, her face wet with tears. "I love you too. Maybe I've loved you for a long time. I don't even know. I'm not—"

"You're not good at understanding your feelings, I know."

"I've always said that but I'm not having any trouble understanding the way I feel about you now." She kissed him and he kissed her back and she forgot that she'd been in a hurry to go back to the house, that she'd wanted this conversation to be brief, to get it over with. All she wanted was now. This. Him. And then she remembered and pulled away. "There's something I need to tell you. Something I need to say." She thought about Rosie and Declan, and how not communicating could lead to assumptions, which could lead to friction and fractures. She didn't want that. Not ever.

"There's something I need to say, too, but you can go first."

She curled her fingers into the front of his coat. "I was never in love with Declan."

"I know."

"You know?" She'd been prepared to repeat herself but it seemed she didn't need to.

"It was obvious to me right from the start that what you were feeling at your sister's wedding was complicated. Your relationship with Rosie is something most people can't imagine. For all your lives you've been each other's significant person, so someone else coming along and disrupting that had to be confusing and unsettling. I did suggest that on the day when you were howling into my shirt, but you were convinced you were in love with Declan so I decided that the best approach was to let you figure it out for yourself. Which I hoped you would in time."

"You're patient."

"Not really. But you're worth waiting for."

"We've wasted so much time."

"Yes, we have. And I don't want to waste any more, which is why I'm not carrying this around a moment longer." He put his hand in his pocket and pulled out a small midnight-blue box, tied with a silver bow. "I could have put it under the Christmas tree, but some gifts are better given in private."

"Will?" She stared at the box, almost too afraid to take it from him, but he pressed it into her hand and she fumbled with ribbon and wrapping before finally lifting the lid. "Oh. *Oh!*"

"If a diamond is too fairy-tale for you, just think of it as carbon atoms."

Carbon atoms.

She didn't know whether to laugh or cry and in the end she did both. "It's not too fairy-tale." It was better than that, because this was real. He was real.

"Will you marry me, Becks? I love you so much. You're my best friend. You've always been my best friend, but now you're so much more than that. You're the only woman I want, and the only woman I'll ever want. If you don't want to get married, we don't have to. Just live with me. Until you're old and can't remember your passwords."

She felt lightheaded. "Is it fake?"

"The ring? No, it's not fake. Nothing about this is fake. Not the ring and not my feelings."

"I can't believe you bought me a ring." The diamond sparkled and shimmered in the winter sunlight. "When?"

"Last year. After Elsie and I broke up I decided this was ridiculous. I was going to tell you how I felt. But then at the wedding you were so sure you were in love with Declan, it just wasn't the right time. Are you going to answer my question any time soon? Because we're both running the risk of frostbite."

She felt a burst of intense happiness. "If I say yes, do I have to wear a scratchy dress with a veil?"

"No. Wear what you like. Wear your hoodie. I'd love you to wear your hoodie. We could get you one with 'Bride' on the front." He was smiling and so was she.

"And you're not just asking me to marry you so that you get in-house tech support for the rest of your life?"

"I can fix my own computer, Becks." He took the ring from its box and slid it onto her finger. "There. You can give it back to me if you don't want it."

"I want it." She clutched her hand to her chest. "Get away from my ring."

"So is that a yes?"

"It's a yes. A big yes. A forever yes."

"Forever yes is what I was hoping for." He kissed her again and she might have carried on kissing him for the rest of Christmas, except that she could feel the ring on her finger and wanted to look at it.

She eased away from him and gazed at her finger. "I love it." She could hardly breathe. "It fits perfectly. Rosie would say that was a sign."

"It's a sign that I checked the size of your finger." He stroked her cheek. "Are you crying?"

"Crying? Me? No, it's the wind."

"That's what I thought."

"And talking of crying, can we forget the fact that I howled at Rosie's wedding? I don't want you to bring it up in twenty years, the way my grandmother does. She waits for the moment that is going to guarantee maximum embarrassment and then she pounces."

"I don't remember you crying." Infinitely gentle, he zipped her coat a little higher and adjusted her hat. "We need to get back indoors. You're freezing."

"Are we going to tell people? About this? About us?"

"Why not?"

"Because our relationship started out as a pretence. It was fake."

He thought about that for a moment.

"It was never really fake, and anyway it doesn't matter how things start," he said, "it only matters how things end."

She slipped her hand into his and they started to walk back to the house. "I like that. I might write it on a sticky note and put it on my laptop. Just to warn you though, you do know Granny is going to ask if I'm pregnant? Because she doesn't know how to not be inappropriate. So apologies in advance."

"After last night, maybe you are."

"Pregnant?" She stopped walking and stared at him. "I hadn't even thought—"

"Neither did I, obviously. Sorry."

"Why are you apologizing? I was equally responsible." Becky did some calculations. "It's probably okay. Possibly. And if it isn't, then Granny will be very happy."

And maybe, she thought, she'd be happy too.

27

Jenny

"You're blocking my view." Rosie pushed Jamie to one side and knelt on the window seat next to Hayley. "Can you see anything?"

"Not really." Hayley squinted. "They're just standing there. They look as if they're talking."

"Talking? Well, who stands outside in below freezing temperatures to conduct a conversation?" Phyllis peered between Hayley and Rosie. "I can't see anything. My eyes aren't good enough. Martin, don't you own binoculars?"

"I do."

"Good. Then perhaps you could fetch them."

"I will not fetch them. And I feel obliged to point out that the entire family pressing their noses to the window watching their every move constitutes a gross invasion of privacy."

Jenny sighed, feeling an equal measure of guilt and hope. "You're right, of course, in normal circumstances—"

"But these are not normal circumstances," her mother finished for her. "Don't be a killjoy, Martin. We're looking out for her, that's all."

"You are not looking out for her, you're looking *at* her. It's different."

"They're kissing," Rosie said, almost bouncing on the seat. "And he's giving her something. Dad, *please* get the binoculars."

"I will not."

"What is going on in here?"

Jenny turned her head and saw her father standing in the doorway, a sheaf of papers in his hand and a bemused expression on his face.

"They're watching Becky and Will on the beach," Martin said, shaking his head as he joined his father-in-law. "Are those the new pages you printed out?"

"Yes. All updated and ready for you to take a look." Brian gazed at the crowd by the window. "What exactly are they hoping to see?"

"I've no idea. I'm assuming they're tired of watching Christmas movies."

"Who wants a movie when you can watch a romance unfolding in real life. He's given her something!" Rosie clutched Hayley's shoulder. "Did you see that?"

"Yes!"

"Could it be a ring?"

"I don't know. They're too far away for me to get a proper look."

Jenny decided she really ought to be the adult in the room and intervene. "Really, whatever is going on, it's between Will and Becky."

"Yes," Martin said. "Don't involve poor Hayley in your family meddling."

"Hayley's part of the family now," Rosie said, "she's part of everything we do. Including meddling."

Martin opened his mouth to protest but then saw Hayley clap her hands.

"It *is* a ring! Look at the way she'd staring down at her

hand. It's a ring!" She and Rosie hugged each other and Jenny felt something unravel inside her as she watched them laughing together.

She glanced at Martin, who gave a slow, despairing shake of his head. But he was also smiling.

"If meddling is part of the job description for joining this family, it looks as if Hayley is going to fit right in." He took Jenny's hand. "Looks as if you were wrong this time."

Jenny was sure she hadn't been wrong. Will had stepped in to help Becky, she was convinced of it. But she didn't need to share that thought with anyone. It didn't matter how they'd reached this point. She was just glad that they had.

"Yes, it looks as if I was wrong."

Rosie turned her head. "Wrong about what?"

"Nothing. It's between your mother and I," Martin said sternly. "Despite what you seem to think, families don't have to tell each other everything."

"But whatever they don't tell you, you can usually find out for yourself if you press your nose to the window," Phyllis said. "Ooh look. They're kissing. And they're still kissing. And still . . . aren't they going to stop to breathe? Jenny, it's time to call Audrey and let her know that her Christmas wish has come true."

28

Jenny

If someone had asked her what her favourite part of Christmas was, she would have said all of it. The chaos, the joy, the unexpected moments, the surprises, the moments of laughter and even the moments when the whole thing was so exhausting she thought *when are they all leaving?*

But really it was Christmas Day. Because somehow the present and the past came together and it became more than this one day. It was this Christmas, and all the Christmases that had ever gone before, and the children were partly responsible for that because they always wanted to do what they'd always done, in the exact order they'd always done it. With one exception. Getting up before it was light.

She remembered years when she'd hear excited giggles in the hallway, the sound of bare feet making the stairs creak as three children tried to creep downstairs without waking their parents, subdued squeals when they saw the stockings and Martin grumbling that it was just too early, and couldn't they at least stay in bed until it was light.

And now, here they were, lying in bed with weak winter

sunlight poking through the blinds, and she was pretty sure that no one else in the house was awake yet.

"Do you miss the days when they used to try and creep downstairs without waking us?"

"No." Martin's eyes were still closed. "This was one of the few days of the year I could actually have a lie-in."

"But now you can lie in every day." She kissed him. "Happy Christmas. I need to put the turkey in the oven."

"Now?"

"If you want to eat at lunchtime, yes, now."

"Can't we just eat when it's ready?"

"We could, yes, but my parents like lunch to be at lunch-time and not at some indeterminate point mid-afternoon. Dad will start snacking and saying things like 'my stomach doesn't know what time of day it is.' Last year I made him scrambled eggs and he stared at it and said 'I don't know what meal this is supposed to be.'"

"Eggs can be any meal. That's the point. We should have trained them better."

"They're too old to change now, and I don't mind. I love them the way they are. I love the fact my dad won't move in the mornings until he's done his crossword, and that my mother uses her age as an excuse for saying things that make me want to hide."

"You hate the fact that she says things that make you want to hide. That's why you hide."

"True." She smiled and tugged at the covers. "But I wouldn't change her. It's all part of the chaos."

"Let's hope the kids feel the same way when she buys them all pregnancy tests for Christmas." He yawned and levered himself upright. "Okay, I'm officially awake. I'll make coffee and take Percy out. Where are you getting your energy from? It was a late night. Yet another late night. Why couldn't our children have made their announcements on the same day so

333

that we could just have one late night celebrating and then get back to normal? What will it be tonight I wonder?"

"It's such great news about Will and Becky." She'd barely slept, smiling to herself in the darkness. "I keep seeing her face. She was glowing."

"That was windchill. The two of them were standing outside in the cold for hours."

"You're so unromantic. I was thinking that next year we should invite Audrey and Paul to stay for Christmas. That way we can guarantee that Will and Becky will be here. And if they're here, the chances are Rosie and Declan will be too. And providing Hayley enjoys herself this Christmas, hopefully she and Jamie will come."

"Where are all these people going to sleep? At this rate I'm going to need to build an extension." He stood up and stretched. "And why are you planning next Christmas when we haven't finished this one yet?"

"Because I don't want to think this will be the last Christmas we'll all be together. I want to know it will happen again."

He sighed and sat down next to her. "You're the one always telling me I have to adapt."

"I never said it was easy."

He pulled her to her feet. "Come on. We're going to stand on the creaky stair and wake the children. It's time the day started. Remind me, when do we do presents?"

"The same time we have always done presents. Stockings before breakfast, main presents afterwards."

They used the bathroom and pulled on clothes, Jenny wearing the festive red dress she wore every year.

They headed down to the kitchen, treading hard on the creaky stair several times until Jamie yelled, "why are you treading on the creaky stair?" to which his father replied "it's revenge," and then they sprinted to the kitchen giggling like children.

Half an hour later when the turkey was in the oven and the smell of fresh coffee filled the kitchen, people started to emerge.

"I mean, if you want to wake us up, Mum, just set an alarm," Rosie said sleepily. "All that creaking made me think I was in a haunted house." She was wearing red pyjamas covered in smiling white snowmen and her hair was tousled from sleep. The innocent effect was slightly ruined by the fact that the top fastened with a single button that was challenged by Rosie's curves.

The back door opened and Percy shot into the kitchen, bringing with him snow and cold air. Martin followed, stamping snow off his boots. "Chilly out there. I hope Santa was wearing his thermals."

"Martin, wipe the dog's paws!" Jenny caught Percy and took him back to the door before he could leave snowy prints through the house.

"Dad, close the door!" Rosie shuddered and moved closer to the oven. "It's freezing. I'm going to get inside the oven with the turkey."

"Why is everyone yelling at me?" Martin closed the door. "Merry Christmas to you too. And you're only freezing because you have flesh showing."

Jenny grabbed the towel and dried Percy. She looked at Rosie, trying to remember the time when she'd had perfect smooth skin. "You're not wearing enough clothing."

"I'm not six, Mum. I can decide what I need to wear. And I was wearing plenty of clothing until Dad decided to open the door."

"Why didn't you get dressed before coming down?"

"Because of all the creaking. You obviously wanted us to get up, so I got up. Like a dutiful daughter. Here I am. Also, I have a special dress and I don't want to drop my breakfast on it."

"Who was going up and down the stairs?" Becky walked

in next, wearing jeans and a hoodie that had *this is a Christmas jumper* emblazoned on the front of it. "It was torture."

Martin removed his boots. "Now you know what you put us through for all those years."

Jamie walked in next, with Hayley. "I just bumped into Granny. She wants to know what the creaking sound was."

"If Granny is up, then you really should get dressed, Rosie." Jenny started laying the table.

"Why? It was Granny who gave me these pyjamas. It will be nice for her to see them."

"You're showing too much boobage," Becky said. "Grandad is too old for that much flesh on display. Why are you laying the table for breakfast? We have to open our stockings first."

Grumbling, Rosie left the room to dress in something more suitable and then they all convened in the living room.

Hayley opened the contents of her stocking and for some reason this was an emotional moment because she and Jamie exchanged looks and Jenny thought to herself that even when you thought you knew your family really well, you could never really know everything and perhaps that was good.

Later, after they'd all consumed breakfast (and her father had commented that it was good to have an actual meal at the right time of day), they went back to the living room to open the gifts piled under the Christmas tree.

And Jenny watched them, her amazing, complicated, surprising, wonderful family, and decided that this was her best gift. Being all together for Christmas. That was what she wanted.

"Why are you gazing at us in that weird way, Mum?" Rosie folded a ribbon. "Like you're going to cry?"

"I'm not going to cry," Jenny said. "It's Christmas. Why would I cry?"

"Because you often cry at Christmas. You say things like 'when you were little' and then you come out with some hideously embarrassing story about something we did when we

336

were little and didn't know better, something that is very probably still being held against us, and then you cry."

"It's true," Jamie said. "You do that, Mum. So maybe this is a good time to give her our present."

Rosie rummaged under the Christmas tree and pulled out a box. "Here," she said. "Happy Christmas. From the three of us. This really will make you cry. Sorry not sorry."

Jenny removed the paper carefully (so that she didn't incur the wrath of her mother) and opened the box. Inside was a large photo album.

"Oh, it's an actual physical album. What a great idea. I'll be able to print some photos instead of having them all living on my phone where I never see them. In the sky, as Granny would say."

"Not just an album," Becky said. "Open it."

She opened it, and there was Jamie aged around five, holding both his sisters on his lap.

She turned the page, and there was Rosie at her first ballet class.

She kept turning the pages, moving through the years and the memories. Child to adult. All the stages. So much of her life, right there in front of her. And at the end was a family photo, the three of them, with Declan, Hayley and Will. Standing on the beach laughing, wind blowing their hair and their smiles so big it made her smile to look at it.

"How did you take that last one? When?"

"Yesterday. Will took it. And we printed it off."

"I should scold you for making your mother cry," Martin said, "but I assume they're happy tears. Good choice."

"Yes, thank you." Jenny was choked, but she managed to hold herself together and join in as everyone took it in turns to open presents. Not that they all made sense to her.

Hayley was opening presents from Jamie and the two of them were laughing.

"Days-of-the-week knickers?"

"Yes. You can wear Monday for a change."

Jenny watched them, mystified as they shared a joke clearly only the two of them understood.

But that wasn't as strange as the moment Declan gave Rosie a box of pink paperclips that for some reason reduced her to tears (*I'd cry too if someone gave me pink paperclips*, Jamie was heard to mutter), and Jenny decided that a gift that was adored by the recipient and not understood by anyone else was probably the perfect present because it was obviously personal and meant something.

She looked up as Martin handed her a box.

"What's this?"

"It's my gift to you."

She opened it and found an old shoe box adorned with a homemade sticker saying *Worry Box*.

"You wanted somewhere to put your worries, so from now on you can write them down, put them in here, and I'll take them. So that you don't have to carry them on your own."

Her throat stung. "You won't look after them properly."

"Yes, I will. I will give them my full attention. In between bins and gutters. If you don't believe me, look inside."

She opened the box and there was a piece of paper with his name on it, but it was crossed out.

She looked at him and he shrugged.

"I know you've been worried, but you don't need to be. Not anymore. You can cross that one off your list. I've had some ideas. We'll talk about them when it's just us again."

And she realised that he did seem like Martin again. Ever since the night of Jamie's party, he'd slowly been regaining energy and interest.

"Worries? Can we help?" Jamie spoke up. "What are you worried about, Mum?"

"Everything," Becky said. "She's Mum. And no, you can't help. You're probably the reason she's worried."

"Well, thanks!"

"If all Dad has given her is an empty cardboard box then we should *all* be worried," Rosie said. "Next year I'm in charge of your gift buying, Dad. I thought I'd trained you better than this. No kitchen equipment. Nothing that's secretly a gift for you. You know the rules."

Jenny clutched the box. "I like my gift."

"When I'm old," Rosie muttered to Declan, "don't even think of giving me a cardboard box."

"Enough!" Martin lifted his hands. "Is nothing private around here? I do have another gift for your mother, so maybe this is a good time to give it." He handed her an envelope and they all waited while she opened it.

"I hope you're not giving her money," Rosie said, "because buying your own gift is seriously overrated. Why are you laughing, Jamie?"

"I'm not laughing. I'm just grateful not to be Declan. The thought of having to choose exactly the right gift for you for the next fifty years would put me in therapy."

"That's because you're not as clever as Declan."

"I always think there's no point in worrying," Phyllis said. "If something is going to happen it will happen."

Ignoring them all, Jenny pulled out a small, stylish brochure. "What's this?"

"It's where we're going for three nights in January. You always say the house feels empty after Christmas when everyone has left, so we're going away. You won't be in an empty house. Someone else will put food in front of you, which will be a nice change after all the cooking and entertaining."

"That's a good idea," Jamie said. "Nice."

"I take it all back, Dad," Rosie said. "That's a great gift."

It was a great gift, because she knew that what he was really giving her was a sign that he was moving forward. That they were moving forward together. That they'd handle this change the way they handled everything else that came their way, by adjusting, however long that took. And her children would come and go and maybe have children of their own or maybe not, but whatever shape her family took, she knew she was lucky to have them.

But that was the future, and for now she intended to stay in the present and enjoy this one day when everyone was together and, for a moment at least, everything was perfect.

She gazed at the Christmas tree and then heard her father clear his throat.

"I don't want to worry anyone," he said, "but is everything fine in the kitchen? I think I can smell burning."

29
Hayley

Jamie? Are you awake?" Hayley lay in the semidarkness, staring up at the ceiling. She'd insisted that they leave the Christmas tree lights on tonight, because she didn't want Christmas to end.

Had it been perfect? Technically, no. Between them they'd forgotten to put the potatoes in the oven so lunch had been late, and Jamie's grandfather had said that given the number of people in the house he didn't see how at least one of them couldn't have got the timing right. Percy had trodden on Rosie's new boots and left a pawprint on the suede, which Declan spent an hour trying to remove, and Jamie accidently knocked Becky's phone on the floor and broke the screen.

But they'd also laughed, swapped gifts, played games, shared anecdotes, eaten too much food, walked on the beach, had a snowball fight and then eaten more food. They'd been a family.

And that part really had been perfect.

"I'm awake." Sleepy, he shifted onto his side so that he could look at her. "Are you all right?"

"I think so." She paused. She'd been wondering how and

when to tell him her news. "Do you think your Granny enjoyed her Christmas?"

"Yes. And I hope she didn't upset you with all her less-than-subtle mentions of babies. You just have to ignore her. That's what we do. No one expects you to get pregnant, Hayley."

"Right." She looked at the lights twinkling on the Christmas tree and smiled. "About that . . ."

★ ★ ★ ★ ★

Acknowledgments

I'm grateful to the publishing teams around the globe who handle my books with enthusiasm and dedication. Getting a book into the hands of readers is a complex operation involving many individuals and departments. I'm grateful to more people than I have room to mention here, but extend particular thanks to Lisa Milton, Manpreet Grewal and the whole UK team, and also Margaret Marbury, Susan Swinwood, Michele Bidelspach and the team in the US.

My thanks to my wonderful editor, Flo Nicoll, whose keen eye makes every book the best it can be, and who manages to bring fun and laughter to the whole process.

My agent, Susan Ginsburg, is an endless source of support and encouragement and I'm grateful to her and to the rest of the team at Writers House.

I doubt I would manage to write a word without the support of my friends, and also my family, who always seem to know when to leave me alone to write and when to provide coffee and chocolate.

I'm grateful to the librarians, booksellers, book reviewers, bloggers and everyone involved in the reading community who share their thoughts on books (and inspire me to buy more, even when my bookshelves can't take the weight!).

Apart from the writing itself, the best part of my job is without doubt engaging with readers, many of whom have been reading my books for years (and sharing amongst the generations). Your enthusiasm, kind messages, gorgeous photos and encouraging words mean so much to me, as do the personal details you so often share when a book has a particular resonance. Thank you for reading my stories. I hope you enjoy this one!

Sarah x

THE NUMBER ONE *SUNDAY TIMES* BESTSELLER

SARAH MORGAN

Brave New Summer

SARAH MORGAN
Read
yourself
happy

1

Evie

Take your career to the next level . . .

Evie stared at the screen. She definitely needed the next level because the current level wasn't working out for her. An upmarket hotel in London known for its luxurious accommodation and impeccable customer service had a vacancy. She should apply.

London. Busy. Anonymous. She'd be able to walk down a street without everyone stopping her to catch up with gossip. No one would notice or care if she arrived home early in the morning wearing the same clothes she'd left the house in the night before. She wouldn't be greeted by winks and knowing looks from the locals or asked for regular updates. She wouldn't have to drive to the next town to find a pharmacist who hadn't known her since she was a toddler. A fresh start. *A new life.*

A new job, where her colleagues wouldn't include people who used to babysit her.

The team members beaming at her from the website seemed happy. Their careers were obviously going well. Unlike hers.

A big red button encouraged her to "apply here." Her finger hovered for a moment and then she sat back with a sigh.

Why was she finding it impossible to make the decision when it was so obviously the right thing to do, particularly given the current circumstances.

Maybe she was having a crisis of confidence.

How was she going to sell herself? How did she gloss over the fact that the hotel where she'd worked since she'd graduated was basically falling apart under her watch? Admittedly she'd only been in this role for a very short time, but knowing none of this was her fault didn't help.

She opened a document on her screen and started to draft a few lines.

"I am a passionate professional—no, that doesn't sound right." Evie deleted the words and tried again, staring at the words on the screen. "I am an *experienced* hospitality professional—yes, that's better—dedicated to delivering the highest standards of guest relations. I pride myself on offering an unforgettable and curated experience to each—"

"Evie?"

Donna, one of the receptionists, appeared in the doorway and Evie slammed her laptop shut and picked up the cup of coffee that had been growing cold next to her.

"Hi. Everything okay?"

"Not really. I need to talk to you." Donna leaned against the door frame and grinned at her. "You should see your face! Picture of guilt. What are you doing on that laptop of yours that's so secretive? I hope it's something that could get you arrested. Your life is much too clean and wholesome."

"Nothing."

Preparing to apply for new jobs, because there's a chance we're all about to lose the one we currently have.

Should she be sharing her fears with the staff? No. That wouldn't be fair. They'd been through enough lately what with

Gerald, the general manager, being so ill and it wasn't as if she had any real evidence to support her fears. No one from head office had actually *said* they were going to be closed down or put up for sale. But it seemed the obvious path to her. The rest of the staff were carrying on as normal, cheerfully oblivious to the economic realities of running a hotel.

And it was frustrating because she truly believed she could change things. She had so many good ideas, but the way things were currently it was impossible to put them into practice.

"Have you joined one of those dating sites?" Donna wasn't easily deflected. "Because I said to Molly last week, I can't remember when our Evie last had sex with anyone. She should join one of those sites. But Molly pointed out that one of the disadvantages of living in a small village is that you already know all the eligible men of the right age on account of having been born here, and if you were going to get together with them it would already have happened. You need to spread your net a bit wider. How would you feel about someone older? Edward Barnes is a nice man."

"Edward Barnes?" Evie spilled coffee on her desk. "Are you talking about Mr Barnes the butcher? Mr Barnes who is sixty and retiring next year? He's more than thirty years older than me." She snatched a bunch of tissues and soaked up the liquid before it could do any damage.

"He's seasoned, that's true, and his hips are giving him problems but he has a very gentle personality and he knows a nice piece of sirloin when he sees it . . ." Donna's voice trailed off and she laughed. "Just kidding. Sort of. Unless you—"

"Enough!" She'd never again be able to walk into the butcher and buy something. She'd have to order online for the rest of her life.

And this whole exchange should make her feel better about being forced to move away from an area she'd lived in all her life and loved. She'd be with people who hadn't known her since birth. People who wouldn't take such an active interest in her sex life.

It might even be possible to *have* a sex life. Which would be a refreshing change.

"I don't have time for sex, Donna."

"Are you listening to yourself? That's tragic. And don't tell me you don't have time. There's always your lunch hour. We could cover for you while you have a quickie in the laundry room."

"If you could say that a little louder Donna—I think the kitchen staff possibly didn't hear you."

"Oh I think they probably did." The deep male voice came from the doorway and she glanced up and met the laughing gaze of Luca, her new head chef.

There was no point in wondering if he'd overheard, because clearly he had.

She didn't know whether to kill Donna or bash her head on the desk.

"Luca."

Recruiting Luca was one of the few things she'd done right recently, partly because he was an excellent chef, but also because he was one of the few people working here who hadn't known her since she was a baby. Until thirty seconds ago she'd had an appropriately professional relationship with him, which had been a novelty.

Unfortunately that professional relationship was now a thing of the past.

She'd never felt so embarrassed in her life, a feeling intensified by the fact he didn't seem embarrassed at all. Judging from the smile on his face he found the situation hilarious.

Or maybe it was the thought of someone wanting her badly enough to have a quickie against a stack of freshly laundered sheets and towels that he found hilarious.

Either way, it was going to be a while until she could have a conversation with him without thinking of laundry cupboards.

Determined not to allow this to become awkward she looked him straight in the eye, trying not to think of him naked.

That part wasn't easy because as well as producing sublime food, Luca was very easy on the eye.

He was above average height and beneath the traditional chef whites his shoulders were wide and powerful. She didn't know whether his physique was the result of a serious gym habit or if he'd been lifting a lot of heavy pans. Maybe that was it. She'd almost put her back out the other night trying to heave her cast iron casserole out of the oven.

She gave what she hoped passed for a professional, detached smile. "Did you need something, Luca?" Seeing the slight lift of his eyebrow she wished she'd phrased that differently.

Still laughing he stepped forward and placed a file on her desk. "The new menu designs. I know which one I prefer, but I'd like your opinion."

Someone wanted her opinion. Someone actually thought she might have something to contribute.

The wilting shoots of her confidence sprang back to life.

"Great. I'll take a look and let you know what I think."

Donna frowned. "What's wrong with the current menu design? Gerald approved it."

Luca transferred his gaze from Evie to Donna. "We're updating the restaurant. We'll be offering a smaller, seasonal menu and we need the design to reflect that. I'm sure Gerald would agree."

Evie almost groaned. She could predict what was coming next. *We've always done it this way . . .*

Donna drew breath. "We've always—"

"Thank you, Donna," Evie interrupted hastily. She didn't want anyone stifling Luca's creativity or he'd end up as exhausted and disillusioned as she was. She patted the file and smiled at him. "I'll take a look at this and get back to you. Great job, Luca."

"And I had some ideas for redesigning the restaurant. We're not making the most of the views."

"Right. Let's arrange a time to talk about that."

She waited until he left the room and closed her eyes. "He heard you. This is terrible."

"Terrible? It's not terrible," Donna said, "it's brilliant. Luca! Why didn't we think of him? We need to add him to our list. True, he's changing things that don't need changing which isn't great, but he is the hottest guy we've had around here in a long time. And talking of hot, your cheeks are flaming. I could fry an egg on them."

"Thanks to you, I already have egg on my face. I don't need more. And what is this list you're talking about?"

"The list of potential men you could date. We spent an hour on it last night when we were in the Smuggler's Inn."

Evie felt a ripple of horror. "You were discussing my sex life in the pub? What if the people at the next table had heard you?"

"Funny you should say that because they did! It was Anthony and Jeff. They were out celebrating the fourth anniversary of the gallery, but they happily joined in."

"Joined in?"

"We had quite a large group on it in the end. The more the merrier, I always say."

"Oh well that's great then. Maybe you could have opened it up to the whole pub. Fixing my love life is more entertaining than quiz night, I'm sure." Evie shook her head in despair. "Don't you have more important things to talk about?"

"More important than you? No. We all care about you."

"Well that's nice, obviously, but I can handle my own romantic life, and right now dating is not a priority. And I'm especially not dating a member of staff."

"Why not? That man is hotter than a chilli pepper, and also he works here which means a rendezvous in the laundry room is a definite possibility. Or one of the empty bedrooms."

And there were far too many of those.

"Stop!" Evie held up a hand. "You have to stop."

"I'll stop if you tell me what secretive thing you're doing on that laptop of yours. And don't say nothing because I know you well enough to know when you're hiding something."

"It's nothing of interest, really." Seeing the speculation on Donna's face, Evie wished she was a better liar. "You said you wanted to talk to me?"

"Is it Pat's anniversary you're planning?" Donna was still peering at Evie's laptop, as if it held the clues to the universe. "Can you believe she has worked here for twenty-five years?"

Yes, she could believe that. She also believed that Pat probably should have moved on to other things at least twenty years ago when she was still feeling fresh and enthusiastic.

"We have a loyal staff," Evie said. And that, of course, was part of the problem. They'd been here for so long they were set in their ways and refused to change. And she had no idea how to motivate them to do things differently.

She adored Gerald, who had been the general manager for the past fifteen years, but after his heart attack she'd stepped up into the GM role in the hotel and what she'd discovered had almost given her a heart attack too.

How could he have let things get so bad? The whole place was a disaster.

For the first month she'd worked eighteen-hour days trying to get a full picture, and once she'd got the full picture she'd spent a few more days in full panic mode before sitting down and trying to form a workable plan to save the place. But her plan required everyone to join together and change the way they did things. Unfortunately most of the staff, though lovely and loyal, liked the way things were done and weren't prepared to change anything bigger than a light bulb.

She didn't have a fraction of Gerald's experience, but even she could see it was only a matter of time until head office made the decision to intervene in a big way. She knew a developer was interested in the site. He'd had the audacity to spend three nights at the hotel, during which he'd poked his thin hooked nose into every corner and asked intrusive question. He reminded Evie of a weasel. She'd managed to resist the urge to give him scratchy sheets or feed him dodgy seafood. What was the point? What difference would it make? The ship was sinking and she was trying to bail it out by herself with a teaspoon.

All she could do was grab herself a lifebelt, which was why she really should be applying for jobs. This was the push she'd needed to do what she probably should have done a long time ago.

Maybe calling herself "an experienced, hospitality professional" was pushing it. If she was being honest she should describe herself as "burned out, disillusioned and hopeless at establishing boundaries with the staff." She'd thought that over time they'd start to respect her experience but that wasn't happening. And maybe it was unrealistic to expect it. To some of them she was still the child who had sat on their laps and watched TV with a glass of milk and a cookie.

She felt a pang, because there were some things she'd miss, of course.

She woke every morning to the sound of waves crashing onto the rocks and the shriek of seagulls. She ran on the beach and bought her fish straight from the boats that landed on the quay.

But she kept those thoughts to herself and tried again to make Donna focus on work. "You came in here to talk to me about something."

"Did I? Oh yes—" Donna nodded, "I'd actually forgotten

for a moment. Mrs Dodds is refusing to pay in full because she says she asked for hypoallergenic bedding and she was given feathers, so she hasn't had a wink of sleep for three nights because her airways have closed up."

"But she always has hypoallergenic bedding. It's on the computer system."

"Mandy says she couldn't find the card, or maybe she forgot to look at it—I can't remember—anyway Mrs Dodds didn't get hypoallergenic bedding. I've told her it was the highest quality down and feathers but that didn't soothe her. She said when this happened last time Gerald comped the whole stay."

"He didn't charge her at all? For the whole week?"

"That's right."

And that, Evie thought wearily, was just one of the reasons the hotel was in trouble.

"All right. I'll deal with this. How bad is it? Should we offer to make her a doctor's appointment?"

"I don't think she wants that. I told her it was a mix up and that we're very sorry, but she seems to just want financial compensation. And one of our towelling robes."

One of the disadvantages of providing top quality bathroom products was that guests had a tendency to walk off with them.

"I'll talk to Mrs Dodds right now, then I need to see Mandy."

Mandy was the head housekeeper. Evie had tried to persuade her to use the computer system that automatically flagged guest preferences, but she was scared of it and preferred to check the old-fashioned card system that had been in place for decades.

"Go easy on her," Donna said. "She's already upset because Mrs Dodds shouted. Honestly, it's not that big a deal. I'm sure she'll stop sneezing if goes for a walk on the beach. Fresh air, that's what she needs. And maybe antihistamine."

"Donna, it's a very big deal," Evie said. "Firstly because we have an unhappy guest, which means we've failed at our job. Secondly because it is much easier to keep guests than it is to cultivate new ones, so losing a guest is bad news. And thirdly as well as losing money by compensating her, we risk a bad review and bad reviews put people off staying here. And they also affect our SEO ranking and—"

"Our what?"

"Never mind. I'll handle it, Donna."

"Right—before you do that, I wanted to ask if I could leave early today. I need to take my mother to a hospital appointment and the journey takes forever at this time of year. I know it's not great timing—"

That was true. They were already short staffed, but what could she say? She knew how hard it was for Donna, caring for her elderly mother at the same time as raising her family and working.

"Of course. How is she?"

"Frail. She just seemed to give up after Dad died. Anyway, such is life. All you can do is carry on carrying on. Thanks, Evie."

Evie wondered if she dared ask Donna to come in early tomorrow to make up the time, but then remembered she had to drop her youngest at school.

Unable to see a solution, she stood up and followed Donna to the front desk where Mrs Dodds was making her discontent known to anyone who would listen and a great number of other people who would probably rather have not listened. Her face was red and blotchy and her tirade was punctuated by sneezing.

Her mouth tightened when she saw Evie. "I have been staying at The Alexandra, Cornwall for—"

"The past ten years. I know Mrs Dodds, and you're a special and valued guest. I'm so sorry this happened. It was a genuine mistake and I assure you it will never happen again." She smoothed and soothed, ignoring the inner voice telling her that the way things were at that moment, it probably would happen again.

"What are you going to do about it? Gerald would have offered me my next holiday free of charge."

"Last night will be complementary, and we are going to offer you a special discounted rate for your booking next year."

"I've been rethinking my booking for next year. I'm not sure I'll be able to look forward to it after what has happened. How can you be sure it won't happen again?"

Good question.

"Because I am personally going to look into it and will be doing some intensive staff training." Which, she could safely predict, would make absolutely no difference at all to the level of service delivered.

It didn't really matter what she promised because she was confident that The Alexandra wouldn't be in business next year. It would have been closed down or sold off to someone who would probably turn it into holiday homes. The thought depressed her. She couldn't imagine strolling through the village and not seeing the hotel nestled in the dip on the headland.

Having pacified Mrs Dodds and offered medical assistance (which was refused), she returned to her office and Mandy appeared a few minutes later.

Evie knew this wasn't going to be an easy conversation.

"Mandy, why don't you take a seat and—"

"You look exhausted, Evie. You're the one who should be taking a seat, you poor lamb. I still can't believe you're all grown up and in charge."

How was she supposed to exert authority when the staff treated her like a favourite pet?

"I'm fine, really. But, Mandy, I need to speak to you about Mrs Dodds."

"Don't you worry your head about that. No one likes to be yelled at and I was upset, that's true, but I'm over it. I'm not one to hold grudges. I'm sure she didn't mean to shout at me the way she did. She obviously woke up in a bad mood."

Evie opened her mouth to say that Mrs Dodds had woken up surrounded by feathers which might have explained her less than sunny disposition, but Mandy was still talking.

"When did you last eat something, Evie? You're always working, that's your problem. Morning noon and night you're in this office slogging away. And you're so serious these days. You used to laugh all the time. You've always been a smiler. I remember your dad pushing you through the village when you were two years old and you were waving your chubby little legs and smiling at everyone. Every trip took him twice as long because we all wanted to cuddle you."

"I'm just trying to do my job, and—"

"You need to be easier on yourself,' Mandy said, 'or you'll go the same way as Gerald, God bless him."

Evie was torn. She was very fond of Gerald, who was kind and avuncular and had ultimately carried the responsibility for the success or failure of the hotel. Unfortunately he'd let things slide and it wasn't until he'd collapsed on that horrible day a couple of months ago that she'd realised how bad things were.

In a way this whole situation was his fault, she thought, although she would never dare to voice that opinion out loud.

She'd been so panicked about it that she'd sent an email to head office, directed to the guy who was in charge of UK operations. She'd had no reply so she'd sent another one, assuming that her first email must have gone into spam.

When there had been no reply to that either, she'd given up.

Perhaps they didn't want to help. Perhaps they'd already sold the hotel and hadn't got round to telling the staff.

In the meantime she had to keep going through the motions.

"I hope I'm in better health than Gerald," she said, "and I'm younger. You don't need to worry."

"But it's a slippery slope. We all think you've been working too hard. So hard you've forgotten what day it is."

Evie stared at her. "What day is it?"

But Mandy already had her head out of the door and was gesturing to whoever was outside.

A moment later her office was full of people. At a rough count it seemed like the entire staff, including Edward, her dad, who had been working as concierge for more than three decades. He was the longest serving member of staff and definitely the most knowledgeable.

Emotion filled her and she felt her throat thicken.

If the hotel was sold, her dad would lose his job and that would be terrible. This place was like a home to him, and the team like a family.

None of them seemed to have any idea how bad things were. They'd trusted Gerald completely.

And now they were all smiling as they produced a large cake with eight candles blazing.

"Today is the eighth anniversary of the day you started working at the hotel," Mandy said, "I mean full time—I'm not counting all the hours you put in here as a teenager. You're so busy holding the fort you've forgotten. And look at you! Sitting in the boss's chair. We can't believe our Evie is all grown up."

"Well I—thanks." The fact that she was sitting in the boss's chair didn't seem to have any impact on the way they saw her.

"We made your favourite cake, Evie! Chocolate sponge with chocolate icing, topped with buttons. I remember making something similar for your fifth birthday. Most of it ended up on your face. I have a photo somewhere. I should try and find it."

"Please don't." Evie stood up and blew out the candles before they could set off the smoke alarm. "How thoughtful of you all. Thank you. Er—who is on reception while you're all in here?"

"No one, but if someone comes, they can wait for five minutes."

359

"It's important to greet guests immediately they arrive, and—"

"Gerald always believed it was important that the staff were relaxed. It makes us seem more welcoming."

"But if no one is manning the desk then it won't be welcoming, and—"

"Stop stressing. You put such pressure on yourself! No wonder you look so tired. Now—" Mandy wielded a large knife "—large slice or small slice?"

"Small is—oh, you're going for large. Right. Thanks." She took the slice of cake. It was bigger than her head. She was starting to understand why Gerald had suffered a heart attack. "I might save it until later and have it with a cup of tea."

"We can make you tea. Or something stronger? You look wrung out."

And this was the problem of course. They were nice people. Generous and kind. Occasionally they were even reasonable at their jobs, but occasionally reasonable wasn't enough to give the hotel the occupancy they needed or the reviews. And every time she tried to address some aspect of improving the guest experience they either reminded her that their approach had worked fine for Gerald, or they mentioned some time in her childhood when she'd committed some hilarious infraction she'd been trying to escape ever since.

Maybe it would be easier if she had a peer she could talk to, but there was no one.

She was on her own with this. She just had to keep going. Keep trying.

Or get out.

"While I have you all here it's the perfect time to remind everyone of the importance of guest records." She tried to sound firm and managerial. "We keep meticulous and detailed records on everyone so that we can make sure we deliver exactly the experience they're looking for, and more. These should be reviewed every evening so that we can prepare for the following day's arrivals. One of the many advantages of having such a long-established staff, is that we have the privilege of getting to know guests over a period of many years. We are more than hotel staff, we are friends and we pride ourselves on the personal touch."

"Don't worry about that now, pet. Eat your cake."

Cake wasn't going to solve her problems, but they weren't going to leave her office until she'd eaten it so she had to make an effort.

"Just a little taste, and I'll save the rest for later—" because they were all watching her with eager expressions she dug her fork into it and ate a small piece. It was heavenly. The flavour. The texture. The softness of the sponge against the creamy filling. It didn't just taste delicious, it actually made her feel better about her life (and that was no small achievement). "Oh . . ." She closed her eyes. "This is—who made this?"

Luca emerged from the back of the crowd. "That would be me."

The laughter in his eyes and the way his cheeks creased when he smiled made her wish she'd done more than simply pull her hair into a scrunchie that morning.

Thanks to Donna she couldn't stop thinking of the laundry cupboard.

She blanked that thought. Who cared that he was hotter than a chilli pepper? What really mattered was that he was an excellent chef. He was so good that she was afraid that once he discovered the truth about the establishment he'd joined, he'd be leaving to work in a top London restaurant.

Still, until that happened she was going to make the most of eating well.

During his interview he'd produced several dishes for her to taste. She'd nibbled her way through tiny strips of seared venison in a blackberry sauce. She'd eaten broccoli that tasted nothing like any broccoli she'd ever cooked at home. By the time she'd tasted his crème brûlée she'd been ready to beg him to take the job.

He'd taken it, and the restaurant had been transformed into an almost overnight success. They even had a waiting list for some evenings.

But it wouldn't be enough, would it? It was too little, too late.

No matter how hard she tried to remain optimistic, it didn't change the fact that the hotel was in trouble. And it also didn't change the fact that no matter what she did, people were always going to see her as "our Evie." She had so much more to give! So much more that she could be contributing. She wanted a chance to prove herself.

She waited until they all finally left the room and opened her laptop again.

With one eye on the door, she finished filling out the application.

Feeling like a traitor, she hit the button and submitted it without allowing herself time to do any more thinking.

There. Done.

She told herself she had no reason to feel guilty. Things would carry on just the way they always had, with or without her. Head office couldn't be planning to sell the hotel or they would have been in touch.

Everything was going to be fine.

Could this Christmas be the start of a whole new chapter?

A long-lasting friendship

Every year, Erica, Claudia, and Anna reunite for their book club holiday. They're bonded by years of friendship and a deep love of books, but there is still so much they keep from each other . . .

A perfect Christmas escape

At the cosy Maple Sugar Inn, Hattie specialises in making her guests' dreams come true, but this Christmas all she wants is to survive the festive season. Between running the inn and being a single mother, Hattie is close to breaking point.

The start of a brand-new story . . . ?

Over the course of an eventful week, Hattie sees that the friends are each carrying around unspoken truths, but nothing prepares her for how deeply her story will become entwined in theirs. Will this Christmas be the end of the book club's story or the start of a whole new chapter?

This is one family Christmas none of them will ever forget!

In the snowy perfection of Aspen, the White family gathers for youngest daughter Rosie's whirlwind Christmas wedding. For the bride's parents, Maggie and Nick, their daughter's marriage is a milestone they are determined to celebrate wholeheartedly, but they are hiding a huge secret of their own. Bride-to-be Rosie loves her fiancé but is having serious second thoughts. Everyone has arrived – how can she tell them she's not sure – but might big sister Katie have guessed her secret fears? As the big day draws near, with emotions running high, will there be a wedding in December?

'SARAH MORGAN IS BACK IN STYLE WITH A PERFECT SNOW-FILLED READ'

Woman & Home

Could the best Christmas gift be a brand new start?

Gayle is a highly successful and motivated business woman, but her success has come at a price – she hasn't spoken to her daughters, Ella and Samantha, for years. But when Gayle has an accident at work, she realises she needs to make amends with her family.

And so she invites herself to join Ella and Samantha for their Christmas in the beautiful Scottish Highlands. The sisters are none too pleased that their mother has inserted herself into their Christmas plans. They have each other – and don't need their mother back in their lives. Or so they think...

As they embark on their first family Christmas together in years, will the three women learn that sometimes facing up to a few home truths is all you need to heal your heart?

'A FEEL-GOOD FAMILY SAGA WITH CHARACTERS THAT LEAP OFF THE PAGE – JUST PERFECTION'

Laura Jane Williams

This Christmas, one family will have secrets to unwrap.

All Suzanne McBride wants for Christmas is her three daughters happy and at home. But when sisters Posy, Hannah and Beth return to their family home in the Scottish Highlands, old tensions and buried secrets start bubbling to the surface. Suzanne is determined to create the perfect family Christmas, but the McBrides must all address some home truths before they can celebrate together...

'DELIGHTFULLY FESTIVE, HEARTWARMING AND THE BEST YET FROM SARAH MORGAN'
Good Housekeeping

Can you find new beginnings with old friends?

Joanna Whitman's high-profile marriage held more secrets than she cares to remember, so when her ex-husband dies, she doesn't know what to feel. But when she discovers that he's left behind a pregnant young woman, Joanna is forced to act. She knows exactly how brutal the spotlight on them both will be...unless she can find a way for them to disappear.

Ashley Blake is amazed when Joanna suggests they lie low at her beach house in her sleepy Californian hometown. Joanna should be hating her, not helping her. But alone and pregnant, Ashley needs all the support she can find.

Joanna's only goal for the summer is privacy. All Ashley wants is space to plan for her and her baby's future. But when an old flame reappears, and secrets spill out under the hot summer sun, this unlikely friendship is put to the test...

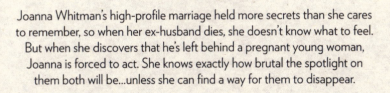

'A PERFECT SLICE OF JOYFUL SUMMER ESCAPISM'
Clare Pooley

It's never too late for adventure...

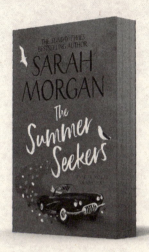

Kathleen is eighty years old. After a run-in with an intruder, her daughter wants her to move into a residential home.

Liza is drowning under the daily stress of family life. The last thing she needs is her mother jetting off on a wild holiday.

Martha is having a quarter-life crisis. Unemployed, unloved and uninspired, she just can't get her life together. When Martha sees Kathleen's advert for a driver and companion to take an epic road trip across America, she decides this job might be the answer to her prayers. Besides, how much trouble can one eighty-year-old woman be?

'THE ROAD TRIP
OF A LIFETIME
– TERRIFIC FUN'

Veronica Henry